The
Cherry
Tree
Café

Heidi Swain

SIMON & SCHUSTER

London · New York · Sydney · Toronto · New Delhi

A CBS COMPANY

First published in Great Britain by Simon & Schuster UK Ltd, 2015
This paperback edition, 2017
A CBS COMPANY

1 3 5 7 9 10 8 6 4 2

Simon & Schuster UK Ltd
1st Floor
222 Gray's Inn Road
London WC1X 8HB

www.simonandschuster.co.uk
www.simonandschuster.com.au
www.simonandschuster.co.in

Simon & Schuster Australia, Sydney
Simon & Schuster India, New Delhi

A CIP catalogue record for this book
is available from the British Library

EBOOK ISBN: 978-1-47114-995-5
PAPERBACK ISBN: 978-1-4711-6802-4

Typeset in Bembo by M Rules
Printed and bound by CPI Group (UK) Ltd, Croydon, CR0 4YY

Simon & Schuster UK Ltd are committed to sourcing paper
that is made from wood grown in sustainable forests and supports the Forest
Stewardship Council, the leading international forest certification organisation.
Our books displaying the FSC logo are printed on FSC certified paper.

To Paul, Oliver & Amelia

Chapter 1

When I was growing up I used to hate my birthday. What use was a birthday two weeks after Christmas? But now, bowling headlong towards my early thirties with Mr Right to snuggle up to, it didn't seem so bad. No, now it wasn't too bad at all. I sighed and stretched out in the luxuriously large bed, then rolled over to snuggle up to his perfectly toned torso for a few more minutes, only to discover that he wasn't there.

No matter, I smiled to myself, as I imagined him sauntering back into the bedroom with a laden breakfast tray and wearing little more than his most seductive smile. Just what, I couldn't help wondering, had he got planned for my birthday, which coincidentally was the same day as our anniversary? Two blissful years since fate had blown him through the doors of the Mermaid pub and into my waiting arms.

Bored with life in Wynbridge, the small East Anglian town where I'd grown up, I was looking for a distraction, anything to stave off the monotony of pulling pints and justifying still living at home, when in breezed Giles Worthington. He introduced himself as a jilted groom, a broken soul in need of a little 'r and r', which I was only too willing to offer. I had him back on his feet in no time and in return he swept me off mine and carried me away to his castle, well, penthouse flat actually.

It wasn't until a few weeks down the line that I discovered that he had actually been the one largely responsible for the jilting, but his fiancée was long gone by then, already seeing someone else (so he said) and I was living the life of a princess, not that any of that really mattered to me. All I cared about was love, head over heels, heart slamming against the ribcage love. I was a firm believer in destiny, fate and all that malarkey and I just knew that Giles Worthington and I were meant to be together, forever.

'Giles,' I purred lustfully, 'hurry up, the bed's getting cold.'

No response. I sat up, shook my red curls away from my face, wrapped the sheet tightly around me and tiptoed to the door to call again. Still nothing, I shuffled back to bed and spotted an envelope propped up against the phone.

My day ran exactly as Giles planned it to. No snuggling up on the sofa guzzling Prosecco and watching old movies for me this year. Instead I was polished and preened at a lavish country house spa and trying my best to enjoy it, despite feeling out of place amongst the glossy, groomed goddesses who, unlike me, were clearly accustomed to such indulgent treatment.

Giles, always so generous, loved to shower me with surprises: lavish bouquets covering my desk at work, exquisite jewellery hidden in boxes of chocolates and last-minute minibreaks, but what I loved best was the time we spent together, just the two of us, snuggled under the duvet with our phones turned off and eyes only for each other. The whole birthday spa experience, although indulgent, just wasn't me. Mindful of appearing ungrateful, however, I plastered on my best smile and thanked my lucky stars that at least I had a man who actually remembered my birthday.

I spent the entire day wrapped in a soft fluffy robe, my every whim catered for before heading to the salon to have my locks straightened whilst a taxi waited on standby to drive me to my favourite rooftop restaurant for dinner with my dream man.

In the run up to the big day I'd become increasingly convinced that Giles was poised to propose, and my hours of intense pampering only served to satisfy the fantasy that endless clandestine conversations with my best mate, Jemma, had fed. I was so close to securing my happy-ever-after I could almost taste it.

'Good evening, Miss Dixon.' The restaurant manager bowed when I arrived.

'Good evening, James,' I blushed.

I still wasn't used to the way people treated me now I was Giles's girlfriend. Wherever we went, everyone knew my name. I knew my mother would have been in seventh heaven to have people falling over themselves for her, but to me it felt weird. I guess deep down I still felt a bit of a fraud living the city high life.

Before Giles whisked me away I was just a barmaid from a small town with no idea of 'how the other half lived' but now I was treated like the Queen of Sheba simply because I happened to grace the arm of Giles Worthington. Talking of whom, where was he?

'Mr Worthington will be arriving shortly,' James the manager said, as I glanced around apprehensively. 'Would you care to follow me to your table?'

I had barely sat down when I saw Giles arrive. I smiled to myself as I watched every woman in the restaurant discreetly shifting in their seats to ensure they secured the best view of the thick dark hair, mahogany eyes and impeccably cut suit that was heading towards my table.

'Lizzie,' he said, bending down and brushing my cheek with the briefest kiss. 'You look gorgeous. How was your day?'

He took the seat opposite mine and dutifully acknowledged the female diners who were still panting for a word from him. I breathed in the lingering scent of his aftershave and tried to draw my mind away from thoughts of getting him back to the flat, loosening his tie and recklessly tearing open the buttons on his designer shirt.

'My day has been utterly sublime,' I breathed, 'but I think tonight is going to surpass it.'

Ordinarily when I made a comment like that Giles would wink or caress my leg under the table and I would know there was no way he was going to wait until we got back to the flat before he would ravish me, but he simply threw me a fleeting smile and picked up his menu.

'Is everything all right?' I ventured.

It wasn't like him not to play along.

'Yes, sorry. It's just been one of those days, you know?'

'Actually I can't say I do,' I tried again, 'because thanks to you I've had the best possible day ever.'

I knew I was pushing the truth a bit too far and that Jemma would shake her head at such gratuitous lying, but I wanted Giles to know how much I appreciated the day he had arranged for me. However, he just nodded vaguely and clicked his fingers to catch the attention of the maître d'.

Two courses later and I was struggling to steady my nerves and keep my frustration in check.

'Can't you just leave it this time,' I begged.

It was the third time Giles's mobile phone had disturbed our meal and it seemed less and less likely with every passing mouthful that he was going to propose and even if he did, I wasn't sure I'd have the good grace to accept, given the filthy mood I'd fallen into as a result of the constant interruptions.

'Surely whatever it is can wait until we've finished our afters.' I whispered.

'It isn't "afters",' Giles snapped, standing up and noisily dropping his spoon, 'this is sweet or pudding or dessert, but not "afters" and no, I can't just leave it.'

Sudden tears stung my eyes as I watched him march across the restaurant. I furiously tried to blink them away and ignore the pang of embarrassment I felt as a result of his harsh words. He'd never corrected anything I'd said before. The Brothers Grimm, as Jemma had named them, Giles's brothers Edward and Charlie, might have done, but not Giles. In the two years I'd known him he'd never been cruel.

I thought back to all the times he'd sat around my parents' dining table enjoying his 'afters'. What the hell was wrong with him? I couldn't believe that he would have gone to all the trouble of arranging the spa and sumptuous meal for my birthday, our anniversary, only to have it all sabotaged with phone calls from work.

'We need to talk,' he said quietly when he finally came back to the table, his expression grave.

'What is it?' I asked, reaching for his hand and feeling determined to make everything better. 'I know there's something wrong, Giles. We've never argued like this before and today of all days.'

I willed myself to forgive his waspish comment and smooth over the cracks in what was supposed to be the happiest moment of my life but there was something in his expression that suggested that today was just another day to him, nothing special at all. Surely he hadn't *really* forgotten?

'I'm sorry, Lizzie,' he stammered, 'I'm just not feeling myself. It's been a very long day.'

'It's OK,' I soothed.

He looked at me for a second then withdrew his hand and took a deep breath.

'Look,' he said, 'there's something I have to tell you.'

I sat back in my chair, ran a pristinely manicured hand over my sleek, straightened curls and tried to return his gaze. This was it. This was the moment he was finally going to ask me. He was just nervous and annoyed that we'd been interrupted.

'So, what is it?' I smiled. 'I'm sure whatever it is can't be that bad.'

Just for a second I was panicked by his unfathomable expression and looked down at the table, then I realised he was fumbling in his pocket for what I presumed was a ring box. I took a deep breath to steady my nerves and looked back up. He was pushing something across the table towards me. Tentatively I stretched out my hand to take it, but it wasn't a ring box or a ring. It was a key. It was Giles's flat door key. I dropped it clumsily back onto the table as if its touch had seared my skin.

'Lizzie, I'm so sorry.' He frowned, his words barely audible. 'But I have to tell you, I've decided I'm going to marry Natasha after all.'

I don't really remember the finer details of what happened after that. I sat and stared, dumbstruck, as Giles's mouth opened and closed and snatches of some of what he said reached me from what felt like light years away.

'I've never really stopped loving her,' I heard him say, 'I know now that when I met you I was just scared of the commitment she and I were about to make.'

'But what about *me*, Giles?' I stammered, bile rising as I refused to acknowledge the voice in my head warning me that the universe was gearing itself up to play an exceptionally cruel hand. 'When we first got together you told me that you and Natasha weren't meant to be. You said that you felt lucky that you got out when you did and that what you felt for me was nothing like what you felt for her. You said you were in love with me!'

'No,' he shrugged, 'I thought I was, but I wasn't. Looking back, I think I just got scared of the thought of being with one person for the rest of my life and I panicked. I should never have split up with Natasha, let alone asked you to move in with me. I just got carried away, and if we're being honest, Lizzie, even you'll admit our relationship has never really worked, has it? I mean, you've never really settled into life here, have you?'

I sat open-mouthed, too stunned to move and too shocked to respond. I had left my job, my family and all my friends in Wynbridge to move to London so I could be with this man. I was crazy about him, would walk through fire for him and I had thought he felt the same about me. Countless times he told me that he loved me, that I was a breath of fresh air, that he'd never met anyone else like me . . .

'Excuse me,' I murmured, pushing back my chair and praying that I'd make it to the ladies before off-loading the contents of my stomach.

I stared at my reflection in the mirrored wall but didn't recognise the person looking back at me. Where had Lizzie Dixon gone? I teased a few of the tortured and tamed curls free and felt heavy tears gathering. I swallowed hard, took a deep breath and splashed my face with cold water to try and temper some of the heat in my flushed cheeks.

'I know this must be one hell of a shock,' Giles whispered, as I rejoined him after a wobbly walk back to our table, 'but I couldn't let it drag on any longer. When I spotted you looking at rings before Christmas, I said to Natasha . . . What?'

'Exactly how long have you been back with her?' I gasped, horrified.

Giles shook his head. 'I don't know, a few months maybe.'

I couldn't bear to hear another word. Jemma's voice was screaming at me to tip his drink over his head and dump his 'afters' in his lap, but I couldn't bring myself to do it. I suddenly realised that this whole meal was a charade and that Giles had pinned all his hopes on me going quietly and not making a fuss and apparently I was going to, but only because I was too shocked to do anything else.

'Can we go please?' I said, standing back up again and clumsily pushing my chair away, 'we'll talk about this at the flat.'

'I'm not coming back to the flat, Lizzie.'

'What?'

'I moved my stuff out today.'

'You sneaky bastard,' I choked, anger threatening to race ahead of shock.

'I just thought it would save a scene. You can stay on there as long as you want. I can even have the lease changed to your name if you want.'

'Oh thanks,' I laughed, sitting back down with a thud, 'you really are all heart!'

'Don't be like that. I'm trying my best to make this as pain-less as possible.'

'For who, Giles? You know I won't be able to pay the rent on my own. I'll have to move out, and what about work? You set me up with that job. Do you really expect me to be able to walk back into that office and carry on as if nothing has happened? I thought you loved me.'

'I'm sorry.'

'So am I. I'm sorry I ever set eyes on you, but credit where it's due, this is certainly one birthday I'll never forget!'

And apparently neither would Giles. One fleeting glance at his handsome face confirmed that he hadn't remembered it was my birthday or our anniversary at all.

Chapter 2

Jemma began ringing soon after eight the following morning. Giles allegedly played squash with a colleague around that time and she knew I'd be home alone. I lay and listened to her breezy answerphone messages which to me, her oldest friend, belied the desperation she felt because I hadn't picked up. I could all too easily imagine the texts backing up on my mobile would be nowhere near as polite.

'Hi guys! It's me again. I guess you aren't in because if you were, you would have picked up by now, wouldn't you?'

If it wasn't all so tragic, I would have laughed. As the morning wore on her tone became increasingly frustrated, but I still couldn't muster the courage to answer.

'Anyway, I'm just popping out to take Ella to her ballet lesson and check on things at the Café,' she gushed airily. *'I'll try and reach you later on your mobile, Lizzie. Hope you're both OK and had a fab evening. Lots of love . . . OK, bye.'*

I slumped back down under the duvet, determined not to have to face the real world for a little while longer and thought about the exciting times Jemma and her husband Tom were enjoying. Unlike me they had never felt any desire to leave Wynbridge. The place was their past, their present and now their future. They had recently bought a business, The Cherry Tree Café, and were deep in renovation and repair mode.

The Café had been an absolute bargain, according to Jemma. The council were in the throes of regenerating the town centre and consequently willing to let some of the smaller shops go for a song. They were pulling out all the stops to tempt the locals away from the out of town retail park, (which had seemed like such a good idea a few years ago), and back to the market square before the place lost its charm and became overrun with pound stores. According to Jemma, 'shop local' were the new buzz-words on everyone's lips.

The Café had been *the* place to be seen when we were growing up and now it was poised to flourish again and provide Jemma with the perfect space to expand her baking empire.

I wrapped myself a little tighter in the covers feeling thoroughly ashamed of the pang of jealousy I felt when thinking about Jemma's perfect life and good fortune. She had a husband who loved her, an adorable daughter and now her dream business; the Café was going to be the cherry on her cupcake.

I managed to get through the rest of the torturous weekend with the comfort of my other two best friends, Ben and Jerry, and I can honestly say it was no sickie that I was planning to pull the following week. My ice cream consumption had reached epic proportions and I was in danger of succumbing to a severe sugar overdose.

Jemma had eventually stopped ringing, probably on the assumption that Giles and I were engaged and consequently otherwise engaged in a marathon weekend shag fest. Which unfortunately we weren't, well, he probably was but with the perfectly pristine Natasha, rather than the frayed around the edges me.

Disconcertingly my mother had also rung a couple of times. Her messages were left in the voice she saved especially for Giles and his family, painstakingly pronouncing every syllable, and along with her nauseating tone there was the added concern that she hardly ever called. Her life was a blur of Wynbridge WI meetings and coffee mornings for orphaned orang-utans. I hoped Jemma hadn't bumped into her and said anything about not being able to get hold of me, but that was highly unlikely. The pair hardly moved in the same social circles.

I finally managed to get to sleep on Sunday night and

unfortunately I stayed asleep. The cunning but face-saving Ferris Bueller style message I'd spent hours devising didn't quite pan out. Blagging myself a few sick days would have given me enough time to compose myself and return to work looking confident, over Giles and with the world at my feet but unfortunately, fate it seemed, wasn't quite finished with me yet.

'It wasn't all me,' I groaned, increasingly convinced that this torturous hell was my comeuppance for so readily forgiving Giles when I discovered that he had been the one who left Natasha at the altar, not the other way round.

'Elizabeth Dixon!' I cringed under the duvet as the voice of my usually calm and kind-hearted boss Henry Glover echoed around the walls of the flat. '*Where the hell are you? In case you've forgotten, you are supposed to be heading up the sales meeting this morning! You have all the data on your computer and no one else can access it! Hurry the fuck up will you, everyone's waiting!'*

Reluctantly I shuffled out of bed, knowing I couldn't put it off any longer.

'Sally,' I sniffed into the receiver, trying to sound more flu-ridden than heartbroken. 'Hi, I'm not going to make it in for a few days. Can you tell Henry for me? I don't think the message I left yesterday got picked up.'

OK, so it was a lie, but given the circumstances, surely I was allowed just one?

'Oh Lizzie, bless your heart. I was hoping you'd ring.'

I swallowed hard but couldn't rid myself of the lump that had recently taken up residence in my throat. Sally, Henry's secretary, knew everything. I could hear it in her voice. If I'd been genuinely ill she would have been sympathetic but brisk. I couldn't stand it. If she knew, then so did everyone else. All the people it had taken months to win over when I first moved in with Giles would now switch allegiance again, wouldn't they? I couldn't say we were ever bosom buddies, but I hated the thought of going back to work and not having *anyone* to talk to.

'Can you tell Henry that I'm sorry? I think it's just a bug,' I lied, struggling to stop my voice cracking. 'I think I must have picked it up over the weekend.'

Sally sighed.

'If it's any consolation, love, no one blames you. It's Giles, the little shit; he's always wanted what he shouldn't have.'

The tension in my shoulders had only just begun to loosen its vice-like grip, when the phone rang again. This time it was Jemma, and I knew I couldn't put off talking to her any longer. It wasn't fair. I took a deep breath, braced myself for the impending storm and answered.

'Finally!' she laughed. 'I was beginning to think you'd left the country! Now, don't tell me, Giles whisked you away to some boutique hotel for the weekend, spoilt you rotten and now you're wearing a princess cut diamond as big as your hand!'

'Not exactly,' I murmured.

'Oh, it's a Lady Di sapphire, is it?'

'Look Jemma, if you'd just shut up for two seconds.'

'What is it? Oh god, don't tell me you eloped! Ella will never forgive you if she's missed the chance to be a bridesmaid! Give me all the details, quick!'

'Well,' I winced, 'the day began with a trip to a country house spa.'

'A country house spa!' Jemma scoffed. 'What was he thinking? You hate that kind of thing! Then what?'

'Then back to the city for dinner.'

'Yes,' she snapped impatiently, 'I guessed there would be food at some point. Jesus, Lizzie, just cut to the good stuff, will you?'

I took a deep breath and forced the three little words I'd been dreading saying aloud out of my mouth and into the world.

'And then . . . he dumped me.'

'*What*?'

'He moved out while I was at the spa and he's gone back to Natasha. They're getting married.'

Silence, then quiet sobbing filled the space that had only seconds before been occupied by my best mate crooning about my future prospects.

'Oh god, don't cry!' I begged. 'I haven't got the energy to try and make you feel better.'

'I'm not. I'm sorry. It's just so horrible.'

'I know. I almost threw up all over the table when he told me.'

I don't know why I was trying to make it sound funny. It certainly didn't lessen the pain or the embarrassment. For weeks Jemma and I had been fantasising about the moment Giles would propose and now I had to explain that what I assumed were nerves about popping the question were actually mass desertion tactics.

'You're not seriously telling me the bastard told you over dinner?' Jemma seethed.

'Yep,' I nodded, unable to stop now I was on a roll, 'but in his defence, it was a very nice dinner even though I did almost end up seeing it in reverse!'

'How can you be making jokes, Lizzie? This is awful!'

'Because if I don't, I think I'll go under completely,' I admitted, 'and I can't do that. I won't give him the satisfaction of knowing how much I'm hurting.'

'What are you going to do?'

'What do you mean?'

'Well, you can't stay there, can you? Have you any idea how excruciating work is going to be?'

'Yes, it had crossed my mind.'

'And what about the rent? You can't possibly manage it on your own.'

'Yes, OK thanks, Jemma,' I grumbled.

Ever since I'd planned to phone in sick, my thoughts had been of little else but I didn't need someone, especially someone I loved, telling me what a struggle my life was going to be from now on. I needed Jemma's support as well as her sympathy.

'I'm sorry,' she sniffed, sounding more like her practical old self. 'It's just such a shock, that's all. Maybe you should come home to Wynbridge for a bit.'

'*What*?'

'Just for a break, until you get your head straight. Come to us if you can't face your mum . . . oh . . .'

'What?'

'Nothing.'

'Don't lie to me, Jemma. What is it?'

'Well, I kind of ran into your mum in town last Friday.'

I slumped down on the sofa, the last of my spirit heading for the door.

'So?' I asked, trying to sound unconcerned.

More silence.

'Jemma, you didn't mention anything about Friday night, did you?' I already knew the answer, courtesy of the answerphone messages.

'I might have mentioned that you were having a birthday treat and that Giles had something special up his sleeve.'

'Oh god,' I groaned.

'I'm so sorry.' Jemma started to cry again.

'Look,' I shrugged, 'don't worry about it, at least you didn't lie.'

'What do you mean?'

'Well, he did have something up his sleeve, didn't he? Just not what we were expecting, that's all.'

I hung up, knowing I couldn't hold back the tide any longer. I was going to have to telephone home and keep everything crossed that Dad, not Mum would pick up. I forced myself to eat a bowl of cereal, then had a shower and washed my hair. There was no point going into battle half-arsed. Where my mother was concerned, you needed all your armour intact before advancing.

'Hello, Dad?'

'Hello, darling . . . oh hang on, your mother wants to talk.'

'No, Dad, wait!'

The sheer relief I had momentarily felt at hearing Dad's voice evaporated as I heard Mum snatching the phone from his grasp and installing herself on the sofa for a cosy chat.

'Lizzie!' she gushed, 'where on earth have you been? I've been trying to get hold of you for days!'

'Mum—'

'Now, tell me. Where did that gorgeous man take you for your birthday? I bumped into Jemma in town and she told me he had something special planned, that's why I didn't ring on the day. Do you know, she had Ella with her and her behaviour was quite appalling?'

I blessed my goddaughter and her ability to shock my mother. I was grateful for anything that would distract her from her current course of interrogation.

'Anywho,' she laughed, 'that's all by the by. When are you both coming home? Can we expect a big announcement?'

I could hear Dad frantically trying to shut her up in the background and the way her voice started cutting in and out suggested that she was wafting him away with a duster much the same as she would a fly.

'We're not,' I said firmly, drawing myself up for the moment of impact, 'and no.'

'Pardon?' She stalled.

'We're not coming home and no, there is no announcement, well, other than that Giles and I are no longer a couple.'

'Sorry, Lizzie,' she murmured faintly, 'I don't understand.'

'Then let me spell it out for you,' I sighed. 'On my birthday Giles moved all his stuff out of the flat while I was at a spa and then in the evening, he took me out to dinner and told me that he didn't love me and that he was getting back with Natasha, his former fiancée and marrying her.'

I stopped to draw breath. It was the first time I'd said the whole thing so plainly and the words tore my heart in two. I still didn't want to believe it had happened.

'Oh, Lizzie!' Mum sobbed. 'Are you absolutely sure?'

I took another deep breath.

'How on earth has this happened?' She sniffed.

'What do you mean?'

'Well, had you been fighting? Had you fallen out with his mother or one of the brothers?'

Sometimes I thought, as I tuned out my mother's disapproving prattle, it would be cool to have a brother or sister. Someone else to conspire with, share the heat and hassle. But then I realised that knowing my luck I'd end up playing second fiddle; I'd be Monica Geller not Ross and that would be undoubtedly worse, wouldn't it? Constant comparison to a saintly sibling was not a comforting thought. Perhaps I should start pinning my hopes on Dad trading in who I'd ended up with for a mother for a kinder, less sharply edged model.

'Lizzie!'

'What? I mean, pardon?'

'I said, are you listening?'

'Of course I'm listening!'

'Then tell me, what did you do?'

'What do you mean, what did I do?'

'Well, you must have done something? Giles wouldn't have just decided this was his only course of action if your relationship was all tickety-boo, would he?'

'Why is everything always my fault?' I retaliated.

'And who is this Natasha person? I had no idea Giles had been engaged before!'

Ah, I'd forgotten about that. Dad and I had decided it would be better all-round if Mum was kept in the dark about that one. When Giles and I first got together we considered it all best left unsaid; shame I hadn't remembered our little plan before I phoned home, really. To be honest, it was a shame that I'd gone along with his little plan at all. My grandmother had always maintained that we reaped what we sowed in life and I was just beginning to understand what she meant.

Chapter 3

It had been the end of December before the first hard frost hit the city, but ever since then the unrelenting arctic blast refused to loosen its grip. The city was on lock-down, like my heart, and the dark, bitter days did nothing to raise my spirits.

If only I had had some clue that would have alerted me to Giles's true feelings then I could have braced myself for when he blew time on our relationship. Having survived the paranoia that accompanied the first few months of our passionate, whirlwind affair, I had foolishly thought the rest would be plain sailing.

Eighteen months in and I had finally convinced Jemma to cast aside her reservations about my dream man and his dodgy relationship credentials. For six months I'd encouraged both our minds to skip merrily ahead, all the way up the aisle and beyond.

*

Somehow I dragged myself back to the office and the cut and thrust world of advertising sales and faced the sympathy, whispering and gradual extrication from the group of people I had so recently almost been tempted to call my 'friends'. However, more worryingly than my lack of chums was the fact that it was little beyond fourteen days since my birthday and my bank balance was already beginning to look as bleak as the winter weather.

'Lizzie,' Henry, my boss, smiled as he called me into his office and discreetly closed the door, 'come in; have a seat.'

I sat as instructed, the tension in my shoulders forcing them up around my ears again as I waited for the death knell on my job to toll.

'I appreciate that this is a rough time for you,' he said, sitting opposite me.

I shook my head, fully prepared to make the 'what is happening in my personal life has absolutely nothing to do with my work' speech, but he cut me off before I'd even launched in. Spare me, his expression said, I've heard it all before.

'And I know everyone's figures take a bit of a dip in the run up to the silly season. However,' he continued, spinning his laptop round so I could see the screen, 'these figures just aren't good enough, Lizzie, and you can't say it's happened recently.'

He pointed to the sharply descending line on the perfectly colour-coded graph he'd created to nail home my ineptitude.

I knew he was right, even without the graphic evidence. I'd gone off the boil around late October after I'd overheard a couple of the other girls, Philippa and Sasha, gossiping in the ladies about who would be seeing in the New Year with a new piece of jewellery. From that day on, my heart simply wasn't in selling advertising space; I was too busy fantasising about floral centrepieces, bridal favours, beautiful babies and insurance policies that would cover gargantuan school fees.

Henry snapped the laptop shut and stared across the desk at me, his expression sympathetic. I knew what was coming.

'I'm really sorry, Lizzie,' he began.

'No, I'm sorry,' I said, wanting to spare him, 'I understand. You think I would be better off working somewhere else . . .'

'No,' Henry interrupted, 'that isn't what I was going to say at all, although if you have decided to move on, then I wouldn't blame you. It can't be easy working here and running the risk of seeing Giles every day.'

'No,' I smiled weakly, 'it isn't.'

'But what I was going to say, and this is strictly between us, is that the powers that be have decided it's time to make some changes. They're going to cut a swathe through the entire advertising department.'

I felt my face redden. Talk about shooting myself in the foot.

'This is just a heads-up, a timely nod to say that everyone's figures are going to be scrutinised in the spring and that you've got time to pick things up before the restructuring plans are made public.'

'Oh,' I said, 'I see. Thanks.'

'I'd hate to lose you, Lizzie,' Henry smiled, 'you're a hard worker and the clients really love you. If you want it, there would be plenty of potential for promotion. You just have to pull these figures round, OK?'

'OK,' I smiled, 'thanks, Henry. I appreciate the warning.'

Henry blushed and not for the first time I wondered how such a soft-hearted guy held his own in the ruthless world of advertising management. When I'd come back to work, he was full of apology for the out of character message he'd left on the answerphone. Henry didn't go in for shouting and swearing so his stress levels that morning must have been, thanks to me, through the roof.

I knew I should have been feeling grateful that he had given me a heads-up, but the plain truth was I hated my job. I'd only accepted the position because it was the first to come up when I moved to London. Giles had seemed thrilled that we were going to be working in the same building and made a great fuss about the long, lazy lunches we'd be able to share, although thinking back they had rarely ever happened. No, selling advertising space just wasn't me. I didn't care enough about projected sales and bottom lines. I was just lucky I got on with people and could talk them into buying space on a page.

However, as much as I hated it, it was a job and because of the constraints of having it I now found myself facing a big decision. Should I stay or should I go? Should I jump before I was pushed, or should I stay and fight just to make life as awkward as I could for the snake who had denied me my fairytale ending and brought my life crashing down around my ears?

'What did you say?' Jemma asked, after I'd explained what Henry had told me. 'Did you tell him to stick it?'

'No, of course I didn't!' I smiled at my friend's militant attitude. 'Henry's one of the good guys, remember?'

'I suppose so, but seriously, Lizzie, what are you going to do?'

'I don't know,' I sighed, 'I'm just not ready to make a decision yet.'

'Well, I'm sorry, mate, but if you don't hurry up you might just find someone else, like the bank manager, has decided for you.'

'There's still time to turn things around,' I mumbled half-heartedly, knowing that what I really wanted to do was pack a bag and run, but to where?

'Yes, but this isn't just about your job, which you suddenly seem to have forgotten you hate; what about the current financial situation?'

I dumped myself down on the sofa and kicked off my

shoes. I hated it when Jemma talked to me in that patient voice she usually saved for Ella, her attention-seeking daughter. I didn't need a well-reasoned argument batted up and down the phone line; I just wanted some sort of escape.

'The last thing you want is to get into debt doing a job you hate, living in a flat with an overinflated rent that's riddled with memories of raw animal sex and an overindulgent lifestyle!'

She was right, of course; the mere sight of the wet room still made me blush and yearn for what I no longer had. If only I could have dished out some revenge and gained some closure; cut the sleeves off his designer shirts, rubbed chilli in his Calvin Klein's, but Giles had been too clever for that. He'd left months before I knew he was actually gone.

'So what do you suggest then, oh wise one?' I snapped sarcastically whilst wracking my brains for an opportunity to vent my wrath.

'Come home.'

I rolled my eyes and reached for the bottle of wine I had had the foresight to open before making the call.

'You know I can't come home. Coming home would be like giving in and I can't admit defeat, Jemma! Mum would never let me forget it. I may have only a teeny tiny shred of self- respect left, but I'm not prepared to give it up without a fight.'

'OK, let me put it another way then. Come back to

Wynbridge, like I suggested before. Come back to me and Tom and Ella, just until you decide what you really want.'

What I *really* wanted was for none of this to have happened, to feel that I still had my life all sewn up with the man of my dreams and that if I did have to go anywhere, it would be with him in tow.

'And where will I live while I make these all important life choices?' I asked, not daring to enlighten Jemma as to the deepest and darkest desires of my heart.

'You could stay at the Café,' she said simply.

'What, amongst the old tables and chairs, with a bed on the counter and my washing in the sink?'

'There's a self-contained flat above,' Jemma went on, ignoring my sarcasm. 'I admit it's seen better days, but there are two bedrooms, a bathroom, kitchen and sitting room at your disposal, if you want it?'

I thought back to all the afternoons we'd spent lazing in the Café gardens and shop. I never realised anyone actually lived there.

'Has the flat always been there?'

'Yes, don't you remember? Old Mrs Taylor sold her house and moved into it so she could inject the last of her savings into the place. It didn't work, of course, not with the burger joints opening up on every corner, but she lived there until the place finally closed and it's still in reasonable order. We're planning to rent it out at some point, god knows we could do with the money, but it's yours if you want it.' I remembered Mrs Taylor with her tight bun, spotless apron and thick hot buttered toast. I felt a pang of guilt as I also remembered how readily we had swapped her simple, homespun service for the endless queues and overpriced under-seasoned patties that were synonymous with 'the new place'.

'So, what do you think?'

I didn't know what to say, I hadn't had time to think.

'It's a really kind offer, Jemma.'

'And one that you'd be stupid to turn down,' she interrupted.

'I'm not turning you down,' I insisted. 'I just need time to get my head round it. There's an awful lot to think about.'

'But is there, really? You work at a job you hate, you sleep in a flat you can't afford and you live in a city where you're all alone!'

'Yes, thanks for that,' I sniffed, 'and there was me thinking life could be worse!'

'I don't care,' Jemma said bluntly, 'you need to see sense and if we have to fall out to make that happen then it'll be worth it because I love you, Lizzie Dixon, and I won't let that slick little shit win!'

'Let me sleep on it,' I told her, for once not contradicting her opinion of Giles, 'let me think about it over the weekend and I promise I'll let you know next week.'

*

Predictably, I didn't sleep that night, but for once I wasn't staring up at the ceiling thinking about Giles and all the ways he had found to deprive me of my eight hours. I was thinking about Jemma's offer, my dreaded job and all the extra time I would have to put in to make amends for my lapsing sales figures.

Bottom line, I didn't want to do it, but the price I was going to have to pay to move to the Café was excruciatingly high. The thought of running into my mother at every turn was not a prospect I was ever going to relish.

During the two previous post-Giles weekends I had stayed in bed until something distracting appeared on TV, but that particular Saturday I was up and out of the flat, full of hope that a brisk, blustery walk would help clear my head and guide me towards making a decision.

The walk was blustery all right and I hadn't ventured far before sharp stinging sleet accompanied it. I ducked into the nearest shop and collided with an impatient-looking woman with a clipboard.

'Oh, you poor love!' she gushed, wide-eyed, 'you look soaked! Here, give me your coat and I'll show you where to go.'

'No,' I stammered, my teeth chattering, 'I'm fine. I'll just wait in here until it dies down a bit, if that's OK?'

'Aren't you Jenny Hudson?' The woman frowned, frantically consulting her clipboard.

I shook my head as another woman ran across the shop floor and lingered at her elbow.

'Oh for goodness' sake, Heather,' the clipboard woman snapped, 'I think we'll just have to start without her!'

'She isn't coming,' Heather squeaked, 'she's just called. Her car's got a flat on the ring road. By the time she gets here it'll be too late.'

'Right, take this.' The clipboard was thrust roughly into diminutive Heather's arms. 'I damn well knew something like this would happen. Every time we've booked her there's been some drama and she hasn't turned up! I'll have to do it, won't I?'

Suddenly her eyes swivelled back to me and she smiled, her expression transformed.

'How are you fixed this morning?' she said. 'Any plans?'

'I beg your pardon?'

'This morning, are you busy? Only, we have a space on our sewing course. No charge. Being a woman down, as it were, leaves someone without a partner and the room's set up so we can work in pairs at individual tables today. You'd be doing me a favour, really.'

An hour and a half later I found myself up to my elbows in triangular off-cuts and chatting to a woman called Fiona. We were making spring-themed bunting and worked companionably as the sleet lashed against the shop window and we drank copious amounts of coffee to wash down the even more copious amounts of cake we had consumed.

Bunting was a bit of an easy project for me, even though it had been months since I'd last been acquainted with a sewing machine and a pair of pinking shears. Consequently I'd finished before the others so I set about embellishing mine with some simple hand-stitched floral embroidery.

Clipboard woman, aka Deborah peered over my shoulder, raised her eyebrows and smiled broadly.

'I take it you've done this sort of thing before?' she laughed, bending down to scrutinise the back as well as the front of my efforts. 'Exquisite technique,' she squinted, looking for a knot or out of place thread.

'My grandmother taught me,' I smiled, 'not just how to sew, but how to knit, crochet, appliqué, all sorts of things. She was a real whizz at sewing.'

'You're not so bad yourself,' Deborah smiled, patting my shoulder as she rushed off to rescue a woman two tables along who had managed to sew her sleeve into her stitches.

'I think she was impressed,' whispered Fiona conspiratorially. 'I come most weeks and she hardly ever says anything nice to anyone!'

By early afternoon the sleet had turned to proper heavy snowfall and the rest of the ladies left the City Crafting Café with various lengths of bunting stowed carefully away in their reusable shoppers. I loitered behind and helped Deborah and Heather clear away. It was the least I could do after such an eye-opening morning.

When I had been living with Giles, immersed in city life, rushing to and from work, out to dinner and seemingly endless parties, I'd forgotten just how much I loved to sew and make. In fact, I don't think Giles ever knew anything about my passion for homemade crafts at all.

When I left school I had studied textiles at college with a view to making and selling my own things. The original plan had been to start small; Jemma was going to sell the baked goods she was becoming mildly famous for and I was going to sell my patchwork bags, bunting and so on, on a market stall before moving into a shop in the town and then of course, world domination would follow close behind.

Having unexpectedly rediscovered my passion, I realised how sad it was that I'd forgotten so much of what I loved, but at least Jemma had hung onto her dream; the Café would be the perfect outlet for her baking and culinary skills. My clever friend really did have it all, whereas I apparently had spent the last few years adrift.

I walked over to the shelves laden with rolls of fabric and pulled out a small bundle from the remnants bin. It would be Ella's birthday soon. This year I would make her something myself rather than rely on the internet to package and deliver.

'I hope you often get the chance to indulge your sewing talents, Lizzie?'

I jumped; Deborah had been watching me. I shook my head.

'No, not at the moment,' I told her, 'this is the first time I've made anything for months.'

She came over and began pulling out reels of coloured cotton that would best match the fabrics I'd chosen.

'Shame,' she said sadly, 'do you live far?'

'Not really. Well, not that far at the moment. I might be moving soon,' I added, my cheeks flushing at the prospect. It was true; the morning I'd spent in the café had helped me sidle closer to making a decision I'd thought it would take weeks to reach.

'You don't fancy a weekend job tutoring classes for me then?' she smiled.

I shook my head. The very idea of me teaching people how to sew was absurd.

'No, I don't think so, but thank you.' I carried my pile of fabrics and threads to the counter.

Heather rang up my bill and deducted the generous discount Deborah scribbled on her clipboard.

'Wow,' I smiled, 'thanks very much.'

'Consider it a little incentive,' she grinned, 'in case you change your mind about the job and by the way,' she added, cocking her head, 'has anyone ever told you, you have beautiful hair?'

Instinctively I touched my head to make sure the curls were still smooth, but of course they weren't. I had fought my way through the worst weather the winter had thrown at the city so far. My hair, left to dry naturally was now a riot of red unruly curls; the sight of which I knew would have made Giles wince. In the early days of our relationship he had loved my hair and constantly told me it was the first thing that drew him to me.

'When I walked in and saw you behind that bar,' he would whisper as we made love, his hands entwined in my curls, 'I knew you were the one for me. I had to have you, Lizzie.'

But when I moved to the city, things had gradually changed. Giles began making various subtle attempts to smarten me up and help me 'fit in and find my feet' as he put it. He suggested I could tone down my freckles with carefully matched foundation and he bought me the most expensive hair straighteners on the planet. Exactly when had he forgotten about the girl he started out loving, I wondered?

'Someone used to tell me they loved my hair all the time,' I told Deborah, tears pricking my eyes, 'but they stopped a long while ago.'

Chapter 4

'OK, I'll come.'

'*What?*'

'I said I'll come.'

'Seriously?'

'Seriously, cross my heart, seriously!'

Just how long, I wondered, was this conversation going to go on? But I could hardly berate Jemma for wanting confirmation. I'd avoided ringing and answering her calls for days, but only because I wanted to be absolutely sure in my own mind before I let her know.

'And you won't change your mind?'

'Couldn't even if I wanted to,' I told her as I lightly fingered the floral bunting I'd haphazardly draped across the kitchen, 'I handed in my notice this morning. I'm supposed to stay for a month but Henry said, given the circumstances, that I can go when I like. I've made him promise not to breathe a word to anyone. I'm just going to slip out at the end of the week and not go back.'

'Oh, Lizzie! I can't believe it. I never in a million years thought you'd say yes!'

'But you are sure it's OK, aren't you?' I swallowed; panicking that she'd only asked me because she thought I'd refuse. 'About the flat, I mean. You and Tom are still happy for me to move in?'

'Of course!' Jemma laughed, before breezily adding, 'There might be a teeny bit more work to do than I first thought, but it'll be fine. Ben's really hands on; nothing's beaten him so far! So, when can we expect you?'

'Ben who?' I gasped, crossing my fingers in the hope that it wasn't the Ben I thought it might be.

'Lovely Ben Fletcher,' she said, 'I thought I'd told you this already? He's just moved back to Wynbridge and is staying with us while we're renovating. He's been a huge help, very hands on.'

'You've already said that,' I snapped.

'Well, anyway there we are, are you *sure* I haven't mentioned him being back before?'

'Must've slipped your mind,' I muttered, my poor broken heart hammering wildly in my chest.

If I'd known about Jemma's other house guest before I'd told her I was moving back then it might have been a different story. I wasn't sure my already fragile emotional state was up to a blast from the past. Not that it was a *real* blast from the past. Jemma and I were the only ones who actually knew about the gargantuan torch I'd carried for Ben Fletcher throughout high school.

'Well, I'm sure you'll be pleased to see him again. He's looking very well,' Jemma said diplomatically, 'and he's bound to be a welcome distraction from . . .'

'Why is he staying with you?' I cut in before she had a chance to remind me what he'd be a welcome distraction from.

'What do you mean?'

'Why haven't you put him in the flat? Surely that would have made more sense than having him squeezing in with you lot.'

'It was Tom's idea,' she said in a rush, 'he wanted to spend some time with his oldest friend and as the flat wasn't quite ready it seemed like the logical thing to do.'

Something about Jemma's answer didn't quite ring true to me. Ben, like the rest of us, had family in Wynbridge, so why wasn't he staying with them?

'And besides,' Jemma added, before I could ask, 'we need him close by to talk about the renovations and his mother's an absolute nightmare. Living with her would drive him potty, well you know what mothers can be like, don't you? He's better off here with us for now. So when can we expect you, then?'

'Friday night.' I said. I was somewhat taken aback by Jemma's breathless response to my questioning but there was no time to delve any deeper. I had more important things on my mind. 'I've only got a couple of suitcases and a few small boxes to pack. All the paperwork and bills connected to the flat are still in Giles's name so I can just load up the car and drive back at the end of the day.'

'Will you take your key to the agent or push it back through the flat door in a dog-poo-filled envelope?' Jemma asked innocently.

'Bloody hell, Jem,' I laughed, all thoughts of buff Ben Fletcher nudged out by Jemma's crudeness, 'that's vile; no wonder your daughter's so out of control. I don't even want to think about how I'd manage to do that and in answer to your question, neither. I'm going to meet Giles and give it back to him in person.'

'Oh, Lizzie, I don't think that's a good idea.'

'No,' I smiled, 'I didn't think you would and that's exactly why I'm so pleased you aren't here to stop me!'

Having finally stumbled upon the best way to secure some closure, I arranged to meet Giles, via his secretary, two days later. It had been an odd day. My car was loaded with my few scant possessions from the flat and miraculously I had marched out of the door for the last time, my heels sounding hollow on the polished floor, and slammed it shut without a pang.

At work I spun out the hours having indulged in a long lunch with Henry who on parting, had tried to kiss me, told me he had always had a 'thing' for me and that if I changed my mind and wanted to stay at work and move in with him, that would be fine. I kissed him fondly on the cheek, told him he was a wonderful, kind man who deserved someone who loved him back and that I was sorry but I wasn't the girl for him because I was through with love and all its complications for the time being or possibly even forever.

I swaggered into the bar having just ostentatiously cleared my desk as my colleagues watched on agog and shrugged their shoulders behind my back. I even had the audacity to throw a cheeky '*see ya,*' over my shoulder as I strutted out.

So much for a discreet departure, I giggled. I hadn't realised going home would be such a pick-me-up but the thought of seeing Jemma and everyone at the end of the day had certainly put a spring in my step.

Then I saw him sitting at a table in the far corner at the back of the bar. Top button undone, tie loosened, glass in hand and looking like he'd just stepped straight off the pages of a Hugo Boss advert.

'Lizzie,' he smiled, standing up as I approached.

He kissed my cheek before I had a chance to duck out of the way and I can't deny there was a flicker of arousal in my stomach as I drank in the familiar manly scent of him, but I had it under control. This meeting was on my terms, not his.

It had been agonising catching glimpses of him in the office every day because it was his territory, but the bar was no one's bolt hole – it was completely neutral and I was more than ready to gain a little ground for myself.

'You look stunning,' he said.

The tone of surprise that accompanied his comment set my teeth on edge, but I let it pass.

'Is that a new dress?'

I ignored him again and sat at the other side of the table, banging down the bag of goodies I had meticulously prepared for the occasion.

'Right,' I said, brushing a wayward curl away from my face, 'let's get this over with.'

'At least let me get you a drink,' he insisted, raising a hand to an obliging barman who came rushing over. 'I really want to tell you how much I admire the way you've handled all this, Lizzie. I've been hoping to get a chance to say how sorry I am that I hurt you and how grateful we are that you haven't made things well . . . difficult.'

'What can I get you?' The barman looked at me expectantly.

'Oh nothing for me thanks,' I said brightly, my tone suggesting Giles's words hadn't touched me at all, 'I'm not staying, but this fella might need something a little stronger before long.'

The barman retreated, smirking as he took in Giles's shocked, flushed expression and furtive glance at the other tables. I smiled as it dawned on him that everyone was whispering and watching.

'So what am I doing here?' Giles hissed, now he'd worked out he wasn't going to have it all his own way. 'I thought you wanted to see me.'

'I do want to see you,' I said innocently as I began rummaging about in the colossal bag. 'I have some stuff to give you.'

'Lizzie, for heaven's sake, stop messing about. Just tell me, why am I here?'

'I have told you,' I laughed, 'I want to give you this stuff back. Now sit back, relax and have another drink for god's sake, you look stressed out, Giles.'

Awkwardly he leant back in his chair and I felt an added thrill, knowing I'd finally got him exactly where I wanted him.

'OK, first this horrible cloying foundation.'

I held it up and read the label, then thumped it down on the table.

'I don't want a flawless, matt finish, Giles. I'm not a feature wall. Believe it or not, I happen to be rather fond of my freckles.'

Next was the Rolex watch he'd made a huge fuss about giving me in the office just a few weeks before. He'd sidled up to my desk, hidden behind a gargantuan floral arrangement then made a great show of checking that it fit snugly on my wrist. The flowers had long gone but the diamond-studded watch was still ticking merrily away, completely unaware of how tempted I'd been to stamp on it.

'Now this,' I smiled, 'this watch is really something but I can't help thinking that along with all the other little trinkets that have come my way recently, they're guilt gifts and I don't want them any more than I want you.'

Forcefully I shoved the watch across the table and continued piling up Pandora boxes, along with several pairs of Louboutins.

It took almost half an hour to pile up all the things Giles had forced on me, the woman he had said he loved because she was 'natural' and 'unique'. Eventually the table was groaning with the spoils of my urban transformation and Giles sat speechless as he stared at the mountain stacked up in front of him.

Whether he was in shock or simply afraid that I would make more of a scene if he protested I couldn't be sure, but it didn't matter because I was loving every second and feeling better with every damn thing I offloaded back onto him. As the bag got lighter my spirit did too and by the time it was empty I felt almost drunk.

I stood up and shook it out just to make sure I hadn't missed anything. The ridiculously expensive salon-worthy straighteners clattered out, scattering make-up and shoes far and wide.

'Ooh!' I squealed in mock excitement. 'How could I have forgotten these? These really are the cherry on the cake, aren't they?'

To say Giles looked gutted in no way did justice to his expression. My actions had said it all; he didn't need to have anything else explained.

'I really hope you're happy, Giles,' I told him, as I mustered the courage to turn my back on him and walk out. 'Because I am. I should thank you, really. If you hadn't dumped me I may very well have lived the rest of my life trying to fit your exacting standards. I would have turned myself inside out to be the woman you wanted me to be and that would have been sad, wouldn't it?'

Giles drained his glass but didn't say anything. I noticed his hand was shaking.

'I really hope married life lives up to your expectations.'

I turned to walk out just as another throng of early evening revellers came crashing through the doors. I heard him stand up, the mess I'd left behind rolling all over the floor as he rushed to catch me up. It was now or never. Without so much as a backward glance I sped up and slipped out into the darkness, vowing that I would never see him again.

Chapter 5

'Oh my god! I can't believe you're really here!' Jemma squealed as she wrenched open the car door. Then, taking a second proper look at me, added, 'Crikey, Lizzie, are you OK?'

Of course I wasn't OK. The cocky confidence that had helped me get through the day had evaporated the second I left the bar. I'd sobbed my way through the entire journey and consequently blown the satisfying little fantasy I'd dreamt up, in which I'd bounce back with enough attitude to make Beyoncé proud. I had hoped for a minute to compose myself as I parked up outside Jemma and Tom's cosy and inviting home, but she had spotted the car and raced out to welcome me before I even had the chance to blow my nose.

'Come on,' she ordered, 'into the house, it's freezing out here.'

'You go in and put the kettle on and I'll get my stuff together and catch you up.'

Jemma gave me another hard stare and just when I thought I was in for a lecture, she twigged. That was one of the nicest things about having a best friend you'd known forever; they could tell when to back off without getting offended and sulky.

'OK,' she smiled, her breath streaming ahead of her in the chill crisp air, 'but don't be too long; you'll catch your death!' She rubbed her hands together and ran back up the steps into the house.

When exactly does that happen? I wondered, as I rummaged in my bag for my compact mirror and face wipes. Is there some miraculous moment during childbirth, just before the baby's head crowns, when all the stupid things your own mother has always said become ingrained in your brain to be trotted out for future use so the rest of the world can shake their heads and tut at you in despair?

I sighed at the sight of my puffy red eyes and pale lips as I rubbed the last smudges of mascara from my cheeks and wondered glumly if I would ever have the chance to say inane things to my own nearest and dearest; would anyone ever roll their eyes and tut at me? A sudden movement in the house caught my attention. I could see Jemma peering out of the bay window and talking animatedly over her shoulder to someone behind her.

Doubtless it was darling Ella, my devilish goddaughter who was poised to pounce upon my sallow complexion with all the tact and subtlety a child could muster. Best at least try and make myself presentable I thought, reaching for my make-up bag.

The front door, which led into the hallway and a welcoming jumble of coats and boots, was slightly ajar and as I quietly slipped inside, the warmth and smell of Jemma's delicious baking wrapped itself around me like a fleecy comfort blanket. Hot tears stung my eyes as I pulled off my jacket and thanked my lucky stars that I had settled for here rather than my parents' house. I was going to need to repair and reinforce my emotional armour before I darkened their door again. I took a deep breath and peeped into the sitting room.

'Hello, hot stuff!' I chirped merrily.

'Hello, cheeky!'

My feet almost left the floor as a man I immediately recognised as Ben Fletcher, my one and only high-school crush, jumped up off the sofa and turned to face me. If possible he was even more appealing than I remembered; a fully formed broad-shouldered, bronzed and bearded specimen of manhood. I felt my face flush and was just about to mumble an apology when Ella appeared from nowhere and jumped into my arms, winding me completely.

'I thought you'd be here hours ago!' she scolded. 'I've been waiting and watching all day!' She pulled away and observed me for what felt like a very long few seconds. 'I've missed you,' she whispered, plugging her thumb in and snuggling her soft blonde curls against my neck. 'I've really missed you.'

'And I've missed you too.' I swallowed, willing myself not to cry.

Ben Fletcher playfully tugged at Ella's foot.

'Oh I see!' he joked, the lines around his eyes crinkling attractively. 'Uncle Ben not good enough for you now, is he, and you haven't been watching all day, madam, you've been at school!'

Ella giggled and wriggled in my arms, but reassuringly made no attempt to escape. I kissed the top of her head and inhaled. She no longer carried with her that seductively sweet baby smell, but I was still comforted by her softness and grateful that she was willing to endure my hug.

'Shall we try again?' Ben smiled. 'I'm Ben, Ben Fletcher. Jemma wasn't sure that you'd remember me. I was in the same year as Tom at school and . . .'

'And you've come back to help with the Café,' I said, aiming for confident and self-assured. 'Yes, Jemma did tell me and of course I remember you,' I gabbled on, 'but you look different, maybe it's the beard. I can't imagine you had it at school, did you?'

'I thought I heard your dulcet tones!' Tom appeared in the doorway grinning broadly, a beer in each hand. 'How are you, chick?'

'Good,' I lied as Ella wriggled free, 'I'm good.'

'You do remember Ben, don't you?' he asked, handing his friend a bottle and offering the other to me. 'Jemma said she didn't think you would, but I didn't believe her.'

Bloody Jemma! I wasn't sure what she was up to but if she carried on making such a fuss about whether I would or wouldn't remember the man in question then I might as well rush to the River Wyn, jump up on the bridge and declare that yes, once upon a time I did indeed have a crush on him.

'Of course I remember him,' I smiled, shaking my head at Jemma's absurd suggestion. 'Although I told him he looks a bit different. I reckon it's the beard that's thrown me.'

Tom held my gaze and just for a second there was something like amusement written across his features, then he turned to watch Ben rub his thickly insulated chin. My heart thumped a little harder and I hoped the truth wasn't written across my flushed face or that Jemma had told him about my tempestuous teenage feelings. I would have been mortified to discover that he knew.

'I still can't decide whether to get rid of it,' Ben sighed.

Tom rolled his eyes, a clear indication that he'd heard the 'for and against debate' about his mate's facial hair many times before.

'Well,' I said reasonably, 'if you shave it all off and change your mind, how long before it gets to this stage again?'

'Oh it'd be months. This all began last year. It was my

contribution to Movember. I had planned to get rid of it, but then I came home and my mother was so appalled by the sight of it that I decided it should stay!'

I laughed out loud, sharp stinging beer bubbles painfully filling my nose and making me snort inelegantly.

'Brilliant!' I spluttered, trying to cover my embarrassment, 'that's exactly what I would have done!'

Why? Why did I say that? I was never going to grow a beard for Movember, was I?

'Lizzie suffers in the mother department as well,' Tom explained on my behalf, 'don't you?'

'You have absolutely no idea!' I coughed.

'Unfortunately,' Ben smiled, raising his eyebrows and fixing me with his intense brown eyes, 'I think I do.'

The fluttering in my stomach and rapid quickening of my pulse as my gaze met his made me feel far headier than the beer I'd been swigging on an empty stomach. I couldn't believe it, a decade and a half after I'd first seen him in the dinner queue and I *still* fancied him. It was ridiculous, I felt like a high-school newbie again and every inch as awkward and unappealing as I had then.

Ella came skipping back in and grabbed Ben's hand.

'Dinner!' she shouted up at us all. 'Mummy says if we don't hurry up she'll give it to the dog!'

'We don't have a dog, Ellie belly,' Tom laughed as he scooped up his impish daughter, 'and we're not getting one, so you can stop all that "we can feed it on leftovers to save money" nonsense!'

Feeling hungrier than I had in weeks, Ella and I led the way into the kitchen and I became uncomfortably aware of furtive whispering going on behind me.

'I told you it would be OK,' I heard Tom hiss as he and Ben fell behind.

'We'll see,' Ben whispered back, 'let's just give it a bit longer before we're saying that, shall we?'

'Jemma, I'm done,' I announced a little later. 'I can't squeeze in another mouthful!'

'Me neither,' Ben puffed, throwing down his napkin and belching discreetly.

Jemma beamed. She had spent the meal swooping around the kitchen, competently filling glasses and replenishing plates. She was the perfect hostess, wife and mother. No, I realised, she was more than that, she was happy. She was settled and content and I couldn't quell the selfish pang of envy I felt as I acknowledged again that my dear friend had achieved so much, whilst I had returned from my endeavours with nothing more than a broken heart and a steadily growing sense of bitterness that would have made my mother proud.

'Well in that case, let's all go and fall asleep in front of the fire,' Jemma laughed.

'What about the clearing up?' I asked. I was hoping to have

a minute with her to ask if she knew what the guys had been whispering about.

'All done!' Jemma beamed. 'I sorted it as we went along.'

'Eat your heart out, Nigella.' Ben grinned, grabbing her and quickly planting a whiskery kiss on her cheek.

'If I didn't know she hated that fuzz, mate,' Tom joked, 'I wouldn't let you get away with that!'

'Actually,' Jemma laughed, 'it is kind of growing on me!'

'Right, that's it!'

This time it was Ella who rolled her eyes as she watched her parents chase each other around the kitchen. I kept my eyes on the table.

'They always do this,' she told me in her most grown-up voice, 'even when we have company.'

'Lizzie's not company,' Tom frowned, skidding to a halt, 'she's family.'

'Yes, and Mummy said she's broken-hearted so I don't think you should mess about like that. It might remind her about her old boyfriend, mightn't it, and what about poor Ben?'

'I'll just go and check the fire,' Ben mumbled, quickly ducking out of the room.

'And you, young lady, can come upstairs for your bath,' said Tom, not daring to look in my direction.

'God, Lizzie, I'm so sorry,' Jemma whispered as she quietly closed the kitchen door. 'I haven't said a word to her, I promise. The little sod must have been eavesdropping.'

'It's OK,' I said, 'honestly.'

'No it isn't,' Jemma frowned, pulling her thick blonde ponytail over her shoulder and hanging on to it.

The gesture made me smile and was a complete giveaway as to how bad she felt. Jemma had been tugging on her ponytail ever since she stepped out in front of my bike and sent me flying after Dad had taken my stabilisers off.

'Look, come on,' I pleaded. 'Please don't make a fuss.'

I was just as embarrassed as everyone else but it was done. I knew being around Ella would mean that this sort of thing would happen occasionally and I'd made sure I factored that in when deciding whether I was going to come back.

'Let's talk about something else,' I suggested, grateful for the opportunity to steer the conversation back to Tom and Ben and the chance to quiz her as to why she'd insisted I wouldn't remember him. 'What's the big secret between the boys,' I said casually, 'and why did you tell Ben that I probably wouldn't recognise him?'

'I was only trying to help,' she pouted, 'I thought that if I said you couldn't remember him it would look as if you weren't interested in him and there is no secret, as far as I know.'

'I'm not interested in him,' I snapped, fighting back the blush that was threatening to bloom, 'but they were definitely whispering as we came in to dinner, something about everything turning out all right.'

'No idea, probably something and nothing,' she shrugged dismissively, 'you know what boys are like.'

'Not really,' I said, wrinkling my nose, 'otherwise I wouldn't be suddenly single, would I?'

The look of horror on Jemma's face was enough to make me regret my flippant comment.

'Oh ignore me!' I laughed.

I could tell that she did know what the guys had been whispering about, but I also knew that once she had made up her mind about something there was no point quizzing her.

'I know,' I suggested. 'How about we go and have a look at the flat? I can't wait to see it.'

'Oh, well,' she stuttered, her cheeks flushing crimson as she fiddled with the edge of the tablecloth, 'I don't think we should go traipsing over there at this time of night.'

'Why not?'

'Well, we've had all this wine for a start!' She gestured towards the two bottles and empty glasses. 'It's getting late and it's freezing out there.'

'And?'

'What do you mean?'

'I mean, and what aren't you telling me?'

I was prepared to let her off with keeping the boys' secret, but withholding details about my future home was something else.

'Nothing!' Jemma's voice was still an octave too high to quell my suspicions.

'Jemma!'

'Oh all right! The boys couldn't get the boiler going today so there's no heating yet, but that's all.'

'Really?'

'Really! I mean, the décor leaves a bit to be desired and the damp needs sorting in the back bedroom but apart from that it'll be fine once you've stretched your creative muscle.'

There was something about the way she carried on fiddling at the table that warned me that perhaps the flat wasn't going to be quite as welcoming as I'd originally hoped.

I remembered the consequences connected to another time she had been cagey about something and hoped this time around things wouldn't be so problematic. Years ago she'd borrowed my first pair of designer leather boots without asking, for a secret date with Tom and somehow snapped the heel off. Consequently I'd looked a right prat when I marched, or should I say hobbled, back to the store shouting about shoddy workmanship only to be told that the heel had been broken before and glued back on.

'Look, I know what you're thinking.'

'No you don't!'

'Yes I do, you're thinking about those bloody boots!'

We both burst out laughing and the atmosphere that only seconds before had been heading towards fraught had dissolved.

'I promise we'll go first thing in the morning,' Jemma said, 'tonight I'll just set up the sofa bed. I'm sure Ben wouldn't mind moving out of the spare room for one night.'

'No,' I insisted, 'the sofa will be fine for me. It'll be a treat with the fire still lit, really snug and peaceful.'

'OK,' Jemma smiled, 'as long as you're sure. Then a fresh start tomorrow, yes?'

'Yes,' I tried to smile back with more confidence than I felt, 'a fresh start tomorrow.'

By the time Ella had finally decided it was time to stay in bed and go to sleep and Tom and Ben had unloaded the dish-washer, I was more than ready to hit the sack. Jemma had closed the sitting-room curtains and thoughtfully warmed up the makeshift bed with Ella's penguin-shaped hot-water bottle. She threw a final log on the fire and told me to help myself to anything I wanted from the kitchen.

'We're so pleased you've come back,' she said kindly, as she wrapped me in a comforting embrace.

'So am I,' I whispered.

'I couldn't have done it,' she admitted, releasing me.

'What do you mean?'

'Come back on my own,' she confided, her body emitting a little tremor, 'I would have gone anywhere but here, any-where other than where everyone knows me.'

She gave me another quick hug and it suddenly dawned on

me that, for the next few weeks at least, my private life was going to be very public. I'd been working in the pub when Giles burst on the scene and there was barely a resident left in the town that my mother hadn't bragged to about my 'high flying' job and well-bred boyfriend. I shrugged my shoulders, thinking it was too late to worry about any of that now. I was here and I was safe amongst friends who had offered me a refuge and a lifeline.

'We'll brazen it out together,' I told her firmly. 'This time next week I'll be old news.'

As I lay alone that night listening to the comforting crackle of the fire, my mind flitted back to Giles and what he had done when I left him at the bar. Had he scooped up the junk I'd dumped on him or had he left it all there? Had he abandoned the mess like he'd abandoned me, on the expectation that someone else would clear it all up and make it presentable again?

I thought about what Ella had said as well. Watching Jemma and Tom in the kitchen brought home to me how 'grown-up' and sensible my relationship with Giles had been. There was no denying the sex was always phenomenally satisfying and well, sexy, but we'd never really messed about or laughed uproariously, never chased each other around the flat or gone in for demonstrative public displays of affection. As I eventually drifted off to sleep I couldn't help wondering if our 'big' relationship had really been worthy of the pedestal I had so readily put it on.

Chapter 6

It was comforting to wake up to the noise and bustle of a house full of people. The building that housed the flat that Giles and I had shared always struck me as exclusive and extravagant with its river views and concierge, but it had no soul. My heels had always sounded hollow on the polished floor and our voices echoed off the empty walls and high ceilings. There was plenty of style attached to the sought-after postcode, but little in the way of substance.

'I'm sorry that Jemma gave you the impression that I wouldn't recognise you, Ben,' I apologised, as I passed him the coffee pot.

I knew it wasn't really necessary to bring the subject up again but to me it still felt like unfinished business and after the humiliation of the beer-bubble snorting and Ella's little faux pas, I just wanted to start our relationship over, wipe the slate clean and get off on the right foot. It was inevitable that we were going to be spending a fair bit of time together over the coming weeks and after the complications I'd left behind in London I was feeling determined to keep life in Wynbridge as simple as possible.

'It's OK,' he shrugged, staring down and pinning me with his seductively dark gaze, 'I'll let you in on a little secret, shall I?'

'What?' I breathed, my stomach turning over as I stared back full of hope that he was going to enlighten me as to what he and Tom had been whispering about.

'It was actually more likely that I wouldn't recognise you!'

'What, when I arrived you mean?'

'No,' Ben smiled wryly, 'with your trademark hair and freckles it could only be you! I meant from the photographs Jemma showed me.'

'Oh,' I said, my eyes now firmly focused on my coffee cup.

I was flattered he had remembered something about me, but it was hardly a compliment; my so-called 'trademark hair and freckles' turned out to be more trouble than they were worth as a rule. For once it would have been nice to be remembered for just being me, for my sparkling conversation and razor-sharp wit. Yeah right. Who was I kidding?

'You looked very sleek and sophisticated,' Ben continued, 'not at all like the girl I used to see around school and working in the pub.'

'Oh,' I said again, my already crushed confidence taking

another knock. At least he'd 'seen me around' but how exactly had I looked then: dull, dowdy, desperate?

Ben took a swig of coffee then banged down his mug.

'Shit,' he muttered, 'sorry, that didn't come out right. I didn't mean you didn't look good before. Sorry, what I meant was . . .'

'It's fine,' I interrupted. 'Don't worry about it.'

I felt even more awkward having guessed which photographs Jemma must have shown him. They were doubtless the set I'd sent her from the company Christmas ball and Ben was right, I had looked sleek and sophisticated. My hair was smooth and straight, my nails polished and my elegant jade dress and matching Jimmy Choos, which had carried a jaw-dropping price tag, immaculate.

'Well, I'm back to my old self now,' I shrugged, tucking my hair behind my ears and desperately trying not to think about anything that was connected to Giles.

'Good,' Ben nodded. His expression was deadly serious as he took in my sloppy pj's and dishevelled curls. 'It never works, does it? I've discovered that for myself recently.' His tone was suddenly bitter and sounded far less friendly.

'What do you mean?'

'Trying to pretend to be someone you're not. It never turns out how you think it will. There's a time limit on pretending. It simply isn't possible to live a lie for long.'

I opened my mouth to say something but couldn't find the words. I was only just beginning to come to terms with how much Giles had changed me and my appearance during the course of our relationship and I certainly didn't need someone I barely knew nudging me to think about all the reasons as to why he might have done it.

'I'm going for a shower,' I mumbled, quickly slipping out of the room and wondering if it was really possible for me to just turn back into my old self. And more importantly, did I actually want to?

'Just remember,' Jemma smiled nervously, 'it isn't as bad as it looks and there's nothing we can't fix, OK?'

'That's it, love,' Tom laughed, giving his wife a gentle shove, 'keep going, you're really selling it to her now! I wish you sounded as confident about overhauling the Café as you do about the flat.'

We rounded the corner, having dropped Ella at her ballet class, and there it was, The Cherry Tree Café or perhaps I should say, the shell of what had once been The Cherry Tree Café.

'So as you can see, the outside needs a bit more work,' Tom faltered, pulling off his hat and scratching his head as we crossed the icy road. 'But Jemma's right, Lizzie, it's not actually as bad as it looks.'

Everything was pretty much as I remembered it. The cute picket fence and cherry tree that covered much of the forecourt was still in situ, only now the fence sported more rot than paint and the once lovely tree looked as though it hadn't been pruned in years.

'We'll go round the back,' Tom suggested, as he took in my expression, 'just focus on the flat for today. Ben's here already. He's gradually working his way through the list of jobs you gave him, isn't he, Jem?'

'He certainly is,' Jemma said, smiling again, 'I've already told Lizzie how hands on he is.'

'Um,' Tom smiled back as he tickled his wife in the ribs, 'I bet you have. Anyway, we won't disturb him for now. Let's go straight up to the flat and look in on him after.'

After our earlier conversation I didn't want to look in on him at all but I was curious to see how the old place was shaping up. I still hadn't worked out if Ben had been having a dig at me back at the house but I was going to have to get over it. I was desperate to get on and start moving my stuff up to the flat, but I wanted to have a look around the Café first, even if Ben Fletcher was there wielding his hammer. Before I could stop them, however, Jemma and Tom had set off down the little path that ran along the side of the building.

'Hey, hang on, guys!' I called after them, 'I want to see the Café first. It can't be that bad surely!'

They walked slowly back and Jemma tentatively reached for the handle and pushed back the door.

'In you go then,' she said nervously, 'see what you make of it. Is it how you remember it?'

I stepped across the threshold and blinked as my eyes became accustomed to the gloom.

'Well?' Jemma whispered close behind me, her change in tone stamping all over her previous enthusiasm about fixing up the flat. 'Oh god, we don't stand a chance, do we?' she groaned.

I spun round to face her as Tom flicked on the lights.

'What do you mean?'

'It's a disaster, isn't it?' she sobbed. 'A dark, dingy nightmare! No one will ever want to eat in here again!'

'You silly sod!' I laughed, wrapping my arms around her. 'It's brilliant, exactly as I remember it, but with bags of potential. You're going to make it so much better than it was before.'

'You really think so?' she sniffed.

'I really do!'

I stepped further in, refusing to see the place as Jemma currently did. I walked the length and width of the Café floor thinking of ways the space could be quickly and cleverly repackaged and relaunched.

The tiled floor was sound and the walls down here at least didn't appear to be damp. A lick of paint, some fresh curtains, one hell of a clean and the place would be back in business.

'Have you thought about a colour scheme?' I asked, lifting down a couple of the chairs that were stacked on the tables.

Jemma opened her mouth to answer but was stopped in her tracks by a barrage of expletives coming from the kitchen.

'Tom!' Ben hollered. 'Is that you? Get your arse in here quick!'

We all dashed around the counter and into the kitchen to find Ben hunched on all fours with his head in a cupboard and a puddle of water spreading with alarming speed across the floor.

'Give us a hand, would you?' he shouted. 'My hands are so cold I can't feel my fingers any more! I think it just needs one more turn.'

He leapt aside and Tom dived into the cupboard and fiddled with something before reappearing shaking his head.

'Just a bit of a leak,' he said, purposefully keeping his tone light as he spotted Jemma's worried expression. 'Nothing we can't sort, hey, Ben?'

'Absolutely,' Ben nodded, his teeth chattering as he rubbed his hands together, 'just thought it best to turn the water off as a precaution. I'll have it sorted by the end of the day, no problem, and the shelves will be up as well so don't worry, Jemma.'

'Assuming you haven't died of hypothermia, of course,' Tom grinned.

'You better get that shirt off,' Jemma said, shaking her head, 'give him your jacket, Tom.'

I turned away as Ben stripped to the waist but not before I'd caught a glimpse of his toned and tanned torso.

'Come back through to the Café with me,' I said to Jemma as I quickly turned and walked away, 'and tell me what you've got planned décor-wise.'

'We haven't got that far,' she admitted as she followed on behind me, blissfully unaware that my insides felt as if they had turned to marshmallow.

'To be honest, Lizzie,' said Tom, following on with Ben, 'we haven't got any idea about how to make it look good. All the money we've saved has been sunk into buying the place and sorting the kitchen and loos and now we can't see the wood for the trees when it comes to making it look appealing. With the constraints of our bank balance, image- and design-wise we've drawn a blank.'

Jemma nodded despondently at his side and Tom took her hand and gave it a reassuring squeeze.

'Well,' I said, brushing down the table I had cleared of chairs, 'if it's saving money you need to be thinking about, then I would definitely re-use everything you've already got in here.'

'Really?' Jemma and Tom chorused.

Ben stood and shook his head as he blew on his numb fingers.

'Of course,' I carried on, 'you can up-cycle all these tables and chairs for a start. Give them a rub down and a fresh lick of paint and they'll be as good as new, better in fact because they'll be a nod to the past but very much about the Café's future. The old clientele will love that.'

Ben thrust his hands in his trouser pockets and began moodily kicking the floor.

'And the counter,' I continued, determined not to be put off by his apparent scepticism, 'that can have the same treatment so it will all match. You need to come up with a design that will complement Jemma's amazing baking of course, that will bring it all together . . . what?' I shouted, as Ben let out a shuddering breath.

'Oh nothing,' he said breezily, 'you just carry on.'

'I take it you don't agree?' I snapped, wishing I'd been privy to his caustic comments and presumptuous personality years ago. I could have saved myself years of yearning. 'You probably think they should bin the lot and start again, is that it? Take out a huge loan and fill the place with brand new soulless stuff instead!'

'Um, not exactly.'

'Well, what then?' I demanded. 'If there's no money left and even less time, then I can't see the harm in using what's to hand . . .'

'Neither can I,' said Ben defiantly.

'What?'

I frowned at Jemma and Tom who stood together looking shame-faced. Tom self-consciously cleared his throat, but it was Jemma who finally answered.

'Ben's been making the same suggestions as you, Lizzie, practically ever since we picked up the keys, actually.'

I sighed and threw my hands up in the air.

'So why haven't you got on with it, then? You've wasted weeks. "We'll be opening in the spring," you told me, Jemma. Why haven't you done anything with all this lot?'

'I guess we couldn't really see it,' Tom admitted. 'But the kitchens and loos are beginning to look tip top! They're almost there actually.'

'Well, that's great,' I nodded sarcastically, 'you'll have all the appropriate licences to hang on the walls, but what's the point if you can't tempt people in to eat?'

'She's got a point,' Tom whispered to his wife who finally looked as if the penny was about to drop.

'I've been so preoccupied with thinking about all the food I'll be able to bake that I kind of got side-tracked. I guess I hadn't really thought about all this,' she gestured, indicating the Café shop floor. 'But you're right, Lizzie; if we can't get customers through the door then no one's going to know how great my cupcakes are, are they?'

'Exactly!' I laughed. I knew how much Jemma's cooking and baking meant to her, but to me the image of the Café would have been of equal, if not higher, priority.

'Sorry, Lizzie,' Jemma smiled, sounding disconcertingly like her daughter.

'Never mind me!' I scolded. 'What about Ben? By the

sounds of it he's been talking to a brick wall for the last few weeks. Where's his apology?'

I couldn't help thinking that I owed him one as well. Just as well he hadn't been privy to my peevish thoughts.

'Sorry, Ben,' Jemma and Tom muttered in unison. 'We should have listened to you, mate.'

'Oh don't worry about me,' Ben rumbled, evidently not seeing the funny side. 'I mean, given my track record, I can understand why you'd think I was talking crap and there's nothing unusual about me not having a say in things of importance, is there?'

'Oh come on, mate,' said Tom, crossing the Café floor and throwing his arm around Ben's shoulders, 'I thought you'd moved on from all that.'

I looked to Jemma for an explanation but she just frowned and shook her head. Clearly there was something I didn't know about our bearded companion, but I wasn't going to find out what it was from her.

'I have, I have,' Ben muttered stiffly. 'Sorry, I'm just having one of those days, you know? For some reason it's all come flooding back.'

He shot what could only be described as a killer stare in my direction and I guessed that my presence wasn't welcome, but what was it exactly that I was supposed to have done? Clearly I wasn't the only one who'd landed on Jemma and Tom's doorstep with more than renovating the Café in mind, but I couldn't see how targeting his aggression towards me was going to help anyone.

Despite his rugged appeal and mesmerising eyes I was beginning to like Ben Fletcher less and less. Clearly he wasn't the person I'd dreamt he was and neither was he going to be the 'getting over Giles' distraction Jemma had hoped for.

'Come on,' she said coaxingly, drawing my attention away from the boys, 'let's have a look at everything else and then we'll go up to the flat!'

The kitchen and loos were shaping up as well as Tom had suggested. Rewired and repainted, there were just the appliances left to install and with a bit of last-minute tweaking and leak-fixing the place would be good to go.

Fortunately, and in spite of Jemma's reservations, the same could be pretty much said for the flat above, however I was still relieved that I'd seen the Café before we headed upstairs. It kind of gave me a heads-up regarding what to expect, and having been so enthusiastic about the shop floor I could hardly refuse to see the potential in the space above, could I?

It was dank and drab, but only because it hadn't been lived in for so long. There was a damp patch in the back bedroom but the large windows offered great views of the Café garden and there were some super vintage kitchen units along with an open fire in the little sitting room. On closer inspection even the damp patch wasn't as bad as I'd been expecting.

'I reckon that could be the result of the dodgy guttering,' Ben frowned, nodding at Tom as they followed me back into the bedroom, 'and now that's been sorted, I reckon if the room's given a decent airing and some gentle heat, it'll sort itself.'

'Yeah,' said Tom, running his hand over the wall, 'I reckon you could be right.'

'There you are then!' I smiled at Jemma who was standing in the doorway. 'Happy days. It's not quite what I've grown accustomed to . . .'

I was just about to add that it was even better because it was so homely, but out of the corner of my eye I spotted Ben rolling his eyes. Was I imagining it or was he still pissed off with me? It wasn't my fault if Jemma and Tom had taken on-board my cheap and cheerful makeover suggestions over his, was it? I watched him walk past her out of the room and turned my attention back to Jemma, who was looking at me expectantly.

'. . . and that's exactly why I love it!' I said. 'This is going to be perfect. Living over the Café will keep me on my toes. It's going to be so busy and exciting that I won't have a chance to sit and brood about everything else that's happened.'

Jemma stepped forward and gave me a hug.

'I just want you to be happy,' she said tearfully.

'I will be,' I told her, squeezing her back, 'just give me time, OK?'

Mercifully the flat walls were painted, not papered, and the carpets would be fine after a good steam clean. I lingered in the kitchen and pictured myself hanging up the bunting I had made whilst the guys had another go at tempting the boiler, which was housed in a cupboard at the top of the stairs, back to life.

'It is small,' said Jemma as she squeezed into the kitchen with me, 'but it's a start, isn't it? I know you've been used to all that space . . .' her voice trailed off as she looked over at me. I knew she was trying to decide if she was pushing her luck.

'To tell you the truth,' I shrugged, 'I never really liked the place. It never felt like home.'

'Not even with Giles there?' she ventured.

'Not even then,' I admitted.

The boiler refused to succumb to the guys' ministrations and as the flat was beginning to feel colder than outside, we admitted defeat and headed back to collect Ella.

'I'll get Bob Skipper who sorted the Café heating to have a look at it on Monday morning, Lizzie,' said Tom.

'Good idea,' said Jemma.

'If I'd known you were coming a bit sooner, I would have got him to sort it when he was here before, but not to worry. However, it does leave us with another problem,' he continued, shaking his head, 'this means you're gonna be stuck with us for a couple more days at least!'

I'd already thought of that.

'You're going to be stuck with me, you mean. Jemma, shall I phone my mum and see if I can go there until the flat defrosts?'

My suggestion was met by a sharp intake of breath from all sides.

'No, you certainly shall not!' Jemma was first to pipe up. 'The whole point of you being here is to rest and recuperate, not endure a grilling.'

Even Ben nodded in agreement.

'Take my word for it, Lizzie; you aren't strong enough for that yet.'

I'd already guessed that Ben's mother and mine were shelled from the same pod but I still couldn't shake off the feeling that everything he said to me was a thinly veiled criticism.

'Ben's right,' Tom joined in, clearly not feeling the same sting from his friend's words as I did, 'give yourself at least a fighting chance! Hey, Jemma, how about we send Ella off to your mum's tonight and head down to the Mermaid?'

'Oh, I don't know,' I began to protest, 'you just said I needed to "give myself a fighting chance" – I'm not ready to face a pub full of locals yet!'

'Band-aid treatment. I've done it, so I'm sure you can,' Ben announced. 'Doesn't apply to overbearing mothers, though.'

'Sorry?' I frowned, wondering what had happened in Ben's

life that meant he too had had to brave a pub full of curiosity and gossiping. '*What* treatment?'

'Band-aid treatment. You know, rip it off quick; get it over and done with.'

'He's right,' Jemma called over her shoulder. 'You can front it out with the help of alcohol in the pub. Your mum, on the other hand, will want you stone-cold sober!'

'Yep,' Tom joined in having the final word, 'you have to work your way up to these things, Lizzie! Pub it is then!'

Chapter 7

To help cushion the impact of walking into a pub full of people I hadn't seen since I floated out of town aboard a heart-shaped cloud, Tom offered to go on ahead with Ben, get a round in and secure a table in a shady corner. Jemma reckoned that if I kept my hood up and my head down I would be able to sneak in and down a couple of stiff ones before anyone recognised me.

As we slipped up the icy pavement that ran alongside the River Wyn and towards the cheerily lit haven at the end of the road, I considered throwing myself into a pot hole in the hope that I would sprain or even break an ankle to avoid the inevitable humiliation which I could feel pulsating towards me with every step. Unfortunately Jemma, my telepathic companion, guessed what was afoot and clung on even tighter. She didn't say anything, but her grasp suggested that if I was going down I was going to have to take her with me.

'Ready?' she asked, her pretty face and long blonde hair lit by the soft glow emanating from the pub windows.

'No,' I smiled nervously. 'Not really. Can we just go home, please?'

'Oh come on! What can possibly go wrong?'

I looked up at the weather-beaten sign as it creaked in the icy breeze and the piercing gaze of the mermaid as she sat upon her rock, haughtily brushing her long locks with a sea shell comb.

'Everything,' I whispered. I stepped back just as Jemma lifted the latch on the heavy wooden door. 'I'm sorry, but I can't do this,' I stammered, 'not yet. I'm just not ready.'

I turned with the intention of rushing back down the road to the sanctuary of Jemma and Tom's welcoming hearth, but the door was thrust open and before I'd taken a single step, I felt myself being helpfully nudged backwards by my 'friend'.

It was inevitable of course that I should lose my footing and fall flat on my backside across the welcome mat. The pub fell silent as Jemma rushed, apologising profusely, to pull me to my feet and dust me down as if it had been Ella who had fallen rather than foolish thirty-something me.

'Well, well, well!' I heard Evelyn Harper, the pub landlady's shrill voice ring out. 'Look what the cat's dragged in!'

Tom and Ben sat as promised, in the shadowy nook next to the fire, nursing their drinks and shaking their heads.

'Hello, Evelyn,' I tried to smile, my face aglow, 'long time no see.'

'Too bloody long!' shouted a voice next to me. It was Evelyn's husband, Jim. 'How the hell are you, girl?'

He spun me round and hugged me tight, my face barely reaching his chest.

'Crikey, Jim!' I spluttered. 'Have you grown?'

As I regained my composure and felt some of the heat in my face recede, I noticed everyone turning back to their own conversations. The babble of chatter in the pub grew steadily louder until it was once again almost impossible to hear yourself think and I was subjected to nothing more agonising than the odd questioning glance. Maybe this wasn't going to be as bad as I first thought.

'I thought you were more interested in grand exits than entrances?' Jim winked as he levered himself to his station behind the bar.

Evelyn, who barely came up to his shoulder but was very much in charge, dug him hard in the ribs.

'You leave her alone!' she snapped. 'Ignore him, my love. You know what an old tease he can be. Now what can I get you – it's on the house?'

Tom and Ben forced their way through the crowd towards the bar where Jemma and I were perched on a couple of stools. Their fireside seats were taken long before they reached us.

'We didn't think there was much point hiding in the corner after that!' Tom laughed. 'Do you girls fancy a song?'

Jemma rolled her eyes and tugged at Tom's sleeve.

'Please not tonight,' she begged, 'can't we just have one night off, one single, solitary trip to the pub that doesn't turn into a bloody Mumford tribute?'

'No,' Tom laughed, kissing the top of her head. 'We thought a bit of a sing-song might take the heat off Lizzie for a bit. Feel free to join in, won't you?' he winked at me.

He disappeared amongst the crowd again with Ben following on behind. He didn't say anything as he passed and I struggled to believe that the impromptu entertainment was really for my benefit and even if it was, it certainly wasn't Ben who had come up with the idea.

'I get the impression Ben doesn't like me!' I shouted to Jemma, after I'd made sure he was out of earshot.

'What do you mean?' she asked, shouting back above the noise.

'I can't explain it,' I shrugged, 'it's just a couple of things he's said.'

Jemma shook her head.

'Don't take it personally,' she insisted, 'he's got a lot on his plate right now.'

'Like what?'

Jemma took a sip of her pint.

'I'm sorry, Lizzie, I'm not supposed to say anything.'

'Oh,' I said, feeling a bit put out.

'Let's just say Ben is pissed off with pretty much everyone and everything right now,' she explained, 'so don't take his comments personally, OK?'

I was intrigued. My hunch at the Café was obviously right.

'That's easy for you to say!' I told her. 'I haven't heard him snap at you!'

'Oh, he's had his moments, believe me.' Jemma smiled.

A thought suddenly struck me.

'He isn't cross because you offered the flat to me, is he? I mean, he was already with you before you asked me if I wanted to move in, wasn't he?'

'No, no! It's nothing like that. I don't think he's planning on hanging around long after the Café's open,' Jemma reassured me. 'He hasn't talked about staying on, anyway.'

'Fair enough,' I muttered. 'I'll try not to take his comments to heart next time.'

Jemma didn't say anything else and I knew I wasn't going to get anything more out of her. It wasn't fair to try and force her to fess up, but I still couldn't help feeling left a little out in the cold. After all, Ben knew why I was sleeping on the sofa in my best friend's sitting room; the least he could do was return the favour and share his woes with me, wasn't it? I'd already worked out we were going to be spending a lot of time together at the Café over the coming weeks and without knowing why he had come back I was bound to put my foot in it and incur his wrath.

Jemma turned to face me again. She was obviously feeling guilty.

'Like I said, he's got a lot on his mind right now. He's coming to terms with some pretty major stuff that's happened in his life, but bear with him. You'll really like him once you get to know him and I dare say he'll fill you in when the time's right.'

I drank a mouthful of my pint and glanced over to where the guys were preparing to entertain the crowd. Tom, sitting at the piano, was grinning broadly and Ben, miraculously smiling, was fiddling intently with the strings on a double bass. A third member of the crowd joined them and cheers went up as he whipped a banjo out from behind his back. I looked around at the ruddy, slightly unfocused faces and thought how the place hadn't changed at all. We were certainly in for a fun evening.

A little while later Jim had somehow tempted me behind the packed bar and I found myself pulling pints with the same dexterity I had achieved when I was a paid member of staff.

'You wouldn't happen to be looking for a bit of part-time work, would you?' Evelyn asked as she squeezed past with a handful of change. 'Only we're a body down at the moment and you've obviously still got the knack.'

'Crikey, I don't know!' I laughed.

This was the second job offer I'd had in days and neither

bore any resemblance to the one I'd just given up. Perhaps Ben was right after all; perhaps I'd been kidding myself all along, trying to be someone other than plain old Lizzie Dixon, but surely if I took Evelyn up on her offer it would feel like the last two years hadn't happened. I would feel like I was admitting, if only to myself, that I would have been better off staying put and pulling pints in Wynbridge.

'I only got back yesterday,' I told Evelyn, 'I don't even know if I'm staying yet.'

I looked over at Jemma, who was now sitting on the stool next to Tom and singing her head off. Another pang of unwanted jealousy hit. Perhaps I'd made a mistake in thinking I would be able to rebuild my life back here? Maybe I would have been better off going somewhere different, somewhere I could be the new girl in town, the only baggage attached to me stowed away in the boot of my car? What if, I cringed, everyone here was thinking the same thing as Ben had suggested. Were they all thinking I deserved what had happened because I'd got ideas above my station?

'Well, have a think about it and let me know,' Evelyn said, her eyes following my gaze. 'I know Jemma's been looking forward to seeing you and I'm sure she could do with a hand with the Café and that little rascal Ella. Your friend has certainly got her hands full at the moment, that's for sure!'

Evelyn was right, of course. I excused myself and headed for the ladies. I wouldn't be much of a friend if I jumped ship when my best mate needed me most, would I? In the past Jemma had always been there for me and now I only had to think about how keen she was to offer me the flat to know that she had my best interests at heart.

'Lizzie Dixon! Well this is a surprise!'

My heart sank as I looked up into the mirror above the sinks.

'Erica Summers,' I smiled through gritted teeth, 'how lovely to see you.'

'Actually, it's Erica Dawson now,' the woman drawled, waving a bejewelled left hand at my reflection. 'I got married last summer.'

'Oh yes, Mum did mention it.' General consensus was that it was the most expensive, extravagant and ostentatious wedding the town had ever seen. 'Congratulations.'

'You next!' she giggled as she primped her hair and reapplied her lip gloss. 'Will you be doing it here?'

'Excuse me?'

'The wedding,' she said, her recent Botox permitting only the merest hint of a raised eyebrow as she stared back at me in the mirror, 'will you be having it here in Wynbridge or is it going to be on Giles's family estate?' she gushed.

'I don't know . . .'

'Don't tell me you haven't decided yet!' she laughed. 'If you don't hurry up you'll never book the caterer or musicians you want or anything! If you aren't careful you'll end up with those buffoons out there!' she laughed, inclining her head back towards the bar door where the distant roar of 'I Will Wait' was being thumped out at full volume. 'Believe me,' she confided in a conspiratorial whisper, 'organising a wedding takes a lot of commitment. I can give you the details of the planner I used, if you like?'

'Erica,' I said, trying not to cry, be sick or show any trace of emotion that would let my old enemy know that she was getting to me. 'I think there's been a mistake.'

'Oh no mistake, your mother . . .'

'My mother,' I interrupted, cursing her under my breath, 'has made a mistake.'

Erica, wide-eyed, blinked slowly and gave her carefully coiffured head a little shake of confusion. I couldn't bring myself to say the words. I couldn't stand there and tell her that I was back in town as a singleton with no romantic prospects or attachments.

I pushed past her back into the bar.

'There's no mistake,' she called close behind me, her voice losing its upmarket tone. 'I read it in the paper!'

The music came to a shuddering halt and everyone clapped and cheered for an encore.

'What?' I shouted above the din.

'We all did!' Erica shouted back, her expression triumphant. 'Everyone knows! Your mother put an announcement in the paper the other week.'

She grabbed the pile of stacked local newspapers from the bar just as Jim lunged for them. Gradually, as the noise subsided, all faces turned to us. Erica rifled through the pile, Jim still ineffectually trying to snatch them from her grasp. Erica held on tight as she finally found her quarry and my heart began beating as if it was chasing the hundred-metre gold.

'Here it is!' she laughed, her cruel voice ringing through the air as the last discarded pages settled around her feet. 'Mr and Mrs Dixon are proud to announce the engagement of their only daughter Elizabeth to Giles Worthington . . .'

She was cut off in mid-flow by Evelyn who had raced around the other side of the counter and snatched the paper from her grasp. I watched on incredulously as she screwed it into a ball and threw it aside.

'You're barred!' she shouted in Erica's face. 'Go on! Out! And this time you won't be coming back!'

She frog-marched Erica through the door and Jemma and Jim led me back behind the bar and into the pub kitchen.

'Why didn't you say anything?'

Jemma shook her head in disbelief as she watched me pacing the floor.

'How could you let me come in here, knowing that was sitting on the bar?' I shouted. 'Whatever must everyone be thinking?'

Still Jemma said nothing.

'I think,' Jim said nervously, 'everyone thought you'd come

in to brazen it out, love. Get it over and done with quick, like,' he added. 'Like pulling off a . . .'

'If you say band-aid, Jim, I'll bloody swing for you,' I seethed, 'I really will.'

Jim gave a wry smile and rubbed his stubbly chin.

'I'll leave you to it,' he said kindly. 'Take your time. You can go out the back way if you like.'

'No way,' I said, shaking my head. 'I'm not hiding now. When I leave it'll be through the front door.'

'Good for you,' he smiled, 'give me a shout if you need anything.'

He backed out of the door and closed it quietly behind him. All the time he'd been talking, Jemma had sat silent and unmoved.

'Well?'

'I don't know what to say,' she said, reaching for her hair.

'How about, I'm sorry?'

'I'm not saying sorry for something I knew nothing about!'

'How could you not have seen it?' I shouted. 'It was there, large as life in black and white. What did you think? That if I knew then I wouldn't come back?'

'I'm telling you,' Jemma said patiently, 'that I, we, didn't know. No one had mentioned it and we don't always get a local paper these days. They're not always delivered and with everything else going on I don't have time to chase the newsagent about it!'

I slumped down in the chair opposite and rested my head on the edge of the table.

'I'm so sorry,' Jemma whispered. 'If I'd had any idea . . .' her words trailed off as the door quietly opened.

'Shall we head off?' It was Tom with our coats.

'Yep,' I said, jumping up, 'I want to get out of here, but I'm not going out the back.'

'I should think not,' Tom smiled. 'Come on, Jemma.'

'And I'll tell you something else,' I said, as I struggled into my coat.

'What's that?'

'By the end of tomorrow, my mother will be wishing I'd never been born!'

Chapter 8

As I had walked defiantly back through the bar, my head held as high as I could lift it, I'd grabbed the page of crumpled newspaper and shoved it in my pocket but now, seeing the pained expression on my dad's face, I couldn't help wishing I'd thrown it on the pub fire instead. I'd just explained to him when I'd arrived back in town and where I was staying, but it was this final blow that had knocked the last bit of wind out of his usually upbeat sails.

'I don't bloody believe it,' he groaned, shaking his head, 'what's the date on it?'

'I don't know,' I told him, 'the top got torn off when Evelyn snatched it out of that cow Erica's hand.'

'And her, of all people!' Dad shouted.

He was off again. It had taken him a good twenty minutes of swearing and shouting to get it out of his system the first time round, and I couldn't help thinking it probably wasn't a bad thing that Mum wasn't there because I think he really would have done her some sort of harm if she'd been standing in front of him.

'When I think of all that Erica girl put you through at school,' he seethed, 'it had to be her, didn't it?'

Erica had been the class bully and my red hair and freckles had been her favourite target throughout primary school and beyond.

'If I'd known about it,' he said, grasping my hand, 'I could have at least warned you, but we don't always get the free paper these days.'

'That's what Jemma said,' I explained.

I was still feeling guilty for accusing her of keeping it from me. Fortunately she had put my harsh words down to shock and forgiven me.

'Although knowing your mother, I wouldn't put it past her to have sabotaged the delivery herself when she realised she'd cocked up,' Dad raged on. 'I can't believe she never said a word. Is she really so deluded that she thought she'd get away with it? That no one would say anything!'

I shrugged my shoulders.

'I wish you'd told us sooner that you were coming back,' he said more quietly, his expression adding to my guilt, 'but,' he added as we heard the front door open and bang shut, 'I do understand why you didn't.'

I smiled an apology and braced myself for the inevitable storm I had unleashed.

'Whose boots are these?' my mother called out. 'They should be on the mat in the porch, not in here. They're soaking the carpet.'

I heard the door open and close again and guessed she had put them in their allotted place.

'Oh hello, darling,' she called when she spotted me. 'When did you arrive? I didn't see the car. I wish you'd called ahead. Are you staying over? There's a load of your grandmother's old junk in your room. It'll take at least all day to sort and then I don't know where we'll put it, but I suppose as you're here now . . .'

'Mum!' I tried to interrupt.

'Now, let me think about dinner. I suppose I could defrost another chop. So how long are you staying? I didn't think you had any holiday left after that nice long break at Christmas . . .'

'Pamela!' Dad bellowed, slamming his fist down on the worktop in frustration and making us all jump.

'Why are you shouting?' Mum asked, looking slightly pained but otherwise unmoved. 'If your only daughter turns up unannounced on your doorstep in the middle of the day, there are things that have to be sorted out. I thought you'd understand that!'

'Oh good god, woman! If you'd just shut up for two seconds then you'd realise that there is nothing to sort out, because Lizzie isn't staying here and after what I've just found out I can't say that I blame her!'

Mum's expression didn't flicker. She was going to try and brazen it out I realised, like she always did but not this time. This time she'd gone too far.

'I don't know what you're talking about, and I'd appreciate it if you didn't shout . . . the neighbours . . .' she breathed, theatrically quiet.

'Right!' I cut in, pulling out a chair and unceremoniously dumping Mum on it. 'Listen. I am not on holiday from work, because I have left my job. The position no longer exists. No, no, no, don't say anything,' I warned, as she tried to interrupt again. 'And I'm not living in the flat any more, either. You didn't see the car because it is parked at Jemma and Tom's. I've been with them since the end of last week and I'm staying with them until the flat above the Café is ready for me to move in.'

I stopped for a second to draw breath, which was of course a huge mistake because it gave her a moment in which to launch off again.

'But why didn't you tell me?' she whined, bottom lip trembling. 'I don't understand. Why aren't you staying here? I'm your mother, Elizabeth; you should have come to me. I should have known these things!'

'Ah yes,' I said, gently releasing the newspaper from Dad's disconcertingly shaky grasp, 'while we're on the subject of things that should be known. What have you got to say about this?'

She knew exactly what it was that I had smoothed out on the table in front of her, but nonetheless took her time rummaging in her bag for her reading glasses before picking up the paper and holding it at arm's length.

'Now in my defence,' she started, 'Jemma did tell me that Giles would doubtless be spoiling you rotten for your birthday and probably taking you to that special place you like so much for a meal.'

'Don't blame Jemma!' I shouted.

'This is Giles Worthington we're talking about, woman!' Dad joined in. 'That's the sort of thing the slick sod was always coming up with. There was nothing out of the ordinary about it at all!'

My attention turned from Mum to Dad as I stared at him open-mouthed.

'Well, I'm sorry, love, but it's true,' he mumbled. 'He was always taking you off for bloody mini-breaks and foreign holidays and putting every other man on the planet to shame.'

'I thought you liked him,' I whispered.

'That's hardly relevant now, is it? The point I'm trying to make is that your mother had no right to assume that a posh day out and a bit of expensive grub meant that your future involved a glittering gown and two point four kids!'

He was right. I turned back to Mum who had gone very

quiet when she thought that I was turning my attention from her to Dad.

'And anyway,' I frowned, 'even if he had asked me, why did you assume that I'd say yes?'

'Well, he's every woman's dream, isn't he?' she said. 'Wealthy family, wonderful salary and connections, great looks and let's face it, you were never going to make a better catch than Giles Worthington. Were you?'

'What do you mean by that?'

'Well, let's be honest, Elizabeth. You haven't exactly made the best of yourself, have you?'

'What?' I shrieked.

'Oh, you know what I mean. Messing about with a sewing course at college instead of A levels and university and then working in a pub of all places.'

I couldn't believe she still hadn't forgiven me for shunning sixth form!

'You can't tell me,' she went on, 'that after finally shrugging off all of that you wouldn't have jumped at the chance of becoming Mrs Giles Worthington?'

'Mum, in case you've forgotten, we all know now that Giles Worthington is a two-timing creep who has broken various hearts in his time, most recently mine, and the fact that you can sit there and belittle the things that I enjoy so much tells me that you don't really know me at all!'

'Well I'm sorry,' she said, 'I thought you were finally

making something of your life and I wanted to share it with the world.'

'Bullshit!'

'Elizabeth!'

'You wanted to brag!' I ranted. 'You wanted to show off to the neighbours. You'd probably even picked out a hat and worked out how much mileage you could get down the WI telling tales about your daughter's fairytale wedding and her happy ever after.'

Mum didn't say anything. She simply sat, her cheeks slightly flushed, which did go some way to suggesting that perhaps she was finally feeling something bordering on shame.

'Can you even begin to imagine how it felt to have this,' I asked her, snatching the paper from her grasp, 'read out in front of a whole pub full of people?'

'I don't go into pubs,' she said quietly.

'You know what I mean!' I snapped. 'I had thought that coming back here would be the best thing for me but, as usual, you've had to stick your nose in and make it all that much harder. Honestly, Mum, you've pulled some stunts in your time but this one really takes the biscuit.'

'It's yours if you want it,' said Dad, as we sat together on the floor in my old bedroom. 'That's why I said to put it in here. Your mother was all for taking it down to the charity shop but I wouldn't let her. I had a feeling you'd come back to it one day.'

I smiled and carried on sorting through the old Lloyd Loom blanket box that had belonged to my grandmother, Dad's mum. The smell that had risen up to meet us when we lifted the padded patterned lid was redolent of lily of the valley, and for a moment heavy tears pricked my eyes as I remembered the comfort of having her close by when I was growing up.

Before Dad noticed, I blinked them away and plunged my hands inside to see what treasures the box would give up. It was packed to the very top, crammed full of her collection of sewing and crafting supplies and encompassing it all was a plethora of memories I hadn't been expecting to face when I dragged myself off Jemma and Tom's sofa bed that morning.

'I know you can't take it all with you today,' Dad said, as he picked through the button tin, 'but as soon as you're settled in the flat I'll drop it round.'

'Do you think it's a good idea,' I asked, 'me coming back to Wynbridge, I mean?'

'Yes I do,' Dad said, 'and not just for selfish reasons. You've got roots here, Lizzie, and they'll help you heal and now you've faced the pub and your mother, there can't be much else left to go wrong. Can there?'

'I'm not going to comment on that,' I laughed, 'because at the moment, just when I think things can't get any worse, they do!'

'Are you staying for lunch, then?' Mum's voice drifted up the stairs.

Dad and I looked at each other in disbelief.

'God, she's got some front,' Dad moaned, shaking his head, 'not a bloody clue! You stay here and I'll go down and set her straight.'

'No, don't worry,' I said. 'I think I will stay. It would be nice to have some time to go through all this properly and besides, there's only so many hours a day that I can cope with Ella jumping all over me!'

During lunch, Mum somehow managed to extricate herself from the engagement announcement debacle. The newspaper cutting had disappeared and by the time we'd cleared our plates, Dad and I were back to rolling our eyes and sighing at her in much the same manner as we always had.

I quickly phoned Jemma to tell her all was OK and that Mum wasn't lying on the hall floor with the kitchen meat cleaver sticking out of her back.

'Promise you'll be back before it gets dark,' she said, just as I was about to ring off.

'Are you serious?' I laughed, again thinking about the ridiculous things mothers say. 'I'm a big girl, Jemma; I think I'll be OK.'

'Ha ha, actually I'm being serious,' she said sarcastically, 'haven't you had the radio on at all? Haven't you heard about the weather?'

'Hey, Lizzie!' Dad called to me, right on cue. 'Come and have a look at this. You'll need to get back to Jemma's before it's dark, otherwise you could be stuck here with your mother for days.'

'I heard that!' Jemma laughed in my ear. 'I guess that's all the incentive you need! See you in a bit then, and watch the pavements!'

The afternoon slipped quickly by and it was almost three when Dad poked his head round the bedroom door to see how I was getting on.

'Found anything that takes your fancy?' he grinned.

'Uh yeah,' I smiled, 'all of it actually.'

I began carefully repacking everything into the box. There were piles of fabrics that were vintage simply because of how long my grandmother had hung on to them, and coloured reels of cotton and embroidery thread along with the treasured button tin. There was even a string of the first bunting I had attempted to make. The fabric triangles, two floral and a gingham, had been cut out with pinking shears to stop them fraying. The only actual sewing involved was one fairly straight line along the top to join it all together.

'Did you do much sewing in London?' Dad asked as he watched me repacking.

'No, afraid not,' I said sadly.

'Perhaps having all this to look through will give you some inspiration to pick it up again?' Dad replied.

'If I get the chance,' I told him, 'I'm going to have to start looking for a job fairly soon. I've got a little bit left in the bank, but it won't last long, especially when I move into the flat. Jemma and Tom haven't said anything, but I'm not expecting to live there rent-free. I think they're already pretty cash-strapped so I'll be paying my way to help out as much as I can.'

Dad came and sat on the bed as I closed the blanket box and with a little nudge passed me an envelope.

'What's this?' I frowned, not wanting to open it.

'It's a cheque. Not a fortune I'm afraid, but it's your share of the sale of my mum's place.'

'But it's yours,' I said, trying to pass the envelope back. 'You should keep it.'

'No,' Dad smiled, 'I always planned to give you a lump sum but I wasn't sure when you should have it. Your mother was all for waiting but I think now is as good a time as any. It will give you the chance and time to make some big decisions and besides, I'd rather see you enjoying it this side of the grave!'

I didn't know what to say. I carefully tore the top off the envelope and peered inside.

'Wow,' I gasped, 'that's a lot of zeros!'

'Like I said, it'll give you the chance to make some big decisions. Just spend it wisely, that's all I ask, and Lizzie?'

'Um?'

'What I said about Giles earlier. It's not that I hated him or anything; I just never really understood how you two worked.

Oh I don't know, I can't explain.' He took a big breath. 'I guess what I mean is that when you were together you were so different, somehow not yourself. Does that make sense?'

I nodded, but didn't answer.

'What have you told Mum about this?' I asked, waving the envelope in front of us.

'Nothing. It isn't something she needs to know about and besides, if she finds out you've got a decent dowry she'll be putting another announcement in the paper!'

I laughed and gave Dad a long hug. It was good to be home, even if it did mean putting up with my mother!

'You'd better be off,' Dad smiled with a nod towards the window and the darkening sky beyond, 'we don't want Jemma sending out a search party, do we?'

Chapter 9

'What do you think of this?' I asked, holding up a piece of fabric. 'Is this the sort of thing you'd like?'

I'd returned from my parents' the evening before with a bag full of things from my grandmother's blanket box that I thought might go some way to helping Jemma and Tom with the Café design dilemma. After a few undisturbed hours' work I'd managed to come up with a couple of pretty ideas using my favourite but recently neglected appliqué, patchwork and cross-stitch techniques, and all with the Café in mind.

The first design incorporated a cherry tree, like those planted around the Café, only this one was already in blossom. Instead of flowers, however, the tree was covered in little cross-stitch cakes, sandwiches and teacups. The colours were predominantly gentle shades of blue, pink and green, which I felt would complement the kind of cake-decorating Jemma favoured, and the sophisticated but cosy atmosphere she and Tom were keen to create.

The second design was a sugary cupcake complete with a cherry on top. The cake case fabric was white with tiny pink hearts and the cherry and frosting had been embellished with tiny beads no bigger than a pinhead. It was very pretty but rather impractical. I had got so carried away and immersed in the act of sewing that I couldn't stop until it looked as sugary and sweet as Jemma's butter icing.

'To be fair,' I said, tilting my head and looking at it from arm's length, 'I have gone a bit over the top with this one, but we could easily strip it back to the basic design if you like it.'

Jemma left her station next to the bay window and perched on the arm of the sofa to admire my handiwork. She had been eagerly watching for Tom and Ben's return from the shops, concern knitting her brow as the day drew to a premature close. As forecast, the snow had fallen steadily all night and then continued on and off throughout the day; a thick white carpet muffled the sounds of the cars as they moved gingerly along the road outside.

'Oh, Lizzie,' Jemma gasped, 'they're both perfect, but how could you have known?'

She pointed at the cupcake design, her expression rapturous.

'Known what?' I asked, passing over the pieces so she could have a proper look at them.

'The signature bake I've been working on for the Café launch!' Jemma laughed through sudden tears. 'It's a cherry and chocolate cupcake! Cherry because of the trees at the Café, of course, and cupcakes and chocolate because, well, everyone loves cupcakes and chocolate!'

I started to laugh with her.

'I didn't know,' I told her, shaking my head, 'they just summed up the Café and your baking to me! I take it you like them, then?'

'I love them,' Jemma cried, 'they're exactly what I would have picked out if I had the choice of a hundred designs!'

We both jumped as we heard the front door slam.

'We're back!' Tom shouted. 'But we're a bit wet. Can you come and give us a hand?'

Later that evening we all sat together in front of the fire discussing plans for the Café launch. Everyone loved the cupcake and cherry tree designs as much as I had loved creating them.

'They're really beautiful,' Ella sighed, as she sneaked yet another toasted marshmallow from the bowl, 'really sparkly. Are you sure you made them all by yourself?'

'I am,' I told her proudly.

'Well I hope you're going to teach me one day,' she begged, 'because Mummy is rotten at that sort of thing.'

'But I'm rotten at cakes,' I reminded her, 'and that's one cupcake you can't eat.'

'That's true,' she grinned, helping herself to the last pink marshmallow. She chewed it thoughtfully, let out a long slow breath and turned to Tom. 'Daddy, I feel a bit icky,' she grimaced, her cheeks rosy from sitting too close to the fire.

'Come on,' said Tom, holding out his hand, 'come and sit on the sofa with me for a few minutes. Let your tummy settle, then it'll be time for bed.'

'Do you think school will be closed tomorrow?' she yawned. 'Do you think it'll be a proper snow day?'

'It might be,' Jemma grinned, 'you never know.'

I looked at my old friend remembering how we used to pray for snow days when we were at school. They didn't happen very often but when they did we'd stay out from first light until dusk, our hands red raw from snowballing and our feet numb. I curled my toes at the memory of the pain a barely warm bath could inflict upon frozen digits.

'These will bring everything together beautifully, Lizzie,' Ben suddenly announced, waking us all up, 'menus, tablecloths . . .'

'Bunting, napkins, curtains, even the wall-light shades could be stamped,' I nodded, instantly swept along by the prospect of seeing the Café so prettily transformed.

I hadn't noticed Ben scrutinising my handiwork and was annoyed to feel even slightly flattered that he had found something positive to say about my contribution to the Café renovation.

Tom stood up and threw another log on the fire.

'I know it's a huge imposition, Lizzie, and I appreciate that your main priority right now has to be finding a job, but it would be a real bonus if you could spare some time to help us with the decorative finishing touches at the Café. You've clearly got an eye for these things.'

'I'd love to,' I jumped in. 'It would be an honour and it would save you a fortune!'

Truth be told, I could already imagine exactly how the Café would look if I had the chance to get my hands on it. With every stitch I'd sewn, I'd been dreading the prospect of Tom and Jemma telling me who would be taking responsibility for its ornamental transformation.

'That isn't why I've asked you,' Tom said quickly. 'God, we don't want you to think we wouldn't pay you!'

'I don't want you to pay me,' I said firmly, shaking my head, 'after all you two have done for me it's the least I can do and besides, it will give me something to do whilst I'm job-hunting. Although in fact, I haven't completely dismissed the idea of working in the pub again,' I admitted, 'assuming I can get past the humiliation of the other night, of course. It might well be the perfect place to earn a bit extra whilst I'm helping you two out.'

'Well, what do you know,' Ben said as he passed back my sewing and drained his pint glass, 'you really are turning back into your old self again, aren't you? Just be wary of handsome strangers this time around.'

'Jesus, Ben!' Tom scowled. 'That's a bit below the belt, mate.'

'Oh, she knows I'm only pulling her leg, don't you, Lizzie?'

I took a deep breath and turned back to Jemma, my eyebrows raised in that 'I told you so' silent form of communication that best friends are famous for.

'Well, as long as you're sure?' Jemma asked, also ignoring Ben's unnecessary comment.

'Just leave it all to me,' I told her.

'Stay where you are, chick,' I beamed at Ella from her bedroom doorway. 'No school for you today!'

'Really?'

'Really! Mummy just checked the website and your school is definitely closed!'

'Oh yes!' she shouted. 'Daddy always says dreams come true but I never really believed him until now. Will you take me out in the snow?'

'Well, I don't know . . .' I faltered, thinking of all the planning I wanted to get done in preparation for the Café transformation.

'Please, *please*, '

'Maybe later,' I gave in, 'if Mummy says it's OK.'

'Yes!'

Ella punched the air, leapt out of bed and began rifling

through her chest of drawers for her snowsuit and I headed down to the kitchen to warn Jemma and Tom of the whirlwind that would be joining them in considerably less than two minutes.

'Grab your wellies, guys!' I laughed but then stopped, my growing excitement halted by the solemn faces of my two best friends. 'Whatever's the matter?'

'We've had a phone call from the bank,' Tom said quietly.

'What, this early?'

It wasn't even eight o'clock.

'Is everything all right?' I ventured, before thinking how intrusive my question was. 'Sorry, don't answer that. It's none of my business.'

'No,' Jemma smiled with a shake of her head, 'it's OK.' She looked to Tom for confirmation.

'The initial loan didn't stretch quite as far as we needed it to,' he explained. 'So we've applied for another. It's not a massive amount but without it we can't finish the Café.'

'It'll cover the rest of the makeover,' Jemma said hopefully, 'and all the bits and pieces we've asked you to help with, Lizzie.'

'And without it you really can't continue?'

'Nope,' sighed Tom, 'there's barely enough left to pay the final bill from the electrician.'

'Then there's the rest of the kitchen equipment to be installed,' Jemma added quietly, biting her lip.

'Well, if the bank says no to the loan could you maybe lease some of the equipment instead?' I suggested, deeply saddened to see my friends looking so defeated, 'just until you begin to turn a profit.'

Tom shook his head and began pulling on his boots.

'I dunno,' he sighed, 'it was the dodgy bloody electrics we inherited that have put us in this position. If things had been done properly in the first place then we wouldn't have been lumbered with someone else's shoddy and frankly dangerous work.'

'There's no point bringing all that up again now,' Jemma snapped. 'It won't alter the fact that we've had to pay to have most of it replaced, will it?'

I loitered awkwardly in the doorway not wanting to interfere but feeling devastated to see my friends arguing and sniping at each other when they should have been getting ready to crack open the champagne.

'Is the kettle on?' Ben yawned behind me. 'I thought I'd make a flask and we could take Ella out on the sledge, unless,' he said as he spotted Jemma and Tom already dressed to go out and clearly not for a snowball fight, 'you've got other plans?'

'We've got to go to the bank,' Jemma explained. 'Do you mind taking her on your own?'

Ben shrugged.

'As long as Ella doesn't mind.'

'Thanks, mate,' Tom said, 'you'll go with them, won't you, Lizzie?'

'Oh, I don't know,' I faltered.

The last thing I wanted was to be stuck with Ben on my own all morning, especially after his catty comment last night. Left to our own devices the silences between us were longer than the Boxing Day queues at Next, and for the time being I just couldn't be bothered with him; I had too many other things on my mind.

'Oh come on,' Ben said, pinning me with one of his intense stares. 'Give me a chance to make up for being such a dick last night, Lizzie.'

Annoyingly, I found myself smiling.

'It was just the beer talking,' he went on, 'I really am sorry. I should never have said it, pissed or sober. I'm surprised you didn't slap me down, to be honest.'

'So am I,' I mumbled.

'Oh go on, Lizzie,' Jemma pleaded, sensing I was about to relent, 'I'll feel better if you both go. You know what a little sod she can be. She can outsmart one of you, but not two.'

'OK,' I reluctantly gave in, 'but there'd better be cake in it.'

'Why aren't you two a couple?' Ella frowned.

I stared hard at the compacted snow beneath my feet, grateful to be focused on staying upright.

'I said . . .'

'We heard what you said,' Ben cut in, scooping Ella up under his arm and passing me the string that was attached to the sledge.

'I think you'd make each other feel better,' Ella continued, her enthusiasm to push Ben and me together completely undiminished, 'you've both had your hearts broken, haven't you? Perhaps you can mend each other?'

'Oh Ella!' Ben moaned. 'Will you stop!' He began tickling her and she screamed to be put down.

To be fair, the morning had been much more fun than I expected. So engrossed in keeping a fearless Ella safe as she repeatedly launched herself down every hill she could find, there had been little time for conversation. We had simply passed the time together, companionably, the wintery wonderland helping us forget our cares for a while.

However, despite Ella's enthusiasm, I wasn't prepared to fall in love again on the strength of a few chilly hours playing in the snow. Cold and exhausted, we gingerly made our way back to the house and hopefully good news with a slice of well-deserved celebratory cake thrown in for good measure.

As we finally turned up the path to the house Ben set Ella back down on the snow and let her walk on her own again, which she did with much drama and squealing.

'She's quite a character, isn't she?' Ben smiled down at me.

'Oh yes,' I grinned back, pleased that he was making light of the situation. 'She's a real drama queen. Is my nose as red as yours?' I asked, trying to wrinkle it. 'Yours is positively glowing!'

Ben nodded.

'Yep and your cheeks. You could give Rudolph a run for his money!'

I was just about to make the obvious 'and you Santa, with that beard' retort, when I lost my footing. Ben reached out to grab me and we landed in a heavy heap on the compacted snow.

'Ouch,' I winced as I tried to disentangle my limbs from his. 'Are you OK?'

'I think so,' he groaned, 'nothing broken, you?'

'I don't think so.'

Eventually finding our feet we stood facing one another, closer than before, our breath sharp in our chests. Ben removed his sodden gloves and gently brushed the snow out of my curls.

'I know you probably won't believe me,' he breathed, his face close to mine and his pupils dangerously dilated, 'but I've actually always loved your hair.'

'Oh?' I said, taking a gulp of freezing air, my eyes locked on his face.

What exactly did he mean by 'always'?

'Um,' he smiled, still a little too close for comfort, 'you stand out from the crowd, Lizzie, you always have. You're unique.'

The spell was broken as quickly as it was cast.

'Don't say that!' I snapped, stepping back and losing my footing again.

'What?' Ben laughed, grabbing my arm to stop me falling. 'Can't I pay you a compliment?'

'It isn't a compliment,' I shouted, shaking my head.

'It was meant to be,' Ben said more gently.

Unwanted shuddering great sobs erupted from nowhere and the tears that I'd been holding back ever since I arrived on Jemma and Tom's doorstep refused to stay unshed a moment longer.

'Hey,' Ben soothed, pulling me into his arms and holding me tight.

'It's what *he* used to say,' I sobbed, trying to pull away, 'before he changed me, before he turned me into someone else. Before he made me fit in with his stupid notions of what a woman should be.'

'God, I'm sorry, Lizzie,' Ben whispered, kissing the top of my head and holding me tighter. 'I had no idea.'

I allowed myself to relax, safe in Ben's solid embrace until my tears stopped flowing. I don't know exactly how long we stood locked in each other's arms, but Ella's little hands were freezing when she reappeared and tugged at my coat.

'Come on!' she shouted. 'They're back! Mummy's made cake!'

The familiar smell of Jemma's famous Devil's Chocolate

Cake, although welcome, warned me that it wasn't good news. That kind of indulgence in Jemma's baking world was equivalent to downing a bottle of Jack Daniel's or chain-smoking twenty cigarettes.

I hid in the utility room on the pretence of sorting coats and boots until I had regained my composure then joined everyone in the kitchen. I glanced over at Ben to gauge his reaction to the cake and from the look he gave me in return I knew he was in on 'the code'.

'What's the matter, Lizzie?' Tom asked the second I appeared. 'Have you been crying?'

'No, of course not,' I laughed dismissively. 'This is how I always look when I've come in from the freezing cold! We were just outside for too long, but we had a great time, didn't we, Ben?'

Ben nodded in agreement and kindly steered the conversation back to Jemma and Tom's appointment at the bank.

'So it wasn't good news, then?' he asked tentatively as he took the loaded plate Jemma offered him.

'Depends on what you mean by good news,' Tom said bitterly. 'We can have the money, but not until we start to turn a profit.'

'But how can they expect you to turn a profit when . . .'

'You can't afford to open,' Ben cut in, finishing my sentence despite having a very sticky mouthful of cake.

I nodded and waved my fork at him.

'Exactly,' I said, my own mouth now crammed with the luscious layers of sponge and creamy frosting.

Jemma dumped herself into a chair and pulled Ella onto her lap. She hadn't even cut herself a slice. This was bad, I realised, really bad. Looking at their expressions, it hit me that they might have to put the Café back on the market and face the heart-ache of seeing someone else capitalising on all their hard work, seeing someone else's name above the door.

'Have you thought about taking on a partner?' I suggested, 'or asking someone to invest?'

Why hadn't I thought of this before they went to the bank?

'Like who?' Tom laughed. 'Our parents have done all they can already.'

'And you know how I'm set,' Ben joined in. 'Sorry, guys.'

Although my curiosity was again piqued as to exactly why Ben, an intelligent and highly qualified architect in his early thirties, was living out of a suitcase in his best mate's house, I knew now was not the time.

'I could do it,' I said quietly.

All eyes turned from Ben to me.

'What?' Jemma frowned.

'I could do it,' I said again, quietly laying my fork on my now empty plate.

'But you're as skint as I am!' Ben frowned. 'And in fact, you're worse off than me. You're sleeping on the sofa. At least I've got a room!'

'Shut up, Ben!' Tom snapped,. 'You can't take out a loan, Lizzie. You've got no way of proving you can pay it back.'

'I wouldn't have to take out a loan,' I smiled, 'I've come into some money. Not a huge fortune but enough to join forces with you at the Café, if you'll have me.'

'But when?' Tom demanded. 'How?'

'Your dad,' Jemma said quietly. 'He's given you some money from your granny's estate, hasn't he?'

I nodded.

'You can't use that, Lizzie. That's your future. There's no guarantee that you'll ever see it again.'

'Jemma's right,' Tom agreed. 'What if it all goes wrong and you lose every penny you've put in? We're best friends, Lizzie. We'd never do anything that would jeopardise our friendship.'

'Then we'd better make sure it's a huge success, hadn't we?' I laughed. 'Because I'm in, and nothing you can say will make me change my mind!'

Chapter 10

We were all so busy with the last minute preparations to the Café that the first signs of spring passed by almost unnoticed. I'd been secretly dreading spending Valentine's Day as a singleton but I needn't have worried. I had barely a spare second in which to reminisce about the hearts and roses fest it had been the year before, or the romantic and totally unexpected trip to New York Giles sprung upon me the year before that.

We were so pressed for time that there was absolutely no time to do anything about the décor in the flat before I moved in either, and as the days quickly turned into weeks I was rather grateful for that. Dad, much to my mum's annoyance, had hung on to some of my grandmother's furniture and the smaller pieces fitted in perfectly with the dated décor and old-fashioned fittings.

My favourite piece was a small wooden painted chair. Dad told me he could remember Granny sitting on it when she bathed David, his younger brother. It wasn't financially valuable but to me it was precious, a treasured family heirloom and it fitted perfectly next to the little sitting-room fire with my childhood ragdoll and knitted cushion adorning it.

The rest of the flat was furnished in a similar fashion and I loved it. Thankfully the damp in the back bedroom had disappeared, as Ben and Tom had predicted, and the boiler was more than capable of keeping the place warm and cosy even on the chilliest spring day.

Living above the Café ensured there was never a dull moment and I had even been brave enough to take on a couple of shifts at the Mermaid. I was thoroughly enjoying settling into my new life back home and looking forward to the Café launch very much, however there was one recent development that was beginning to prey on my mind a little more than it probably should and was a clear indication that Wynbridge was already helping me see the sunny side of life again.

'Your phone's buzzing!' Ben called to me from the Café kitchen.

'Just leave it!' I called back as I straightened up to admire my painting skills.

'It might be the print guy!'

'He phoned this morning!'

'Well, what about the jam woman? Jemma said we weren't to miss the jam woman!'

'She hasn't got my mobile number. Just leave it.'

Ben wandered through from the kitchen.

'It's stopped.'

I nodded as he placed it on the counter and struggled to ignore the urge to see if whoever had called had left a message. A number I didn't recognise had registered a week before and called every day since. I'd never managed to answer before it rang off and as yet no message had been left, but part of me was considering the obvious: was it Giles? There was nothing out of the ordinary about me not recognising his number. He was constantly changing his phone so my theory was perfectly plausible, but if it was him, what did he want? And more importantly, why was my pulse rate even slightly agitated by the thought that it might be him, when I was so contentedly settled in Wynbridge?

Helping to renovate the Café had been the perfect distraction for my broken heart, but these mystery phone calls had stirred up my emotional cauldron and bubbling away on the surface was the idea that Giles might be trying to get in touch to ask me to take him back.

At night I dreamt of all the good times we had shared; the trips we'd taken and the way I couldn't even glance at something without it appearing gift-wrapped a few days later, but more importantly than all the material and social trappings were the memories of the way he looked after me, the way he made me feel so safe.

I couldn't deny I'd *always* been a fully paid-up member of

the 'one true love club' and now my fickle heart was deliberating whether my new life would be even better if I gave an old love a chance to play a part in it.

I hadn't forgotten that Giles had treated me badly in the run up to our break-up or that he'd gone out of his way to change me, but he had never behaved like that when we were together in Wynbridge. If my hunch was right and if I could tempt him to leave London for my hometown, then perhaps there might just be a way for us to rekindle the magic we'd had at the beginning.

My embrace with Ben had resurrected feelings I had naively thought I was going to be able to lock away forever. Weak perhaps, to admit it, but I missed Giles. I missed the intimacy and warmth of having a man in my bed. I looked at Jemma and Tom and knew, deep down, that I wanted what they'd got. I wanted my very own happy ever after.

'What do you think?' I asked, shoving the paintbrush back in the pot and turning away from the phone and my weakening resolve to cut Giles out of my life for good. 'Not come up too bad, have they?'

'They look great,' Ben agreed, 'really great, and it won't matter if they get a bit chipped and distressed – that will just enhance the look. The best thing is they've cost practically nothing. Jemma and Tom will love them!'

'I hope they will!' I laughed. 'They've taken long enough but it was your idea, remember?'

Ben looked at the carefully prepared and painted Café tables and chairs. Where there had once been battered orange pine there was now a sea of pristine matt cream. It was amazing how much lighter and airier the whole Café felt now it was rid of its dark furniture and heavy curtains. Simple blinds and tablecloths had been ordered with my cupcake design printed on them and The Cherry Tree Café sign had been carefully stencilled on the door. The place was coming together just as I'd imagined it would.

'You thought of it as well,' Ben said generously.

'But you came up with it first,' I reminded him.

Ben nodded but didn't say anything else. Our relationship since the snow day had thankfully shifted from tense to the comfortable side of tolerant. Even though we hadn't talked about what had happened, the air between us was considerably clearer and I couldn't help thinking that he had got over his unfathomable reason for disliking me. Any probing as to why he had moved back to town however, no matter how gentle, was quickly brushed aside and I was still none the wiser.

'Are you coming to the pub tonight?' I asked.

'Maybe, I'm out for dinner but I might wander down after.'

'Hot date?' I teased.

'Just a meal with my mother,' Ben said. 'I've been putting it off but I reckon I'm about due another grilling.'

I thought back to the first night I'd arrived and how we'd compared maternal notes.

'Does she have your father tucked away somewhere?' I asked, fighting the urge to ask what the grilling would be about. 'Mine's allowed some respite courtesy of the garden shed, but not for long.'

Ben shook his head.

'No,' he replied, 'my father lives in Spain. He'd had enough of her by the time I'd grown up and left. He took early retirement to the sun and now enjoys the company of Rosita, my stepmother who is actually young enough to be my sister!'

'Go Dad!' I laughed, imagining the absurdity of my own father moving abroad with a tanned young beauty.

'That accounts for a lot of my mother's bitterness,' Ben sighed, 'and now of course I'm a huge disappointment as well.'

'I don't see why,' I said, hoping he was finally going to explain the mystery behind his return.

'No,' he smiled, 'I know you don't. I still can't believe Jemma hasn't told you anything, but I'm grateful she hasn't.'

'She's a loyal friend,' I agreed. 'She hasn't told me a thing.'

'She and Tom are the best.'

I nodded.

'You see, the thing is, Lizzie . . .'

'Oh well done, you've finished! God they look amazing! Don't they look amazing, Tom?'

Tom staggered in behind Jemma and gently lowered his precarious pile of boxes on to the counter top.

'I can't believe these are the same ones!' Jemma carried on.

'Are you sure you haven't traded them in, because I can't believe these are the ones you started out with.'

'You've already said that!' Tom interrupted, rolling his eyes.

'But look Tom,' she breathed, 'it's all coming together! This is really going to happen, isn't it?'

I wandered over and gave my friend a quick squeeze and Tom a sympathetic glance.

'And you're living with this, aren't you, mate?' I laughed.

'It's like having two Ellas in the house,' Tom groaned, 'and I can't get away from either of them! I've got Jemma jumping up and down about the Café and Ella bouncing about like Tigger because it's almost her birthday. I'm exhausted,' he admitted. 'Ben, I have no idea how you're coping but I promise that when you move out you'll get a medal for all you've had to put up with!'

'I'd be disappointed if it was any different,' Ben smiled as he disappeared back into the kitchen.

'Are you OK?' Jemma asked, as she helped me clear up the paint and newspapers.

'Of course,' I nodded, 'I'm fine. Over the moon about all this!'

'But?'

'There is no "but", I'm fine.'

Jemma didn't budge. I looked at her and sighed. There would be no shifting her until I'd offered some sort of explanation.

'I think Ben was about to tell me something when you burst in,' I said quietly, 'and now he's clammed up again and we're back to square one.'

'Oh Lizzie,' she frowned, 'I'm sorry. I know it seems unfair that we know what happened and you don't but I can't break his confidence. He made Tom and me swear not to tell a soul.'

'I'm not asking you to tell me,' I smiled, 'of course I'm curious, but not to the point where I'd try and drag it out of you!'

'I still can't believe he hasn't told you *anything* about it at all,' Jemma frowned.

'Funnily enough, he said the same about you.'

'What do you mean?'

'I think he thought that perhaps you might have told me something because we're so close.'

'But he asked me not to.'

'That's what I told him! You're a true friend through and through!'

'Hey, what are you two whispering about now?' Tom scowled, creeping over.

'Nothing!' we chorused and burst out laughing.

Ella's birthday was now just days away and if I didn't have a paintbrush or a pint glass in my hand I was wielding a fistful of pins and the sewing machine. Utilising some of the pretty fabrics I had bought after my fateful morning in the City Crafting Café, I had made Ella a ragdoll of her own, complete with a range of outfits and her own teddy bear. I was delighted with the result of my labours and hoped Ella would be too.

'What do you think of this for an idea?' Jemma asked a few days before the Café launch. 'How about we ask a few of Ella's friends to tea at the Café on her birthday?'

'But it won't be open,' I frowned. 'Her birthday is days before the launch party.'

'I know,' Jemma nodded, 'but we have all the paperwork and certificates to say that we can open by then and there's barely anything left to do, so I was thinking it might be the ideal opportunity to have a trial run sort of thing. See how the kitchen works; get a feel for the layout of the place before we're expecting people to pay for our services . . . and my baking,' she added nervously.

'Sort of a trial by toddler you mean?'

'Ella's hardly a toddler!' Jemma laughed. 'Although having been on the receiving end of her tantrum this morning, I do see what you mean!'

'I think it's a great idea,' I smiled. 'You could even ask the other mums to stay and we could try out some of the more daring tea choices Tom ordered.'

'Exactly!' Jemma giggled. 'And it will help us decide if we need to employ any waiting staff.'

We'd already put our heads together and discussed whether we should take on some part-time help but we hadn't been able to make a decision. Jemma planned to run the kitchen and I was going to do as much front of house ordering, serving and clearing as I could between working shifts at the Mermaid, but that meant there would still be times when there was no one actually in the Café with the customers.

Originally Tom had planned to help out for the first few months, to gauge demand, but with money being so tight, when he was offered a permanent job with the local council he simply had to take it. It wasn't exactly how they had planned things would be, but at least now he and Jemma had one regular, steady income they could rely on.

'You're right,' I said, 'I can't help thinking you're going to need someone, even if it is only for the lunchtime rush and on a Saturday.'

I had been toying with the idea of giving up my shifts at the pub so I could be on hand on a more regular basis. Jemma was going to be at the Café from eight every morning, having first dropped Ella with Tom's mum, then she would open at nine and remain open until around four-thirty. Some days Ella would stay at the after-school club and on other days, such as Saturdays, she would burn off some energy at her ballet class then either go home with her nan or one of us would collect her and keep her at the Café or in the flat.

I had been thinking that if I gave up my pub shifts then I'd be an extra body but I was holding back on making the suggestion and I wasn't proud of the reason why. The mystery phone calls might have tailed off but they'd left something behind. A lingering feeling that I didn't want Jemma or Tom to start relying on me too much in case, for some reason, I was going to need to commit some time to something else.

It didn't take a genius to work out that the 'something else' might be my potentially rekindled relationship with Giles. He may well have broken my heart but I was still entertaining the possibility of him walking back into my life and picking up the threads of what we'd once had. My unwillingness to really commit anything more than money to the Café told me that I still wasn't over him and that if he suddenly swaggered back into the Mermaid then I'd do everything within my power to keep him in Wynbridge and rebuild the relationship we had when he first arrived. I hated myself for harbouring such feelings but I couldn't help it. I wanted what Jemma and Tom had. I wanted to be loved, and if that meant sacrificing my time helping out at the Café then so be it.

Ella's sixth birthday dawned bright, clear and full of feverish excitement.

'Happy birthday to you!'

'OK, Ella, on three!' Jemma shouted above the din. 'One, two, three!'

Ella leant over the table and with perhaps rather more gusto than was really necessary, blew out the candles on her beautiful birthday cake.

Jemma had spent hours creating the pastel pink and lilac princess castle cake complete with turrets and a glittering moat. She said she was trying out the working arrangement of the Café kitchen but I knew that for this birthday more than any other she wanted Ella to feel like the little princess she thought she was.

Being an entrepreneurial mum was no easy option, I had come to realise since my move home, and Jemma was finding it hard to adjust to managing a home and family life along with a business. It was obvious to me that on top of everything else she had a big dollop of guilt to contend with and that Ella's elaborate birthday tea was her way of making up for all the extra hours she and Tom had been putting into getting the Café ready for opening.

'I can't believe this is the same place!' chorused the little group of mums Jemma had invited to stay. 'You've done an amazing job and these are delicious!'

Jemma and I swooped between the tables offering neatly cut sandwiches and delicate iced fancies to the grown-ups and bowlfuls of sweet treats and cheese straws to the party-goers. Ella was in her element at the head of the table whilst Tom did the rounds with endless beakers of milk and juice.

'And where did you get these?' Sarah, one of the mums asked Jemma, tugging at the corner of her cupcake-patterned apron.

Jemma pointed at me and grinned.

'Lizzie made them from a vintage pattern. The frilly heart-shaped pocket was one of her ideas and she came up with the cupcake design for the Café as well!'

'Were you responsible for anything else, by any chance?' Sarah laughed, looking around.

Before I had chance to do anything beyond blush, Jemma launched off.

'She did everything, Sarah! The design on the door, the tablecloths and lampshades, literally everything! I don't think my cakes would taste half as good if they weren't being served in these pretty surroundings!'

'Well, I wouldn't go that far!' I said, my face glowing.

'Could you make me one of the aprons?' Rachel, one of the other mothers asked. 'I'll get the fabric and I'd love some bunting for the kitchen if you can spare the time!'

'I don't know,' I stammered, 'I haven't really thought about carrying on making things now the Café's finished.'

'Oh you must!' Sarah cajoled. 'You wouldn't believe how inept we all are at this sort of thing. You simply have to help us out, Lizzie.'

Jemma raised her eyebrows and fixed me with her 'I told you so' stare. I could tell she was thinking back to our college days when our heads were first filled with dreams of starting our own business together.

'Maybe she could teach you instead,' Tom joked, joining Jemma from behind the counter.

'Teach them!' I laughed.

This was the second time I'd heard that ludicrous suggestion and it didn't sound any more likely this time round.

'Hey, that's not a bad idea,' Sarah said thoughtfully. 'Give a man a fish and you feed him for a day . . .'

'What?'

'Well, you could make the things for us, of course, and that would be lovely, but if you taught us how to make them ourselves then we'd have the sewing skills forever, wouldn't we? It would be much more fun if you could teach us, wouldn't it?'

'I don't know,' I stammered, 'I'm not a teacher, I'm just handy with a needle and thread.'

'You think about it,' Rachel smiled as she stood to gather up her children, 'I think Sarah's really on to something. I for one would sign up straightaway!'

Chapter 11

I hardly slept that night. After Ella's friends had left, each weighed down with a princess party bag and a slice of the only turret on the cake Ella would allow to be cut, we cleared the Café and went up to the flat to eat the soup and crusty bread Jemma had had the foresight to make earlier in the day.

'You could always use the area where the adults sat,' Ben mused, having been brought up to speed about what had been said at the party. 'I mean, the space at the back there is more than adequate, isn't it?'

Tom nodded in agreement.

'We could still seat a dozen or so regular customers, Lizzie, and give you room for what, say half a dozen students? We haven't found anything to put in the cupboards that run the length of that wall so you could use the space for storage and supplies.'

I didn't know what to say. The whole idea still felt like a bit of a joke to me.

'We could offer a package deal,' Jemma suggested, eyeing me speculatively, 'include lunch or a snack in with the price of the crafting session.'

'Are you *really* going to be a teacher?' Ella chirped up. 'You don't look like a teacher!'

She was sitting on the floor in front of the fire carefully undressing the ragdoll I had made and getting her ready for bed.

'Have you thought of a name for her yet?' I asked, trying to draw the conversation away from my potential professional future, 'she looks like a Bonnie to me.'

Ella shook her head and wrinkled her pretty pink nose.

'You didn't answer my question,' she scowled. 'If you're really going to be a teacher you'll have to watch your manners!'

'Right. Come on, madam,' said Jemma, scooping up her daughter along with her belongings. 'Time for bed. I can always tell how tired you're feeling by how rude you are.'

'But Lizzie didn't answer my question,' Ella sighed, plugging in her thumb, 'did she?'

'Sorry, Ella,' I smiled, 'I don't know yet. I'll have to think about it.'

'Make sure you do,' said Tom, bending to kiss my cheek, 'I think it sounds like an amazing idea.'

'For what it's worth,' Ben joined in as he pulled on his coat, 'so do I.'

Still refusing to get drawn in to the conversation, I turned my attention back to Ella.

'Did you have a nice party?'

'It was the best,' she whispered sleepily, 'and Mummy's cake is the prettiest one I've ever seen. Even prettier than Rosie's Hello Kitty Island one and that's saying something!'

After they'd all gone I took myself off to bed and lay staring up at the ceiling, thinking about the possibility of actually running sewing and crafting courses at the Cherry Tree. I hadn't mentioned my bunting-making session in the City Crafting Café but my mind had been full of it ever since Sarah hit upon the idea of me doing something similar. Deborah, the woman who managed the City Café, thought I had the skills and talent to teach so maybe the idea wasn't so ridiculous after all.

The City Crafting Café was perfectly equipped and provided the ideal ambience in which to learn new craft skills and although the Cherry Tree was much smaller I could already visualise the area Tom had suggested up and running; lengths of bunting and patchwork cushions in abundance. I was disconcerted to realise that I could picture it as clearly as I had the Café transformation, and look how quickly that had come to fruition.

If I was really going to take the idea seriously, I thought, as

I tried to thump the pillows into a more sleep-inducing shape, then I was going to have to dial that mystery caller's number and find out once and for all if it was Giles who had been trying to get back in touch.

I wasn't sure how he'd feel about a future living in Wynbridge with a girlfriend whose idea of a career was spending hours sitting in front of a sewing machine rather than a computer screen. However, convinced as I was that an old love had the potential to make my new life complete, I didn't want to start walking the patchwork path to sewing nirvana, only to find myself unpicking stitches a few weeks down the line.

The final few days before the Café launch party passed by in something of a daze and I barely had time to think about either making the call or the potential sewing tuition the mums had been clamouring for at Ella's party. Jemma and Tom had finally decided that they were going to need extra help in the Café, especially during lunchtimes and on Saturdays and employed Ruby Smith, a local girl who was studying for her A levels and biding her time at home until she could fly off to university.

'Are you sure you can fit the work around your studies, Ruby?' Tom had frowned as he watched her lay the tables on the day of the launch, 'only I don't want your dad on my case if your grades drop off.'

Ruby rolled her prettily kohl-rimmed eyes and carried on

preparing serviettes and cutlery. Jemma and I exchanged knowing glances, both of us thinking back to when we were keen to find our feet and not let school or college responsibilities stand in our way.

'It'll be fine,' Ruby said stubbornly. 'Mum wouldn't have let me do it if she thought it would interfere with my timetable, would she?'

'It's not your mum I'm worried about,' muttered Tom, holding the door open for yet another delivery.

'Don't worry about Dad!' Ruby laughed coquettishly. 'I can wrap him round my little finger!'

I smiled to myself and carried on setting out the plates of Jemma's cakes and delicate fancies. Rather than take individual orders for the launch, we'd decided to dress the tables with a variety of afternoon tea treats from the menu. That way she and Tom wouldn't be spending the whole time running in and out of the kitchen. It was important that they mingled with the customers and hopefully the local press, whilst Ruby and I served drinks.

Excitement was at fever pitch as we stood in our matching aprons waiting for the town clock to strike one, which was when Jemma was going to cut the ribbon and invite everyone inside.

'Thank you for this,' she smiled at me, as we gathered under the branches of the now blossoming cherry tree, 'if it wasn't for you we wouldn't be doing this.'

'Yes you would,' I smiled back, dismissing her gratitude and not wanting a fuss, 'you'd have found a way.'

'No we wouldn't,' she said, tears suddenly appearing, 'we wouldn't. Without your help and investment the only thing we'd be doing now is looking at a For Sale board!'

'Oh god, she isn't crying again is she?'

Tom and Ben had appeared with celebratory bottles of local elderflower cordial. I turned to face Jemma and scrutinised her expression. She laughed and pulled her handkerchief from her apron pocket.

'Almost!' I announced. 'It was a close run thing but I think the crisis has been averted!'

Right on cue, the crowd that had gathered began counting down, the press arrived and the sun began to shine. It felt like spring had really arrived and I couldn't help thinking about how much we'd achieved in such a short space of time.

'This is a wonderful thing you've done,' Ben whispered in my ear.

His face was close to mine as he bent to make himself heard above the crowd. I took a step back, trying to avoid his gaze.

'You would have done the same,' I whispered. 'They've done so much for us, individually I mean, over the last few months. All this is the least I could do.'

'But even so,' Ben smiled, 'it's still a wonderful thing.'

'Five, four, three, two, one!'

Jemma snipped the ribbon to rapturous applause and Tom, having quickly passed Ben the bottles of cordial, swept his wife off her feet and carried her across the threshold.

'We declare,' they laughed together, 'The Cherry Tree Café open for business!'

The crowd cheered and the photographers snapped away as we jostled back inside to begin our new adventure.

'So,' said Jay, the freelance reporter who was covering the launch for the local paper, 'Tom tells me that you're going to be running some sort of sewing courses here in the future. Is that right?'

I looked across the Café to where Tom was clearing tables and laughing with Ben about something or other.

'Nothing's been decided yet,' I told him honestly, 'it was just an idea a friend of Jemma's came up with.'

'Well, I got the impression that it was more than just an idea! Apparently people have been asking about when they can sign up and what you'll be offering all afternoon.'

'What?' I frowned.

I knew that customers had been asking about the designs I had come up with, but I had no idea the crafting course rumour was still running amok amongst the local population. I could feel a heady mix of fear, apprehension and excitement creeping up as the idea once again took hold of my imagination.

'Hello, darling!' My mother sidled up. 'Congratulations! You've done an amazing job. Jemma tells me you've done all this! It looks like you've transformed the place single-handedly.'

'Not quite,' I muttered.

'Is this your sister, Lizzie?' Jay asked innocently.

I wanted to cry when I heard him say that. There would be no stopping her now. I spotted Dad loitering by the door, clearly ready to go. 'Sorry!' he mouthed with a shrug.

'No,' I smiled through gritted teeth, 'my mother actually.'

'And is she the clever lady who taught you how to sew?'

'No,' I said, more bluntly this time. 'It isn't. My gran, that is my dad's mum, taught me how to . . .'

'Well, I must have taught you something, darling!' Mum cut in, clearly wounded that I wasn't prepared to let her take any of the credit.

'Mother,' I declared sternly, 'you know perfectly well that only a few weeks ago you told me that messing about with sewing was a waste of time.'

'Oh no,' Jay smirked, understanding the situation perfectly, 'surely not! Your daughter is clearly extremely talented! As I understand it customers are crying out for . . .'

'Well anyway,' I said, desperate that Jay wouldn't say another word.

I didn't want Mum knowing anything about the potential courses. It was still, in my mind, unlikely that they would really happen and I certainly didn't want to give her anymore 'wasted opportunity' ammunition! She had a barrel full already.

'Right, we're off!' Dad said, giving me a quick kiss and forcibly steering mum by the elbow towards the door. 'Well done with everything, darling, it looks wonderful. Thank you for a lovely afternoon, Jemma! See you later, Tom.'

I let out a relieved sigh as they disappeared through the door and Jay began packing away his camera.

'If you do decide to run those courses,' he smiled, 'give me a bell.'

'Why?' I asked. 'You don't look like the crocheting kind.'

We both started to laugh and I looked at him properly for the first time: piercing blue eyes and just the right amount of stubble, nice. However, I couldn't help thinking he would have looked more at home amongst the ranks of the paparazzi than the dowdy offices of the local rag. I felt myself blush as I realised he might have seen my faux engagement announcement a few weeks back.

'No, I'm not the crocheting kind,' he laughed, 'but I might know someone who would be interested in covering the story for you. I thought perhaps I could tempt you with a bit of free advertising.'

He held out his card but I didn't take it.

'I don't even know if the courses will be happening yet,' I murmured, shaking my head. 'It all seems a bit pie-in-the-sky to me.'

'Well, take it anyway,' he said, carefully laying the card on the table. 'Maybe you'll decide to call me even if the courses don't go ahead.'

'I think,' said Tom, draining his champagne flute for the third time, 'that was what you call a raging success!'

The Saturday launch afternoon had flown by so quickly and we were so exhausted after clearing up that our own private celebration took place the next day in the Café garden. The sky was bright and clear and for the first time it was possible to feel some real warmth from the sun.

We sat together under the cherry blossom with blankets around our legs, sipping champagne, the excitement already mounting for the next day when the Café would open properly for the first time. Jemma had spent the morning baking and prepping whilst I tidied and primped with the boys and now there was little left to do besides count down and see who would be first through the doors.

'Have you thought any more about the crafting courses, Lizzie?' Tom asked, holding up his hand to shield his eyes from the glare of the spring sun as he scrutinised me.

'She's thought of little else!' Jemma laughed, without even glancing in my direction.

'Yes, Tom,' I answered, totally ignoring Jemma and her telepathic powers. 'I have been giving the idea some consideration.'

'And?'

'Well,' I began.

'She wants to give it a shot,' Jemma cut in, 'but she's going to find an excuse to begin with. For example, she's going to tell us that she thinks we should wait and see how the Café does first. She wants to give it a couple of weeks and see what business is like.'

There was an edge of 'know it all' sarcasm to her tone that I really didn't appreciate but unfortunately as always, she had hit the nail on the head. Along with unmasking the mysterious caller, I had been thinking that it would be a good idea to see how well the Café took off before making a decision, but apparently Jemma wasn't prepared to settle for such a flimsy reason for not pushing on and taking the plunge.

'Of course, the problem with that,' she continued in a singsong voice, 'is that everyone who was interested may well have forgotten about the idea or got so fed up with waiting that they will have found somewhere else further afield to go to and in the meantime forgotten all about our little Café.'

That was actually a very good point and one that I had failed to consider.

'I think,' Jemma finished cunningly, 'that if people knew Lizzie was really planning to offer these sessions from the word go then we'd have an edge. We'd be offering added value from the very first time we open the door. We'd stand out as offering something extra and currently unique in this area. However, if we wait even just a few weeks,' she added sadly, her theatrical pout reminding me of Ella, 'it might look as if the Café was struggling and we were tacking the courses on, no pun intended, to try and turn things around.'

I opened my mouth to say something but no words were forthcoming. Tom sniggered and leant forward to pat my leg and give me a knowing wink.

'She's good, isn't she?' he smiled proudly. 'Definitely the brains of the outfit!'

I brushed him off and turned my attention to Ben. Would he be a more cautionary adversary, I wondered?

'What do you think, Ben?' I asked.

'Oh, I completely agree with Jemma,' he said, without stopping for even a second to think it over. 'I mean, you've got a financial interest in the place now so you're in it for the long haul, aren't you?'

'Well yes . . .' I began, but Ben cut me off.

'I would have thought you'd be desperate to see it succeed and Jemma has often spoken about the plans you had when you left college, so it's hardly a bolt out of the blue, is it? The idea seems like a rather logical progression to me.'

I glared at him and he raised his eyebrows and smiled back in what I can only describe as a flirtatious manner. My stomach flipped and I quickly looked away but it was too late. I let my hair swing forward to cover the tell-tale blush that flooded my face. No wait and see cautionary advice there, then. Deep down I knew everyone's opinions made perfect sense but of course they weren't privy to my other little secret, were they?

'So that's settled!' Tom announced, swaying slightly as he stood to refill our glasses. 'Lizzie will be running crafting courses with immediate effect! Better let the local press know! They or should I say, a certain someone who works for them, will be clamouring to hear the news!'

'Tom!' Jemma shouted. 'Sit down, for goodness' sake!'

'No, hang on,' I cut in, 'what exactly do you mean by that, Tom?'

'Jay,' Tom whispered conspiratorially, trying to tap the side of his nose but missing, 'he phoned last night begging for your number. I think you've got yourself an admirer, Lizzie!'

I could feel myself blushing again and bit my lip to keep myself quiet.

'What, Jay as in the press guy you used to play football with?' Ben frowned. 'The one who was at the launch?'

'The very same!' Tom grinned.

'He's a total prick,' Ben scowled, 'I've never could stand him, on or off the pitch.'

I stole a furtive look at Ben, curious as to why he had reacted so aggressively to Tom's admission. His jaw was set hard and his steely glare focused on the poor crystal champagne flute that looked ready to buckle in his uncompromising grasp.

'Well,' Tom continued, apparently unaware of his friend's

disapproval, 'he's sharpening his pencil for you, Lizzie, so you'd better watch out.'

'Ignore the pair of them,' Jemma snapped. 'I told Tom not to say anything.' She shot her husband a fearsome glance. 'He's just being an arse. He's always like this after champagne. Obviously I didn't give Jay your number, Lizzie.'

I didn't know what to say to any of them. Now, not only did I have the mystery caller to identify, but it also transpired that I had unwittingly aggravated Ben and was going to have to contend with the unwanted advances of the local rag man on top of everything else.

Chapter 12

The Cherry Tree Café's first week of trading was a huge success and business was brisk. Every day ran like clockwork, thanks to Jemma's organisational skills, and her observations about the potential of the courses were spot on as well. Barely a day went by without someone mentioning them, and by the end of the week she and Ruby had somehow convinced me to commit to offering a taster session the following Friday.

'Left side down a bit,' Ruby shouted at me through the Café window, 'that's it. Stick it there and then everyone'll see it.'

I stuck as instructed and joined her outside to see how the poster looked. I let out a long breath as I stood staring at it and wondered just what I was letting myself in for.

'Looks good!' Ruby beamed, linking arms with me. 'I bet you'll be fully booked by the end of the day.'

'That's what worries me,' I told her, 'I'm still not really sure about all this.'

'It's bunting!' Ruby laughed. 'Jemma told me you've been making bunting practically since you could walk! It's not exactly rocket science, is it?'

'No,' I agreed, 'and that's the whole point. Why are people going to want to pay me to show them how easy it is to make, when they can buy metres of it for a few quid in any of the shops in town?'

'Don't you ever watch TV?' Ruby frowned.

'Sometimes,' I admitted.

'Well then, I'm sure you've seen the likes of Kirstie Allsopp spouting on about upcycling and the joys of making your own, haven't you?'

I nodded at my youthful companion's wise and intuitive words.

'And besides, it isn't just about money or convenience. It's a social thing, isn't it?'

'I guess so,' I murmured, thinking back to the City Crafting Café and the laughter the customers had shared during their morning together.

Ruby was right, of course. I adored the length of bunting I had made that day because it was unique. I had selected the fabrics, I had been responsible for every snip and stitch and I loved it all the more for those very reasons. But of course I already understood all this, didn't I? Afternoons spent with

Granny had taught me all of that; how could I have forgotten so much of what she had taught me?

'Finally!'

I spun round to find Sarah peering over my shoulder for a better view of the poster.

'I was beginning to think you'd given up on the idea!' she laughed. 'Put my name down, will you? You'd better put Rachel down as well, actually. She'd never forgive me if she missed out on your tutoring debut!'

'Oh please don't put it like that!' I groaned, my insides squirming again.

'Oh you'll be fine!' Sarah grinned. 'You're amongst friends, Lizzie! Now, what do we need to bring?'

'Nothing,' I told her.

I had already decided that it would be easier all round if I supplied everything myself and because it was a simple project the outlay would be minimal.

'I'll have a variety of fabrics for you to choose from and we can take it in turns to use the two sewing machines I've managed to borrow. If the afternoon's a success and people want to do more then I'll draw up a list of potential projects and supplies and offer you the choice of sourcing your own things or buying from the selection I'll have to hand in the Café.'

Suddenly I realised just how much thought and effort I had been putting into planning the venture and for the first time

I felt a real surge of excitement at the thought of being responsible for the sessions. I let out a long calming breath, knowing that deep down I really did want it all to work out, and a few seconds later when Ruby gave me a playful nudge I was smiling broadly.

'Well, I hope those aprons will be on the list!' Sarah said as she backed towards the gate. 'I can just see myself flouncing about in the kitchen in one of those! It might even convince Mark that I am actually making some commitment to the household chores!'

As Ruby predicted, all six spaces were booked by the end of the afternoon and along with my nerves my increasing sense of excitement had grown with every name that had been added to the list. There was just one thing left for me to do before I allowed myself to get completely carried away.

'Are you sure you don't want to come to us for dinner?' Jemma frowned. 'I don't like to think of you in the flat on your own every night.'

'It's fine,' I told her, 'honestly. Now I've got the internet connected I'm going to spend a bit more time planning next Friday's taster session.'

Jemma looked at me, her eyes shining. I could tell she was exhausted but she was also on a real high. So far the thrill of running the Café had exceeded all her expectations and she was loving every minute of it.

'Well fair enough then,' she beamed, 'I'm so pleased you've decided to give it a go, Lizzie.'

I nodded, hating myself for not being completely honest with her. I was going to spend some of the evening organising the sewing session, but I had also decided that tonight was the night I was going to phone the mystery caller's number and find out if it was Giles wanting me to take him back and if it was, would he be willing to move to Wynbridge.

I knew I had to do it before next Friday because, assuming the session was a success, there was the thrilling possibility that it would take my life in a completely different direction. There was a huge part of me that still wanted my sewing and crafting to be a very key part of my future but there at the back of my foolish mind was still the faintest glimmer of hope that Giles might have changed his mind and if he had, then I might need to focus my attention on repairing our relationship and helping him settle into life in a small town rather than making bunting.

In total I must have dialled the number a dozen times before I actually plucked up the courage to let it ring. Sitting on the sofa in my cosy flat I waited, my breath tight in my chest and the value of all that I had achieved and been a part of during the last few weeks pushed to the very periphery of my mind.

Finally I let it ring and agonising seconds passed.

There was no answer.

The recorded message kicked in and informed me that the phone was switched off.

Coupled with crippling disappointment there was the tiniest twinge of relief, but still I couldn't shrug off the feeling that I had really wanted it to be Giles. My head was trying to tell me that I was better off without him, that he had broken my faith in men and shattered each and every one of my romantic dreams, but my heart . . . well, that was another story.

'I'm ever so sorry to let you down at such short notice, Evelyn, but this will be the only chance I get to go.'

'Well, it can't be helped, I suppose,' she sighed, 'and I know how much this idea means to Jemma. You go, my love, and we'll see you next week.'

I climbed back into my car and turned the key hoping that Jemma would be as easy to convince.

She wasn't.

'But I don't understand,' she frowned. 'Surely there are places closer to here that you can go to for fabrics?'

I should have known better.

'Yes, of course there are,' I explained again, 'but it isn't just about buying fabrics. Deborah is already running the kind of sessions that we want to offer at the Cherry Tree. Her Crafting Café is a total hit and she's too good a contact to ignore. This is the perfect opportunity for me to pick her brains before we really get going!'

'So tell me again, when exactly did you meet this woman?'

I explained as patiently as I could, with one eye on the kitchen clock, about how I had stumbled across Deborah and the City Crafting Café and the influence she and the place had on my initial decision to move back to the town.

I had phoned her on a whim after drawing a blank with the mystery caller the previous evening, and arranged to meet and discuss my prospective business plans the following day. I was amazed Deborah even remembered me, but she insisted that with my hair and exquisite embroidery skills I'd been hard to forget.

'It's fate!' Jemma laughed excitedly as she finally began to see the sense in what I was cunningly suggesting. 'Perhaps I should come with you?' she added enthusiastically.

'You can't!' I panicked. 'Who would run the Café tomorrow?'

'Well, what about taking Tom then, or even Ben? He's at a loose end right now. He's finished the list of jobs I gave him and it would be a chance for the pair of you to spend some time together. He might even tell you a bit about why he's back in Wynbridge.'

As tempting as Jemma made that sound I shook my head knowing that her suggestion simply wasn't compatible with what I really had in mind. Unbeknown to my dear friend, I had also arranged to spend the night at my former boss Henry's flat, with the sneaky intention of picking his brains about Giles. The longer I stood talking to Jemma, the worse I felt, so I began stealthily edging back down the hall towards the front door and the sanctuary of my car.

'No, I'll be fine,' I insisted. 'I'm going to stay at Henry's and he only has room for one guest. He sounded a bit down in the dumps actually; I think he needs cheering up a bit. Given the circumstances, I'm pretty sure he wouldn't appreciate a complete stranger tagging along. I'll take him out to dinner after I've seen Deborah tomorrow and then drive straight back the next morning.'

'OK,' Jemma shrugged, 'just as long as you're sure.'

She eyed me beadily and I knew it was time to go.

'I'll see you Monday, OK?'

'Just let me know you've arrived safely, won't you?'

'Of course.'

The journey to London was hellish. Not only did I not enjoy the drive, I was also crippled with guilt every time I thought about Jemma's enthusiastic reaction to my implied efforts at market research and developing contacts. She was my oldest friend and I was keeping her in the dark about my biggest secret, but I knew that if I told her about the plan I had formulated to reignite my relationship with Giles by bringing him back to Wynbridge, she would have told me to get a grip.

She would have reminded me just how badly he'd treated

me, how long it had taken me to heal the heart he had wrenched in two, but it was all right for her. She had Tom. I didn't need to hear her telling me to see sense and get on with my life when she had the comfort of the love of her life standing firmly next to her. No, far better she found out after this visit, when Giles and I were reunited and she could see first-hand exactly what it was I was trying to achieve.

It was almost midnight by the time I parked up outside Henry's flat. Already in his pyjamas he buzzed me in to the building and waited tentatively on the threshold to welcome me.

'Hello, old thing,' he smiled. 'Gosh, don't you look well!'

I gave him a swift hug wishing I could return the compliment and felt some of my guilt evaporate as I realised Henry really did look like he needed a shoulder to cry on.

'Thank you,' I smiled. 'It's really good to see you, Henry.'

He ushered me inside and I followed him to the kitchen.

'Crikey!' I blurted out without thinking. The shock of looking at him from behind revealed why his usually all-encompassing hug had felt so different. 'However much weight have you lost, Henry? You look almost thin!'

'Tell me about it,' he said sadly. 'It's all stress, I'm afraid, nothing to do with a healthy new lifestyle.'

'Oh dear,' I sympathised, 'is it really that bad?'

'You got out just in time, Lizzie,' he told me. 'It's all far worse than I initially thought it was going to be.'

I sat at the tiny kitchen table and waited for him to continue.

'The department restructuring is really taking its toll,' he explained glumly. 'Everyone's neck is on the block. There's no knowing who's going to get the chop next. You wouldn't recognise the place; it's practically empty. Would you like a cup of tea or coffee or something stronger?' he offered.

'Tea please,' I smiled, 'if it's no bother.'

I watched Henry making the tea for me and pouring himself a large whisky and thought about my old job. Truth be told, I hadn't given it a second thought since I'd left and that went a long way to reinforce my conviction that it had never been right for me, but Henry on the other hand was crestfallen. He loved his job, he was committed to the company and passionate about providing a professional service for his clients, but now he looked as if he'd had the rug pulled out from under him.

'So have you considered looking for another job?' I prompted.

From my very first glance at Henry I knew it would be insensitive to reveal my real intentions for my impromptu visit straight away. I decided it would be best to get work woes discussed and then I could spend the rest of the time endeavouring to lift his sagging spirits and weave my ulterior motive into the conversation gradually. I might want to question him about Giles, but I wasn't so obsessed that I didn't give any credence to timing.

'You aren't worried you might be next?'

'Oh no,' said Henry, draining his glass in one mouthful. 'They won't get rid of me.'

'Well, I should think not,' I told him robustly, changing track, 'you're an integral part of the company machine!' I laughed; it sounded funny reeling off the old managerial mantra that I had never cared a jot for.

Henry laughed with me but there was an underlying bitterness to his tone that I had never heard before.

'Perhaps I should have said they won't get rid of me *yet*,' he added.

'Really? So you think you're for the chop as well, do you?'

Henry nodded resignedly.

'I will be,' he said sadly, 'but not just yet, not until I've finished getting rid of everyone else on their behalf. They've designated me as the hatchet man, you see. I'm the one who's responsible for the firing. I hate it.'

'Oh, Henry!'

'It is hell, Lizzie, it really is.'

'So why don't you quit? Get out now before they push you?'

'I can't,' he sighed, 'I think it'd be even worse if my own team were being culled by someone else. I'm trying to let them down gently, but at the end of the day it isn't really making any difference. I'm still the one telling them they won't be able to pay the mortgage next month, aren't I?'

The poor guy really was in a bad way. There was no one in the company with as much heart as Henry and I couldn't help wishing that some of his compassion and consideration had rubbed off on Giles.

'What time are you meeting your friend tomorrow?' Henry asked, tossing back another gargantuan nightcap.

'Early,' I said, 'around seven. Deborah and I agreed it would be easier to talk before the shop opens. I hope that's OK? I won't disturb you, will I?'

Henry shook his head.

'Don't worry about me,' he sighed, 'but you better take this.'

He threw me a key from a hook below the light switch.

'Just in case,' he sighed. 'I don't tend to surface very early at the weekends these days; nothing worth getting up for.'

'Not even me, Henry!' I joked. 'After I've come all this way!'

'Yes well,' he said with a grim smile, 'I've got a feeling you aren't really here for me, are you? But we'll talk about that tomorrow as well.'

Chapter 13

Not surprisingly I didn't sleep well that night. Henry obviously knew exactly why I had blagged a night at his flat and his words and hurt expression stuck in my mind as I tossed and turned in his sparse spare room. I could quite easily have fallen asleep around five but forced myself out of bed and into the shower, determined not to be late for my smokescreen meeting.

Deborah was already at the Crafting Café when I arrived just before seven. She looked as daunting and efficient as I remembered, but her welcome was warm and her advice both concise and practical.

'Stick to what you know to begin with,' she told me, 'the sort of thing you can do standing on your head. Yes?'

I nodded enthusiastically and made frantic notes in the pretty fabric covered notebook she had presented me with on my arrival.

'It's all very well making things for yourself in the comfort of your own kitchen or sitting room but when you're showing someone else, who has practically no skill with a needle, how to do it, well you'll soon discover you need the patience of a saint and the confidence of a king!' she warned me. 'People will be paying you, Lizzie, never forget that. They'll be expecting to learn something and they'll want to create something they are proud of, something they can really use or display.'

'I'm starting with bunting,' I told her feebly.

I couldn't help feeling a bit of a fraud as I sat and listened to this confident and accomplished businesswoman whose achievements I was going to try to emulate. Fortunately, Deborah didn't seem to notice my lack of self-assurance and rushed on.

'Perfect!' she shouted, as she hurried to unlock the door for Heather who had appeared, weighed down with bags from the supermarket.

'Good morning, my dear,' Heather smiled at me, 'Deborah said you were coming today. How are you?'

'Yes, yes,' Deborah interrupted before I had time to answer, 'there'll be plenty of time to chat later Heather. Put the kettle on would you? I'll be through in a minute.'

Heather bobbed through the shop into the kitchen and Deborah came and sat back down.

'Now,' she said, 'bunting. That was what you made the morning you joined us, wasn't it?'

I nodded.

'Nice simple cutting and sewing skills,' she smiled, 'and hugely satisfying. It's quick and easy so everyone will take something complete away with them and it doesn't matter if any of the triangles are a bit wonky. No one notices when it's strung up.'

'I thought if the session goes well, we could move on to things like Lavender bags and cushions, then drawstring bags and aprons,' I suggested, 'then perhaps peg bags, hot-water bottle covers, maybe even some simple felt brooches and other accessories.'

I stopped abruptly feeling both surprised and concerned that my enthusiasm had got the better of me but I wanted Deborah to know I had given the idea some real thought and that I wasn't taking up her precious time solely to get ideas and answers to questions I should have been able to fathom out myself.

'That sounds like a nice logical progression and quite a varied mix. You've clearly thought it all through,' Deborah reassured me, 'but what about embellishment? Have you thought about something like machine embroidery? How about offering tuition in some of the finer skills?'

I shook my head and swallowed hard.

'I think I'll wait and see how the taster session goes before I even consider any of that.'

'Well, I wouldn't leave it too long,' Deborah insisted. 'Word spreads fast and it wouldn't surprise me in the slightest if you found yourself inundated and running some sort of group every day before you know it.'

'Really?' I frowned. 'I just thought this would be something I could offer once, maybe twice a week to amateur enthusiasts.'

'Where's your ambition, Lizzie?' Deborah laughed, shaking her head. 'The beauty of running these sessions in a Café is that you will attract all sorts of people very quickly. You won't need to worry about advertising either: the Café itself and word of mouth will be enough to get things going.'

'Do you really think so?' I swallowed again.

At least that would keep Jay at bay I thought sagely, whilst at the same time I realised that Deborah's own ambition and ideas were fast outpacing mine and I had neither the courage nor the business skills to keep up.

'Of course,' Deborah continued, blithely unaware of my growing doubt, 'there'll be the mums who have signed up for your first session. From what you've told me they have limited skills and time but then there will be the older people, pensioners, who pop in for a coffee during their weekly shopping trip.'

I took a deep breath and carried on scribbling.

'They'll be a totally different skill set and probably won't want tutoring but would appreciate some sort of regular opportunity to get together for a chat and the space to get on with projects they've already started.'

'A knit and natter session you mean?'

'Exactly! You could quite easily offer a weekly knitting and crocheting circle.'

Everything Deborah was suggesting made perfect sense, but it sounded very much to me like the crafting could end up taking over the Café and I wasn't sure how Jemma and Tom or Giles for that matter, would feel about that.

'How long has the Café been open?' Deborah asked, after I briefly explained my concerns about hijacking Jemma's dream.

'Only a week,' I told her.

'No matter,' she smiled, drumming her fingers on the table, 'I dare say you can already see peaks and troughs, busy times and quiet times during the day?'

'Definitely. Around the school run it's pretty quiet and there's certainly a lull after the lunch rush. The place is never empty but there are already fairly well defined quieter times.'

Deborah raised her eyebrows but didn't say anything.

'Oh I get it, I get it!' I nodded enthusiastically. 'You're suggesting I schedule the sessions during the quiet times and then that way the Café will be busy even during those normally slacker times. Is that right?'

'Exactly! The knit and natter gatherings wouldn't be a paid-for session as such, but you can guarantee that customers are going to be tempted by the delicious cakes on offer when they get there. I can't imagine your friend would have any objections to that!'

'No, I'm sure she wouldn't,' I said, gratefully taking on board the benefit of Deborah's huge wealth of knowledge and business acumen.

'And you might even want to think about an evening session for people who are working and can't make it during the day.'

I sat back in my chair as Heather bustled through with a laden tea tray and a plate of very tempting buttery crumpets.

'Do you mind if I join you?' she asked. 'Only I haven't stopped this morning and I could really do with a cuppa.'

'Of course you can join us!' Deborah boomed. 'I'm not going to deny you your breakfast, am I?'

Heather looked at me and smiled sheepishly.

'By all means see how you feel about things after the taster session,' Deborah concluded as she poured the tea and passed around the crumpets, 'but I have no doubt that you're going to love it.'

'I think you'll be brilliant, Lizzie,' Heather smiled warmly.

'Get yourself signed up to one of the free local business courses or if you're too busy to commit to that go for one that's online. There's plenty to choose from,' Deborah carried on. 'You might want to give some thought to running the venture independently of the Café but even if you don't, the courses are invaluable. They'll flag up no end of things you won't have thought of.'

Later that morning, I found myself walking back along the bustling pavements towards Henry's flat, my emotions pinging off in all directions.

'Don't let fear get the better of you!' Deborah had warned as I got ready to leave. 'From what you've told me it sounds like you have the perfect set-up to make the venture work. Of course, we already knew you had the skills,' she added with a laugh, 'and don't forget, if you feel like tutoring here every now and again, my offer still stands!'

'I'll keep you posted,' I told her, 'and thank you again for all your help and advice. I still can't really believe you remembered me!'

'I couldn't forget stitches like that in a hurry,' she laughed, 'and as for the advice, well, let's see how things go before you decide whether to be grateful or not.'

'Goodbye, my dear,' Heather said, 'you look after yourself, won't you? And make sure you keep on sewing, whatever else you decide to do. A talent like yours shouldn't be left to languish! You need to keep using it, promise me you will?'

'I promise,' I told her.

Those last words from Heather were a timely reminder of the kind of life I had led whilst I was in a relationship with Giles and living in the city. I had abandoned my sewing skills and left them to languish without a second thought along with all my other interests and passions. I had twisted and contorted my personality as well as my looks to fit the required mould that would turn me into an acceptable partner for him. How could I have forgotten all of that?

My time at The Cherry Tree Café and in the flat really had softened my memories of our break-up, but as I was shoved and pushed along the pavements back towards Henry's flat the scales finally began to drop and I could see my crazy plan to bring Giles back to Wynbridge for the fantasy it was. Yes, I missed his body in the bed next to mine and yes, I still craved the comfort of having him there to wash my back in the shower, but it was extremely unlikely that he was going to give up the affluent urban lifestyle he loved and move to Wynbridge to be with me. A huge part of me still wanted to be loved, to be one half of a whole like Jemma and Tom, but there was something pressing that I wanted more. I had a new and exciting future on the horizon now, a future I had once abandoned and never thought I'd see again, a future that was now mine for the taking if I could just dig deep enough to find the courage to grasp it.

As I turned the key in Henry's door I decided I wasn't going to mention Giles or my crazy plan at all. I knew Henry had already guessed the real motive behind my visit and I felt guilty at the thought of using my old boss, who had always been such a stalwart friend for me, so readily. I would convince him that the sole reason for my visit was my new sewing business, which ironically was exactly what it had turned out to be.

*

'I suppose you want to talk about Giles, then,' Henry said astutely as he passed me the box of noodles that evening.

We had decided not to go out for dinner and ordered a takeaway that we could eat in front of the TV instead.

'No,' I said, heaping another spoonful onto my plate, 'not really.'

Having decided that I wouldn't mention Giles, I hadn't taken into account that Henry might and now the dreaded subject had been broached I wasn't sure how to play it. Blasé could actually be interpreted as eager but then indifference, denial or vehement resistance could all suggest the same. What exactly could I do or say to convince Henry that I didn't care?

'Unless he's met with a sticky end!' I added breezily, aiming for a touch of dismissive humour.

Judging by Henry's expression my foolish attempt to make light of the situation had failed miserably.

'It's OK,' he said glumly, 'I know that's why you're *really* here.'

The words hit me square in the stomach like a blow from a prize fighter. Henry was no fool and I knew I had to come clean. I owed him that at least.

'OK I admit it,' I began. 'Originally I had asked to come and stay so I could pick your brains about Giles.'

Henry shook his head.

'Let me finish,' I begged, 'but now things have changed.

My meeting this morning has made me realise I've got more going in my life than trying to rekindle something that I should have let die out properly when I moved back home.'

'Like what?'

I took my time explaining to Henry about the Cherry Tree, my passion for sewing and my potential new business. I also – as I felt he deserved a full and proper explanation – told him about the mystery phone calls and how they had been responsible for reigniting my interest in Giles.

'What was the number?' Henry asked.

I wiped my hands down my jeans and unlocked my phone, then found the call log screen and passed it over.

'That's Natasha's number,' Henry said bluntly.

'What?' I choked. 'Why would *she* be ringing me?'

'When did the calls start?'

I took the phone back and scrolled through the list, giving Henry the dates of when they started and ended.

'That's when Giles went AWOL,' Henry explained, 'a few days before the wedding he just disappeared.'

'And Natasha thought he was with me?' I questioned, pushing the thought that Giles and Natasha were now married to the back of my mind.

'Obviously,' Henry shrugged, 'and she probably wasn't the only one.'

'Is that what you thought as well?' I asked, my face glowing.

'Well, I'm not being funny but he does have a bit of a track record for buggering off before the big day, doesn't he?'

I felt the colour spread to my neck as I thought how desperate Natasha must have felt when she realised her fiancé had done a bunk again. During all the time Giles and I were a couple I had done my utmost not to think about Natasha and how it must have felt to be jilted as she was about to practically walk down the aisle, but now I couldn't get the image of her out of my head.

If it had been Giles who had been calling me I realised, and if he had wanted me back, then there was every possibility that I would have stamped all over the poor woman's heart again. It was a shame that I'd never found a way of harvesting the hold that Giles had over the women in his life because it was potent stuff and doubtless worth a fortune.

'So,' I said tentatively, unable to stop myself asking the next question, 'I take it he came back then?'

'Oh yes,' Henry said, 'no one got to the bottom of where he went but they're on their honeymoon now. Mauritius, I think or maybe the Seychelles, so she must have forgiven him . . . again.'

I swallowed hard and drank a mouthful of the lager we had ordered with the takeaway.

'I'm sorry, Lizzie,' Henry said, reaching across and grabbing my hand, 'I take no pleasure in being the one to tell you that.'

'It's OK,' I smiled, 'really. If I'd found out yesterday I would have been in a heap but after this morning and a good think about everything on the walk back, it's all good. I'm glad they're married.'

Henry raised his eyebrows.

'No, I mean it,' I said, 'Natasha finally got her man, despite my interference.'

'But Giles was the bastard!' Henry burst out. 'He was the one who lied to you and broke it off with her!'

'Like I said,' I told him with a shrug, 'Natasha got her man. They suit one another and they were meant to be together. Giles is part of my past and right now I'm more interested in the future but just keep those drinks coming, OK?'

Chapter 14

'Do you want all the tables pushed together or would they be better in pairs?'

Ridiculously early the following Friday morning, I stood in the area designated for the trial bunting-making session, hands on my hips, head on one side, riddled with doubt and on the brink of ripping down the poster and scrawling 'cancelled' across the middle of it in thick black marker pen. Where had the week gone? I asked myself. How was it possible that today was *the* day and I still, despite all my preparations, didn't feel ready?

'Here,' Jemma nudged, thrusting a steaming mug into my hand, 'drink this – you look like you're about to pass out.'

'I think I am,' I said, my hands grasping the mug tightly but shaking so badly that the contents were in danger of ending up all over the floor. 'I can't believe you talked me into doing this,' I scowled.

'Right, come on,' she shouted to Tom and Ben who had been helping. 'We've got to get Ella from Mum's and I think Lizzie could do with a few minutes to gather her thoughts.'

'I thought Tom's mum took her to school on a Friday.'

Jemma gently released the mug from my unsteady grip and put it on a nearby table.

'She does normally but we've had a phone call from the school. Miss Grey, Ella's teacher, has asked us to pop in before registration this morning.'

I bit my lip.

'It isn't funny, Lizzie!' Jemma scolded.

'Sorry,' I smiled, trying not to. 'I'm sure it's nothing. I'll see you later.'

She and Tom quickly disappeared through the Café door, but Ben was still rooted to the spot.

'What are you planning to do with this?' he asked, holding up the string of bunting that I had made at the City Crafting Café.

'I thought I might use it as an example this afternoon,' I told him. 'Just to make sure everyone is totally clear about what we're making.'

'Good idea,' he smiled. 'There's certainly plenty of it.'

I had been adding to it in the evenings and now it was probably long enough to go around the entire crafting area.

'You know, I think it would look even better if you hang it,' Ben suggested, climbing up the ladder and holding it up so

I could see the effect. 'Let it really define what this area of the Café's going to be.'

I wasn't sure.

'How about I hang it whilst you get going with everything else?' he smiled kindly. 'If you don't like it, I'll take it down. I promise I won't make a sound,' he added, noting my hesitation.

'Go on then,' I said reluctantly. 'I'm popping back upstairs to get the other boxes, so don't fall off the ladder, will you?'

A little later we stood back and surveyed our handiwork. Despite my reservations, the bunting looked perfect and was easily long enough to fill the walls around the top of the crafting area. The sewing equipment including scissors, tape measures, pins and so on were arranged along the top of the cupboards that ran the length of the back wall and displayed in upcycled tin cans all painted in pastel shades to match the rest of the Café décor. The fabrics, ribbons and cottons each had their own similarly painted wicker baskets and the two sewing machines were housed in a little recess, which helped muffle some of their noise. The tables, for the purpose of this particular session had been pushed together as there were only six students and there was room for me their tutor, behind a table of my own.

'It's perfect,' I whispered, willing myself not to cry. 'Exactly as I imagined it.'

Ben put a friendly arm around my shoulders and gave me a squeeze.

'Having seen how beautifully you transformed the rest of the Café,' he said with a smile, 'this is pretty much how I imagined it too.'

Without thinking, I leant into the comforting warmth of his body. Ben had been on hand all week to help me with the preparations, not in an intrusive or overbearing way; he was more subtle than that. He had discreetly come up with endless clever solutions to the hundreds of little problems that, left unsolved, I would have obsessed over and blown up out of all proportion.

I was grateful that our initially fraught friendship had turned a corner and I couldn't help wondering what would have happened after our little tumble in the snow if Ella hadn't interrupted. Even though I was still feeling raw and bruised from my aborted attempt to lure Giles back to Wynbridge, I couldn't deny that I missed the intimacy and physical closeness of having a man in my life.

Ben and I might have got off to a shaky start but I was beginning to appreciate that, on the evidence of the last few days at least, he really seemed to 'get me'; he understood what I was dreaming of achieving.

'Thank you for all your help this week,' I said, 'I couldn't have done it without you.'

Ben shook his head dismissively.

'Oh yes you could.'

'Well all right then, let's just say, I wouldn't have wanted to muddle my way through it all without you on my side.'

'It means a lot to you doesn't it, all this?' Ben smiled.

Yes, I realised, he really did 'get me'.

'It's what I've always wanted,' I replied honestly, 'I was dreaming of this even when we were at school.'

'I remember.'

'Do you?' I frowned.

'Oh yes, I remember a lot of things, Lizzie. Sometimes it's a curse, to be honest; my memories remind me of my regrets.'

'What do you regret then?'

'Oh I dunno.'

'No, come on, tell me. I want examples!'

'Well, for a start, all the things my shyness stopped me doing when I was younger, I guess.'

'You? Shy?' I exclaimed, taking a step back and losing myself in his deep, ponderous gaze. 'I was the shy one. I was the one hidden away in my room whenever Jemma went off with Tom and you and your merry band. You played in the bloody band, remember?'

'Yes,' Ben laughed, 'but I never sang.'

I wasn't quite sure what he meant by that and was about to ask, but he cut me off before I had a chance.

'So how come you've never done all this before?' Ben

asked, pointing at the crafting area. 'There's more than a decade between leaving school and now.'

'I know,' I sighed resignedly, 'I don't generally go in for regrets myself, but now I do wish I'd got on with things sooner. After college I just drifted. Mum had convinced me I was wasting my time with my sewing and I just fell into the routine of working shifts in the pub, then Jemma and Tom got engaged and oh, I don't know, it just never happened.'

'Did you not think about setting up something like this when you were living in London?'

'God no!' I laughed. 'I never gave any of this a second thought. As you're well aware, I was too busy trying to pretend to be someone I wasn't.'

I stopped abruptly and moved a little further away. I was somewhat taken aback by the edge of bitterness that had crept into my response.

'But what about you?' I asked. 'Can you honestly say that you're living the dream?'

Today was supposed to represent a fresh start for me and I had no desire to dredge up the past and start thinking about why I'd blown back to Wynbridge. I knew that any talk of Ben's private life usually stopped him in his tracks and so that was the path I took. It was a cheap shot but I didn't want anything other than a few wobbly stitches taking the edge off my day.

'I'm not like you,' he said, 'I don't think I ever had one big dream as a kid, just lots of smaller ones that would take me all over the world on lots of different adventures.'

'And have you lived them all?' I asked. 'Have you ticked them all off?'

Ben began to laugh. He leant back against the edge of a table and thrust his hands in his jeans pockets. He looked infuriatingly relaxed.

'I've ticked some off,' he smiled, 'but nowhere near all of them. Why are you so angry and defensive all of a sudden?'

'I'm not!' I half shouted, stubbornly thrusting out my chin.

'Yes you are!'

'Well if I am, it's because you always do this!'

'Do what?'

'You just have this way of making me say things; making me feel things and then when I ask for something in return you clam up or make a joke of it. You know every detail of my excruciating homecoming, yet I don't know why you've come back! You never actually give me a straight answer . . . to anything!'

'But you've never asked me?'

There was no denying that. It was Jemma and Tom who had wrapped him up in cottonwool, not Ben himself. I had never asked him because *they* had warned me off.

'So, why have you come back then?'

'Come on! Come on! Action stations! There's only twenty minutes until we're open!' Jemma charged through the Café and into the kitchens. 'Why haven't you put the water on?' she shouted.

'Damn it,' I muttered.

Ben shrugged his shoulders and pushed himself upright.

'It'll keep,' he smiled, 'I'm not planning on going anywhere, are you?'

The morning passed all too quickly and before I knew it, Sarah and Rachel were hovering in the doorway ten minutes before the taster session was due to start.

'Come in, come in,' Jemma smiled, 'Lizzie's just putting the finishing touches on everything.'

What I was actually trying to do was not throw up all over the prettily prepared tables as I checked and rechecked that every person had access to everything they were going to need in order to complete their string of bunting within the allotted time. I smoothed my unruly curls behind my ears one last time and stepped out to meet my first two attendees.

'What about this one with the little boats and beach huts on?' I suggested, holding up a long strip of fabric for Rachel's scrutiny. 'If we're careful, we can line the template up to make sure you don't lose any of the designs?'

'Perfect!' she laughed, clapping her hands together. 'Lizzie, you've got such an eye for these things!'

Feeling much more settled, I handed over the fabric and

continued my rounds of the tables offering words of encouragement and advice as necessary. What I had assumed would be a quick, simple make was turning out to be quite a challenge for some but they all looked as if they were enjoying themselves.

'We'll stagger the refreshments,' I told Jemma, 'that way there won't be a queue for the sewing machines.'

Five of the six people who booked had turned up. Helen, the third musketeer in Sarah and Rachel's clan, had had to cancel courtesy of her young son who was unwell and needed collecting from school.

'Try this,' I said, passing Rachel a transparent template, 'you can see the pattern through this one so you can see exactly what you're outlining.'

I'd made everyone a triangle and rectangle template and they were now enthusiastically cutting out the shapes they had chosen and drawn around ready to sew them together.

'If you weren't bothered about the bunting being double-sided,' I explained, 'you could cut the fabric with pinking shears to stop it fraying. That way you wouldn't have to worry about edging it.'

'So if it was going to be hung flat against a wall or something you could use that technique, couldn't you?'

'Exactly,' I smiled.

Jackie and Sandra were both making bunting for their grandchildren and sat companionably comparing notes on their toddlers' development and prowess in the playground. Rachel's string was destined for the bathroom, whilst Sarah's floral masterpiece was earmarked for the summerhouse.

'Have you got anywhere in mind for yours, Angela?' I asked as I gathered offcuts to see if there were any scraps worth salvaging.

'I thought it might look nice above the sink in the kitchen,' she smiled shyly. 'But I'm not sure.'

I sat next to her in the seat that should have been occupied by Helen and looked about me. Everyone was chatting away across the table, sharing news and gossip, but still absorbed in their own project.

'How's it going?' Ruby whispered, as she set about clearing the Café tables.

'Great!' I beamed. 'Brilliant. Exactly how I hoped it would.'

I turned back to the group to monitor their progress.

'Now,' I called, 'who knows how to thread a sewing machine?'

Two hours later it was all over and the group were getting ready to leave. Each had a brown paper bag, stamped with The Cherry Tree Café logo and a tiny silver bell threaded through the handles, clutched to their chests.

'I still can't believe I've made this!' Sarah giggled, peeping inside the bag. 'Mark will never believe that I haven't been down the shops and bought it!'

'What's next?' Rachel asked. 'I can't wait to have a go at something else!'

'I don't know!' I laughed. 'I wanted to see how today went before I decided whether it was worth planning anything else.'

'Its crafts and cakes, Lizzie,' Jackie laughed, 'nowhere else around here offers such a tempting combination. What on earth did you think would go wrong?'

I held open the door and watched them disappear down the path, their chatter and laughter still reaching me long after they were out of sight. The Café was almost empty and I went back to the crafting area to finish tidying away.

'I just wanted to say thank you again, Lizzie,' Angela said quietly.

'I'm sorry, Angela. I thought you'd gone out with the rest. I'm so pleased you enjoyed yourself.'

'This afternoon has really meant a lot to me,' she said, her voice so quiet I could barely hear her. 'This is the first time I've done anything like this since my Roger died.'

I didn't know what to say.

'I haven't been out much at all, really. We'd only moved here a few weeks before he passed and I haven't had the chance to get to know anyone beyond the neighbours.'

'Why don't you sit down?' I said, pulling out a chair.

'No, I won't stop,' she smiled. 'I just wanted to say thank you. It's been lovely doing something to take my mind off things for a while. Promise you'll let me know if you decide to do something else, won't you?'

'Of course,' I nodded, remembering how Deborah had told me people would enjoy the opportunity to socialise as much as sew. 'I'll keep you posted, but do pop in and say hello any time, won't you? I'm always here.'

I watched as she headed out the door, the silver bell on her bag tinkling gently as she disappeared.

'So?'

'So what?'

'So much to talk about,' Jemma laughed, 'that I hardly know where to start!'

'How about you start by telling us just what your wayward daughter has been up to this time!' Ben suggested as he handed around the plates of spaghetti bolognese that I was serving up and passing him.

Ella was spending the night with Tom's mum so we could have a Café catch-up and general discussion about how the taster session had gone.

'Oh yes!' I teased. 'You never said when you came back. What's she been up to now?'

Jemma and Tom exchanged glances.

'She got in a bit of an argument at playtime yesterday.'

'Not again!' Ben and I chorused together. 'What about this time?'

Playground differences were becoming almost a weekly grievance in Ella's little world and I hoped the impact of having so little time with Jemma wasn't the reason behind it. I was about to say something, but catching the concern on her face, decided against it.

'I bumped into Sarah and Rachel when I went to collect Ella from school,' Ben smiled, successfully steering the conversation back to the business in hand. 'They were both grinning like Cheshire cats.'

We all walked back to the sitting room and sat, our plates balanced precariously. 'Perhaps this wasn't the best idea!' I joked, trying to spin spaghetti onto my fork without spilling it.

'Never mind that,' Ben scolded, 'how do you think the session went, Lizzie?'

'It was brilliant!' I beamed. 'A total success. Everyone had a great time. In fact, they were all clamouring to know what we could make next!'

Looking back, I couldn't imagine why I'd been so worried. I'd finally got the opportunity to do something I was passionate about in the company of some lovely people and eventually, if everything went to plan I would be able to make a living at it. The only twinge of doubt in the back of my mind revolved around Jemma and whether she would want different groups meeting in the Café on a weekly basis.

'That is assuming there's going to be a next time,' I added.

'What do you mean?' Tom asked, wiping his tomato-stained chin on his shirt sleeve.

'Well, Jemma might not want half the Café taken over every week by a raucous group of unruly craft enthusiasts!'

I was trying to make light of the situation but my heart was hammering in my chest.

'No,' she said, 'I don't.'

I swallowed hard and nodded, forcing myself to remember that the Café was her dream and Tom's. I was going to have to look elsewhere to fulfil mine.

'I want it taken over every day!' she laughed. 'This afternoon was amazing, Lizzie. It was everything we ever dreamt of; no, actually it was so much more than that! I don't see why you can't run a different group every afternoon and maybe even establish the knit and natter thing you were on about at the same time.'

'Really?' I choked. 'You really want me to carry on?'

'Of course, you silly mare!' Tom laughed. 'We know a golden opportunity when we see it, don't we, Jemma?'

Chapter 15

The 'meeting' that evening lasted far longer than we expected and it was almost midnight before Jemma and Tom said their goodbyes and headed home to bed. Ben lingered behind, ostensibly to help me with the dishes, but I could tell there was something else he wanted to say.

'So you really enjoyed yourself this afternoon?' he asked, as we stood at the sink, me washing and him drying.

'It was fantastic,' I nodded, 'I can't believe I was so nervous, though! You must have thought I was a right idiot.'

'Not at all,' he smiled, 'I was relieved actually.'

'What do you mean?'

'Oh I don't know. I guess it was a relief to see that you were taking it all so seriously.'

'Why would you think I wasn't?'

'You just seemed different after the Café opened,' he said hesitantly, 'distracted almost. To tell you the truth, we all thought you were thinking about leaving again. Then when you went to stay with your old boss last weekend we half wondered if you'd come back.'

'But I told Jemma I was going to see Deborah at the Crafting Café,' I frowned. 'The trip was all about my commitment to the Cherry Tree.'

I kept my eyes on the sink full of dishes, unwilling to return Ben's penetrating gaze.

'We know that now,' he said gently, 'and I don't want you thinking we were talking about you behind your back, Lizzie. It wasn't like that. I promise. We were just worried about you.'

I nodded, dried my hands on the towel and spread it across the radiator to dry.

'Do you want a coffee?' I offered.

Even though it was late I didn't want to be on my own. I knew that if Ben left now I would go to bed and start stewing over imaginary and bitchy conversations that he, Jemma and Tom might have had about me, which of course they hadn't.

'Yeah, thanks. Coffee would be good.'

We stoked up the fire and sat in the siting room staring at the flames.

'About what you asked me earlier,' Ben said, breaking the silence, his voice thick in his throat, 'about why I've come back.'

I held up my hand to stop him.

'It's fine,' I insisted, 'you don't have to tell me anything. It's your business. I know how it feels to have the world and his wife talking about you, so please don't feel obliged to explain anything just to make me feel better. I didn't mean to sound so tetchy earlier, I was just nervous.'

'It's OK,' he whispered, 'I want to tell you. I want you to know.'

'Well that's different,' I said.

He took a deep breath and set his mug of coffee down on the table.

'I came home because, like you, I had a relationship break-up,' he said tentatively. 'The girl I was seeing smashed my heart into a thousand pieces and I couldn't bear to be any-where near where she was.'

I tucked my feet under me and sat back in the chair ready to listen.

'Another broken heart,' I sympathised.

'Another broken heart,' Ben repeated.

Seconds passed.

'Do you want to tell me what she did?' I said eventually.

Ben looked at me for a second then back to the fire. I think, lost in his thoughts, he'd forgotten I was even there.

'I don't know where to start,' he laughed.

'Well, how about the beginning?'

'Oh no, you wouldn't like the beginning.'

'Then why don't you tell me what she did to break your

heart, assuming it isn't too close to the beginning?' I suggested, trying to help him.

'I thought she was ill,' he began quickly. 'For weeks she'd seemed pale and tired but there was nothing I could put my finger on. I knew she was working too hard, but she was always working too hard.'

He stopped for a second, cleared his throat and ran his hands through his hair.

'She came home from work one day and told me she was going to France for a few days, some business conference. I told her she wasn't well enough but she said she had to go, that the whole thing depended on her being there.'

He stopped again and stared into the fire, the memory of it all clearly playing out in his mind.

'Did she go?' I whispered, an assumption that she had had an affair with a colleague already forming in my mind.

Ben nodded.

'Yes, she went,' he said bitterly. 'The morning after she left, I set about tidying the flat. I took the rubbish down to the bins and the bag split. Amongst the detritus I found a pregnancy test.' He took a swig of coffee. 'It was positive.'

I let out a long slow breath, my heart rate picking up with every word I heard.

'Was that why she seemed ill? Did she have morning sickness?'

'I guess so. I was angry at first. Angry that she hadn't told me, I thought she was going to try and trap me. I didn't want a kid; I wasn't ready to have a kid.'

Typical, I thought.

'But as the days went on and I waited for her to come back, the idea began to grow on me. I mean, I was in love with the girl, wasn't I? Yes, it was sooner than I expected but there were worse things to be than a father.'

I nodded and retracted my uncharitable thought, but didn't say anything.

'Anyway she came back looking even paler and more tired than ever. I looked after her. Took her home and put her to bed. She agreed to take a week off work and that seemed to help. Every day she looked better and grew stronger and all the time I waited for her to tell me.'

'And did she?' I couldn't see where any of what he was telling me was heading now.

'The evening before she went back to work I couldn't stand it any more so I showed her the pregnancy test. I told her not to worry, that I was pleased, that I would support her and the baby.'

'What did she say?' I asked, leaning forward in my chair.

'She told me she hadn't been on a business trip. She'd checked into a clinic and had an abortion.'

'Oh god,' I gasped, 'how could she? How could she do that?'

Ben shook his head.

'I don't know.'

'Oh Ben, I'm so sorry.'

'I told myself that day,' he continued bitterly, 'that I would never trust another woman again, that I would never love another woman again and I hate her for that. I hate her for taking the possibility of loving someone again away from me.'

I didn't say anything, but I knew exactly how he felt. My relationship turned car crash with Giles had ruined love and trust for me too. My coffee was cold when I reached for the mug and I put it back down again. Ben was sitting with his head in his hands and his shoulders shaking. I moved to the sofa and took one of his hands and kissed it. This was doubtless what he meant about having regrets. He was probably thinking that he should have been a father by now, that he should have had a family of his own.

When he finally looked up his expression was utterly forlorn but his skin was seductively warm, the smell of him masculine and desirable. Without speaking, without thinking we moved together and began to kiss, our bodies entwined on the sofa. I moaned and arched my back to meet him as he hungrily tore at the buttons on my shirt. I wrapped my legs around his back, pulling him hard down on to me. I was desperate to feel all of him, to shut out the rest of the world and give in to desire. In that moment I wasn't looking for love and tenderness; I just wanted to feel taken over, if only for a while.

'No,' Ben gasped, pushing me away, 'we can't. Not like this.'

I tried to kiss him again, but he pulled further away.

'Lizzie, we can't. We'd be doing it for all the wrong reasons. I think more of you than that.'

The fragile bubble of intensity that had surrounded us burst and along with it our moment of spontaneous passion. I didn't say anything. I didn't move. I just watched him walk away.

I didn't go down to the Café the next morning. I knew Ruby was coming in early to help Jemma so there was no need for me to put in an appearance until mid-morning when the rush would begin. I told myself I could begin planning the next sewing session, but what I actually did was wander aimlessly from room to room thinking about Ben and everything he'd told me.

It was little wonder he wasn't the life and soul of the party. He probably spent most of his days with one eye on the calendar trying to work out exactly when he should have become a father. I couldn't imagine why any girl would do that to him. I mean, it wasn't as if it was some one-night stand that had resulted in her pregnancy. From what I could gather they were living together as a couple, so why would she do that? On what planet did she think her actions were acceptable? Ultimately of course the final decision would have been hers, but surely Ben had a right to know, surely he deserved the chance to offer an opinion?

I couldn't get our feverish embrace out of my mind either. We had been drawn together out of sympathy, a mutual understanding of what each of us had endured in the name of love over the last few months, but those kisses, the lust his hands awoke in me meant much more than a quick sympathy fumble.

'Can I come in?'

It was Jemma and she already had.

'Are you OK?' she asked, leaning against the kitchen doorframe. 'Only, you've normally put in an appearance by now.'

She stopped suddenly, her eyebrows raised.

'Oh,' she smirked, 'feeling a bit tired, are we?'

'I didn't sleep particularly well, but what do you mean?'

'Haven't you looked in a mirror this morning?'

I frowned and crossed the room to look at my reflection in the mirror hanging above the fireplace.

'Or maybe you have,' she giggled, 'and that's the reason why you haven't come down. I could be mistaken,' she concluded smugly, 'but that to me looks very much like the kind of raw skin you'd get from snogging someone who sports a fine crop of facial hair!'

She was right and I was mortified. My neck and chin looked red raw. I cursed Ben and his beard. There could be no denying what had happened after Jemma and Tom left us alone now. I was just about to try to find something to say that would explain my tell-tale appearance when I heard another set of feet thundering up the stairs.

Ben stopped in the doorway panting and red-faced.

'Don't mind me,' Jemma laughed, backing out of the room. 'I'm just popping down to the chemist to get Lizzie some calamine. See you later.'

'What was that about?' Ben frowned. 'Are you hurt?'

I turned to face him.

'Oh,' he said, 'sorry about that, occupational hazard I guess. You're the first girl I've kissed since – well, let's just say – since I started growing it. I wasn't sure what the impact would be. Does it hurt?'

'Don't worry about my face,' I told him, brushing aside his concern in my eagerness to talk, 'look, about what happened.'

Ben shook his head looking embarrassed.

'I'm really sorry about everything,' he interrupted, 'I don't know what came over me. Maybe it was the shock of telling you everything, I dunno.'

Clearly he regretted what had passed between us and although I was disappointed, I was still determined to be honest with him. At around three that morning I had decided that I needed to explain the truth behind my London trip and wanted to get it over with as quickly as possible. I knew I didn't *have* to, but I didn't want there to be any confusion or doubt over my commitment to the Cherry Tree.

'Have you got time for a coffee?' I asked.

Ben gave his trademark shrug and I went to fill the kettle.

'Let's take this down to the garden, shall we?' I suggested, passing him a tray loaded with the coffee pot, mugs and milk jug.

The spring day was bright and breezy and the air refreshing but warm with the promise of increased heat to come. We sat under the cherry tree with our backs to the Café, safe from prying eyes and ears.

'Before we even get into what happened last night,' I ventured, 'I want to talk to you about my London trip.'

Ben finished pouring the coffee and passed me my mug.

'It wasn't just about the Café was it?' he said. 'I didn't think it was.'

I could already feel my face beginning to colour with shame but I was desperate to completely clear the air that for some reason had been tainted ever since we first met.

I didn't know if our moment of passion on the sofa would ever lead to anything more but I had to admit, if only to myself, that I still liked Ben a lot and that being honest with him was paramount. My relationship with Giles had been shrouded in trickery, secrecy and lies from the outset and look how that had turned out. I couldn't put myself through that kind of deception again.

'No,' I said, 'it wasn't just about the Café, although in my defence I did learn a lot the morning I spent with my contact Deborah.'

'Stop beating about the bush, Lizzie.' Ben frowned. 'Why did you really go?'

'OK,' I said, taking a deep breath. 'Before the Café launch I started getting these calls to my mobile. I never answered them and I didn't recognise the number but I thought—'

'You thought it might be Giles,' Ben interrupted.

'Yes,' I admitted, 'I thought it might be Giles.'

'So you went to London to find out.'

'So I went to London to find out.'

'And was it Giles?' he demanded bluntly.

'If you would just let me explain without interrupting!' I chastised.

Ben lifted his hands in surrender, picked up his mug and sat back in his seat.

'No,' I said, 'it wasn't Giles.'

Ben raised his eyebrows in surprise but didn't say anything.

'It was Natasha,' I continued, 'Giles's fiancée.'

'How did you find that out?' Ben rumbled, his vow of silence quickly forgotten as his voice thundered around the garden. 'How can you be sure it was her?'

'Henry, my old boss, recognised the number,' I explained. 'When I told him the dates of when the calls came through, he told me that during that time Giles had gone AWOL.'

'So?'

'So I guess Natasha assumed he might have been with me. It was only a couple of weeks before their wedding and he already had a track record for disappearing at inopportune moments, hadn't he? I mean, a week before their original wedding date was when he hooked up with me the first time.'

'Did he go back?' Ben demanded. 'Did he turn up?'

'Yes,' I said, unnerved by Ben's almost explosive anger. 'They were on their honeymoon when I stayed with Henry. No one knew where Giles had disappeared to, but Natasha forgave him and they were married as planned.'

Ben banged his mug back on the tray and quickly stood up. I looked up at him, my hand shielding my eyes from the glare of the sun. Distractedly he ran his hands through his hair. For a moment I thought he was going to ask how I felt but his expression suggested otherwise.

'I can't believe you cared enough to find out,' he said, staring down at me sternly. He looked repulsed by what I had done. 'After everything he put you through.'

'Neither can I,' I swallowed, 'I let my heart rule my head; it was a moment of weakness.'

'And if it had have been him, then what?' Ben asked sharply.

I resented his judgemental tone and stood to face him.

'I don't know,' I lied, thinking of my silly plan to lure Giles back to Wynbridge. 'What would you have done if you thought your girlfriend had been trying to get in touch with you?' I snapped. 'Could you have dismissed her so easily? Would you have listened to your heart, or don't you have one?'

Ben's expression was unforgettable and I knew instantly that I had gone too far.

'Sorry,' I mumbled, 'I had no right to say that.'

Ben said nothing.

'I really am sorry,' I said again.

Jemma had invited me to lunch the next day and I was hoping to see Ben and apologise again for my despicable comment. Tom's mum Maureen had also been invited and the plan was to have an afternoon off from the Café but I reckoned it would be less than half an hour before the conversation took its natural course and led us back through the door.

'Can you help Ella lay the table?' Tom asked as soon as I arrived. 'She can't manage on her own but she won't let me help.'

'He's in her bad books again,' Jemma smiled, cuffing him playfully with the oven gloves.

'Not another row about a canine companion, is it?'

'Yes,' said Tom wearily, 'she's trying to use the fact that we're busy with work and the Café as leverage now.'

'But surely she understands there's no one here all day to look after a dog?'

'Nope, according to Ella a dog would fill the gap in her life that her working parents can no longer fill.'

'Oh,' I said. 'I see.'

I took the proffered basket of cutlery and headed into the dining room to help my wayward goddaughter.

'Did you have a dog when you were little?' was her opening gambit.

'Nope, sorry,' I said, 'you're out of luck trying me. I didn't have so much as a goldfish.'

'How come?'

'Because pets are smelly, noisy, messy things,' I told her.

'No they're not!'

'I know that,' I said, 'but that's what my mum always used to say.'

Ella didn't say anything else. Clearly I wasn't worth investing any more time in.

'Hang on, chick, you haven't laid enough places,' I told her as I counted the haphazardly laid placemats.'We're one short.'

'No we're not!' Ella scowled, marching around the table tapping every setting and announcing who it belonged to.

'You've missed Ben out,' I said, 'or has he been naughty and has to eat in his room?'

'He's not here.'

'Oh,' I said. 'OK.'

'He's gone to Spain,' Ella announced.

'Of course he hasn't,' I laughed, thinking Ella had misunderstood. She had a reputation for misinterpreting information gleaned whilst eavesdropping.

'He has,' she insisted, pouting and folding her arms. 'Daddy took him to the airport last night. Didn't you, Daddy?' she asked innocently, batting her eyelashes at her father who had just come in with assorted plates and bowls.

'Didn't Daddy what?' he asked hesitantly.

'Take Ben to the airport, of course!'

'Yes,' he said, 'I did.'

'There!' said Ella. 'I told you, Lizzie, he's gone to Spain.'

I didn't know what to say. I stood and stared at the pair of them, the cutlery I was supposed to be setting frozen in mid-air. Suddenly I felt very hot, my heart was hammering and I could feel hot stinging tears pricking the back of my eyes.

Why hadn't he told me?

'He's gone to stay with his dad,' Tom frowned. 'Surely he told you? He said he was going to tell you.'

I shook my head.

'He said he had some stuff to think through, that he needed a bit of space to come to terms with a few things.'

'It doesn't matter,' I smiled.

Tom opened his mouth to say something else but I cut him off.

'It really doesn't matter,' I said again but rather too brightly this time, 'I'm not his keeper. It's not up to me whether he stays or goes.'

I began carefully laying out the cutlery again and Tom bent down and scooped Ella up in his arms.

'Come on,' he said, jiggling her up and down and giving me a sidelong glance, 'come and be my lookout for Nanny Maureen.'

Chapter 16

I knew I had no real reason to resent Ben leaving, that there was nothing real, nothing tangible between us that meant he *had* to stay, but nonetheless his disappearance wormed its way into my ego and steadily chipped away at my already fragile self-confidence. Frustratingly his absence from the pub in the evenings also took the edge off my willingness to carry on with my shifts and, coupled with my desire to focus on the sewing courses, it wasn't many days after he went that I made my excuses and resigned.

'We're really sorry to see you go,' Evelyn told me as we cleared away after my last shift, 'but I'm pleased about the Café. It's good that you and Jemma have found a way to realise your dreams. Too many people forget what they started out wanting or lose faith and give up. I'm really proud of you, Lizzie. You've both worked really hard and Tom, of course. I hope it's a huge success for all of you.'

'Thanks, Evelyn,' I smiled, 'so do I.'

As Deborah suggested, I had signed up to an online small business start-up course and told myself, as I worked steadily through the information, that running another session was the *real* reason why I was giving up the shifts in the pub. I had a nice little nest egg sitting in the bank so money wasn't a problem and I knew that being able to dedicate all my time to the new venture was a total luxury. I didn't mention my tumultuous feelings about Ben Fletcher to anyone.

'So I guess I'll see you Friday then,' Evelyn said as she began cashing up. 'Are you fully booked?'

'No, not yet,' I told her. 'There's still room for a couple more people, but I'm not too worried if all the spaces aren't taken. To be honest I hadn't been expecting to run another session so soon!'

'So who has signed up so far?'

'Well there's Helen, of course,' I explained. 'She missed out first time round because her son was sick. She was the person who asked if I'd consider running it again, actually. Apparently Sarah and Rachel haven't stopped going on about how much fun they had. Then there's a lady called Angela, she was on the first course and enjoyed it so much that she wanted to come again.'

'Sounds like you made quite an impression!' Evelyn laughed.

'Then there's a woman called Alison,' I continued, 'but I've no idea who she is.'

'Oh, that'll be Ali Fletcher,' Evelyn nodded, 'she's the only Alison round here.'

'Ali who?'

'Fletcher,' Evelyn said again. 'Ben's mum. I dare say she's missing him now he's rushed off to be with his father and you never know, what with her being such an old gossip,' she said, eyeing me astutely, 'we might even find out why he went off in such a hurry.'

'Oh, I'm sure he had his reasons,' I said evasively.

'Well anyway,' Evelyn laughed, thankfully abandoning the subject, 'I'm not so sure you'll be able to get me to sew in a straight line, but we'll give it a go. I've been meaning to find a way of doing something with this place for ages,' she said, looking around her, 'but I never seem to have the time. Some of that bunting stuff will be lovely strung around the bar. I want rectangles though,' she added fiercely, 'and nothing frilly!'

'Lizzie!'

'What?'

'There's someone to see you!'

'Can they come back later?'

'No! Hurry up will you?'

Of all the mornings to be running late, and now I had a visitor to contend with on top of everything else. So far I was managing to keep my nerves in check this time around and I felt barely a flicker as my mind ran through the plans for the session. No, now it was something else that was causing me problems and typically, on the one morning I couldn't afford to, I'd overslept.

'Who is it?' I hissed as I thundered down the stairs and through the beaded curtain that separated home from work.

'Oh, hello.'

I stopped in my tracks as I came face to face with Jay, the journalist from the Café launch.

'Hello, Lizzie,' he smiled disarmingly, 'you never called.'

'I've been busy,' I told him, brushing past and scowling at Jemma for good measure.

'I asked Tom for your number,' Jay continued, following doggedly on behind, 'but he wouldn't give it to me.'

'I should think not!' I snapped. 'I don't know you from Adam. You could be a stalker or a complete psycho for all I know.'

'But I'm not,' he grinned. 'You know I'm not.'

'Look, I'm sorry, but I'm really busy. Was there something in particular you wanted? I have a group this afternoon and loads to do.' I knew I sounded rude, but I was cross.

I could see Jemma and Tom peeping through from the kitchen like a couple of kids and I guessed that they had set this meeting up. Unwittingly they were offering me Jay as a Ben alternative, but I had no desire to compromise.

'Jemma told me you'd decided to go ahead with the sewing

sessions,' Jay explained. 'She showed me the photos from the other Friday.'

'What photos?' I frowned. 'I didn't take any photographs.'

'These,' he grinned, lifting a large parcel on to the table and effectively stopping me from carrying on setting out the materials for the afternoon.

'What's this?' I pointed.

'Open it,' he smiled.

'Tell me again,' I frowned, 'why exactly are you here?'

'Just open it,' he laughed, his bright blue eyes sparkling mis-chievously.

It was the only way I was going to get rid of him, so I tore off the paper and gasped in surprise. I'd been meaning to ask Jemma what had happened to the cherry cupcake design I'd created and here it was, beautifully displayed in a pine box frame with a pastel pink mount, the photos of the first bunting session artfully arranged around it.

'Oh my god!' I laughed, my hands flying up to cover my face. 'That's amazing!'

Jemma and Tom came rushing out of the kitchen to join us.

'That looks fantastic, mate!' Tom beamed, slapping Jay on the back and shaking his hand.

'Was this your idea?' I said to Jemma.

'Nope,' she laughed. 'Jay thought of it. He took the cup-cake design with him on launch day and I gave him the photos I'd managed to sneak a few days ago to see if he could include them.'

'Wow,' I smiled, 'it's stunning, really beautiful. Thank you.'

I genuinely meant what I said. The picture was so pretty; exactly the sort of thing I loved.

'Come on then,' Tom laughed, 'let's hang it before we open up, then I really must get off to work.'

He climbed on top of the cupboard, hammered in the picture hook he had magically produced from his shirt pocket and then lifted the frame into position. We all took a step back and admired our combined handiwork. It looked stunning. The tiny beads I'd used to decorate the frosting caught the light and the darker strands of thread used to embroider The Cherry Tree Café name stood out beautifully. The choice of frame and the colour of the mount complemented the design perfectly and I was feeling suitably chastened as I turned my attention back to Jay.

'Were you responsible for all this, then?' I asked. 'Or are you just the delivery man?'

'Guilty of both charges actually,' he smiled.

'But I thought you were just a journalist,' I frowned.

'And I thought you were just a barmaid,' he grinned.

'Touché!' I laughed back. 'Sorry, I should know better than that, shouldn't I? It's gorgeous. Thank you, and you guys!' I called as Tom went off to work and Jemma disappeared back into the kitchen.

'You're welcome!' she called over her shoulder before starting up the mixer.

'It really is lovely,' I smiled at Jay. I realised it was suddenly just the two of us again and hastily made my excuses to get back to setting up. 'But I'm ever so sorry, I really must get on. I still have to prepare for this afternoon and the Café will be open in a minute.'

'Have you any spaces left?' he asked, as he began to fold the paper the picture had been wrapped in.

'Just the one now,' I told him, 'Tom's mum Maureen decided to take a spot at the last minute. She's got to bring Ella with her though, so that will be interesting.'

'Ah yes, the enchanting Ella!' Jay laughed.

'You know Ella?'

'Oh yes. Whenever I go to the house she always tells me I wear too much aftershave!'

In a flash my initial dislike of Jay was explained and all thanks to the blunt and frankly rude comments of my goddaughter. It was the aftershave. Jay wore the same Hugo Boss as Giles. How absurd that a smell could initiate such strength of feeling.

'That sounds like Ella,' I said, unnerved by the realisation that I had totally misjudged this perfectly kind, thoughtful man because he smelt like a toad from my past.

'Anyway,' he said, 'I can see you're busy and I have to be somewhere.'

'OK,' I called after him, 'and thanks again. The picture really is beautiful.'

He stopped at the door and turned back.

'Can I see you again later?' he asked.

'I'm not sure,' I hesitated, unwilling to commit to anything. 'I'm busy here all afternoon.'

'What a brilliant idea!' he beamed.

'What?'

'Well, you said you had a space left, didn't you?'

'Yes,' I frowned.

'Well put me down for it then!'

'Are you serious?' I laughed. 'You want me to put your name down for the bunting-making session I'm running in the Café this afternoon?'

'Why not?' he replied. 'If you do decide you want some publicity you'll want someone with experience helping you out, won't you?'

He'd gone before I could think of a suitable answer.

'You didn't tell me Jay was such a good family friend,' I whispered to Jemma as she carried through a tray laden with cakes and biscuits later that afternoon.

Everyone except Maureen and Ella was settled at the tables, busily selecting fabrics. Surreptitiously I had been watching Ben's mother but I was struggling to see her as 'the viper with a thin veneer' he had always described her as when we compared maternal notes. For the moment, she was seated at a table alone but chatting companionably with the women either side of her as she tried to decide which template to use.

'He isn't really a family friend,' Jemma whispered back. 'He and Tom used to play football together on a Saturday morning and the friendship just seemed to stick after the team folded. We don't see him often but for some reason Ella is always shockingly rude to him!'

'He told me.'

'Talking of Ella, where are they? Honestly, what a day to pick to close the school for staff training! Where's Harry?' she called to Helen. 'You could have brought him with you.'

'No fear!' Helen called back. 'I've been looking forward to this for ages. He's gone to play at Rachel's. I'm picking him up later.'

'Here they are,' I said, pointing to the window as I spotted Ella trotting along, with Maureen looking flustered in her wake.

'Sorry, sorry,' she grimaced, struggling out of her coat, 'I know we're late but I had such a job getting a certain someone off the swings.'

Jemma quickly took her wayward daughter by the hand and led her out into the kitchen.

'Don't worry, Maureen,' I smiled, pulling out a chair, 'we've barely started. We're still selecting fabrics. Why don't you sit here with Mrs Fletcher and take a moment to catch your breath?'

'Please, call me Ali,' Ben's mother smiled, 'Mrs Fletcher makes me feel so old!'

'Ali then,' I smiled back, 'how are you getting on with that template?'

'So you're the famous Lizzie Dixon are you?' she said, looking me up and down appraisingly and ignoring the template completely. 'Of course I would have known you even without Ben's description. It's the hair, love, makes you stand out a mile.'

'Yes,' I said tentatively, 'believe it or not you aren't the first person to pass comment.'

I chose my words with care, suddenly on guard and slightly afraid that the viper was drawing herself up to strike.

'I wasn't sure whether I should come today,' she continued just loud enough for me alone to hear. 'It all rather depended on where Ben was on his sliding scale.'

'His what?'

'His "Dixon Dilemma" scale.' She said it as though she assumed I knew what she was talking about. 'The whole "one minute he loves you and the next he hates you" debacle, but then he buggered off to Spain and I thought, why not?'

'And have you heard from him since he's been gone?' I asked, the words escaping before I could bite my tongue.

'No,' Ali laughed, shaking her head, 'he's having too much

fun with his father and the new girlfriend to worry about his poor old mum.'

'Sorry,' I said, rewinding the conversation in my head, 'what did you just say, the "Dixon Dilemma"? I don't understand.'

Suddenly my mind was reeling. What the hell was this whole love–hate thing she was going on about? It was his ex who had pummelled his heart into a thousand pieces. Surely he should have hated her, not me!

'Well, at school he said he loved you, although he never plucked up the courage to tell you.' Her tone suggested she was sick of the whole thing. 'He knew you avoided him so it was obvious you didn't feel the same way and now he's come through the latest crisis and is apparently falling for you again. Although how he's managed to see beyond the whole situation amazes me. I couldn't have moved on, but then . . .'

'Lizzie!' Evelyn suddenly shouted from the back of the room. 'Is this machine supposed to sound like this?'

All the while Ali had been talking, I'd forgotten I was in the Café supposedly tutoring and making bunting. What the hell was the woman talking about? Ben had never loved me. She was clearly deluded, or unbalanced, or both.

'I'm coming, Evelyn,' I called, amazed that my voice sounded so normal because my mind was pinging off in all directions and none of them I could understand. 'I'm coming.'

When I came back to interrogate Ali further, she and her belongings had mysteriously disappeared.

'Where's she gone?' I hissed at Jemma, who stood on sentry next to the now empty space.

'Who?'

'Ben's mother,' I said as calmly as I could manage, 'Ali Fletcher.'

'Oh, she had to go. She wasn't feeling well, was she, Maureen?'

Maureen nodded but didn't look up.

'What do you think of this, Lizzie?' Jay called. 'How do you think this would look in my sister's kitchen?'

Just what exactly was going on? One minute I'm listening to Ali Fletcher telling me that her son had always had feelings for me and now I'm staring at an empty space and there's no trace of the woman anywhere. Perhaps I'd dreamt the whole thing. Perhaps I'd had a psychotic episode and would wake up in a minute and find myself in the shower! I turned to Jay, remembering my duties as sewing session manager.

'Well, that would rather depend on your sister,' I told him bluntly, 'wouldn't it?'

'Now then, young man,' Evelyn teased, 'we don't want you monopolising the teacher all afternoon just because you're the only man here!'

Everyone giggled and I felt myself blush, but Jay didn't turn a hair. I worked my way around the room correcting and congratulating wherever necessary but my mind couldn't have been further from The Cherry Tree Café.

By the time Jemma let Ella back out of the kitchen everyone was almost ready for a turn at the sewing machines.

'You smell different today,' Ella declared, striding up to Jay and openly sniffing at his shirt in some sort of strange juvenile challenge.

'Better different or worse different?' he asked her seriously. He didn't even glance in her direction, just carried on tacking his triangles together.

'Better different,' she said solemnly.

'Good,' he smiled. 'I made a point of showering and toning down the aftershave when I heard you'd be here.'

Ella couldn't work out how to respond but a slight blush rose in her cheeks as she carried on surveying his skill with a needle.

'Why are you sewing?' she asked, clearly frustrated that she couldn't get a rise out of him. 'I thought sewing was for girls.'

'Did you now!' he said sternly. 'I see I need to have a word with your mother.'

'Oh no please don't,' she begged, 'I'm in enough trouble already. I only meant I've never seen a man doing sewing before.'

'Fair enough,' Jay shrugged, reaching for the scissors and giving her a nudge.

The session finally drew to a close and again everyone left with their afternoon's accomplishments carefully stowed away in the bespoke Café bags.

'You did very well,' I smiled, as I let Jay out the door, 'considering you had Ella to contend with as well, I mean.'

'Believe it or not I've had a ball!' he laughed. 'Bye, Ella!' he called over his shoulder, blowing her a kiss. 'See you, Lizzie.'

'Bye,' I grinned. 'I'm glad you had a good time.'

He turned and left and I was grateful he hadn't asked to meet me in the pub to watch Evelyn's grand bunting unveiling.

'Don't worry about all that, Angela,' I called as I closed the door. 'You get off.'

'No, no, I don't mind,' she said, scurrying about amongst the tables picking up scraps and dropped pins. 'I've had a lovely time again,' she confided. 'I'm sending what I've made to my daughter this time. She lives in Australia now, you know.'

'Oh, my goodness, you don't see her often then?'

'No I don't, not any more and she's been so worried about me but when I told her that I'd done this a couple of weeks ago she was over the moon. It isn't easy for her being so far away and she worries even more now it's just me on my own.'

'Have you ever thought of moving out to be with her?' I asked.

From the look on Angela's face you would have thought I'd asked her if she'd considered moving to another galaxy.

'No,' she said firmly, 'I'm not like you young ones, jetting off at the drop of a hat. Take Alison's boy Ben, for instance.'

'I'd rather not,' I muttered without meaning to.

Angela eyed me speculatively and opened her mouth to say something else but was cut off.

'Did I tell you Ruby's leaving?' Jemma announced as she came through from the kitchen and dumped herself down on an empty chair. 'Her parents are worried she isn't spending enough time studying.'

'I bet she loved that!' I said, thinking of Ruby's militant teenage attitude.

'Actually,' Jemma replied, 'she didn't put up much resistance.'

'Why?' I frowned. 'What did you say to her?'

'Nothing much really, just that if she didn't knuckle down and get her grades then she wouldn't be going to college or university. She'd be serving tea with us for the rest of her life.'

'I can think of worse things!' Angela chirped up from behind the sewing machine recess.

I raised my eyebrows at Jemma and inclined my head in Angela's direction.

'Oh really?' said Jemma.

'Oh yes,' Angela smiled, joining us at the table, 'I'd love a little job in a place like this. Just a few hours a week to get me out of the house,' she said dreamily.

'OK then, you're on!' Jemma laughed, holding out her hand for Angela to shake.

Angela began to chuckle and roll about on her seat, as round and shrill as an agitated blue tit.

'Don't be silly!' she chuckled, knocking away Jemma's hand. 'Don't be daft!'

'I'm not being silly,' Jemma told her seriously, 'the job's yours if you want it, Angela.'

'Really?' she asked wide-eyed and suddenly pale. 'Do you mean it?'

'Of course I do! I wouldn't have said it otherwise, would I? What do you think?'

'Oh, go on then,' Angela said, her cheeks flushing crimson, 'I'll take it.'

'In that case, welcome to the team!' I smiled and reaching for a cupcake, plonked it in front of her to seal the deal.

Chapter 17

'Any chance you could stay behind for a minute?' I asked Jemma as she set the washing-machine timer in the utility area. 'Only I think we need to have a little chat, don't you?'

'I'd love to, Lizzie,' she said, picking up her keys and a stack of invoices, 'but I've got to get Ella sorted. You saw how she was this afternoon. She's run poor Maureen off her feet.'

I had no choice but to let her go. Maureen had looked less than thrilled at the prospect of taking her granddaughter home with her and I couldn't blame her.

'All right,' I sighed, 'but we do need to talk, Jemma. This won't keep.'

After she'd gone I dimmed the Café lights and stood for a moment staring at the wonderful cupcake picture Jay had framed so beautifully.

Handsome, creative, good with kids and a cracking sense of humour.

That would be how his lonely hearts ad would read. All the single girls I knew would have snapped him up in a heartbeat and a few of the married ones as well! He was the perfect guy to get over Giles with and if it weren't for this strange twist in the Ben Fletcher saga I probably would have flung myself at him without a second thought. However, there was no denying there was a twist in that particular tale and I was determined to iron it out once and for all.

I could, of course, have ignored my desire to get to the bottom of things and just gone for it with Jay. I mean, his incessant requests for my mobile number, the wonderful picture presentation and his willingness to join the crafting session suggested he was genuinely keen, but if I had made a play for him it would have only been because I was trying to make myself feel better about what had happened with Ben.

His willingness to get to grips with the sewing machine amongst a group full of teasing women was proof enough that he genuinely liked me, so it would have been totally wrong to lead him on in an attempt to bolster my self-confidence which was now reeling from what I interpreted as rejection from two men rather than one.

I grabbed a handful of flyers, flicked off the Café lights and headed out of the door. I didn't really feel like going out but Evelyn's bunting unveiling was too good a PR opportunity to miss and I was sure she and Jim wouldn't mind me drumming up some potential future trade for the Café crafting sessions.

The pub was already packed and it took me a couple of minutes to squeeze my way through the crowd to the bar. It felt like everyone in the town had got wind of the fact that Evelyn had tuned into her feminine side and were all cat-calling to see what she had made.

'You should have come round the back, Lizzie!' Jim shouted over to me.

'I wasn't sure I was allowed to use the tradesman's entrance now I'm not on the staff!' I called back.

'What can I get you, love?'

'Half a bitter please,' I requested, fumbling for some change.

'On the house!' Jim winked then added conspiratorially, 'Evelyn's been talking about joining you on a regular basis down at the Café. Can you imagine the peace?'

'I'm right here, Jim!' Evelyn shouted, giving her husband a playful cuff. 'I'm doing it for my benefit, not yours. There'll be plenty you can get on with while I'm gone!'

'That's what you think!' Jim shouted back.

Listening to their banter made everyone laugh but I couldn't help feeling a little jealous. The sparky duo sparred continuously, their snapping and snarling was part of the pub entertainment but they loved each other dearly. Any fool could see that. Their comfortable and practised companionship wasn't something I could never imagine having in my own life.

'Lizzie! Come and have a seat!'

'Dad,' I smiled, 'I didn't see you. What have you done to deserve a trip to the pub?'

Dad was sitting on his own at the far end of the bar nursing a pint, and judging by his complexion it wasn't his first.

'Your mother's organising some coffee morning thing and apparently I was getting in the way.'

'So she told you to come to the pub?'

'Not exactly,' he grinned. 'She said I should get out from under her feet. She didn't specify a destination so I thought I'd make the most of it!'

'You know you'll be in trouble, don't you?'

'I do,' he said, 'that's why I'm taking the chance and downing a few of these quick. With any luck she'll be so appalled she won't be able to speak.'

I shook my head, not convinced his tactic would work.

'She'll never lose the ability to scold,' I told him, 'you know that!'

'I do,' he said resignedly, 'but I live in hope. What have you got there?' he asked, pointing at the pile of flyers.

I held one up for him to read.

'Cupcakes and Crafting at The Cherry Tree Café,' he said quietly, in an instant his expression had changed to one of paternal pride. 'Evelyn told me she was with you this afternoon. She had a wonderful time. Apparently,' he added, standing to peer over the top of the crowd, 'she's supposed to be showing off what she made tonight.'

Right on cue Jim began to ring the bell he kept above the bar.

'As many of you know,' he bellowed, 'it's been quite a long time since the Mermaid was last decorated!'

'Too bloody long!' someone shouted and everyone cheered.

Jim raised his hands to quieten his audience.

'But what you don't know,' he said, shaking his head in despair, 'is that I had a little wager with the wife.'

'You bloody fool!'

'I know, I know. Anyway, Evelyn's never been much of a one for making things herself. She prefers to go down the shops and spend my hard-earned cash so I thought I was on to a good thing when I told her the pub could have a makeover when she'd mastered a needle and thread.'

He threw a glance in my direction and suddenly the puzzle pieces regarding Evelyn's out of character appearance at a sewing circle fell into place.

'You must be more of a fool than I am, Jim!' someone jeered and the crowd began cheering again.

Everyone welcomed the Mermaid's pirate-themed bunting and enthusiastically toasted Evelyn's ingenuity in ensuring the pub received the makeover she had spent the last half a decade nagging Jim for. My pile of flyers quickly disappeared amidst a flurry of enquiries and I realised that Deborah had been right. Word of mouth, especially in a local watering hole, was the best advertising a new business could get.

'Do you want another?' Dad asked, holding aloft his empty glass.

I was just about to say yes when out of the corner of my eye I spotted Jay sitting in the nook next to the fireplace. He was alone, checking his phone and looking like he could do with a bit of company.

'Thanks, but not right now,' I told Dad. 'Maybe later.'

'Well, don't leave it too long!' he laughed. 'I'm off home in a bit, walking back with Alan from next door. We're taking the path of the condemned men together! Wish us luck!'

I patted him on the back and levered myself away from the bar. Having seen Jay sitting all alone it would have been rude not to thank him for the picture and congratulate him on his sewing prowess.

I had almost reached him when he was joined by a young woman, a very beautiful young woman with shining blonde hair and ridiculously long slender legs. Jay shuffled along the seat and she sat next to him, smiling broadly as he passed her a glass. I took her timely appearance as my cue to call it a day and turned back towards Dad and bumped straight into Tom.

'Aha,' I said. 'Just the man. I didn't know you were here.'

'Jemma and I were in the restaurant,' he said sheepishly. His guilty expression left me in no doubt that I was the last person he wanted to bump into. 'We thought we'd celebrate the end of the week with a meal. Do you want to walk back with us? Jemma's already outside.'

'Yes, great,' I said. 'As you probably already know, I was hoping to have a quick word.'

Unfortunately Jemma was in much the same state as my dad and the walk back to the Café quickly turned into a nightmare. Every few paces she giddily reached for her husband and kissed him drunkenly with much slurring about how she 'couldn't wait to get him home'. Asking them to spill the beans about Ali Fletcher's inexplicable comments was impossible with the pair of them falling over each other, so in the end I said my goodbyes and went home alone. I don't think Jemma even realised I'd gone.

The next morning neither Jemma nor Tom were answering their mobiles or the house phone and I knew I wasn't going to get a straight answer out of either of them before the new week dawned.

'Come and have some lunch with us, Lizzie,' my mother commanded when I stupidly snatched up the phone before checking the caller display.

I was desperate to say no. I'd been planning to cocoon myself away from the world for the day, watch rubbish on TV and eat things out of tins, but Mum's tone had a 'defy me if you dare' edge to it that well, basically, I didn't dare defy.

'Your dad's feeling a bit under the weather,' she carried on, 'and I've got a huge pork joint for us to get through.'

So much for wanting to spend some quality bonding time together; Mum was clearly more concerned that she'd over-ordered at the butcher's. This was all Dad's fault. Had he stayed sober he would have been able to talk her out of ringing me by requesting cold cuts and one of her famous meat pies.

'OK,' I gave in, knowing resistance was futile, 'but I can't stay late. I've fallen a bit behind with this online business course I'm taking and want to catch up.'

'That's fine,' she said airily, 'I know how busy you are these days. You can just eat and run. I won't even ask for any help with the dishes.'

And the guilt sealed the call!

'Go and call your father would you?' Mum asked the second I closed the front door. 'I'm rushing around here like I don't know what whilst he's still lazing in the bath!'

Poor old Dad. I bet he was already regretting his night of drunken self-indulgence, if you could call a few pints with a mate in the pub a night of drunken self-indulgence. My mum clearly could, and that would explain his unusual desire to linger over his ablutions.

I couldn't help wondering at exactly what age Mum had stopped enjoying being married. When exactly was it that she decided married life had become a chore, something to be worked around, the elephant in the room that threatened her precious clubs, meetings and coffee mornings?

'Dad!' I bellowed up the stairs just as she walked through from the kitchen with the gravy boat.

'Elizabeth!' she snapped sharply. 'I asked you to go and call him not cat-call from the bottom of the stairs like some common navvy!'

'Sorry,' I muttered.

'On my way!' Dad shouted back down somewhat feebly, but given the circumstances that was hardly surprising.

By the time he joined us at the table Mum had finished carving and was hurriedly piling roast potatoes on to my plate and offering me the bowl of apple sauce. I bit my tongue knowing that she had purposefully rushed just to make Dad feel bad about the food getting cold. As much as I resented her childish behaviour, I was determined not to say anything and give her further ammunition to use against him and his one night of heady freedom.

I took a hasty sideward glance to see how he was holding up but didn't like the look of him at all.

'You needn't look like that,' Mum swooped in, having spotted my crafty glance, 'it's all his own doing. I hope the state he's got himself in shows you just what a waste of time and money these trips to that damn pub are?'

'Are you OK, Dad?' I asked, laying down my cutlery.

'Of course he's not all right! Look at the state of him! He's been complaining of a headache. Hardly any wonder, is it? Out until all hours drinking and with a neighbour as well!'

'Shut up, Mum!' I snapped.

'I beg your pardon?'

'What is it, Dad?' I asked again, the little remaining colour visibly draining from his face as I watched. 'Do you feel sick?'

'I can't feel my arm,' he whispered, 'everything's spinning.'

'Well, it will be!' Mum laughed knowingly. 'What do you expect? You can't even speak properly! Listen to you slurring your words, your system's still saturated!'

'Mum,' I said, rushing to Dad's side, 'go and phone an ambulance.'

'What?'

'Go and phone an ambulance. I think Dad's having a stroke.'

'You go in the ambulance and I'll follow on in the car,' I told Mum as I locked the front door and steered her down the path.

'No,' she said shakily, 'I'll drive in with you.'

'Are you sure?' I asked quickly, mindful that every second was vital.

'Yes,' she said, 'yes, I'll come in with you.'

'Is that OK,' I asked the paramedic, 'if mum stays with me?'

The paramedic nodded.

'Probably best,' he said, 'she looks like she's had a quite a shock. Don't worry, my love; we'll get him there in no time.'

His last words were clearly directed at Mum, but she appeared not to have heard. He gave me a sympathetic smile and swung the ambulance door shut.

'Come on, then,' I said, holding open the passenger door of my car, 'get in.'

Within seconds we'd lost sight of the ambulance which seemed to cut through the traffic like a hot knife through butter.

'I thought it was just a hangover,' Mum said for the hundredth time, 'I thought he'd be all right by this afternoon.'

I focused my attention on the road ahead and the throng of Sunday drivers heading out of town to the retail park.

'He'll be fine,' I told her, braking sharply as the traffic lights changed just as I reached them.

'But what if you hadn't come round for dinner?' she said, an edge of desperation creeping into her voice. 'What if you'd been too busy and said no?'

She reached up her sleeve and pulled out her handkerchief.

'He could have collapsed in front of me and I would have still been blaming his bingeing session!'

I didn't know what to say. Part of me wanted to say that yes, Dad would probably have fallen at her feet and she would have moaned about him cluttering up the floor space but I could see she was in shock. He had finally achieved the impossible and made her question her attitude.

The hospital car park was heaving with visitors and it took seemingly endless trips round to find a parking space.

'Why don't you hop out and I'll catch you up as soon as I've parked,' I encouraged.

Mum sat tight and vehemently shook her head.

'Look, the A and E department is right there,' I said, pointing. 'That's where they'll take him first, I'm sure of it.'

Still she refused to budge.

'I'm scared, Elizabeth,' she said quietly, 'I don't want to go in there on my own.'

Frustrating as it was, I did understand her reluctance to move. Dad's own father had died in this hospital after a massive stroke that no one had seen coming and I knew that she was terrified that Dad was facing the same fate. I was terrified too, but knew I wouldn't be any use to anyone if I gave in to my fears.

Eventually we squeezed into a space and I reached into my bag for my mobile.

'Are you going to phone Jemma?' Mum asked. 'Let her know what's happened?'

'No,' I said, 'I'm just turning my phone off before we go in. There's no point phoning anyone until we know exactly what we're dealing with. Come on,' I said firmly, 'let's go and find him.'

Mum shook as we entered the hospital and I took off my jacket and wrapped it around her shoulders in a moment of strange role reversal. She was deathly pale and clearly terrified. Obviously, for now at least, I was the one in charge.

'We're looking for Mr Dixon,' I told the nurse behind the reception desk. 'He came in in an ambulance a little while ago. I'm his daughter, Lizzie Dixon.'

'If you take a seat, Miss Dixon, I'll see what I can find out.'

'Thank you,' I smiled, desperate not to be a nuisance in this place filled with Sunday sports players and their oddly angled limbs and pained expressions. 'Come on, Mum.'

Two plastic cups of grey tea later and we were still waiting. Some of the colour had come back in Mum's face and she had laid my jacket over the back of her chair.

'I don't know if this waiting is a good or bad thing,' she said yet again.

I nodded but didn't comment. My thoughts had drifted back to the house and the dining table set for Sunday dinner. Ordinarily she would have been fretting over the wasted food and dirty dishes but she hadn't uttered a word even if she had thought about it. I was beginning to feel as concerned for Mum's welfare as Dad's.

Any stranger privy to my thoughts would have doubtless been puzzled; a woman showing concern for her husband's health was only to be expected. A certain level of fear and trepidation was only natural, wasn't it? Well, yes, but this was my mother I was dealing with and at times there appeared to be very little of anything 'natural' about her at all.

'Mrs and Miss Dixon?'

'Yes!' Mum and I chorused together, jumping up.

'The consultant will see you now.'

I gave Mum's arm a reassuring squeeze and we followed the nurse through the labyrinth of corridors to a sparse but spotless room.

'Good afternoon, my name is Mr Hanif. Please, take a seat.'

I sat in the chair next to Mum, a lump the size of a golf ball forming in my throat as she took my hand and held it tight in her own.

'Your husband is currently having a scan, Mrs Dixon, then he will be taken up to the Bluebell ward.'

I heard Mum let out a long slow breath. The relief in the room was palpable and I knew then that like me, until that very moment, Mum hadn't been sure that Dad had survived the journey.

'He has suffered a transient ischemic attack,' Mr Hanif explained, 'or more simply put, a mild stroke.'

Mum squeezed my hand again and gave me what could only be described as a grateful look. Noticing the gesture, Mr Hanif added, 'Your daughter did the right thing, Mrs Dixon. She called the ambulance straightaway. In situations like this, timing is crucial.'

'Yes well,' said Mum, clearing her throat, 'she's a very clever girl.'

Chapter 18

It was horrid seeing Dad lying in a hospital bed. He looked tired and pale and disconcertingly old as Mum stroked his head and planted a tender kiss on his lips. For a second I had to look away. My parents had never been demonstrably affectionate and this intimate exchange was more shocking than Mum's earlier acknowledgement that I had done the right thing by calling the ambulance.

'How are you feeling?' I asked.

'Not too bad,' Dad croaked, 'tired, but otherwise not too bad. I've still got a bit of a headache but everything seems to be working OK. On balance I think I've got off rather lightly.'

He closed his eyes and Mum moved to the chair at the side of the bed.

'Why don't you go and ask where we can get another chair, Lizzie?' she whispered.

'I'll just go and phone Jemma first,' I told her, 'let her know what's happened. You can guarantee the grapevine will have gone into overdrive when the ambulance turned up.'

'Pound to a penny they'll be having a whipround in the pub this afternoon for my funeral flowers!' Dad chirped up without opening his eyes. 'Better go and put them out of their misery, Lizzie. Tell them to raise the flag again.'

Mum tutted loudly but didn't comment.

'I'll be back in a minute,' I said.

The air outside hit me full in the face and felt a good ten degrees cooler than inside. I shivered as I waited for my phone to wake up then smiled knowingly as half a dozen missed calls and messages pinged into my inbox.

'Lizzie!' Jemma must have had the phone in her hand. 'What on earth's happened?'

'Dad's had a mild stroke,' I explained, the seriousness of the situation hitting home as I said the words aloud. 'Mum asked me round for lunch and I knew he wasn't right as soon as I saw him.'

'Is he OK now?' she demanded. 'Is he going to be OK?'

'I think so,' I said shakily, suddenly aware that I didn't really know. 'We haven't been told much yet other than that it was very mild. He's talking and everything,' I added to try to reassure myself as much as her. 'Before I left he was even joking about funeral flowers.'

'Sounds about right. Do you want me to come to the hospital?'

'No, we'll be fine, but thanks. I drove Mum here so there'll be no problem getting home. I'll ring you again later.'

I stopped and cleared my throat, close to tears.

'Well, we're here if you need us, OK? If there's anything that any of you need then just ring.'

'OK,' I croaked, 'thanks.'

'Oh, and Lizzie?'

'Yes?'

'I know this is really horrible timing but Ben phoned earlier. He asked if you could call him.'

'Ben called you or you called him?' I asked, guessing that she had gone ahead and warned him about what had happened with his mother.

'Tom called him actually,' she admitted guiltily.

'Why did he do that?' I demanded. 'He had no right, and why are you telling me this now? I really don't need to be even thinking about any of this at the moment.'

'I know and I'm sorry, Lizzie. We just thought the pair of you should clear the air as soon as possible, but you're right, I shouldn't have mentioned it, especially now.'

Back on the ward the curtains were drawn around Dad's bed. I lingered awkwardly, not knowing whether to go back in or not. There was nothing to knock on so I just stood, shuffling from one foot to another; a new spectacle for the rest of the patients to stare at and mulled over whether I could face talking to Ben on top of everything else.

'Right,' I heard a woman's voice ring out, 'I'll leave you for a bit, Mr Dixon. Don't keep nattering on, will you? You need your rest.'

The curtains twitched back along the rails and a nurse stepped out with test tubes of blood rattling around on a tray.

'Is everything all right?' I asked. 'He's my dad.'

'Everything's fine,' the nurse smiled. 'You can go back in, but not for too long. I've given your mum a list of a few things you might want to bring in for him.'

'OK,' I said. 'Thanks.'

If possible Dad looked even paler now and the red rings around Mum's eyes were a complete giveaway.

'Jemma sends her love,' I told them. 'She said to let her know if we need her to do anything.'

'That's very kind of her,' Mum said graciously, 'given how busy she is with the Café and everything.'

Ordinarily this would have been the moment she would launch into a bitter rant about my best friend's inability to control her daughter and how the situation would only get worse now she was a working mum, but she simply smiled.

'She's always been kind-hearted,' she said. 'Take the flat, for instance. She could have offered that to anyone, couldn't she? I dare say she and Tom could have charged a much higher rent given the location and everything.'

'I am paying my way,' I said, feeling slightly nettled that she might think I was freeloading. 'I do pay rent.'

'Don't misunderstand me,' Mum said mildly, 'I just meant that it was kind of her to think of you and your situation.'

I felt suitably chastened and realised this subdued vision masquerading as my mum was going to take some getting used to. I looked over at Dad and by the way he raised his eyebrows I could tell he was equally as shocked. Part of me couldn't help hoping the change would be permanent, but I knew deep down that she would be back to her old self as soon as his health improved.

'Right,' she announced, standing up and passing me my jacket, 'I think we'll pop back to the house and get you these things now.' She waved the list the nurse had given her. 'I can't bear the sight of you in that gown even if it is only for a day or so.'

'What, this old thing?' Dad wheezed, plucking at the blue fabric with his healthy arm. 'I just threw this on!'

Mum shook her head.

'We'll be back in a bit,' she said and kissed him again.

The first thing we saw when we opened the house door was the flashing light on the answerphone.

'I know exactly who that'll be,' Mum said coldly. 'Why don't you put the kettle on, Lizzie? I don't know about you but I could do with a cup of tea and there's some cake left in the tin.'

'What shall I do with the dinner?' I whispered, pointing at the dining room.

'Just bin it all.'

'Even the meat?'

'All of it,' Mum nodded. 'I haven't got time to worry about leftovers. Oh hello, Jennifer . . .'

I left her to her call and scraped the congealed plates and tureens full of food into the bin. I was so hungry that even the roast potatoes looked appetising despite their soggy state.

'Well, that hardly matters now, does it!' I could hear Mum shouting as I dumped the bin bag in the wheelie bin next to the garage which was quite a distance from the house.

'I don't care what you tell her! I've explained the situation to you; if you can't understand then that's your problem!'

I ventured back inside and began to wolf down the cake.

'Of course I can't! I'm going to be at the hospital! Who exactly do you think you are, questioning my priorities like that?'

I don't think I'd ever heard Mum so angry. Not even when Dad attempted to make champagne and the bottles exploded in the cupboard under the stairs.

'I don't care whether it's a mild stroke or a major one! He's my husband and his health comes first. Well, if that's how you feel, I'll resign!'

I was all ears as I poured the tea. Mum was obviously on the phone to Jennifer Summers, bitchy Erica's mother and leader of every group and committee Mum held dear.

'Yes, Jennifer!' she concluded triumphantly. 'That is my

final bloody word! You can stick your sodding coffee morning up your arse!'

She banged down the phone, took one look at my expression and burst out laughing.

On the journey back, Mum sat methodically ticking items off the hospital list.

'I know they're only expecting to keep him in for a couple of days,' she said fussily, 'but I want him to have everything he needs.'

'Is this what happened to Granddad?' I asked, finally daring to voice the question that had been on my mind ever since I realised what was happening to Dad.

'Oh no,' Mum said, 'there was no warning like your dad's had. One massive stroke and it was all over.'

I didn't know if that made me feel better or worse. Dad had been a very young man when his father died, much younger than me.

'You and Dad had just got engaged when it happened, hadn't you?'

'Yes,' Mum nodded, 'we had. We hadn't even set a date for the wedding.'

I guessed that was probably when Mum's dislike of her soon-to-be mother-in-law set in. Dad was so protective, always visiting and sorting Gran's problems before ours. That couldn't have been easy, suddenly having to share your other half. I adored my gran and was eternally grateful for all the things she had taught me, but seeing her relationship with Dad from Mum's perspective gave me a fresh understanding of where her resentment might have sprung from.

'Of course things are very different now,' Mum carried on, 'there are lots of new things they can do. I've always dreaded that this would happen, but we'll manage.'

'I'm sure you will,' I smiled. 'He's in the best possible hands.'

'I was wondering if it would be all right if I slept at the flat tonight?' she asked hesitantly.

'What?' I frowned, almost swerving off the road. 'My flat?'

'Only if it's convenient; I don't really fancy being in the house on my own.'

'Of course,' I replied, taking a quick mental tour of the rooms. 'No problem.'

'I'm not going to worry about whether you've tidied, Lizzie,' Mum smiled, guessing my thoughts. 'It's your home; I'm not going to judge it or you. I could just do with the company.'

'Mum's staying at mine tonight,' I whispered in Dad's ear as soon as Mum was out of range, 'she says she wants the company.'

'Good god!' Dad choked. 'I should have done this a decade ago!'

I bit my lip and tried not to smile. It was good to hear him cracking jokes, even inappropriate ones.

'I hope you aren't drying your pants on the radiators, old girl, you know how she hates that! She'll have your guts for garters!'

'No she won't!' Mum said as she appeared seemingly from thin air; 'I've already told Lizzie that I'm looking forward to seeing the flat. Her housewifery skills, competent or otherwise, are not my concern. I imparted what knowledge I could, what she has chosen to do with it is up to her.'

She began fussily straightening the blankets and let Dad kiss her hand as I watched on agog.

'Sorry if I gave you both a fright,' Dad said, 'I feel fine now. It's silly they won't let me home really.'

'No it is not,' Mum and I chorused together.

'You're not going anywhere until all those tests come back,' Mum said sternly. 'And I'll be back first thing tomorrow to make sure of that.'

'But what about your coffee morning?' Dad said seriously. 'You've been planning this one for weeks.'

'Don't you worry about that,' she said, throwing me a warning glance, 'I've rescheduled it.'

'I bet old Summers loved that!' Dad snorted.

Mum chewed her lip but didn't say anything. Her idol really had fallen out of favour! Ordinarily we weren't allowed as much as a sneer in her direction.

'Now,' she said, 'we'll be back first thing to find out what they're going to do with you.'

'I'll go and sort the parking,' I said shakily, not wanting to say a proper goodbye, 'see you tomorrow, Dad.'

'See you tomorrow, old girl,' Dad winked, 'and remember to get those pants off the radiator!'

Chapter 19

With Mum staying in the flat there was no chance to phone Ben, which turned out to be a blessing. Left to my own devices, in my eagerness to find out just what the hell was going on I would doubtless have called him straightaway and run the risk of appearing too eager. Which of course I was, but I didn't want him knowing that.

I might have been secretly thrilled that my high-school crush had reciprocal feelings, but his mother had also said he had gone through phases of hating me and I had absolutely no idea why. I was, however, perfectly clear in my mind that when I did get a moment's peace in which to call him, the conversation was going to be messy, probably loud and potentially emotionally destructive and it was therefore best conducted in private.

When I surfaced the next morning, the sight of Mum sitting at the kitchen table wearing my fleecy dressing gown and sharing a plate of toast with Ella was a clear enough indication that this was not going to be an ordinary week.

'Where's Jemma?' I asked, pouring myself a cup of tea and buttering a slice of toast.

'Mummy's checking an order,' Ella explained, 'I was helping her but Nanny Pam said she needed me up here.'

'Did she now?' I smiled at Mum wondering where 'Nanny Pam' had sprung from.

'Yes,' Ella carried on in her most matter-of-fact voice, 'she needed help to find the breakfast things because she hadn't actually been in your kitchen before.'

'Oh, I see and you found everything for her, Ella, did you?'

Ella nodded and gave a toothy grin as she crammed in the crumbly remains of her slice of very jammy toast.

'Mouth closed, darling,' Mum said automatically and Ella obeyed, just like that. I was stunned.

'How did you sleep, Mum?' I asked.

'Surprisingly well,' she smiled, 'I haven't slept in a single bed since I got married. I thought it would feel a bit cramped but I just went out like a light.'

'Well, it was a tiring day,' I yawned.

'I've had a good look round the flat while you had your lie in.'

'Oh,' I said.

It was only seven fifteen.

'And I have to say you've done a lovely job. It isn't at all how I'd imagined it.'

'How did you think it would look then?'

Mum shrugged and swirled the teapot before pouring herself another cup.

'More modern,' she said decidedly, 'much more modern. This feels like your grandmother's house and not just because you've got some of her things. It's comfortable and cosy, Lizzie. Really lovely. I like it a lot.'

'I helped with some of the painting,' Ella chipped in.

'Yes, well we won't go into that!' Jemma laughed, appearing in the doorway looking flustered. 'Thanks for taking Ella, Mrs Dixon. I knew that driver hadn't offloaded everything.'

'Please call me Pamela,' Mum insisted. 'What did he forget, dear?'

'Half a dozen of the big bags of flour and it isn't the first time,' Jemma complained. 'I reckon he leaves something off every other order then sells it on! But I've called his bluff this time. I know where he's delivering next and Tom's gone to have it out with him.'

'Good for you!' Mum told her. 'These things have to be nipped in the bud!'

'Nip!' squealed Ella ecstatically and squirted honey all over my best tablecloth.

*

By the time we'd welcomed Angela to her first shift working in the Café and dropped Ella off at Maureen's to walk up to school, it was rush hour and slow going towards the hospital.

Dad was sitting up in bed when we finally arrived, neat and clean, and looking every inch the man he'd always been. He'd even got some of his colour back. Mum and I exchanged a fleeting glance, both of us clearly relieved to find him so apparently recovered.

'Well?' he smiled. 'What did you think?'

'To what?' Mum frowned as she peered into the locker next to the bed to check all was shipshape.

'To the flat, of course! Was it the student slum I predicted?'

'Absolutely not,' Mum said, wagging an accusing finger, then added with a sigh, 'actually, your mother's things all fit a treat.'

'Well I'll be—' Dad began but was cut off by the appearance of Mr Hanif at the end of the ward.

We watched and sat quietly as he wound his way around his patients, until he finally came and stood at the foot of Dad's bed.

'In a high proportion of cases, Mr Dixon, a mini stroke, like the one you had yesterday, turns out to be a warning of what's to come.'

'I was afraid of that,' stammered Mum, reaching for her handkerchief.

Mr Hanif looked at her and shook his head.

'I can assure you, Mrs Dixon, that quite often these first forerunners are missed, however, in your husband's case, your daughter's vigilance has been a huge help. Now we know what may be lurking on the horizon, we can do our utmost to prevent it happening or limit the trauma if it does.'

Mum took a deep breath and nodded bravely.

'So,' she said, 'what have we got to do with him?'

'Naturally I will prescribe some medication but there are other things that, after my earlier conversation with Mr Dixon this morning, will I feel go a long way to helping prevent another more potentially serious stroke.'

'Such as?' Mum asked, leaning forward in her seat.

I glanced at Dad. He was looking increasingly tense.

'Wait for it,' he mouthed silently.

'Certain simple diet and lifestyle changes can all have a huge impact on reducing the risk of strokes,' Mr Hanif carried on, 'I suggest you and your husband have a think about the food you eat, as well as the amount of exercise you take.'

I braced myself for the blow, fully expecting Mum to launch off at the suggestion that her decades of rich, hearty cooking might have played some part in putting Dad in a hospital bed, but she said nothing.

'I take it neither of you smoke or drink?' Mr Hanif asked, his eyebrows raised in Dad's direction.

'I like a sherry before lunch on a Sunday,' Mum confessed,

'but I've never been a smoker and he gave up years ago. Didn't you, love?'

Dad didn't say anything.

'Well,' said Mr Hanif moving away from the bed. 'I'll leave you these leaflets and providing you behave yourself today, we'll discharge you tomorrow, Mr Dixon. How does that sound?'

'Perfect,' Dad smiled. 'Thank you, Mr Hanif.'

'What was all that about?' I hissed, as Mum went to borrow another chair from the patient in the next bed.

'I never gave up,' Dad hissed back, 'what did you think I was doing in the garden all the live-long day? It isn't exactly Monty Don standard, is it?'

'There, Lizzie,' Mum said, pointing at the chair, 'you sit there.'

I sat as instructed and began flicking through the leaflets trying to pretend I wasn't going to listen to what was said next.

'Well I hope you've learnt your lesson, Tony Dixon,' Mum said sternly.

'What do you mean?'

'I'll gladly take some of the blame but I'm not shouldering your damaged lungs on top of all the cream and butter we get through!'

'What do you mean by that?'

'All the cigarettes you smoke when you're supposedly

gardening. I didn't say anything in front of Mr Hanif because I didn't know if you'd told him the truth, but it ends now. No more cigarettes.'

Dad looked like a child who had been caught with his fingers in the penny sweets.

'How did you know?' he gaped indignantly. 'I've always made sure my clothes have had a good airing before I come back in and I use a mouth wash!'

'Exactly!' Mum said, her lips a thin set line. 'Who pops out to do a bit of weeding and comes back in minty fresh?'

We all looked at each other and laughed, but it wasn't funny. It was time they started taking a bit more care of themselves. It was a shock to acknowledge it, but they weren't getting any younger.

'Perhaps I'll take up golf or walking,' Dad said wistfully.

'No,' said Mum, 'perhaps *we'll* take up golf or walking or both.'

'But how are you going to fit all that in with your coffee mornings and committee meetings?'

'I'm giving all that up,' Mum said determinedly, 'it's high time I spent a few more hours with my husband.'

'Well, I'll be . . .' Dad said again.

'Do you know what you're going to say?' Jemma asked, as we set up the laptop in the flat kitchen. 'Have you gone through it all in your head?'

'A hundred times,' I admitted, 'at least.'

'I'm sorry it's come to this,' she said sadly, 'I really am. Tom's asked him to come back, but he says he just can't do it. I can't believe he's agreed to do this, to be honest.'

'Neither can I,' I said, squinting at the monitor. 'If it wasn't for Dad being ill, I would have jumped on a plane and gone over there myself, but I guess this is the next best thing.'

'Well, it's a start,' she smiled, giving me a squeeze. 'Good luck. I'm pleased we're OK again, Lizzie. We are, aren't we?'

'Of course we are,' I said, hugging her back, 'I do understand why you and Tom don't want to tell me anything. This is Ben's business and it's up to him to take care of it.'

'Promise you'll call later and let me know what he said?'

'I promise.'

Because jetting off to sunny Spain wasn't an option, I'd asked Tom to arrange a Skype session with Ben. At least that way I could see the whites of his eyes when I demanded to be told what the hell his mother had been prattling on about but now, as I counted the seconds down I couldn't help feeling a little vulnerable myself. There was nowhere to hide with the screen right in front of me but it was too late to back out.

'Hi!'

'Hello.' I swallowed.

The picture wasn't great but it was unmistakably him. Tanned and no longer sporting a beard, he looked disconcertingly like the boy I had fallen in love with at school.

'Sorry to hear about your dad.'.

'Thanks,' I croaked, my voice thick in my throat.

'Tom told me,' he added.

I nodded at the screen, my actions slightly out of sync with my words.

'What happened to the beard?'

'Oh it had to go,' he smiled, 'too hot out here, you know?'

I nodded.

'Did Tom tell you why I wanted to talk?'

'Yes, and I had an email from my mother. She said she had a feeling she might have put her foot in it a bit.'

Understatement of the century!

'What an interesting character she is,' I said diplomatically.

Ben grinned sheepishly.

'Oh yes, she's a real keeper.'

'She speaks very highly of your father and the new love in his life.'

'Yeah, I bet she does,' Ben laughed.

It was harder than I thought, trying to find the words and ask the right questions. It would have been far easier by text, away from those delicious dark eyes.

'So . . .'

'So,' I responded, trying to find the courage, 'she said . . .' I faltered.

How could I ask him to explain without making it sound like a playground drama?

'She said you had feelings for me when we were at school,' I said simply.

Ben nodded.

'I did,' he said with a sigh. 'You were my high-school crush, Lizzie.'

I couldn't believe it. Straight from the horse's mouth: the very words that I'd used to describe him to myself only weeks before. My heart was beating a tattoo in my chest as I thought how fantastic school could have been if only we'd been brave enough to seek each other out.

'But it's OK,' he carried on when I didn't say anything, 'I know you didn't like me. You always made a point of staying out of the way when I was around so I got the message, but it didn't alter the fact that I liked you.'

'Why didn't you ever say anything?' I asked.

'Because you made it so obvious, like I just said, you always stayed out of the way. Even after we left school you seemed to do everything you could to avoid me, didn't you?'

'Yes,' I nodded, 'I suppose I did.'

It wasn't a lie. I did avoid him, but I couldn't face putting my feelings on the line and telling him why, although it probably would have been different if his mother hadn't mentioned that he also hated me!

'I liked you right up until Giles swept you off your feet actually,' Ben bravely admitted.

Despite the tan and blurry picture I could still make out a

slight rosy tinge lighting up his cheeks. Why couldn't I be as brave as him? Maybe it was the Giles effect? Maybe the toad really had tainted me for life and left me incapable of being honest about my feelings for fear of ridicule and reprisal.

'I guess it's just water under the bridge now,' Ben shrugged.

'Not quite,' I said, trying to see beyond my own regret, 'the sliding scale, the "Dixon Dilemma" as your mother called it, it has a more sinister side to it, doesn't it? She said it had slipped from love to hate fairly recently.'

Ben swallowed, but didn't say anything.

'So what was that about?' I demanded, beginning to lose patience.

'I'm not sure we should talk about that like this,' he said, indicating the screen. 'It doesn't feel right, it's not fair.'

'Oh none of this is fair, Ben!' I scowled. 'Believe me!'

'I know. I'm sorry,' he ran his hands through his hair, sat up straighter and took a deep breath. 'OK . . .' he began.

He opened his mouth to answer, but whatever he was trying to say was drowned out by music blasting through the computer speakers and filling the room. A girl in a sarong and little else appeared in the shot. She draped her arms around Ben's neck and kissed him on the cheek.

'Hola!' she beamed at the screen then began to try to pull Ben to his feet. 'Come and dance!' she shouted, gyrating her tanned hips in his direction. 'Ben, come on! Come and dance!'

'You better go,' I said, 'looks like quite a party.'

'No it isn't,' Ben shouted, 'it isn't a party.'

'See you, Ben.'

I flicked the monitor switch and he was gone. Well, that was it. It didn't really matter why Ben hated me, after seeing that, I could live without knowing. Obviously he'd moved on with his life and it was high time I did the same. Yes, we'd had feelings for each other in the past but as Ben said, it was all water under the bridge.

We weren't like Jemma and Tom. We'd missed our chance and now it was time for me to stop believing in fate and the romance of one true love and focus on my future. I had a fledging business to nurture and if a relationship of some kind did magically materialise, then it would have to be prepared to take second place to my first true love.

Chapter 20

It wasn't easy getting used to the idea that Dad had a potentially life threatening medical malfunction looming on the horizon. Every time the phone rang, I sprang to answer it and if more than a couple of hours passed I was calling the house to make sure everything was OK.

'What you need is a distraction,' suggested Angela, 'and I don't just mean from worrying about your dad,' she added knowingly.

Angela had fitted in to the Café routine seamlessly. She was even allowed to help Jemma in the kitchen and for my control freak of a friend that was a major step forward.

'Like what?' I asked, passing her a tray of dishes over the counter and ignoring the implication that she knew I was still stewing over the unsatisfactory Skype fiasco.

'I think it's high time you offered another sewing session,' she said. 'I know you've been worried about your dad amongst other things, but life has to go on, Lizzie. You only have to look at what your parents have been up to see that!'

'She's right,' Jemma chipped in. 'Since the cigarette-burning ritual they haven't looked back. You're the one constantly hanging on the end of the phone! What you need is to launch this business properly. Draw up a schedule of what you want to run and when and we'll take it from there.'

They were both right, of course. My own life had been running a little off the tracks since Dad's stroke and Ben's departure from my life. I'd given Jemma a blow by blow account of what had happened with Ben but had made her swear not to talk about it to anyone or mention his name when I was around. I knew it was tough on her because she knew all the answers and I didn't, but I was doing a grand job of convincing myself that I didn't care and that I had far bigger fish to fry.

People were still asking when I was going to get started properly and I knew I couldn't expect them to show interest indefinitely, especially if I didn't have even a sketchy suggestion to offer them, but suddenly it felt like such a huge step. What I needed was another Deborah top-up, I realised; another little coaching session to get me back on the right path.

'You know you are right,' I told the two eager faces peering at me over the counter. 'I don't want to end up a "what if", do I? I think I'll ask Deborah to travel up and have a look at the set-up. How does that sound?'

'Perfect!' Angela beamed.

'Whatever it takes,' Jemma agreed.

Deborah was ecstatic when I phoned and told her how things had gone with the second session and subsequent flyer distribution in the pub.

'I'm sorry about your father, Lizzie, I really am, but you mustn't let life's little hiccups throw you off course. If you really want to make a go of this you have to do your absolute utmost to get it going, put in the hard work and the hours and most importantly, don't give up when you hit a hurdle or two!'

I knew what she was saying made perfect sense, but Dad's stroke had felt like more than just a hurdle to me.

'I know you probably think I'm a hard-faced old boot,' Deborah carried on, obviously having heard my sigh, 'but I want you to succeed, Lizzie. I really think you've got what it takes.'

'So you'll come?' I asked hopefully. 'I can make arrangements for you to stay and I'll pay your train fare.'

'You'll do no such thing!' Deborah boomed but then her tone softened, 'Heather's been a bit under the weather recently, the poor love. A little break will do us both good. I've someone here who's more than capable of running the show for a few days. We'll take a bit of a tour and see you mid-week. How does that sound?'

'Perfect!' I smiled. 'And thank you so much. I can't wait to show you everything I've done!'

The morning Deborah and Heather were due to arrive I was more nervous than before the first bunting session, and this wasn't something that went unnoticed by Jay who happened to pop in for a quick bite as he was passing through town. I hadn't clapped eyes on him since the night in the pub but in quieter moments, when I was cursing men and their associated complications, the thought of him and the leggy blonde had loitered uncomfortably in the recesses of my mind.

'I'm sorry to hear about what happened to your dad, Lizzie,' he said kindly, whilst staring pointedly at my shaking hands as I fussed and fiddled, making final adjustments to the crafting area.

An instant wave of guilt crashed over me. For the last hour or so Dad and his problems hadn't been at the forefront of my mind at all. My sudden attack of nerves was solely down to Deborah's imminent visit and subsequent judgement on my efforts to impress her.

'I didn't know what had happened until last night,' Jay continued when I failed to answer, 'I've been working away and only found out when I popped into the Mermaid for a quick drink.'

'He's much better now,' I said, throwing what I hoped was an appreciative smile in his direction, 'thanks for asking.'

Thankfully Dad really was much better. Since he had been discharged from the hospital, Mum had put him and herself on a strict new diet and fitness regime. The exercise had gently increased as the dairy and other fats diminished and half the time they looked like a pair of love-struck teenagers. It was beginning to look like Dad's stroke had re-ignited their flagging marital spark and I was overjoyed for them on all fronts.

'Don't mind the state of her, Jay,' Jemma teased as she set out the cutlery and cruets, 'it's a big day. Come back tomorrow, normal service will have been resumed by then.'

'Oh?' Jay questioned. 'What's going on? I can't leave you girls alone for five minutes, can I?'

I shot Jemma a fearsome glance. She knew I didn't want to make a big fuss about Deborah's visit.

'Lizzie's friend from London is paying an official visit,' she carried on regardless. 'She's a real crafting-café aficionado, isn't she, Lizzie?'

I opened my mouth to answer, but again she didn't give me the chance.

'If she gives Lizzie the thumbs-up then it'll be all systems go!'

'What I don't get is why you're still hanging back, Lizzie,' Jay frowned. 'The Café is spot on and you only have to look at the picture up there to see that you have the skills! Everything is perfect, even you.'

How could I explain that my confidence levels just needed a bit of a boost without sounding all feeble and needy? It had been a while since the last session and although everything was, as Jay so enthusiastically pointed out, looking perfect, I still doubted my ability and wanted Deborah to see me in situ before I took the plunge and officially launched the business.

The fact that Jay had just called *me* perfect sent all my collated thoughts scattering and I was left red-faced, shuffling my feet and feeling confused. What exactly had he meant by that? Was he suggesting that I was the perfect image of womanhood and loveliness or did he mean that I had the perfect personality and business skills to make the venture succeed?

'Don't waste your breath!' Jemma shouted, coming to my rescue. 'We keep telling her all that but she won't believe us. She's got the perfect set-up here but she's still holding back.'

'That isn't quite what I meant,' Jay mumbled, suddenly more interested in looking around the Café than at either of us.

'What did you mean then?' Jemma asked mischievously, raising her eyebrows in expectation of a quick and concise answer.

'Never mind,' he stammered, 'it doesn't matter. I'll pop back later to see how you've got on.'

I watched him rush through the door, then turned back around and carried on fussing as if nothing had happened.

'Why didn't you say anything?' Jemma scowled. 'You can't keep this ridiculous man ban in place forever you know!'

'I don't see why not,' I shot back, annoyingly thinking of Ben, 'besides I don't trust him. He was with a tall blonde girl the other night in the pub. Why is he trying to make a play for me if he's already got someone else? You of all people should know I wouldn't fall for that one; once bitten and all that.'

Jemma rolled her eyes and flicked me lightly with the tea towel that she seemed to have permanently attached to her person these days.

'That's his sister, you idiot!' she laughed. 'The one he was making the bunting for!'

Chapter 21

'Lizzie darling, it all looks absolutely charming!' Deborah boomed, as she burst through the Café door.

'You've only seen the outside!' I laughed, then stopped as I caught sight of Heather teetering rather than trotting along behind in Deborah's enthusiastic wake.

Seeing my change of expression, Deborah quickly turned around and ushered her friend inside.

'Hello, Lizzie,' Heather said, 'this all looks fabulous, so pretty with the trees outside and the little picket fence.'

I nodded and stared then realised what I was doing and fumbled for something to say that would cover my shock.

'Hello, Heather, Deborah tells me you haven't been well lately.'

Oh, well done. Zero out of ten for discretion, Lizzie. Heather however, always so accommodating, smiled weakly.

'No,' she said, 'I haven't been well, but I'm feeling better for getting out of London and seeing a bit of countryside.'

'Would you like to go up to the flat?' I offered. 'Have a bit of a rest from your travels while I show Deborah around?'

'Top idea!' Deborah agreed. 'Lead the way, Lizzie, then we'll get down to business. Come on, old girl,' she smiled, tenderly taking Heather's hand, 'up the wooden hill to Bedfordshire.'

With Heather settled in the spare room Deborah and I went down to the Café and shared the cake and biscuits Jemma had thoughtfully laid out in the crafting area.

'Are you all right?' I tentatively asked, not at all sure how to react to Deborah's thoughtful expression and unusual lack of words.

She let out a long slow breath.

'Not really,' she admitted with a shake of her head. 'It's been hell, Lizzie, sheer hell, but we'll talk about all that later. Give me a few minutes to have a look around this beautiful Café and then we'll talk business.'

I left Deborah to have a proper look at everything and took the tray back to Jemma in the kitchen.

'How's it going?' she whispered. 'What does she think?'

'I don't know yet,' I explained, 'Heather's been unwell and by the looks of it, it's knocked the wind out of both their sails.'

'Look out!' Jemma hissed as Deborah appeared in the doorway.

'Well, congratulations, girls!' she smiled, 'this is quite a place! I adore all these cupcakes and the cherry tree design on the door is precious. I'm guessing they're all your work, Lizzie, am I right?'

'Yep,' I nodded proudly, 'they do look great, don't they?'

Deborah nodded.

'And the crafting area is perfectly situated in the recess. Just far enough away not to interfere with Café business, but close enough to make it part of the place. Spot on!'

I beamed in response to Deborah's positive reaction and rejoined her at the crafting table where I had laid out some of the ideas and potential projects I had put together along with my business plan.

'Now about Heather,' I said gently as we finished looking through everything.

'Could be cancer,' Deborah blurted out, her eyes never leaving the paperwork in front of her, 'don't know yet. Get the results back next Friday.'

I didn't know what to say. My relationship with these women, although freshly formed, had been hugely instrumental in getting over my post-Giles heartbreak and the thought of either of them suffering in any way was horrid.

'Might not be, of course,' Deborah added bravely, 'either way,' she said, sitting up and finally meeting my eyes, 'I've decided the time has come to sell the Crafting Café.'

'What?' I gasped. 'Why?'

Deborah chuckled at my reaction.

'Do you know how long Heather and I have been together?' she asked.

'No,' I shook my head, my mind still reeling from the shock of her selling up. 'No idea.'

The City Crafting Café was Deborah's life. She had built it up from nothing on a shoestring. The thought of her being able even to consider parting with it seemed impossible to me.

'Thirty-five years,' she said with a smile. 'For the last thirty five years Heather has supported me. She's never complained or questioned; she's put up with my moods and my tantrums and with never a moment's thought for her own happiness or hopes and dreams.'

'Because she loves you,' I began to say.

'But love shouldn't be a one-way street, should it?' Deborah burst out. 'Loving someone should be about give and take. I know that Heather has given for the last thirty-five years and I've done little other than take and that is shocking, Lizzie, shocking.'

'I can't believe that's true, Deborah.'

'It is,' she said, her tone suggesting I shouldn't dare contradict what she was saying, 'but not any more. Neither of us is getting any younger and no matter what the results are next week, Heather and I have decided, together for once, that we're leaving London.'

'But where will you go?' I asked, struggling to picture either of them living anywhere other than the urban jungle.

'Heather's always fancied the coast,' Deborah smiled. 'When she was little, her parents always took her to the seaside for their summer holidays. Norfolk or Suffolk we thought.'

I didn't know what to say.

'We might even get a little dog,' she carried on wistfully, clearly caught up in her dreams of what the next stage of her and Heather's life together could be.

The thought of Heather not being well enough to see their dreams come true was too much to bear and I knew that if it didn't happen then Deborah would be haunted by her guilt for the rest of her life.

'I was rather hoping,' she said, with a heavy sigh, 'in my typically selfish way, of course, that this place would be a disaster. A struggling little business in a rotten location that looked destined to fold in a few months, but I can see that is not the case at all.'

In the time we'd been sitting in the crafting area, the tables had filled with shoppers and Jemma and Angela were bustling about taking orders and chatting to customers who were more than happy to make the Café a regular stop when they popped into town.

'I don't quite know what to say to that,' I told Deborah honestly.

She'd always been so enthusiastic and encouraging about my plans.

'Sorry,' she said with a shake of her head, 'I'm not explaining myself very well, am I? The truth is,' she said, clearing her throat and sounding much more like her old self, 'I wanted to offer you first refusal on the City Crafting Café, Lizzie. I wondered if you would consider buying it from me.'

Deborah and Heather left after an early lunch and I can only say that I was relieved by their departure. I had asked whether they had considered putting in a manager to run the place but Deborah was having none of it.

'A clean sweep with a new broom, eh, Heather?' she boomed, almost making the flat windows rattle in their frames. 'That's the best way. Time to do all the things that being tied to the old place has stopped us doing.'

I wanted to ask about the person running it while they were away. Deborah had said they were more than competent so perhaps they would fancy taking it on with her as a silent partner, but one look at Heather's face silenced me. Mingled with her sadness and pain I could see hope. Hope that she would be a part of the new venture her lifelong companion was so meticulously planning. I couldn't be the one to put a spanner in the works, so I said nothing.

'Promise you'll let me know how Friday goes, won't you?' I insisted as they got ready to leave.

'Of course,' said Deborah, 'as long as you promise to come and see us before you make a final decision. I can see that you've got the perfect set-up here but if you were feeling a hankering for the old smoke, then this might be the perfect opportunity to come back.'

There and then I didn't have an answer to give her. I hadn't missed the city at all and my trip back to see Henry had made me realise just how much nicer the sedate calm of my little hometown was. But perhaps, said a little voice at the back of my mind, perhaps you would like it if you were the owner of the City Crafting Café, fulfilling your dreams on a much larger scale.

'I'll try,' I promised, 'if I can get away, I'll come.'

'So,' said Jemma, sidling over as I waved the pair of them off, 'what did Deborah say? Did she give you the seal of approval?'

Jemma was another one full of hope. I looked at the expectation in her eyes. She and Tom were doing their utmost to make a success of the Cherry Tree and were undoubtedly frustrated by my reluctance to commit to more regular sessions.

'She loved it,' I told her honestly. 'She loved the Café and the crafting area.'

Jemma clapped her hands together and let out an excited little squeal.

'As far as Deborah is concerned there's absolutely no reason why I shouldn't get going and set up some regular meetings.'

'So?' Jemma asked, plucking at my elbow, 'are you going to get on with it? You did say that now your dad is on the mend and if Deborah said yes, then you would get cracking before everyone lost interest, didn't you?'

'I did,' I nodded. What else could I say? 'I'm going to start preparing my next session right now, as long as you can spare me?'

'Of course she can spare you,' Angela said as she swooped past with someone's lunch order. 'We can manage.'

'There you are then!' Jemma laughed as she ushered me across the Café floor. 'Off you go, get planning!'

I looked at the array of ideas and materials spread across the tables but my mind was no closer to deciding what we would be making next than it was to saying yes or no to Deborah's gargantuan suggestion.

I surreptitiously watched Jemma and Angela at work in the Café. The pair already operated like a well-oiled machine. I could see that Angela had lost her pale, pasty pallor and she had also gained a few pounds, although I had no idea how; she never stood still long enough to let the calories pile up. By contrast Jemma was looking a little peaky, but it wasn't easy juggling the Café, a home, a marriage and an Ella.

She was the one person in my life I had always been able to talk to about my professional hopes and dreams without fear of question or ridicule, but not this time. There was no way

I could even hint at Deborah's suggestion to either her or Tom. I knew I was going to have to figure this one out on my own.

'Have you finished already?' Jemma asked as she watched me tidying up and pulling on a jumper. 'That was quick!'

'Almost,' I lied. 'I'm just popping out to see Mum and Dad.'

'OK,' she beamed, 'but don't be too long. If you hurry we could get the posters copied and up by the end of the day.'

I found Mum and Dad in the garden, sitting together on the swinging seat I had bought them as a wedding anniversary present a couple of years before.

'Hello, you,' Dad smiled, levering himself upright and patting the empty space next to him. 'This is a lovely surprise. We haven't seen you since, oh now let's think, yesterday wasn't it, Pam?'

'Don't be like that,' Mum chastised, 'you should be grateful she cares! I saw Ben's mum in the butcher's at the weekend. She says she hasn't had even so much as a postcard from him since he went to Spain to see his father.'

I had been doing my utmost not to think about him but the mere mention of his name and the memory of how our Skype session had ended sent the colour flooding back to my face and neck.

'I didn't know you knew his mother.' I swallowed.

'I don't particularly well. We used to sit next to each other at the WI meetings sometimes,' Mum sniffed by way of explanation.

Mum had been true to her word and given up all her clubs and meetings to look after Dad and I couldn't help wondering if she missed it all or regretted making such a speedy and dramatic swathe of cuts through her social life.

'Are you missing it, Mum, all your friends and coffee mornings and things?'

'Nope,' she said firmly, standing up and straightening her lilac linen shirt, 'I still see my friends when I want to. To be honest, darling, I'm rather enjoying the freedom and spending all the extra time with Daddy.'

Daddy! She bent down and gave him the kind of kiss no offspring should be privy to.

'I'll go and make some green tea,' she said coquettishly, flashing Dad a little smile over her shoulder when she reached the house.

This was the first time Dad and I had been alone together since he'd been discharged from the hospital and I sat waiting for him to tell me what a nightmare it was having Mum in his pocket all day, but he said no such thing.

'So,' I sighed, 'how's it all going? How are the pair of you getting on together?'

'Fine,' he laughed, 'great actually! It's like we've turned the clock back thirty years. I should have had a stroke years ago.'

I scowled at him, but didn't say anything. It wasn't the first time he'd said that and it still wasn't funny.

'Sorry,' he nudged, 'what's up with you? You look a bit down in the dumps. I thought your friends were coming up from London today. Have they gone already?'

'Yes and yes,' I nodded as Mum returned with the tea and some healthy nibbles in a bowl. 'No cake?'

'No, Lizzie,' she frowned, 'no cake and you should be thinking about your health a bit more, you know. You have your dad's genes as well as mine.'

'She's right, love,' Dad agreed.

Oh great. This was all I needed, the pair of them ganging up on me. Next they'd be asking how loud my biological clock was ticking and the afternoon would be complete. I grabbed a handful of what looked like sawdust and slumped back on the seat.

'So,' said Dad, picking up the thread, 'what did your friends think of the Cherry Tree? I take it from your expression it wasn't a successful trip?'

'No, it was fine, more than fine actually,' I told them, 'they loved the place. Deborah said there was no reason why I couldn't turn the sewing and crafting into a very successful little business.'

'But?' Mum asked, looking at me expectantly over the top of her glasses.

'No, but, well not really; she dropped a couple of bombshells that's all and they've set me thinking.'

I explained to Mum and Dad about Heather's illness and Deborah's suggestion that I could buy the City Crafting Café myself. They sat quietly and listened. Mum didn't interrupt once.

'So that's it,' I shrugged, 'obviously I haven't mentioned her idea to Jemma or Tom; they'd be devastated if they knew I was even considering it.'

'Well,' said Dad, 'I can see why you're looking so glum! You've had quite a confusing day, old girl. What do you think, Pam?'

Mum set down her cup and saucer, deep in thought. I was sure she was going to tell me to think big and go for it. The purchase and subsequent ownership of the City Crafting Café in London of all places would have been something she would have taken huge delight in boasting about in the 'olden days'.

'So,' she said, 'your friend has already established this business and it's running successfully in London with a regular client base.'

Here we go, I smiled, old habits die hard.

'All you have to do is sign the paperwork, pick up the keys and carry on where she leaves off, is that right?'

'Yes,' I confirmed. I could see her point. It was a peach of an offer. 'Exactly.'

'But then there's nothing there for you to do, darling!' she laughed. 'I thought you'd joined forces with Jemma and Tom because you wanted to build something from scratch, something creative that you could truly call your own.'

Oh my god! So she did understand. Talk about a thunderbolt.

'But this place has a reputation already,' Dad chipped in, 'and Lizzie could make some changes and turn it into what she would want it to be.'

'But will this regular client base share her vision?' Mum said with a shake of her head. 'What if they don't like the changes and go elsewhere and in the time it takes to re-establish, the finances take a dip. It's a very big risk.'

They both turned to me, but I didn't have an answer. I could see the sense in what they were both saying. The Cherry Tree offered the potential to do things my way, from scratch, but it was going to be a hard slog to make it succeed and raise enough of an income to live off and there was always the risk that one day Ben might walk back through the door and take custody of my heart all over again.

The City Crafting Café, on the other hand, was good to go. I could just walk in and keep it ticking over, but was that, as Mum suggested, going to be enough? Even though I had some money behind me, buying Deborah out would be a huge financial risk and I didn't know if I was willing to take on that amount of pressure or commitment.

Chapter 22

A few days passed and I was still no closer to making a decision, but I had spoken to Deborah nonetheless and found her uncharacteristically tearful, her voice full of relief.

'Not cancer,' she breathed a definite wobble in her voice, 'it's definitely not cancer. They've still got to figure out exactly what is wrong, but it isn't the worst.'

'Oh, Deborah,' I exclaimed, 'that's wonderful news! Can I talk to Heather? Is she there?'

'No, she's at the hospital having more tests.'

'She must be so relieved!' I smiled.

'You wouldn't believe the change in her,' Deborah laughed, 'she almost looks like my old girl again. It's such a weight off her shoulders – both our shoulders.'

'And how are things with the business?' There was no point beating about the bush.

'Ticking over. Have you thought any more about it?'

'To be honest I've thought of little else,' I admitted, 'but I still haven't come to any kind of decision. Is that all right?'

'Of course it is. You take your time. I have one other interested party but I promise I won't do a thing until you give me the nod either way.'

'Thanks, Deborah,' I said gratefully, 'I appreciate your understanding.'

'Of course,' she said sensibly, 'it's an enormous decision for you to make, I understand that. But whatever you decide, it won't alter our friendship, I hope you realise that, Lizzie?'

I ended the call with mixed feelings. I was overjoyed that Heather's illness was not as serious as first thought but felt surprisingly alarmed to learn that someone else was poking around the Crafting Café, but who could blame them? The sale was a unique opportunity to buy a thriving bang-on-trend business in a prime location *and* with an established and highly prized reputation. Anyone with half a brain looking for a retail opportunity would be clamouring to get their hands on the place.

Now the pressure was really on and I felt my stress levels crank up a notch as I thrashed out the pros and cons of the situation. What I really needed was a chat with my best friend. Perhaps it was time to risk sounding Jemma out, whatever the consequences. As long as I reassured her that I had no intention of withdrawing the money I'd already invested in the Cherry Tree, then surely she'd understand, wouldn't she?

'Ella, you said that if I let you come to the Café today you would sit and colour and not get in the way!'

Jemma's tone suggested now perhaps wasn't the best time for a heart to heart after all. It was far earlier than she usually arrived and she never had Ella in tow, even during the holidays.

'But I want to go in the garden and play! Why can't I go outside? You can see me from the window!'

'I said no!'

I popped my head around the door and took in the unusually chaotic scene that met my eyes. The kitchen, always so meticulously tidy, was in total disarray. Jemma's hair was flecked with flour and her frown was equally matched by Ella's.

'Need a hand?' I offered. 'Where's Angela?'

'She's not starting until we open today,' Jemma said, sounding tearful. 'Tom was supposed to be looking after Ella so I could make an early start, but he's had to go into the office and his mum's gone away for a couple of days.'

She stopped for a second and took a deep breath. Something was obviously troubling her and it wasn't just Ella playing up that had got her in such a muddle.

'What is it, Jemma?' I asked. 'What's wrong? You look shattered.'

She shook her head and took another shuddering breath.

'I've got this huge order for cupcakes,' she said eventually, 'and there's no way I can get it done with Ella messing about. I can't blame her for wanting to be outside but I can't be in two places at once, can I?'

I knew whatever it was that had upset her had nothing to do with cupcakes and I also knew I wasn't going to be any use in the kitchen so I suggested the only thing that I could think of that would help save my friend's sanity.

'How about I take Ella to the park and leave you to get on in peace for a while?'

'Oh, would you really?' she gasped. 'Oh, Lizzie, that would be such a help. If I can just get a couple of uninterrupted hours to complete this order then I'm sure I'll feel much better.'

'Come on, madam,' I smiled, holding out my hand to Ella, 'let's go and find your water bottle, it's getting warmer out there.'

It was peaceful in the park. I sat on a bench and watched Ella tearing around burning off some of her seemingly endless energy. I envied her a little and found myself wishing that I was as full of exuberance and as carefree as she was, my major preoccupation in life whether to go on the swings or the slide first. The whole 'where to set up my dream business' situation was playing havoc with my sleeping pattern and I felt exhausted by the mental mind games I couldn't fathom out how to win.

If I was being brutally honest, I knew that had Ben not

buggered off to Spain then I wouldn't have been even considering the idea of moving again because we would have 'had it out' (as my mum would have put it) face to face, and moved on.

Obviously I could appreciate that he had painful relationship stuff to work through but running away hadn't actually solved anything. I ignored the little voice in my head that told me that that was exactly what I had done when Giles dumped me, but I'd run home, hadn't I?

I'd chosen to come back to the people who could help me heal and isn't that what Ben had initially done as well? Deep down I did feel unsatisfied that I didn't know all the details of the whole love slash hate saga but I was still hell-bent on convincing myself that I didn't care. The fact that I had, in quieter moments, actually considered knocking on Alison Fletcher's door and demanding an explanation was most telling, but there was no guarantee that she would have been willing to tell me the truth.

'Mind if I sit down?'

'Jesus,' I swore under my breath, the colour flooding my face as my feet left the path.

'Sorry, I shouldn't have crept up on you like that.'

It was Jay. He was trying not to laugh so I must have looked ridiculous.

'It's fine,' I lied, resenting his intrusion, 'I was miles away. Probably wouldn't have heard a bomb go off to be honest.'

'You've obviously got something on your mind,' he said, 'I'll leave you to it. I hope your friend's visit was a success?'

'No, honestly it's fine,' I relented, my manners getting the better of me, 'and yes, thanks, her visit was a complete success.'

'Brilliant,' he beamed, sitting down; 'I didn't manage to get back to the Café to ask. I'm sorry.'

He looked at me intently, his blue eyes staring blatantly into mine.

'You probably think I make a habit of breaking promises, don't you?'

'What do you mean?'

'Well, every time I say I'll see you later I never seem to manage to and you still haven't given me your mobile number so I can't even text or ring and explain why.'

To be honest I hadn't realised. My interest in him wasn't *that* piqued, hence the fact that I still hadn't given him my number.

'It's my work,' he explained when I didn't rush to get my phone out; 'I never know where I'm going to be from one hour to the next. Today for example I wasn't supposed to be working for the paper at all, but I got a call asking me to photograph the park graffiti and so here I am. Thought I'd better turn up early, though,' he added. 'It doesn't really look good, does it? A grown bloke running round a kiddie's park taking photos.'

He'd got a point.

'So what would you have been doing today instead then?' I asked politely.

'I have a couple of framing commissions to complete,' he said proudly, 'I was hoping to get them finished. I'm a bit like you really, Lizzie.'

'You are?' I asked, turning my attention from Ella to focus on him. 'In what way?'

'My little framing side-line,' he explained. 'I want to set it up as a proper business. I want to make a go of it, but I can't quite muster the courage to take the plunge and go full time.'

'You mean set up a business framing things like the Cherry Tree pieces you created for me?'

Jay nodded. The picture was exquisite and not a day had gone by when I hadn't stopped and looked at it. It was perfect. The way he had mounted the design and cleverly displayed the photographs and little pieces of sewing paraphernalia around the outside made it more than just a picture; it was like a memory box, a wall-mounted memory box. I was sure, given the current interest in crafts and anything handmade, that Jay would make a success of it. Weddings alone could make up a huge part of his business.

'Can't you do both?' I asked. 'Work for the newspaper and carry on framing whilst you build up the business a bit? If you're freelance at the paper and part-time I can't see that they'd have any objection.'

'Maybe,' he nodded again, 'but what I really need is an injection of capital,' he sighed. 'I'm sure if I had some financial backing then I could make it all happen so much faster.'

'It'll be worth the wait,' I told him. 'Look at me! I've waited almost half a lifetime.'

'And yet you still have doubts, don't you?' he reminded me with a nudge. 'You're still dithering about. I thought Jemma said it'd be all systems go if this friend of yours gave you the thumbs up and yet here you sit looking as miserable as sin!'

'Yes well,' I sighed, 'something else has come up now.'

'Do you want to talk about it?'

I did want to talk about it, but not particularly with him. My parents had been far too practical and level-headed and I didn't know Jay well enough to confide in him, did I? It was Jemma I really needed, vested interest or not.

'Drink please!' Ella gasped as she collapsed on the bench between us. 'I'm dying.'

'You are not dying, Ellie belly!' I told her. 'But you do need to slow up a bit.'

I smoothed her curls away from her face and felt the heat coming off her rosy cheeks.

'Just sit here for a bit,' I told her, 'until you get your breath back.'

She was too out of breath to object and slurped away contentedly at her water bottle.

'I'd better get on,' Jay smiled, 'let me know if you want to talk, OK? A problem shared and all that.'

'What problem?' Ella pounced. 'Who's got a problem?'

I shook my head and gave her a quick tickle to try to distract her.

'It's just a saying,' I told her, but she wouldn't leave it. Ella was like a dog with a flea when she sensed intrigue.

'Perhaps you could talk about it over dinner,' she suggested innocently, 'that's what grown-ups do, isn't it? Mummy and Daddy are always sending me to bed so they can talk.'

She looked from one of us to the other, waiting for either of us to say something. Jay caved first.

'Well, would you like to have dinner, Lizzie? I'm free tonight as it happens.'

'OK, if you like,' I agreed reluctantly, 'dinner it is.'

'Hadn't you better swap numbers or something,' Ella jumped in, 'otherwise you won't know where and when.'

She rolled her eyes and shook her head pityingly. I took out my phone and Jay did the same. While we exchanged numbers and arranged to meet in the pub, Ella tore off for one final lap of the playground.

'She's quite the little matchmaker, isn't she?' Jay laughed.

'Oh yes,' I smiled, remembering how she had tried to push me and Ben together. 'She's a regular little cupid. Not that I'm suggesting that this is a dinner date in the romantic sense,'

I laughed, then seeing the hurt expression on Jay's face blurted, 'or perhaps it is.'

He looked at me quizzically and I realised I couldn't have made more of a fool of myself if I tried.

'I'll see you in the pub at seven then,' he teased, 'just look out for the roses and champagne!'

On the way back to the Café we called in to see Mum and Dad.

'Nanny Pam!' Ella gushed, leaping into mum's arms and planting a kiss on her cheek. 'I haven't seen you for so long!'

Mum looked quite tearful as she carried Ella through the hall and into the kitchen. Perhaps her relationship with my goddaughter wasn't one to nurture after all. The last thing I needed was the pressure to procreate on top of anything else. Besides first I'd need a suitable sperm donor and, despite Ella's meddling, I couldn't imagine Jay and I as a bona fide couple somehow. Now Ben on the other hand; his eyes and my hair combo would be precious.

'So,' Dad smiled as mum unceremoniously plonked Ella next to him, 'what have you two been up to?'

'We've been to the park,' Ella announced whilst methodically picking the raisins out of the snack bowl, 'and Lizzie has a date.'

'Does she now?' Dad asked, turning his attention to me.

'She wouldn't have if I hadn't helped her get it, though.

Between you and me, she's pretty useless when it comes to men.'

'Oh?' I said, torn between outrage and amusement. 'Am I really?'

'Yes you are,' she said sternly, 'I heard Mummy saying so to Daddy.'

Dad shot me a glance and Mum left the drinks to join him and Ella at the table.

'Mummy said that if you didn't pull your finger out with Jay then he'd move onto someone else and then you'd be left with no one.'

I swallowed hard, but couldn't think what to say in response.

'Daddy told her off for that,' Ella continued conspiratorially, 'but I think he's just disappointed about what happened with Ben.'

'Nothing happened with Ben,' I snapped defensively.

'Exactly,' Ella nodded, her mouth now crammed with raisins, 'because of all the baggage.'

'What baggage?'

'Oh I don't know; something about it all being too complicated and the pair of you sharing too much stuff. It's all mixed up or something. Don't ask me!' she added indignantly. 'I'm only little.'

I didn't know what to say. Part of me was furious that my love life had been up for discussion and the rest was just downright confused. What did Jemma and Tom mean by 'shared baggage'? Did they think that because Ben and I were both such complete emotional screw-ups that we couldn't make a relationship together work or was there more to it than that? And what about the dinner date I'd just set up with Jay? I didn't want Jemma looking all smug and congratulatory because she thought I'd finally 'pulled my finger out'.

I dropped Ella back at the Café, grateful that Mum hadn't for once chipped in to the conversation. Whatever had happened to her since Dad's stroke, I liked it. This toned down version of my mother was an absolute joy compared to the old model.

Back inside the Café kitchen I couldn't look at Jemma. I didn't trust myself to keep my mouth shut.

'They look great,' I told her, glancing over at the much tidier counter and boxes of sugary delights. 'Really great, you got them all finished then?'

'Yes!' Jemma smiled, looking heaps better than she had earlier, 'I knew I could do it; I just needed the time. Thanks, Lizzie, I really appreciate your help this morning. I hope she didn't play you up too much?'

She threw an accusatory glance in her daughter's direction.

'No, she was fine,' I said lightly.

There was no way I was going to tell her what Ella had said. If my goddaughter got in trouble for spilling the beans she might not want to tell me anything again and she was one channel of communication that I was determined to keep open.

'She did exactly as she was told and we had a great time, didn't we, Ella?'

Ella nodded and carried on with her colouring, clearly not sure whether she was in trouble or not.

'Now if you'll excuse me,' I said, 'I have to make a phone call.'

Chapter 23

That afternoon I called Jay's mobile number at least a dozen times, but to no avail. He didn't answer and he didn't reply to any of my text messages either. As the time wore on I realised I was lumbered with a dinner date I hadn't wanted in the first place and which would doubtless be scrutinised in minute detail by my so-called 'best friend'.

I had no option but to walk down to the Mermaid with some lame excuse in tow and tell Jay that the evening was off. For a few minutes I toyed with the idea of calling the pub and asking Jim or Evelyn to do the dirty deed for me but that would mean involving more people and it was hardly fair on Jay who was completely oblivious of the scheming that was underway to make sure our one and only date culminated in a brisk walk down the aisle.

I didn't bother getting changed or fixing my hair or make-up. I was going to be five minutes max, so what was the point? I grabbed my jacket and then ran back for my purse. The least I could do was offer to buy him a consolation pint.

'Straight through to the restaurant, Lizzie,' Evelyn commanded the moment my face appeared around the door. 'He's already got you a drink.'

'Shit,' I muttered under my breath.

I had been hoping, as I was a good few minutes early, that Jay would still be sitting at the bar. It would have been far easier to duck out after a quick drink and chat but now, with him already sitting at a table, it was going to look like a proper stand-up job.

'Thanks,' I mumbled, heading into the restaurant.

Jay was sitting all alone at a table tucked away in the furthermost corner from the bar. He was reading something, the menu I guessed, and I was surprised to see he was wearing glasses. Suddenly his face took on a new perspective and his personality a wholly different slant. I imagined him working away in his framing workshop, meticulous and focused. It was a kind of Superman revelation but in reverse. I'd been aware of his rough and rugged exterior first but now his softer side had come to the fore.

Sensing my presence, he looked up and smiled then quickly whipped off his glasses and hurriedly stuffed them in his shirt pocket.

'Lizzie,' he croaked, 'sorry, I didn't see you.'

He jumped up, his knees colliding with the underside of

the table and almost upsetting the drinks as he rushed round to pull out a chair for me. I didn't sit down.

'Look, Jay,' I began shamefacedly, 'I'm ever so sorry but something's come up. Can we do this another night?'

'Oh,' he looked crestfallen, 'OK.'

He pushed the chair back and began shuffling together the papers and photographs, which I could see now were not the menu at all, but some kind of portfolio.

'I really am sorry,' I said again, my resolve weakened by his disappointment.

'Have you at least got time for a quick drink?' he asked, all puppy-dog eyes that were filled with hope. 'Evelyn said you were rather partial to cider.'

He pointed at the glass already on the table and I knew I had no choice. It would be churlish to turn down a drink he had already bought and paid for.

'Of course,' I nodded, 'thanks.'

I hung my jacket over the back of the chair and sat poised on the very edge of my seat ready to make a quick getaway before anyone saw us and reported back to Jemma, the town's resident relationship expert.

'I hope it isn't anything to do with your dad?' Jay asked.

'No god no,' I said, shaking my head and feeling more guilty by the second, 'nothing like that.'

I didn't offer any further explanation because I didn't have one to give. I didn't go in for lying as a rule and in my haste to get to the pub early I hadn't had a chance to dream up a credible excuse for cancelling. I took a long sip of my cider to buy me a few seconds and did all I could to avoid Jay's piercing gaze. My eyes fell on the papers he had been reading.

'What have you got there?' I asked.

'Oh it's nothing,' he blushed, 'it'll keep.'

'No, come on,' I pleaded, 'I've got a few minutes and it's obviously something you wanted to show me.'

We sat together and pored over the beautiful photographs and outline business plan that Jay had been getting together in preparation for launching his bespoke framing business. He explained that he had attended evening classes to get the basics right but the artistic flair and idea of adapting the frames had been all his own work. He was obviously proud of his idea and his passion and enthusiasm made him look like a far more appealing romantic prospect than when he was just a local 'journo' looking for a lead.

'Like I said this afternoon,' he concluded with a shuddering sigh, 'it all comes down to funding, or lack of it.'

'Doesn't it always?' I said with an understanding smile.

If it hadn't been for Dad's timely generosity there was no way I could have even allowed myself the luxury of dreaming about crafting at the Cherry Tree.

'If I could just lay my hands on enough to tide me over for a couple of months I'm sure I could make a go of it,' Jay continued.

'So folks, what can I get you?' Evelyn asked. 'I take it you are eating?' she added, throwing me a quizzical gaze.

Jay looked at me expectantly. He was wearing his glasses again and I had to admit they really did enhance his appeal considerably.

'Oh go on then,' I smiled, then quickly added, 'a couple of hours won't hurt. I can sort out what I was supposed to be doing tomorrow as easily as tonight.'

'As long as you're sure?' Jay asked, his sparkling blue eyes searching my face. 'Date back on?'

'Date back on,' I confirmed.

We ordered quickly. I hadn't realised just how hungry I was, but after Evelyn left us the thread of conversation was lost and we sat for a few moments in awkward silence.

'So it's all systems go with the crafting classes now then, is it,' Jay asked eventually, 'or do I still detect a glimmer of hesitation?'

He looked at me intently, his observation too astute to be anything near comfortable and I turned again to my cider, my second cider. I gave myself a moment in which to consider whether I knew him well enough to confide in him. Did I trust him enough to share my current conundrum?

In many ways, as he had suggested earlier, we were the same; both passionate about handcrafted and homemade and both about to embark upon the self-employment path with all its associated excitement and pitfalls. Surely it would be OK to talk to him about the City Crafting Café and Deborah's proposals, wouldn't it? In the absence of my best friend and faced with such inner turmoil I didn't see that I had much choice if I didn't want to go completely mad.

'Something has come up,' I began tentatively, 'something that might mean a change of plan for me.'

'Go on,' Jay encouraged, taking off his glasses and cleaning them on his napkin.

I explained about Deborah's business, Heather's health scare and the fact that I now had first option on the place if I wanted to buy it.

'But what about the Cherry Tree?' he asked as he picked up his knife and fork. 'What about Jemma and Tom?'

'I haven't dared mention it to either of them yet,' I cringed, colour flooding my face, 'I don't want to say anything until I've made a decision and if I do decide against it I probably won't say anything at all to be honest.'

'Why upset the apple cart,' Jay nodded in agreement.

'Exactly, but even if I do go ahead it won't impact on the Cherry Tree financially. I wouldn't dream of pulling out the money I've already invested.'

'I didn't know you had invested,' Jay said, his eyebrows raised.

I coloured an even deeper shade as I realised how indiscreet I had been to mention the Café's financial arrangements.

'Oh not much,' I said casually, 'I just wanted to help get the place going and of course if I do decide to stay then I've secured myself a share in the business as well as a roof over my head, haven't I?'

I shut up then. Playing back in my head what I had just said, my words sounded calculated and callous and that wasn't how I felt about the Cherry Tree at all. I'd invested because I loved the place, like I loved Jemma and Tom and Ella. My interest in the Café was bound up with far deeper emotions, with family and friendship and you couldn't and shouldn't ever put a price on that.

'So what's the latest scandal at the paper?' I asked, draining my glass and steering the conversation in to safer waters.

By half ten I was yawning and soon discovered I was more than a little tipsy when I stood up to leave. My earlier plan to cancel our date had turned into dinner, dessert and a couple more drinks and I wasn't entirely sure how it had happened.

'No,' Jay insisted as I pulled out my purse to go halves on the meal, 'this one is on me. I asked you, remember?'

I stuffed my purse away and leant across the table on tip-toe to kiss him on the cheek as a thank you for what had turned out to be such a lovely evening. However, just at the crucial moment he turned his head and what should have been a light peck turned into a full on kiss, complete with eye contact, a quickened pulse and a definite flicker of desire that started in my toes and blazed a trail towards my stomach.

'Now then, you two!' Jim boomed as he came through with the bill. 'Break it up, will you? It isn't that kind of establishment!'

As soon as I opened my eyes the next morning I knew something was wrong. I couldn't see properly for a start, everything was fuzzy and out of focus.

'Here, I thought you'd probably need this.'

I pulled myself upright, far too quickly, according to the way my stomach complained, and took the mug Jay proffered with a sheepish grin.

'Thanks,' I croaked. Apparently my voice had come out in sympathy with my eyes.

I sat back and breathed in the rejuvenating smell of the strong, black coffee he had made.

'How're you feeling?'

'I've been better,' I whispered, self-consciously pulling the duvet tighter around me.

'You were pretty drunk last night!' Jay laughed, his words hitting my tender head like a sledge hammer, 'and you'd only had a few halves of cider!'

'I don't usually drink it any more,' I said weakly. 'I learnt the hard way what kind of effect it has on me.'

Jay smirked and patted my leg sympathetically. I couldn't remember getting home; in fact, I couldn't remember anything much beyond the kiss in the pub.

'Did you stay?' I asked, fearing the worst.

I gingerly moved my legs in the bed and was relieved the sense of touch hadn't deserted me. I still had my jeans on and my top. It could have been worse.

'Yes,' Jay smiled. 'I slept on the sofa. I didn't like to leave you on your own. I hope that was OK?'

I nodded my thanks and took a sip of the hot bitter coffee.

'We talked for hours,' Jay explained, beginning to fill in the gaps. 'Can't you remember anything?'

Embarrassed by the state I must have been in, I shook my head.

'Oh well, that's a shame,' Jay said, standing up.

'You'll have to help me out, I'm afraid.'

'No, it doesn't matter,' he said, moving to the door.

'No please,' I insisted, 'go on. I hope I didn't embarrass myself,' I cringed, 'I didn't suggest anything inappropriate, did I?'

'You offered to put some money in towards the launch of my framing business actually, but if you can't remember.'

Had I? Had I *really* offered to do that? It certainly didn't sound like the sort of thing I would do, but then I had been drunk, very drunk. I didn't know what to say.

'Don't worry about it,' Jay said with a shrug, 'it doesn't matter. I've got an appointment with the bank. I'm going to see if I can get a loan.'

'But when we looked through your portfolio you told me you didn't want to start the business beholden to the bank.'

Now *that* I could remember; we had been talking about it early on in the evening. I wracked my brains but still couldn't remember the part where I'd apparently jumped in to save the day.

'Is there really no other way?' I frowned, feeling increasingly guilty that I had dashed Jay's hopes, especially now that I was beginning to find him so attractive. 'Is there no one else you could ask, family perhaps?'

'No, I'm afraid not. You really were my last hope, Lizzie.'

'Well, in that case I feel even more sorry,' I said.

He came back into the room and sat next to me on the edge of the bed.

'I should never have said I'd help and being drunk was no excuse.'

'Then you really can't help?' he asked, pushing my guilt level up another excruciating notch. 'Not even a couple of thousand?'

I couldn't believe he'd asked. Surely he could see how bad I felt? If he was trying to guilt me into making another offer he was making a right hash of it. I didn't say anything and he stood up again.

'Sorry,' he said, colour flooding his face, 'I didn't mean to ask you like that. It's just that last night I really thought I was there, but it's not your fault. I'll go to the bank.'

'I really am sorry, Jay,' I said again, 'I never meant to make you feel like this.'

'I know,' he said sadly. 'I'll see you later.'

By mid-morning my head had stopped spinning so I went down to the Café. I didn't really want to in my fragile state, but I was worried about Jemma. Yes, I was annoyed she had been talking so freely about my love life in front of Ella but she was still my best friend and I knew there was something bugging her besides cupcake orders. I wondered if she knew there was something bugging me too.

'Help yourself to coffee,' she smirked as soon as I appeared, 'something tells me you need it this morning!'

My concern was stamped out in a second. She looked far too smug for my liking and I didn't think I could take one of her 'I told you so' lectures about my love life with such a gargantuan hangover in tow.

'So,' she said, drying her hands and joining me at the counter, 'how was your evening?'

Bloody Jim! That unfortunate kiss was probably the hottest gossip the pub had been a party to since I did a bunk with Giles. I really needed to kick this unfortunate habit of providing the town with their regular supply of tittle-tattle.

'It was OK,' I said tentatively, 'but whatever Jim has been saying, you can guarantee . . .'

'I haven't spoken to Jim,' Jemma interrupted, 'although I know now I probably should if I want all the goss! I saw Jay leaving the flat this morning.'

That was even worse. I could hardly tell Jemma the truth, could I? I couldn't imagine that she would be thrilled to learn how I had blabbed about my investment in the Café and how I had then gone on to offer Jay, the guy I had only just met and shared one fleeting kiss with, the same level of financial commitment!

'We met in the pub,' I explained lamely, 'and I had a bit too much to drink. Jay stayed at the flat to make sure I was OK. Nothing happened,' I added feebly.

Jemma held up her hands and laughed.

'It's nothing to do with me!' she grinned. 'I'm not your mother.'

'I just didn't want you to think—'

'What?'

'Oh I don't know. I didn't want you to think it meant anything. Yes, I admit I like him but I'm not about to jump into a relationship – let alone bed – with him.'

I knew I was rambling and the more drivel I spouted the more it looked like I had something to hide. I waited for Jemma to continue teasing but the mention of relationships and beds seemed to have halted her in her tracks.

'Can you come round to the house for dinner tonight?' she asked seriously. 'It's important.'

'Sure,' I told her, my concern rushing back, 'is everything all right?'

'Everything's fine,' she smiled, 'it just seems like ages since we had a chance to chat properly without Café business getting in the way. Talking of which, you haven't got time to help me clear a couple of tables have you?'

Chapter 24

Later that day during a long, hot soak, I grabbed the opportunity to have a long, hard think about all the things that were happening in my life and try to marshal them into some sort of order. As I lay immersed in a Soap and Glory bubble bath complete with cup of tea and a slice of Jemma's delectable red velvet cake, I realised it was high time I stopped floundering about. If I didn't get my act together and make some decisions soon then I was in real danger of missing out. I'd come a long way in the months since my break-up with Giles, but I wasn't home and dry yet; there were still hurdles to face and conquer.

There could be no denying that I had fallen head over heels in love with my little flat, The Cherry Tree Café, and all its associated opportunities. I had not, however, fallen head over heels in love with Jay, because annoyingly my heart still belonged to Ben. As I turned from smooth goddess to prune and the water became more tepid than tempting, I had to admit that in spite of everything that had happened I was still as crazy about him as I had been when we were at school.

I loved Ben, body and soul, and it didn't matter that he wasn't around or that our Skype session had been a disastrous fail; my heart had been touched and I still wasn't over the boy I'd lusted after in the school canteen and beyond. My heart was apparently the one part of my anatomy that refused to toe the line.

I leant forward, turned the hot tap and felt the wave of warm water wash over me. Last night I had been tempted, with the assistance of too much cider, to kiss Jay but I still wasn't convinced that I had offered him any money. Dad had taught me to be careful with the little I had and I couldn't imagine that I'd been so drunk that I'd been tempted to throw caution to the wind and offer to fritter away Granny's life savings, but how could I be sure? Cider had always had a funny effect on both my body and my behaviour.

And what about the City Crafting Café? Yes, I loved the place; it had healed and soothed me on one of my darkest post-Giles days, but did I want to buy it? Did I want it to be my future? Did I really want to move back to the bustle of the city or was I happier here in Wynbridge? Surely being close to family and friends was of more value than anything else, wasn't it?

As I pulled the plug and reached for my towel I knew I had finally made up my mind.

Bottle of Prosecco in hand, I opened the gate and walked up the little path to Jemma and Tom's front door. Ella banged on the bay window and waved, bouncing up and down excitedly. I could see her mouth opening and closing, her warm breath on the window and wondered why she was so thrilled by my arrival. Before I had a chance to raise the knocker, the door was snatched open.

'Hello, Lizzie.'

I stood open mouthed, the bottle slipping a little in my grasp as I took in the tanned vision before me. It was all I could do to stop myself from jumping up and throwing my arms around his neck. It was such a jolt to see him, a wholly pleasurable jolt according to my traitorous heart and it started in the soles of my feet and spread with alarming speed throughout my entire body. Over and over again a little voice in my head kept repeating '*he loved you once, he loved you once*' whilst a more cautionary adversary fought back with '*and he hated you too and he hated you too.*'

'Oh,' I said, ignoring them both, 'hello. Still no beard then.'

'Still no beard,' Ben smiled guardedly. 'I couldn't cope with the tan lines.'

I craned my neck to look around him, fully expecting to

see the Spanish bikini clad beauty who had been doing her utmost to get him dancing, but the hallway was empty.

'I didn't know you were coming back,' I said.

'About that,' he began, 'I know . . .'

'But then if it was left to you,' I cut in, 'I still wouldn't know that you'd gone, would I?'

Ben nodded. His eyes fixed firmly on mine.

'Yes, I'm sorry about that. I know I should have told you. I had planned to, but it was all such a rush. A spur of the moment thing really and then the Skype session was such a disaster.'

'No matter,' I interrupted with a shrug. I thrust the bottle into his hand and brushed past into the hall. 'You're a free agent. It's nothing to do with me and like you're so fond of saying, it's all water under the bridge, isn't it?'

Less than an hour ago I had been lying in a bubble bath privately admitting that I was head over heels in love with this man, but now, faced with the reality of him, I was terrified of falling so obviously under his spell, especially as we shared such apparently cataclysmic 'baggage', the details of which I still knew very little about. I took a deep breath and warned my brain and my heart not to become befuddled by the tantalisingly tanned features and reassuring presence of the man who had vanished without giving me a second thought.

'Lizzie!' Ella suddenly shouted as she raced up the stairs. 'Will you come and read me a bedtime story?'

'Of course I will, poppet, hang on.'

I trotted up the stairs after her and away from danger before I was completely ensnared.

'Did you know he was coming back?' I hissed at Jemma, when I finally joined her in the kitchen. 'Is this why you asked me to come to dinner tonight?'

'Yes,' she answered shortly, 'we did know.'

'You panicked this morning when I mentioned Jay and bed in the same sentence, didn't you?' I whispered, not picking up on her frosty tone. 'You thought I was going to fall for him and you wanted to give me one last chance with Ben?'

'Maybe,' she muttered, 'but now something else has come up and it's all gone rather sour. I'm going to check on Ella and after dinner we need to talk. Stir this, would you?'

I stirred the risotto as instructed whilst Tom set the table and Ben opened the Prosecco. I tried to avoid looking at either of them and wondered what had happened to put Jemma in such a foul mood.

'I'm only going to apologise so many times,' Ben whispered as he leant past me to reach the glasses. 'I've actually come back to tell you why I went in the first place and to explain my mother's silly comments.'

'Honestly, I'm not bothered,' I lied, feeling secretly pleased that his clandestine exit had played on his mind. 'You should have saved yourself the air fare. You could have sent me a text or set up another Skype session if you were that worried.'

'I'm being serious,' he snapped, 'there are things I need to tell you.'

'Like how you've fallen in love with the sarong-wearing dance partner?' I said lightly.

'The what?'

'The girl in the club or wherever you were!'

'Actually I was in my dad's bar,' he frowned, 'crammed in the only spot where you can get a fairly decent internet signal, and the sarong-wearer was my prospective step-mother. I told you she was young.'

Before I had a chance to say anything, Jemma marched back in and began clattering plates and bowls.

We merely picked at the dinner she had gone to the trouble of making and our glasses still stood half-full, even after the meal had ended. To be honest, having jumped to the wrong conclusion about Ben and his Spanish senorita, I was grateful for a few minutes' silence in which to recover, no matter how awkward. I forced myself to look only at my plate and the wall opposite.

'Shall we move?' Tom finally suggested in an overly cheery tone. 'Go and have our coffee in the sitting room?'

'No,' said Jemma, 'I want to stay in here.'

I didn't know what was wrong, but she was hardly the hospitable hostess who had asked me to dinner earlier in the day. I wondered if she was annoyed that I still hadn't made a decision about the crafting sessions at the Café and thought what a relief it would be all round when I told her and Tom I was finally good to go. I wasn't going to let the fact that Ben was back change anything as far as the Cherry Tree was concerned.

'I saw Jay earlier,' she said before I had a chance to make my announcement. 'He popped into the Café. He said he was sorry about the potential change of plan and asked if he could use the crafting space to display his frames. He offered me a healthy commission, said it might help bring in some extra revenue if the space became empty. I got the impression that he seemed to think you might not be with us for much longer, Lizzie.'

I looked from her to Tom and back again.

'*What*?'

'He didn't say anything specific but I'd already guessed something was going on after the visit from your city friends and it didn't take long for me to join the dots. The City Crafting Café, it's called, isn't it? According to the agent I spoke to this afternoon it's already attracted a fair few enquiries, but the current owner is holding off and we all know why that is, don't we?'

Jemma looked straight at me. I didn't know what to say.

'You'll need to give us a bit of warning about when you want your money back,' Tom joined in, but not able to meet my gaze. 'It'll take us a while to raise it but don't worry; you'll get back every penny.'

I was too stunned to speak. It suddenly dawned on me that Jay after our – what I thought was confidential – conversation, had seen a prospective business opportunity and jumped at the chance. He'd gone straight round to Jemma just to spite me because I refused to offer him the money he wanted. The petty bastard! Suddenly those glasses didn't make him look so appealing any more.

'And you believe this, do you?' I said to Jemma, ignoring Tom's comment about the money. 'You never thought to ask me if what Jay was suggesting was true? You just took his word for it?'

'I know your friend is selling her business, Lizzie, and you must have talked to her about it when she came to see you the other week.'

'So that means I'm buying the place, does it?' I said unsteadily. 'I haven't been to view it, I haven't even got the agent's details let alone the funds, but apparently I'm off!'

For a split-second a flicker of doubt crossed Jemma's face but I didn't stick around long enough to see if the penny dropped.

I went to bed as soon as I got back to the flat but I didn't sleep. I tossed and turned until the duvet was wrapped so tightly around my body I could have been mistaken for an Egyptian mummy. I was devastated that Jemma and Tom had taken the word of Jay, a former football teammate, over mine – their lifelong friend and confidante.

I understood now why Ella was always so rude to him. Kids, I realised, were far shrewder when judging character than adults. They could see through all the layers of bullshit we shielded ourselves with. I couldn't believe it was only hours ago that I had decided I was staying here for good and now I was teetering on the brink again.

'Hello?'

I'd rung Jay's mobile, but hadn't really been expecting him to answer.

'Hi, Jay. It's Lizzie. Don't hang up;' I instructed, sounding braver than I felt; 'I think you owe me an explanation.'

I heard him sigh and I crossed my fingers in the hope that he would at least have the guts to offer some kind of justification for his despicable behaviour.

'I want to know why you went to Jemma behind my back. I thought I could trust you.'

'I'm sorry, Lizzie, I really am.'

'So why did you do it? You've put me in a really difficult position! I told you that I didn't know what I was going to do and I also told you that if I decided to stay then I wouldn't say anything to Jemma and Tom. What right did you think you had to stir all this up?'

'To tell you the truth, Lizzie, I can't believe I did it either. I don't know what came over me. Can I come round? Can I see you?'

Half an hour later, Jay sat at the kitchen table looking as

guilty as it was possible for a man to look. If I wasn't so angry I would have felt sorry for him, but I was still fuming.

'The other night,' he explained, 'when you told me you'd lend me some money to get my business started, I thought all my Christmases had come at once. You'd already told me you'd invested in the Café so I thought it would be fine. I've wanted this for so long, Lizzie, but I've never been able to quite make it work, you know?'

'Go on.' I still couldn't believe I'd made the offer in the first place but cider did funny things to my system; my student photos were proof enough of that.

'So when you then said it wasn't possible I could see it all slipping away from me again and I saw red.'

'You mean you wanted to get back at me?'

'I just wanted to make things uncomfortable for you, I guess,' he admitted awkwardly. 'I began to tell Jemma in a roundabout way what you'd told me but I realised what an idiot I was being and I stopped. That was when I thought I might be able to use the crafting space myself. I was just trying to make the best of what had turned into a huge disappointment.'

'But Jemma's not stupid!' I shouted. 'She was straight on the internet, then the phone. She knows exactly what's going on. She and Tom think it's a done deal. They think I'm already packing to go!'

'Oh, Lizzie, I'm so sorry. Let me go round and straighten it out. I made the problem, let me solve it.'

'No,' I said quietly, 'just leave it.'

'But they've got it all wrong. I should have kept my mouth shut.'

'Yes,' I said, 'you should, but you didn't and for some reason they've decided to take your word over mine, and if they can jump to conclusions over something as important as my commitment to the Cherry Tree then perhaps they aren't the friends I thought they were after all.'

I didn't think the morning could get much worse, but after Jay left, Ben arrived.

'Have you got time to talk?' he asked. 'It's important.'

'If you've come to tell me that Jemma and Tom have finally worked out the truth,' I sniped, 'then forget it. I'm in no mood to hear it.'

'This has nothing to do with them,' he insisted. 'This is about us.'

Reluctantly I opened the door and let him in.

'Do you want a drink?' I called from the kitchen, having deposited him on the sofa.

'Please,' he answered, 'coffee would be great.'

'OK,' I passed Ben a mug and sat in the chair opposite, 'what is it you want to talk to me about? I think we're beyond gossiping about high-school crushes, don't you?'

Ben didn't say anything but there was a definite rosy glow to his face that hadn't been there when he arrived. It was a low blow considering my own feelings, but I was still feeling raw and bruised and he was a sitting duck.

'No,' he said, 'I'm not interested in what could or should have happened when we were kids.'

'Well, whatever you've come to tell me, I'm not really interested.'

'Look, Lizzie, I want to tell you about why I went, rather than keep apologising for the way I went,' he said quietly, 'and I'm sorry, but I do think you need to know why Mum said what she did.'

'You went because you were upset about what you told me,' I said bluntly, 'about your girlfriend and the terrible thing she did.'

'That was partly the reason,' he agreed, 'but you only know half the story, Lizzie.'

'OK,' I took a deep breath and put my mug on the hearth, 'but you don't owe me an explanation, Ben. This really has nothing to do with me, does it? It's ancient history.'

'It has everything to do with you and if you'll give me half a chance and not interrupt or fly off the handle then you'll see why.'

I sat back in my chair not unlike Ella waiting for her bedtime story. There was nothing that Ben could tell me that would have an impact. After everything else that had happened in the last twenty-four hours I was immune to further shock.

'My girlfriend,' Ben said, looking straight at me and making my stomach do a loop-the-loop, 'the one who disappeared and had the termination . . .'

'I remember,' I said. 'You don't need to spell it all out again.'

'I probably should've mentioned her name.'

I shrugged and reached for my mug.

'I don't see why,' I told him blankly.

Ben leant across the space between us, took my mug and set it back on the hearth. He held my hands tight in his and looked straight at me.

'It was Natasha.'

'What?' I laughed, snatching my hands away as my stomach launched off on the rollercoaster again but for a very different reason this time. I didn't understand. Surely the name was just a coincidence? It had to be.

'It was Natasha,' he said again.

I sat and stared at him, my head and heart struggling for synchronicity.

'What, you mean Natasha, as in Giles and Natasha?'

Ben nodded.

I thought I was going to be sick.

'But when, how?'

Why was I asking? Why did I want to know?

'A few days after Giles first turned up in the Mermaid and swept you off your feet, Natasha came looking for him.

Apparently she'd found out where he'd been staying and was hell-bent on revenge. I mean, she'd practically been left at the altar; she was entitled to some kind of explanation.'

'So where was I?'

'You'd gone away with Giles. Didn't he whisk you off on some mini break or something? Anyway it doesn't matter. Neither of you were here when she turned up.'

Ah yes, I remembered. Giles had roped Mum in on that one. He'd gone to the house and together they'd packed a suitcase and found my passport and I'd been picked up after my shift at the pub and driven off to the airport. Everyone had thought the gesture was the ultimate in romance; just as well they hadn't got wind of the fact that Giles was already spoken for. He would have been lynched . . .

'Lizzie?'

'Um? Sorry. So how exactly do you fit into all this? How did you meet Natasha?'

'I was in the pub when she turned up. She never told anyone else who she really was. She was too embarrassed when she heard the locals talking about how their barmaid had been whisked off her feet by a slick city type. It didn't take a genius to work out who they were talking about. You can imagine the state she was in, can't you?'

'What and you swooped in and picked up the pieces?' I snapped scathingly, trying not to think about Natasha. 'You were little better than me then, were you?'

'It wasn't like that,' Ben thundered, moving back to his chair, 'I didn't swoop in at all. I was just a shoulder to cry on. I never meant to fall for her, it just happened. I felt sorry for her to start with.'

I snorted derisively, picturing the scene.

'Our relationship was nothing like yours and Giles's,' Ben frowned. 'We were friends a long time before we were lovers which is more than I can say for you!'

'So how come our paths never crossed in London?' I questioned, ignoring his slur on my morals. 'How come we never ended up at the same parties and events in the city?'

'Natasha went out of her way to make sure she and Giles were never going to be anywhere together. Work was a nightmare for her, but socially it was just as awkward. You know the kind of circles they moved in.'

'And now they're moving in them again,' I said resignedly, 'only now they're together. They really were meant for each other, weren't they?'

I was struggling to take it all in. It sounded like a Jeremy Kyle episode but with designer labels instead of trainers and tracksuits.

'What about the baby?' I asked without thinking. 'If she loved you, then why did she have an abortion?'

'She obviously loved Giles more, didn't she? She was already back with him when she found out she was pregnant. She promised me she hadn't slept with him, though. That's how she knew the baby was mine and that was why she had the termination. Giles wouldn't have taken her back if he knew she was carrying someone else's child, would he?'

'Did he even know she was pregnant?'

'No. She made sure both the baby and me were well out of the way before she began seeing him *properly* again.'

'I'm guessing this wasn't all that long before Christmas, was it?'

'How did you know?'

I shrugged but didn't answer. Giles himself had told me he'd spotted me looking at engagement rings and panicked. That had been enough to send him scurrying back to the elegant arms of Natasha, but it didn't matter. None of that mattered any more. They were married now, both of them lost to me and Ben, and good riddance to the pair of them.

I couldn't believe how calm I felt, how untouched. I looked down at my mug on the hearth. I should have been smashing it against the wall, shouldn't I? Tearing my hair out in fistfuls and wailing like a banshee, but what would have been the point?

'Why didn't you tell me this before?' I asked, wishing I'd known the full story all those weeks ago when he had seen fit to fill me in on the first instalment.

'I had planned to, but the longer I left it, the harder it got. I found myself starting to like you again, Lizzie, and then, just when you were beginning to move on, you were hurt all over again as a result of those bloody mysterious phone calls. I didn't want to add to your pain so I kept my mouth shut.'

Was I supposed to feel grateful?

'And I presume this explains the whole hating me phase and making my first few days back here as awkward as arse, does it?'

'Yes, I'm sorry. I just couldn't stop thinking that if you hadn't fallen for Giles then Natasha would never have come looking for him. I got it all a bit twisted in my head and I saw you as the villain rather than the victim. I'm sorry, Lizzie, but when you arrived back at Jemma and Tom's it tipped me back over the edge. I thought it would be OK, but it wasn't. The sight of you and the thought of them brought it all back again.'

At last everything was explained and the jumbled puzzle pieces finally slid smoothly into place. I collected my mug from the hearth, took it to the kitchen and rinsed it out. There had been nothing but conflict and crossed wires associated with every aspect of my relationship with Ben Fletcher and it had always been like that, even at school. It was time to draw a line.

It was up to me to be the bigger person here, forgive Ben for his anger and suggest it was time we both moved on with our lives. After all, I couldn't deny that it was me who had chosen not to break it off with Giles when I discovered he was engaged. But then another more disturbing thought occurred to me.

'Did Jemma and Tom know about all of this?' I stammered, rushing back to the sofa, my bottom lip threatening to betray me. 'Did they know that Natasha was the girl who had broken your heart?'

Ben didn't say anything. He ran his hands through his hair and stared at the carpet. At least now I understood what Jemma had meant by 'baggage'. I couldn't believe she and Tom had kept this from me. Not only had Jemma, my oldest friend, believed Jay about the City Crafting Café, she had also kept me in the dark about Ben's biggest secret, even though she knew how much I liked him. Suddenly it felt as though I didn't have a friend left in the world.

Chapter 25

'I won't be gone long,' I called to Mum as she saw me off at the train station. 'Give my love to Dad and promise you'll look after each other!'

'You are sure this is what you want, aren't you?' Mum shouted. 'You aren't just going because you're cross?'

I shook my head and smiled.

'No,' I called back, 'this is the right thing to do. I just needed a little nudge to help me find my courage,' I reassured her. 'I finally know what it is that I want!'

I waved and smiled, forcing myself to watch until Mum's silhouette on the platform became nothing more than a distant speck. Only then, I told myself, could I cry; only then, with Wynbridge behind me, would I give in to my turbulent emotions, but the funny thing was I didn't feel like crying any more.

Anger had stamped all over the shock of what had

happened during the last few days and now I felt determined to embrace the opportunity that I had finally found the nerve to grab. I may have been leaving the Cherry Tree behind but I knew that had I not lived there, had I not tried out my little business, then I wouldn't be sitting on a train, poised to super-size my dreams. My time at the Café had been an essential part of my journey but now life's path had turned another corner and I was pushing on to see what lay ahead.

Deborah had been delighted when I phoned and said I wanted to meet and discuss the sale in more detail. In her enthusiasm to make sure I was the one who took over the reins she had even offered me a gradual buy-out option; half now and the rest in two years' time. Now I couldn't even use my fear of funding the project as a reason not to try to secure it.

I banged the window shut, sat down and reached inside my sewing bag. Having decided not to drive down to London, I had the opportunity to dedicate the journey to working on the crocheted mice with long tails which were my current little project. I had already made a whole family of them in different sizes, in the hope that I could introduce them at the Cherry Tree crochet circle I'd been planning, but I figured they would feel just as much at home in the city as they were in the town.

'Oh these are precious!' Heather squeaked mouse-like herself, as she scooped them up off the counter when I finally arrived.

Deborah was more reserved and discerning and took her time scrutinising the stitches and finish before pronouncing with a smile that they were 'beautifully constructed' and 'ideal for beginners'.

'That's what I hoped,' I explained. 'I thought they would be just the thing for a crochet taster session.'

'I agree,' Deborah said. 'Quick to finish and pretty to look at. Far more interesting than the square mats for the dressing table that I made when I was learning.'

I had hailed a taxi and gone straight to the Crafting Café when the train arrived, keen to see the place in all its glory on a busy weekday afternoon. A knit and natter session was in full swing and the place was buzzing with cake, conversation and customers popping in off the street. I was thrilled to find Heather behind the counter looking much the same as she always had, only on this occasion being fussed over by Deborah rather than vice versa.

'I've set out all the books in the back office,' Deborah told me keenly, 'and the accounts. Access all areas, Lizzie, and if there's anything I haven't covered just give me a shout, OK?'

'OK,' I smiled nervously.

'Right, we'll leave you to it then!'

It felt strange being in the store in my capacity as potential owner. I browsed around, pulling books off shelves, fabric samples from rolls and various kits and remnants from the sale crates and all under the watchful eye of my two friends. Front of house was the area I really loved and in which I felt most comfortable, but I knew I couldn't put off trying to get my head around the managerial aspect and eventually I ducked into the office feeling something of a fraud.

I sat at Deborah's organised desk and ran my fingers down the columns and columns of neat, pristine figures and stared at the screen, equally neat, that displayed the more recent accounts and bills. The reality and enormity associated with running the Café struck me like a hammer blow.

This was all a far cry from setting up a few tables and teaching someone how to sew in a straight line. If I bought the place, assuming the bank would lend me enough to make up the initial fifty per cent; I wouldn't know what to do with all this. The whole point of starting small was to find my feet and make my own way, wasn't it? I had no idea about what half of the figures and columns meant. I jumped as Heather knocked on the door and appeared with a laden lunch tray.

'I know it all looks a bit complicated, Lizzie,' she said astutely, 'but it isn't really and we'll be around until you get the hang of things. Deborah's very keen that you shouldn't feel overwhelmed by it all. She's planning a smooth and steady handover with everything explained, everything ship-shape and as simple as possible, and of course we have a great accountant.'

I nodded and took a bite of the delectable smoked-salmon sandwich she offered me.

'This place is all about passion,' she beamed as she poured me a much needed cup of tea. 'Passion for sewing and crafts, and I know you've got that in abundance, along with your amazing skills, of course. We really believe you can take this place further, Lizzie. You're young, with fresh ideas and a whole new perspective and understanding about what people want. Those little mice of yours for a start.'

'They were just an idea,' I said, 'something a bit different.'

'Exactly! Different ideas are just what this place needs to attract new customers! Don't get me wrong, there's nothing amiss with our current customer base and turnover, but it's time for a clean sweep and we're sure you're just the broom the place needs!'

By the end of the afternoon I was feeling more settled in my mind, but I still wasn't prepared to make a final decision.

'I'm sorry I'm taking so long.'

Deborah shook her head.

'I wouldn't think much of you if you weren't! If you'd rushed in here this morning and told me you were ready to sign on the dotted line I'd have turned you away.'

'Really?'

'Really!' she boomed. 'Please don't worry about taking your time. The only stipulation I have is that you'll keep on the kitchen and waiting staff if you do go ahead. They're a good crew and all hard workers. I'd hate to think of any of them being out of work.'

'Of course,' I nodded and smiled.

It was a real jolt to acknowledge that taking on the business would also make me responsible for the livelihoods of a small army of staff. If I cocked this up it wouldn't be just my neck on the line.

I had hoped to stay with Henry again during my visit but, like mine, his life had moved on since we last met and I was thrilled to hear about the new love in his life.

'I'm sorry I won't be here, Lizzie,' he told me when I phoned to ask if I could stay. He sounded far from sorry, but I didn't mind. To be honest it was a relief to hear him sounding so happy. 'I've met this girl, you see, and we're planning to go away for a few days.'

We chatted at length about Cass, the new girl in his life and touched briefly on work, which finally seemed to be shaking down after all the recent upheaval.

'We'll catch up soon, though,' he promised. 'The last thing I want to do is lose touch.'

'Of course,' I said. 'Have a lovely break, Henry.'

Fortunately there was a Premier Inn not too far from the Café so I booked myself in there. Deborah and Heather had offered to accommodate me in their little house but I needed some space; some time away from the intensity of the situation to gain a little perspective.

Once I was cocooned in my room and had enjoyed a

refreshing shower I decided, as I was still full from my lunch at the Café, that I didn't want any dinner. I sat on the bed surrounded by paperwork and lists, a tinge of excitement and enthusiasm staving off the fear that had threatened to engulf me earlier and send me scurrying home.

Now I knew Deborah and Heather weren't going to disappear without a trace as soon as I took over I felt much better, and my mind was awash with potential plans and ideas. I knew they would help set my course steady and true and then only retreat like Dad had when he took the stabilisers off my bike. He had held on tight until he was sure I could manage to do it on my own and I knew that Deborah and Heather would be the same when it came to the business.

I eagerly read through my plethora of lists and began prioritising jobs. The Café had no online presence beyond the details the agent had posted and that was one of the first things I wanted to address. A buzzing Twitter account would help spread the word and was vital for modern day networking. The shop décor needed a bit of updating as well. The place was looking more than a little jaded but with some new lighting and a fresh lick of paint I could drag it into the new crafting era, no problem.

With television programmes such as the Great British Sewing Bee currently topping the ratings there was no time to lose. I only had to think of the positive impact the small changes the Cherry Tree had had, to realise the potentiality that a makeover offered.

I tried to make a rough estimate of how much my sketchy plans would cost. As ever with every new venture, money was an issue, whether it was a couple of thousand as Jay needed or a figure with a few more zeros attached. If it all worked out, I might even consider offering Jay some space to display his frames, I thought charitably, just to show there were no hard feelings. If I really could pull this off then his sneaky little chat with Jemma might turn out to be most fortuitous for me and it was only fair I repaid the compliment.

I looked down the list of figures I had come up with and sighed. No matter how well I could sew and paint and no matter how much I wanted to make a success of this venture, if I couldn't find the money then I'd be sunk.

My phone started buzzing and I reached down the side of the bed to pull it out of my bag. I could see the unread messages were piling up but I ignored them and checked the caller ID. My parents' number flashed on the screen and I answered, thinking it would be Mum making sure I had reached my destination safe and sound.

'Lizzie?'

'Hey Dad, is everything OK?'

Funnily enough it hadn't been Dad who I'd gone running to when Ben had left me shell-shocked, it was Mum. I'd begged her not to say anything to Dad until I left.

'But that's silly, Elizabeth,' she scolded, 'you haven't done anything wrong.'

'But it doesn't feel like that to me,' I confessed. 'If I hadn't been tempted by Giles and his flashy ways in the first place then none of this other mess would have happened, would it?'

'Well, perhaps not,' she said honestly, 'but that has nothing to do with the fact that Jemma and Tom believed what Jay said without even asking for your side of the story, does it?'

'I guess not.'

'And it doesn't alter the fact that they knew that Ben had been in a relationship with this Natasha person. I think you've got every right to feel upset, darling.'

It was shocking to have my mother agreeing with me but she was absolutely right; my feelings were more than justified. I didn't think I could trust any of them any more. They'd all had endless opportunities to tell me that the woman in Ben's life had been Natasha before he buggered off to Spain and they hadn't said a word. I felt like their second choice, knowing they'd promised to keep such a secret, and now this added business with Jay had pushed me right down the friendship list.

'Everything's fine,' Dad said, 'apart from the fact that you aren't here and I've only just found out why.'

'Yes, I'm sorry about that,' I winced, biting my lip. 'Don't blame Mum. She said I should tell you, but I felt such an idiot, I just had to get away.'

'But you haven't done anything wrong.'

I had. I'd given Giles my heart on a plate and now I was being made to pay the price. Not only had our break-up cost me my job, it had also cost me my friends, my home, my business and the man who I'd spent my formative years imagining would be the love of my life.

'Oh, Dad,' I sighed, 'I think you and I both know that's not true.'

'Well maybe, but that isn't why I've called you. Your mother's warned me not to go on about it,' he confessed. 'So, this place you're visiting in London,' he continued, 'is this the kind of thing you really want?'

'Yes, I think so.'

'Mum says it's a bit like the Cherry Tree on steroids; has she got that right?'

'Yes,' I laughed, 'I suppose she has. It's pretty much the same, just on a much larger scale, that's all. There's an empty flat above which is also larger and if I needed to I could rent out the spare bedroom to bring in some extra income.'

'Have you thought about how you could fund the purchase?'

I explained about the change of plan Deborah had come up with.

'In that case why don't you let me loan you the money for the first fifty per cent?' Dad offered. 'Interest free.'

'No!' I gasped. 'I couldn't let you do that.'

'Of course you could!' he laughed. 'It really is ridiculous having the money sitting in the bank doing nothing when it could be put to good use.'

'But what would Mum say?'

'Actually it was her idea. Look, I know it's a lot to think about, so sleep on it, OK? Go back tomorrow and have another look and we'll talk again soon. How does that sound?'

'OK,' I whispered, 'thanks, Dad.'

Compared to the Cherry Tree, the flat above the Crafting Café felt colossal. The living and kitchen area was open plan and overlooked the road at the front whilst the two double bedrooms and bathroom were situated at the back. I guessed the plan had been to make the sleeping areas quieter, but even with the triple glazed windows firmly shut you could still hear the noise and bustle of the road. Every window was overlooked and there was no outside space.

'I imagine this feels a bit different to the Cherry Tree,' Heather ventured as she showed me around, 'but to be honest you'll be so busy you'll hardly ever be up here!'

She was right, of course. The Café was going to keep me on my toes, but I couldn't help thinking about my little sitting-room fire and the vintage kitchen units that I had become so fond of. Even with all my creative acumen I couldn't imagine this open, blank space ever feeling like home.

'And having enough space to share is a real bonus,' Heather rushed on. 'I can't think why Deborah never let the place on a permanent basis before instead of going in for the few troublesome short-term tenancies we've had. It seems silly now to have had it empty for practically all this time!'

I nodded in agreement as I tried to imagine myself living here with some other girl. But I didn't really want to live with some other girl; I liked living on my own. If a song I loved came on the radio, I could dance about like a loon in my underwear and no one was any the wiser. I wouldn't be able to do that with some young executive watching my every move.

'So what do you think?' Heather asked.

'I think it would be fine,' I replied. 'I'd probably want to see how I felt living on my own initially, give the place a bit of a spruce up and then think about letting out the spare room.'

'Good idea,' Heather beamed, patting my arm. 'No harm in giving yourself a bit of time to settle in. Are you staying for the day?'

'Yes,' I smiled nervously, 'and travelling home later, but first I have to pay a call.'

Chapter 26

When I had called Henry and asked if I could stay with him I also told him of the extra little visit I'd scheduled into my London trip. He choked on whatever it was he happened to have a mouthful of and spluttered, 'Are you completely mad?'

'Probably,' I answered, trying to sound as if this was the sort of thing I did all the time. 'Just give me the address, Henry, will you, before I completely lose my nerve.'

'You already know it, old girl, they're still at the flat.'

'My flat?' I asked incredulously then quickly added, 'I don't mean my flat, I mean, oh you know what I mean. Why are they still there? I would have thought Natasha wouldn't want to even admit the place existed, let alone begin married life living in it!'

'They did try and find somewhere else,' Henry explained, 'but they couldn't find anything like as exclusive. You know how much the right postcode means to some people!'

It was a relief knowing that I hadn't got to go trawling halfway across London to find them; I wasn't sure my nerve would hold if I had to get out the A–Z, but it was going to be strange going back.

'OK, thanks Henry,' I said, grateful for the information. 'Wish me luck.'

'No I shall not,' Henry scolded. 'I think you must be mad to even consider it.'

Ignoring Henry's warning which had nonetheless been ringing in my ears ever since I spoke to him, I knew my first problem was going to be how to gain access to the flat. It was months since I'd been inside the building and I was well aware that the security code was changed on a regular basis. Fortunately, however, I needn't have worried; I'd picked the right day to blag my way in. The door was immediately opened upon my arrival and I was greeted like a long lost friend.

'Well, well, Miss Dixon. Long time no see!'

'Hello, Frank,' I smiled, taking the hand of quite possibly the oldest concierge in the known free world.

Fortunately he'd always had a soft spot for me and I felt only fleetingly guilty about abusing the fact.

'You here to see old gorgeous, then?' he asked with a sniff.

I smirked as I remembered he had nicknames for practically every inhabitant of the building.

'I am.'

'He's out,' Frank said dismissively, 'but she's in.'

No love lost there then I guessed.

'Shall I buzz her?'

'No!' I said far too quickly. 'This is more of a surprise visit.'

'I thought as much,' he smiled. 'Go on then. If anyone asks, I never saw you!'

I pressed the lift button to the top floor and took a deep breath. Purposefully I had left my hair in its unruly natural state and made no effort to cover or tone down my freckles. I didn't want or need any armour for this little visit. It was all about me just turning up as me.

'What makes you think I'm going to let you in?' Natasha asked, once she'd got over the shock that I was standing the other side of her front door.

'I know about you and Ben Fletcher,' I said. I knew it was a cheap shot, especially as I wasn't there to talk about him at all, but I needed some sort of leverage to get inside.

'Wait a minute.'

I heard the chain slide back and watched the handle turn. Slowly the door opened.

'Hello, Natasha,' I swallowed, looking up at the sleek-heeled goddess before me.

'You'd better come in,' she said, taking in my own ruffled appearance with a look of disdain.

Little had changed inside the flat. It was still bare, hollow and unwelcoming, hardly a newlyweds' love nest. I can honestly say I felt no connection to the place at all, no hankering to pick up the threads of the life I had once lived there. Perhaps if I'd taken a peek at the wet room I might have felt differently . . .

'What do you want, Lizzie?' Natasha scowled, narrowing her feline eyes. 'What has Ben told you?'

'Everything,' I said simply, 'but he isn't the real reason I'm here.'

I explained my plans to buy the City Crafting Café and the fact that it was little further than a stone's throw from the flat.

'I know it,' Natasha said casually. 'My mother and sister attend some of the classes there. They're very fond of it. But what has any of this got to do with me? You aren't here touting for business, are you? I'm not really the crafting kind,' she added scathingly.

'No,' I said, 'I can see that. I just didn't want you to think that I was trying to muscle in on your patch or that I was still in any way interested in Giles, because I'm not. I'm really not.'

Natasha threw me a withering look and began to laugh, her glossy curtain of hair neatly swept aside with a deft flick.

'I don't think we'd really need worry about that even if you were, do you?'

Comparing her to me, I guessed not. We were in different leagues, different stratospheres in fact, but she didn't need to make me feel like such a bargain-basement bit of rough. But then again, why shouldn't she? This was her one chance to be as mean and scathing as she liked. I couldn't blame her for wanting to make me feel like I belonged in a jumble sale so consequently her next words were something of a shock.

'Actually,' she said, her voice taking on a softer edge as she placed two glasses on the marble worktop and took a bottle of wine out of the walk-in fridge, 'I've been meaning to get in touch with you to say thank you.'

'What on earth for?'

'Well, ever since Giles came crawling back he's been practically falling over himself to keep me happy,' she divulged. 'There's nothing he won't give me, nothing he won't do for me. It's been heaven.'

'But what about the phone calls before the wedding?' I asked agog.

'Oh yes, I forgot about those,' she smiled, her eyebrows raised as she deftly poured and passed me a glass. 'I take it you know they were from me, then?'

I nodded and took a sip of the crisp, chilled wine.

'I admit I was suspicious,' she explained, 'but I shouldn't have been. You won't believe where he was!'

'Where?' I asked, my head spinning. This wasn't how I envisaged our meeting turning out at all.

'He was having counselling!' she laughed. 'He booked himself into some rehab place he'd heard about from a friend. Spent the week getting his head cleared and his baggage sorted and came back with his tail between his legs, good as gold, ready for the big day!'

I couldn't help but laugh along with her. The thought of Giles even admitting that *he* had a problem was inconceivable but the fact that he was prepared to have counselling to sort it was most telling. We raised our glasses and toasted Giles, the man who loved Natasha so much it turned out that he was prepared to do anything to make sure their marriage, albeit second time around, actually happened.

'Well, I'm glad it's all worked out,' I said, feeling some of the guilt lifting from my shoulders, 'but I'm still sorry about everything that happened with Ben. Neither of you deserved to go through any of that.'

For a split second Natasha's veneer crinkled.

'You won't ever say anything about it to Giles, will you?' she begged.

'No of course not,' I said earnestly, 'it's none of my business.'

The flat door opened and in an instant Natasha was back to her polished confident self.

'That'll be Giles,' she smiled. 'Watch his expression. This will be priceless.'

'Fucking, shitty traffic!' We heard him sling his keys on the table in the hallway. 'Do we have to go out to this dinner, I . . .'

He stopped dead when he spotted me, his ex-lover,

perched next to his wife in the kitchen, sharing a bottle of wine. Natasha was right, his expression was priceless. I only wish I'd had my phone out ready to take a photo. It certainly would have been one for the album!

'What the hell?' he gaped.

'It's all right,' I said, putting down my glass and picking up my bag, 'I was just leaving.'

Ever since I'd decided that I would track the pair of them down, I'd wondered how I would feel seeing him again. How was I going to react when I gazed upon the gorgeous face of the man who had broken my heart and dashed my naive notions of romance? Could I trust myself not to jump into his arms and beg him to come back to Wynbridge with me?

Apparently I could. Yes, he was still handsome and polished, oozing wealth, status and urban sophistication, but he definitely wasn't the man for me. It was easy to see how I, a young woman bored witless and working shifts in the local pub had been swept off my feet and carried away by him, but I wasn't that woman any more. I felt nothing. My heart behaved itself; my stomach didn't fall through the floor, my palms remained dry and my loins unstirred. I was over him, completely and utterly over him.

'What are you doing here?' he asked.

He looked absolutely panic-stricken as did Natasha. She obviously still thought I was going to say something about Ben. Just a couple of months ago I might have done but now, having experienced for myself the trauma and heartache that descends when someone meddles in business they know nothing about, I wouldn't have dreamt of doing it. The complications that had arisen as a result of Jay's interfering in my life ensured my lips were sealed. What happened between Ben and Natasha was their business, nothing to do with me or anyone else for that matter.

'I just came to congratulate you both on making it down the aisle,' I said graciously.

The expression on Giles's face ranged from shock to suspicion to disbelief and back again and all in a split second. He turned to Natasha, who simply shrugged her designer-clad shoulders and took another long sip of wine.

'And I'm moving back to London,' I elaborated to help him out a bit. 'I'm thinking of buying the City Crafting Café up the road. I've been going through the books and so on and saw Natasha's mother and sister attend some of the classes there. I didn't want there to be any confusion about what I was doing here if word got back to her that I was running the place.'

'Oh right,' Giles frowned, running a hand through his hair, 'I see.'

But I could see he didn't. He had no reason to associate me with sewing and crafts, let alone buying myself a business in the city, but there was no need to explain. The purpose of my visit had been to talk to Natasha and I'd done that now.

'Well, I'll be off,' I smiled. 'I have a train to catch.'

'OK.'

'Bye, Natasha, and thanks for the wine. If you fancy taking up crocheting or making a patchwork quilt, then you know where I am.'

We both laughed as Giles turned from one of us to the other again, shock and bewilderment still etched across his face.

'I might take you up on that,' she laughed, 'oh and, Lizzie?'

'Yes?'

'Thank you.'

Chapter 27

I'd never enjoyed the upheaval of packing and this particular move was proving to be the worst I'd lived through so far. I'd only been living in the flat above the Cherry Tree for a few months but the place felt more like home than anywhere else I'd ever lived and it certainly seemed fuller.

Now I'd set my heart on the Crafting Café and was planning to move back to London and a much larger flat, I knew I was going to need all the 'stuff' I could lay my hands on to make it feel welcoming but I was still torn about what to take. I couldn't somehow picture any of Granny's treasured belongings in the London flat. It just didn't sit right with me at all.

'You can put some things back in your old room until you make up your mind if you like,' Mum reassured me.

'Are you sure? I don't want to clutter up the place.'

'It'll be fine,' she said. 'Your father and I are going to be away for a few weeks, remember, so we won't even notice it's here.'

'Thanks, Mum,' I smiled, giving her a hug.

I'd had to get out of the flat for the afternoon. I could hear the Café was buzzing and I hated sitting upstairs all on my own. Jemma and Tom hadn't made any attempt to make amends for keeping me in the dark about Ben's gargantuan secret and I was doing my utmost to stay out of their way as much as possible.

The evening I arrived back from London, I had sneaked downstairs and sat on my own in the crafting area. The perfection of the place was overwhelming. It was the perfect size and set-up; it was what I'd always dreamt of and I knew that supersizing my goals by taking on the City Crafting Café so soon was going to take some getting used to.

'So,' said Mum, 'run me through it all again. Exactly how long are you going to be away for?'

'Just a month to begin with, that's why I'm not taking everything all at once. The bigger furniture belongs in the flat anyway. I'll just clear out the personal bits, but thanks for the storage offer. It would be such a waste to take everything if it all goes wrong.'

'Don't be such a pessimist, Lizzie!' Mum scolded. 'Nothing's going to go wrong!'

I wished I could share her optimism. Deborah had agreed to let me run the City Crafting Café for a month on a trial basis, just so I could be sure that it was what I wanted. It was a huge sacrifice on her part. The other interested buyer had disappeared when Deborah explained the set-up and I knew that she and Heather were itching to move permanently to the little flint cottage they had fallen in love with on the North Norfolk coast. It felt selfish asking them to put their lives on hold for me, but as Heather kindly reminded me: 'Deborah will never settle if she thinks things aren't right at the Café, and think about what she'll put me through with all her agonising!'

'So tell me about this cruise again,' I said, reaching for the brochure and itinerary Mum had set out on the kitchen table. 'It'll take my mind off packing.'

Dad was looking forward to the trip just as much as Mum. He had had the go-ahead from his consultant that it was safe for him to travel and had already employed the services of a local gardener to keep the lawns in trim and the borders weed-free until he got back.

'It'll certainly make a change from a wet week in Morecambe!' he chuckled as mum trotted upstairs to change into the outfit she had bought for the night they would be dining at the Captain's table. 'But it's bad timing for you, Lizzie. I'm sorry, love.'

'I've told you it's fine,' I said for the hundredth time. 'It'll be easier to leave with you not here to wave me off, to be honest.'

Dad took my hand and gave it a quick squeeze.

'It isn't too late to change your mind, you know?'

'What do you mean?'

'To make it all right between you and Jemma. I know I don't know the ins and outs of everything that's gone on, but you've been friends forever, Lizzie. I hope the pair of you aren't throwing your friendship away over something silly like those damn boots she borrowed all those years ago.'

'No,' I shook my head sadly, 'believe me, Dad, this is nothing as trivial as that.'

'I really appreciate you doing this, Jay,' I said, as we unloaded the last of the boxes from the back of the van.

'It's the least I could do,' he insisted, 'I really am sorry that I've caused so much trouble, Lizzie. It breaks my heart to think that you've left the Cherry Tree because of my stupidity.'

'No,' I told him again, 'what you told Jemma was just the tip of the iceberg. Please don't worry about it. If anything, I should be thanking you for helping me find my courage!'

'Oh well in that case, just call me Dorothy!' he laughed, batting his eyelashes.

I hadn't told him how Jemma and Tom had kept me in the dark about Ben's big secret. It wasn't my secret after all and there was no way I was going to lower myself to their standards and involve Jay in their web of deceit.

'So,' I said arms outstretched, 'what do you think?'

'Very impressive,' Jay smiled as he looked down into the street. 'You've really fallen on your feet with this one, Lizzie!'

'Yes,' I agreed, 'I have rather, haven't I?'

'I wish you the very best of luck.'

'Thanks,' I said, 'I'm going to need it. Do you want to have a look around downstairs?'

'Well,' Jay laughed, as we made our way back up to the flat after the grand tour, 'no one could ever accuse you of not taking a risk, Lizzie! No wonder you didn't have the funds to help me out when you had this place in the pipeline!'

I didn't say anything, but my expression must have been enough to show him what I thought of his sly comment.

'I'm sorry,' he teased, 'I'm only kidding, besides my interview with the bank went really well. Fingers crossed, the loan will be approved and even if it isn't, I'll find a way. Now you've moved out of the Cherry Tree I might even ask Jemma about displaying in the crafting space again, as long as you don't mind.'

'Of course I don't,' I said flippantly. 'It's nothing to do with me.'

I left Jay arranging the few smaller pieces of furniture I had decided to bring and went to the kitchen in search of the kettle. I was doing my utmost to keep busy and focused. I wouldn't allow myself to picture either the flat or the crafting area at the Cherry Tree as I had left them; barren and forlorn with my keys in an envelope on the counter. I had considered writing Jemma a letter to accompany them, but I couldn't think of a single nice thing I wanted to say.

'So you're going for good, then?' she asked when I told her that I was moving out of the flat.

'Just for a month to begin with,' I explained, 'but I won't be moving back here even if it doesn't work out.'

She didn't look at me, just carried on buttering bread.

'I'll tell Tom to put an ad in the paper for a new tenant then,' she said. 'Don't forget to leave both sets of keys will you?'

So that was it. According to Jemma, my lifelong friend, I was just one tenant who could be replaced with another. My absence from the Cherry Tree made no apparent difference to her whatsoever. A lump the size of a golf ball lodged itself in my throat as I thought back to our sour exchange. I hastily swallowed it away and carried on filling the kettle.

'Where did you magic that little lot from?' Jay laughed as I rejoined him with a tray full of sandwiches, tea and slices of delectable looking cake.

'Deborah and Heather have stocked the fridge,' I said, 'and they left all this with a welcome note and a promise that they'll call in later.'

'Something tells me you won't be going hungry during the

next few weeks!' Jay laughed, reaching for the largest slice of coffee and walnut he could lay his hands on.

'You will ring me if you need anything, won't you?' he asked as he was getting ready to go later that day, 'anything at all.'

'I will,' I said, 'of course.'

'I don't like to think of you all alone in the big city!'

'I'll be fine,' I laughed. 'I lived in London before, remember? There are plenty of people I can call up and go partying with!'

Henry was hardly the partying kind and I didn't think Giles's heart could cope with the thought of me having a night on the tiles with his new bride, but come to that, Natasha's probably couldn't either. The look of disdain she had given me when she took in my hair and creased shirt suggested that our paths were highly unlikely to cross in the future.

'I'll be off then,' Jay shouted as he turned over the engine. 'You are sure you'll be OK, aren't you?'

'Honestly,' I shouted back, 'I'll be fine. I can't wait to get started!'

Deborah and Heather didn't make it to the flat that evening but Deborah did ring.

'We've only just arrived back,' she seethed. 'The traffic was awful.'

She and Heather had been to the cottage in Norfolk to oversee some building work they were having done.

'Don't worry,' I told her, 'I'll see you in the morning. Everything's fine here. Thanks for the food parcel by the way; it was much appreciated.'

'Oh, don't mention it. And you really don't mind if we don't come tonight?'

'Not at all,' I said again, 'it's been one hell of a day. Shower and an early night before the big day I think.'

'Good plan!' she boomed. 'Fair enough. We'll see you in the morning. Six thirty sound OK?'

'Six thirty will be fine.'

It had taken me so long to get to sleep that night, what with wailing sirens, barking dogs and someone shouting, that the realisation that at five in the morning I was being pulled out of oblivion again was not welcome. I lay in bed watching the shadows of passing cars dance across the ceiling in the sitting room and listened intently.

I could hear muffled voices and distant clattering, definite movement coming from downstairs. I was certain it wasn't burglars because they were making far too much noise but nonetheless I was still nervous about having to investigate.

I crept down and tentatively opened the door behind the shop counter. There were lights on in the kitchen; I could see them under the door. I was just about to retreat to the safety of the flat and telephone Deborah when I heard someone behind me.

'I knew we'd wake you. I said we'd wake you but oh no, she said if we were quiet which she never is, then we'd be fine!'

I stood open-mouthed and too shocked to scream, rooted to the spot staring down at the face of a tiny woman who was beaming up at me.

'I'm Sophia,' she informed me, 'I work in the kitchen with my sister, Maria. We're waiting for the bread guy,' she explained. 'He should have been here by now but he's always late on a Monday. Come and meet Maria.'

I followed dumbly on behind, feeling a complete idiot. Heather had told me there would be staff turning up early to begin work in the kitchen, but in my drowsy state I'd completely forgotten. I tried to smooth my curls behind my ears and wrap my dressing gown a little more securely. This was not how I wanted to introduce myself to the staff on my first morning, or any morning for that matter!

There hadn't been time for introductions to the team the last time I came and I had set my sights on making the right impression when I came back in my official capacity, however it clearly wasn't meant to be and I was going to have to make the best of the situation.

'Hey, Maria!' Sophia called across the sparkling kitchen. 'Look who I found!'

Maria appeared from behind one of the fridges, her face an exact replica of her sister's. They were twins, I realised, and seemingly identical in every way.

'We woke you!' she said aghast. 'I told Sophia we would but she said if we were quiet which she never is, that it'd be fine. I knew it wouldn't be. I did try and tell her!'

'It's fine,' I told her, an overwhelming sense of déjà vu descending, 'I needed to get up anyway.'

'Bread guy's here!' Sophia bawled from the shop floor. 'Finally! He's gonna get a piece of my mind.'

'Help yourself to coffee,' Maria nodded, 'we'll be back in a minute. This guy's gonna get a piece of my mind.'

'I'll grab one in a minute!' I called after them, my head spinning as I wondered if they always repeated what the other said and if so, how did they decide who got to say it first. 'I'm just going to get dressed, but thanks!'

'OK, good morning, everyone,' Deborah beamed at her assembled team. 'As you know, today is going to be something of a red letter day for the City Crafting Café.'

I took a deep breath and offered what I hoped was a confident and reassuring smile. This was it; this was my first day working at the Crafting Café and in spite of my earlier faux pas I was determined to regain some ground and secure myself that all important good first impression.

'Firstly let me begin by introducing you to Lizzie Dixon.'

I widened my smile a little and gave a nod.

'As you know, Lizzie will hopefully be taking over the Café in a few weeks but is joining us now so she can see how things operate.'

'We've met her already,' chirped up Maria and Sophia in unison.

'And we have cakes in the oven,' continued Maria.

'And buns to be iced,' backed up Sophia.

'So if you don't mind?'

'No, ladies, that's fine,' Deborah said, somewhat non-plussed, 'we'll catch up with you in a minute.'

Maria and Sophia disappeared back into the kitchen and we were left with just three other members of staff.

'OK, this is Janice,' Deborah said, introducing me to a smart middle-aged woman who did not look at all pleased to see me.

'Hello, Janice,' I smiled.

'Hi,' she replied frostily.

'Janice is my right-hand woman,' Deborah elaborated. 'She runs the counter on the crafting side, as well as lending a hand in the Café when we're really busy. Sometimes I wonder how she manages with just one pair of hands!'

Janice was still smiling, but no hand-shake was forth-coming.

'And then we have Sasha and Rob who wait on the tables and help Sophia and Maria in the kitchens.'

'Pleased to meet you,' Rob smiled shyly.

'Love your hair,' Sasha beamed, her own a riot of colour.

'Thanks,' I smiled; at least there were two people here who might listen to what I had to say.

Janice was clearly not impressed by my presence and the terrible twins I could tell already would stand for no interference in their kitchen.

'So!' Deborah boomed. 'Felting this morning, knit and natter over lunch and quilting this afternoon. Any problems?'

'If I could just have a quick word about the felting workshop, Deborah?'

'Of course but you better talk to Lizzie. She's the one in charge!'

Oh god, oh god! Please don't let there be a problem already!

'We have no tutor,' Janice said bluntly. 'Annabel phoned me at home last night. Her daughter isn't well so she can't make it.'

Deborah groaned.

'You should have called last night,' she moaned.

Janice looked as if she was well aware of that but, knowing it was my first day, had no intention of making life easy for me.

'I could take the session,' I offered. 'Admittedly I haven't felted anything for a while but if you show me where everything is, Janice, then I'm sure it'll all come back to me. What time does the session begin?'

'Nine thirty,' said Janice, clearly disappointed that I hadn't crumbled.

'Plenty of time,' I smiled, 'let's get on then.'

Ideally I could have done with a few extra hours to get my felting technique back up to speed but I stumbled through the session and thanked my lucky stars that it was a beginners' slot. The knit and natter pretty much ran itself and I had the chance to introduce myself to some of the customers and quiz them about what they loved about the Café and whether there was anything they would change.

The only thing they suggested was that the menu was a little lacking in variety. Needless to say, the thought of tackling Maria and Sophia filled my heart with dread but such problems could be dealt with further down the line.

The afternoon quilting session was an intermediary skill slot so the ladies attending only needed minor input and it soon became clear that they could teach me as much as I could teach them.

'So,' said Sasha, at the end of the day as she sat on one of the tables swinging her legs, 'how was your first day? Did you like it?'

'It was different and very busy,' I told her seriously.

'Good different or bad different?' she quizzed.

'I'll let you know when my head stops spinning!'

'Cool. Right I'm off. I'm gigging tonight.'

'What?' I snorted. 'After a day like this you still have the energy to gig?'

'Oh, this has been nothing!' she laughed. 'You wait until Saturday! You won't know what's hit you!'

Chapter 28

Sasha wasn't wrong. By the end of Saturday afternoon when I finally flipped the shop sign from Open to Closed I was almost dead on my feet. During the previous five days I had partaken in every conceivable craft Granny had taught me, waited on dozens of tables, dealt with a handful of queries, checked what seemed like a thousand orders and had at least half a dozen run-ins with Janice whose dislike of me seemed to be growing daily.

'So,' smiled Heather as we sat together in the Café eating the lasagne and salad Maria and Sophia had kindly plated up, 'any thoughts? How are you finding it?'

'Absolutely exhausting,' I admitted, 'and exhilarating and absolutely nothing like I expected!'

'How do you mean?' Deborah asked.

'It's just so busy,' I said, 'all the time!'

Deborah and Heather laughed and exchanged glances.

'And this is a quiet time,' Deborah told me. 'You wait until the winter. We're inundated from October until, well, March really. Aren't we, Heather?'

Heather nodded in agreement and not for the first time I felt a little knot in my stomach and a question forming in my mind. I hastily brushed both aside, thinking I just needed to up my game, get back up to London-speed rather than the casual laid-back small town pace I'd slipped into at the Cherry Tree.

'How are you finding the staff?' Heather asked tentatively.

'Sasha's a blast and Rob is lovely,' I began, 'Maria and Sophia are fantastic. I didn't know what to make of them to begin with, always arguing with each other and sniping but they seem to run like a well-oiled machine as does the kitchen. However,' I winced, 'I think I might like to make some changes to the menu. Mix things up a bit. What do you think?'

Deborah and Heather exchanged further glances but this time didn't comment.

'How about Janice?' Deborah asked. 'Has she been giving you any trouble?'

'Well, you've been here, Deborah,' I said, deciding not to hold back, 'sometimes she's been downright rude and in front of the customers. I don't know what I've done to upset her but if she's the same next week I'm going to have to say something. Is that OK?'

This time it was Heather who spoke up.

'We perhaps should have mentioned it before,' she began but Deborah cut her off.

'What Heather wants to say and I should have let her say it before you came really.'

'Yes?'

'Is that Janice was the other interested party.'

'You mean she wanted to buy this place?' I gasped. 'She was the other buyer who was hanging on?'

Deborah and Heather nodded.

'God, I wish I'd known. Why didn't you say anything?'

'We didn't want to make it awkward for you,' Heather said.

'And we thought she'd be OK,' Deborah chimed in.

'But she isn't OK, is she?' I frowned. 'How long has she worked for you, Deborah?'

'About fifteen years.'

'And did she have any reason to think that you might sell to her?'

'We had touched on it in the past, but not in any detail.'

'So she thinks I've just elbowed my way in and taken the opportunity that should've been hers! The poor woman, no wonder she can't stand the sight of me.'

This was clearly a problem that needed addressing. If I was going to buy the Crafting Café, any issues between us were going to have to be resolved. Janice was fantastic at her job and the customers clearly loved her. I couldn't afford to lose her. I decided to wait another week to see if the dust settled and then, if it didn't, I'd have to say something.

The following week passed in much the same vein as the first. Thankfully Janice did relent a little in her assault, but to be honest, every day was so packed I probably wouldn't have noticed if she hadn't. With courses running both mornings and afternoons and then a more sociable, less structured event over lunch, there was hardly time during the day to draw breath.

As I ticked the days off on my calendar, it became increasingly obvious that I was never going to have any time to do any crafting myself. I had been planning to make things to sell in the shop but at the end of every day I was just too tired and had to accept that that was never going to happen.

The second week I'd been less involved with the crafting sessions as well. Various tutors had appeared and taken charge of the classes leaving me to deal with the mountains of paperwork and seemingly endless invoices that would be my responsibility when Deborah finally cut the apron strings.

I had hoped to catch up with Henry and see a bit of the city at some point, but I was at the mercy of the Café and its incessant demands and any free time I did manage to squeeze out of the day was no good for him and his new girlfriend.

'We really do want to see you, Lizzie,' he told me, 'but Sundays are a definite no-go, I'm afraid.'

'Don't worry,' I told him, willing my tired self not to cry, 'I'll probably be asleep all day anyway.'

'When are your parents back?' he asked brightly. 'Can't they come and see you?'

'No,' I said, 'they're not due back before my month here is up.'

'Well, what about that Jay chap? You said you weren't holding a grudge, especially after he helped you with the move. Why don't you ask him?'

So I did.

I think Jay was a little overwhelmed by the reception he received when he turned up at the flat the following Saturday evening. It had been one hell of a week and as the pressure had built up I was beginning to feel more and more homesick, and not just for the Cherry Tree and my flat either.

I couldn't deny that I was missing Jemma and Tom and Ella, and of course Ben. It didn't matter that they'd all deceived me and kept me in the dark – if any of them had turned up and offered to take me home I would have jumped at the chance, but they didn't, so I made do with the next best thing Wynbridge could offer.

'How was your journey?' I asked, standing on tip-toe and kissing him on the cheek.

'It was OK,' he frowned, clearly confused by my demonstrative welcome. 'How are you?'

I shrugged and let out a long breath. I wanted to tell him everything; that it wasn't what I expected, that it was beginning to dawn on me that it wasn't what I wanted, that actually I just wanted to go home, but that had all been hard enough to admit to myself and given Jay's track record I wasn't sure he wouldn't go running home on Monday morning and tell everyone else.

'I'm good,' I said wearily, 'I'm knackered but I'm good.'

'You look knackered,' he said, staring down at me.

'Oh thanks.'

'Sorry, you know what I mean.'

'Yeah, you mean I look knackered! Don't worry about it. I know I do. Getting back up to London speed is taking a bit longer than I thought.'

'How about we stay in tonight then?' Jay suggested.

His words were music to my ears.

'And eat takeaway out of the containers?' I asked hopefully.

'And drink this?' he grinned, producing a very tempting-looking bottle of Prosecco from his bag. 'A little bird told me you like it and I thought it might do you more good than cider!'

By nine thirty I was stuffed, sleepy and a little squiffy. We had talked about nothing important, opting instead to watch the TV rather than chat while we ate but I couldn't put it off any longer. I couldn't go to bed not knowing.

'So how are things at the Cherry Tree?' I asked, picking up a stray strand of noodle from the floor. 'Have you been in at all?'

'A couple of times,' Jay shrugged, draining his glass, 'it all looks a bit sad what with the crafting area still empty and everything.'

My heart thumped a little harder at the thought that it was still there, just waiting for me to bring it back to life again.

'Everyone was gutted when they found out you'd gone. I think Tom's tried to find someone else to take it over but had no luck and as far as I know it's the same with the flat.'

'That's a shame,' I said, feeling torn between disappointment and delight, 'but what about your frames? Aren't you going to display them in the Café now?'

I thought about the solitary framed picture that I had left behind. I'd desperately wanted to bring it with me but I hadn't. I couldn't bear the thought of having such an emotionally charged reminder of the place and it didn't really belong to me anyway; it was part of the Café and besides, it would have looked out of place here in the flat which was more like a modern loft apartment.

'I haven't seen Jemma much,' Jay carried on, 'I did ask her the first week you'd gone and she said she'd think about it, but she hasn't been in touch since.'

'Well, I hope she makes up her mind soon,' I told him. 'That long back wall would be perfect for you and they could quite easily extend the Café tables if they can't find anyone to take over the crafting.'

I couldn't understand why they hadn't just got on with it already. It wouldn't take much effort to switch things around.

'How did you get on with the bank?' I asked, suddenly remembering Jay's loan appointment. 'Are you finally up and running?'

'They said no,' he murmured, pouring the last dregs of Prosecco into my glass. 'They turned me down.'

'But why?' I gaped. 'I thought it was a done deal.'

'So did I,' Jay said sadly. 'So no, it's still not happening, I'm afraid.'

I was sorry Jay hadn't got his money and his dream. Part of me still felt responsible for dashing his hopes.

'Would it be any help while you're waiting for Jemma to make up her mind, if I asked Deborah to offer you some wall space downstairs?' I suggested. 'I'm sure we could move things around so you could display at least four or five and then when I take over you could have more.'

'I don't know,' Jay frowned, rubbing his chin.

'It would be better than nothing,' I told him, 'Londoners are always prepared to pay a premium and I'm sure you'd get a really good take-up rate,' I continued, warming to my theme. 'The Café is bound to attract the sort of people who would be interested in what you have to offer. Come on, let's go down now and have a look.'

The wall opposite the counter was the perfect spot for Jay's frames and there was even some room in the Café area.

'You know, I might take you up on this idea,' Jay said, scanning the potential spot I was suggesting. 'Even if people are just popping in for a minute, they'll still see them up there, won't they?'

'Exactly,' I smiled, leaning against the counter, 'and you could have some cards or leaflets made up and we can give them out to anyone who enquires. It's definitely worth considering, don't you think?'

'If I can find the money to make up some samples then I'll definitely take you up on it,' he replied.

Gently he slipped his hands around my waist and pulled me to him. I swallowed. This wasn't what I had in mind when I asked him to visit but as he tucked a stray curl behind my ear and bent to kiss me, his lips brushing mine so softly that I felt my knees buckle, I knew it was now.

Sleeping late on a Sunday was one luxury I had really come to appreciate over the last couple of weekends and that morning was no exception. I stretched in the bed, my memories of the night before still a hazy blur but I knew, as I felt my bare skin touching the sheets, that last night I had definitely gone further with Jay than I had during my cider-soaked encounter.

I reached out to draw him close but my grasp met only a

cold bed sheet and my head was immediately filled with a terrible sense of foreboding. The last time I'd been in bed with a man and awoken to find his side of the mattress empty, things had not ended well for me.

I slipped into my dressing gown and after exploring the flat to make sure Jay hadn't deserted me completely I realised he must have gone back downstairs to look at the space I'd suggested for displaying his frames.

'Jay?' I whispered, as I entered the Café.

He wasn't there and neither were the keys to the office. I crept behind the counter as quietly as I could, the fact that I had gone into stealth mode already telling me that whatever he was up to, I knew it wasn't going to be good. I could see he was in the office because the door was slightly ajar. On the desk in front of him along with the now empty petty cash tin, I could make out the Crafting Café accounts and a pile of bank statements.

I couldn't think what to do and didn't know how he would react if I tackled him in such a confined space so I crept back upstairs and climbed into bed, feigning sleep until he reappeared and slipped in beside me.

'Morning, sleepy head,' he smiled, running a hand lightly down my back.

I shivered slightly but knew I had to keep up the pretence.

'Morning,' I yawned, rolling over and keeping the sheet tight around me.

'How are you feeling?' he asked, a smile playing around his lips.

'Not as hung over as I was after the cider,' I admitted.

'I'm not surprised,' he replied, 'you've been asleep for hours. You've probably slept it off!'

'I have?'

'Can't you remember?' he grinned. 'By the time I came out of the bathroom last night you were in bed fast asleep!'

'Oh,' I said, feeling hugely relieved.

'You really can't remember?' Jay laughed.

I shook my head.

'Well,' he said, 'if it's any consolation I was the perfect gentleman, as always.'

And that, given the sordid little scene I'd just witnessed downstairs, was something I was very grateful for.

'I'm going to have a quick shower,' I told him, 'then we'll go out for lunch, if you like. I know the perfect place.'

There was a certain irony to the fact that I'd picked the same bar to tackle Jay in as I had chosen to give Giles back all the crap he had piled on me in his efforts to transform me when we lived together.

'This place looks nice,' Jay said as he pulled out my chair, 'I could get used to living in London.'

I didn't say anything. I wanted to hear what he was going to suggest next.

'Actually,' he said ponderously, as if the idea had just come to him, 'that spare room of yours . . .'

'What about it?' I asked innocently.

'Well, if you ever want to fill it, put me top of the list would you?'

'What a brilliant idea!' I smiled enthusiastically. 'I'm sure you'd get loads of freelance journo work here in the city and you'd be right on hand for the framing business if you did decide to display them in the City Crafting Café.'

'Crikey,' he said, wide-eyed. 'Yeah, I hadn't thought of that!'

'I'd actually been toying with the idea of renting out the spare room,' I told him seriously. 'I'm thinking of making some changes to the Café, you see, and I was worried there might be a dip in turnover for a while, but if you were paying city rent that wouldn't be half as much of a concern.'

The change in him was barely noticeable, but I noticed. His expression and demeanour told me he wasn't planning on paying rent at all.

'I'll go and get us a drink,' he said. 'What do you fancy?'

'Red wine, please.'

With our meal ordered and glasses half empty I led the conversation back to the night we'd spent together at the Cherry Tree.

'I still feel bad about letting you down over the money you needed,' I told him, reaching across the table to take his hand. 'I never meant to get your hopes up.'

Jay didn't say anything but shifted a little in his seat.

'It's just so unlike me, you see,' I pushed on. 'My dad has always taught me to be so cautious about lending money. I guess I'd had a bit more cider than I realised!'

'Never mind about that now,' Jay said, patting my hand, 'everything to do with the Cherry Tree is best forgotten, if you ask me, especially now you've got bigger fish to fry and besides you might have a change of heart again when you've bought the Crafting Café and are making the changes you mentioned. I bet the place is making a pretty penny already, isn't it?'

'It's holding its own,' I smiled sweetly, 'but you already know that, don't you?'

'What do you mean?'

'You already know exactly how much the business is making, along with how much was in the petty cash tin.'

'What are you talking about?' he said, colour flooding his face.

'Jay, I saw you this morning,' I said resignedly, 'I saw you in the office going through the Café papers and accounts.'

Jay placed his glass back on the table and sat back in his chair.

'Look,' he said, recovering in less than a second, 'I know it looks really bad, but I was just worried about you, that's all.'

'How do you work that one out?' I frowned.

'I was worried that you wouldn't really know what you were looking at when it came to the money side of the business and I wanted to make sure you weren't investing in something that was heading for a fall.'

'You patronising git!'

'Jesus, I was only trying to help. You do have something of a reputation for letting your heart rule your head when it comes to money, Lizzie, don't you?'

'What the hell does that mean?'

'Well, the Cherry Tree for a start. You haven't exactly made the best judgement call there, have you? You'll be lucky to see a penny of your granny's inheritance again.'

'How do you know about my inheritance?'

'People talk, Lizzie, especially in the pub. Everyone knows you've come into some money since you came back.'

'But what business is that of yours?' I scowled. 'What makes you think you have any right to interfere in what I decide to do with one penny of my money?'

'Look, I really like you, Lizzie, and I just don't want to see you make another mistake.'

'Because if I do then you know I won't have enough to help you out, is that it?'

Jay didn't say anything else; he just shrugged. He knew the game was up and clearly he couldn't be bothered to invest any more time trying to cover his tracks or make me believe his cock and bull story. He was a fraudster, a trickster a con man and a thief on the look-out for an easy target and a way of making a fast buck.

'Are you actually interested in setting up a framing business at all?' I asked him, my heart sinking as I realised what an idiot I must have looked.

'No,' he laughed, 'of course not. Do I look like the sort of bloke who can frame a bloody picture?'

'But what about the Cherry Tree frame?' I demanded. 'How did you pull that one off?'

'I have an uncle in the trade,' he said casually. 'He knocked it up for me and together we made it look pretty.'

I was devastated. I'd genuinely believed Jay had a real talent and a potentially successful business up his sleeve, but it turned out he was just on the take. What a fool he had made me look – made us all look.

'Perhaps you should introduce me to him then,' I said scathingly, 'he's got quite a gift, it would be a shame to waste it.'

Chapter 29

I didn't say anything to Deborah and Heather about Jay's visit. Obviously I was embarrassed to have been duped, but worse than that, I was terrified that if I hadn't seen through Jay's scheme to fund his 'once in a lifetime trip around the globe', then the City Crafting Café would have been financially ruined. I decided to keep quiet, cut Jay out of my life completely and carry on regardless.

I replaced the money he'd taken from the petty cash tin and took all the business paperwork out of the office and up to the flat for further scrutiny. Every evening during the following week I sat going through the books, walking around the Café and trying to find a commercial rather than an emotional reason for not wanting to take the business on.

Jay's scathing remark about my heart ruling my head had wormed its way into my brain and sat there festering. I knew that if I didn't take the plunge and commit to the City

Crafting Café it would be because I had let my heart get the upper hand again. Now was the time to dig deep, I realised, and I did my best to swing into 'focused and driven business-woman mode' before I did something I would possibly regret in later life.

Creating a better working relationship with Janice was top of the list that I frantically penned as I tried to rediscover my excitement for the project. If I wanted there to be a smooth transition between Deborah and myself, then I knew her input would be key.

'How would you feel about managing the shop one day a week, Janice,' I asked in as friendly a tone as I could, 'possibly two?'

I had been trying to find a way to schedule some free time into my week. Of course when I said 'free time' what I really meant was time to spend on my own crafting projects. If I was really going to make the commitment and sign on the dotted line then there were certain things that I was not prepared to sacrifice and some private sewing time was one of them.

After much thought, I had settled on asking Janice to help out as the ideal solution. Not only would I claw back some hours, but my suggestion would also, hopefully, go some way to reassuring her that I wasn't going to shoe-horn her out at the earliest possible opportunity.

'How much will you pay me?' she sniffed.

'Pardon?'

'To manage the shop. You wouldn't expect me to take on the extra responsibility and not pay me for it, would you?'

'No, of course not,' I blushed, my proposition already in tatters, 'I was just asking to see how you would feel about it in theory, that's all.'

'Well, if it's just a theory,' she shrugged, 'I suppose I wouldn't mind, assuming I'm still here of course,' she added mysteriously.

'Is there any reason why you wouldn't be?' I asked, trying not to show my concern.

Panic set in at the thought of taking over without Janice at her station behind the counter. We might not have hit it off exactly but at least she knew how the place ran! I was still way too far behind even to consider flying solo. She looked at what must have been my stricken expression and miraculously her face softened slightly.

'There's a shop become available in the parade,' she said, blushing slightly, 'might be too good an opportunity to miss but please don't say anything to Deborah,' she added. 'It might come to nothing if the rent's too high.'

I nodded and sighed, wishing not for the first time that we could have got along. Janice's business acumen rivalled Deborah's and coupled with my passion for crafting we would have ensured the Café's future. I was sure of that. I looked up, expecting her to have gone back to the shop floor, but she hadn't moved.

'I'm sorry I've been such a cow,' she said, quietly closing the door, 'it isn't you; I know you're a lovely girl and I'm sure you'll be very successful. It's just that—'

'You thought you were going to be sitting this side of the desk when Deborah decided to move on?'

'Exactly,' she nodded sadly, 'but she picked you. I know it's my own fault and I shouldn't be taking it out on you. I am sorry.'

'There's no need to apologise,' I smiled, 'I do understand. If I was in your shoes I'd feel exactly the same, but tell me, Janice, what makes you say that it's your fault?'

'Well, for a start I never really rushed to tell Deborah that I might want to take over when she first hinted that she was ready to move on.'

'But I thought that you were the other interested party?'

'Oh I was,' she sighed, 'but to be honest it was such a huge decision that it took me a while to make up my mind and get the ball rolling and by that time she'd been to see you.'

'But I never said yes straightaway,' I said, 'I told Deborah that I'd think about it, that was all.'

'Well, you know Deborah when she's got her heart set on something. She was sure you were the one and I hadn't the heart to make a fuss. I didn't want to rock the boat. When she said that you were coming for a month's trial and that we'd talk again after that I thought it would be OK. I love working here,

Lizzie, you know I've been here forever and I didn't want to jeopardise my job so I just withdrew my interest and let Deborah get on with things.'

'But you do still want the place really, don't you?'

Janice nodded.

'If she offered it to me now,' she admitted, 'I'd snatch her hand off but I took one look at you and I knew it was too late. You're just what this place needs, Lizzie.'

'I'm not so sure about that,' I smiled. I was unsure as to where these great ideas about me had sprung from. 'You know what people want as much as I do. I dare say you're glued to the Sewing Bee and read every crafting magazine on the market, don't you?'

'Well actually,' she whispered, leaning forward in her seat, 'I have got one or two new ideas.'

Having cleared the air with Janice, my heart and head were back in sync and I knew what I was going to do. The City Crafting Café was one hell of a business but it was too much for me. I felt a huge weight lift as I reached my final decision, but then it descended again at the thought of telling Deborah and Heather.

'I assume this is good news!' Deborah boomed as I welcomed her and Heather into the flat later that day. 'You've made up your mind, haven't you? And still with a week to go!' she laughed. 'You certainly haven't let the grass grow, Lizzie, I'll say that for you!'

'Deborah dear,' Heather smiled gently touching Deborah's arm, 'why don't you let her speak, my love?'

'Sorry!' Deborah said, shaking her head, 'I'm just so . . .'

'Deborah,' Heather interjected a little more forcefully this time.

'OK,' I smiled nervously as they squeezed together on the tiny sofa, 'OK. Crikey, I'm not quite sure where to start.'

I looked from Deborah to Heather and took a deep breath. The look of expectation on Deborah's face almost made me change my mind, but I had to stand firm.

'Well,' I swallowed, sitting down and rubbing my damp palms together, 'I've really enjoyed my time at the Café. It's been a definite eye-opener and the place is fantastic, but—'

'But?' Deborah demanded.

'But it isn't for you, is it?' Heather said gently.

'No,' I said shakily, 'it isn't.'

'I didn't think so,' she said, quietly, squeezing Deborah's hand.

'It's nothing to do with the staff,' I babbled, 'or any of the courses, it's just . . .'

'Too much?' Heather suggested.

I nodded.

'Don't get me wrong,' I carried on, 'the place is buzzing and I love what you offer but I just don't want to be a manager. I want to be more hands-on, running all the courses and getting really involved and I'm not sure I can face moving back to London either.'

'Home is where the heart is,' Heather added for good measure.

'Yes,' I smiled, 'I couldn't have put it better myself.'

Deborah hadn't said a word. She sat still and silent next to Heather, her complexion growing darker with every word she heard. Any second, I was poised to throw myself over the back of the chair and take cover.

'Well,' she said eventually, 'all I can say, Lizzie, is that I'm sorry.'

'Sorry?' I asked, completely thrown. 'For what?'

'When I came to see you at the Cherry Tree,' she explained, 'I could see how happy you were, how you'd created the perfect space for what you wanted your business to be.'

'I had,' I said sadly, an image of the crafting area, complete with bunting and pastel painted tins swam before my eyes.

'And I took advantage of what you'd achieved.'

'How?'

'By assuming you'd want more. I thought you'd jump at the chance to take on this place but I can see now that you already had what you really wanted. You'd achieved what you'd always dreamt of and you'd got the balance just right. If I hadn't offered you this place so forthrightly you never would have considered moving on, would you?'

'No,' I said uncertainly, still mindful of all the other reasons behind my decision to leave. 'I guess not.'

'And now I've blown it for you,' Deborah said sadly.

I couldn't allow that.

'No, Deborah,' I told her firmly, 'things were spoilt at the Cherry Tree, but not by you. Even if you hadn't proposed I took on the Crafting Café I probably still wouldn't be there. Too many other things had happened behind the scenes to make it viable for me to carry on.'

'So what will you do now?' Heather asked.

'I honestly don't know,' I said resignedly, 'I can't get my head around the future right now, deciding not to buy this place has been enough for one day but more to the point, what will you do?'

'Go back to the agent, I guess,' Deborah shrugged, 'get the place back on the market.'

'No,' I said, 'I wouldn't do that if I were you.'

'Well, what do you suggest then?' Deborah said, a hint of annoyance creeping in for the first time since we all sat down together. 'We're not giving up the cottage. I promised Heather we'd retire and we are!'

'I'm not suggesting you give anything up!' I laughed. 'Just go and talk to Janice.'

'She's not really interested in the place,' Deborah frowned.

'I think you'll find she is,' Heather said, patting her companion's knee. 'Are you coming back down, Lizzie?'

'No, I don't think I will, if that's OK. Now I've made up my mind I'm not going to buy I'm going to get packed and get out of your hair.'

'You don't have to!' Deborah insisted. 'There's no rush, and besides you said yourself you hadn't made up your mind what you're going to do, so where will you go?'

'I think I need a break,' I said, suddenly remembering Jay's dream of seeing the world. 'My stuff can go back to my parents' place and then I think I might take off for a while. Have a little holiday and stop thinking about everything so much.'

'Sounds like a good idea to me,' Heather smiled. 'Have you got anywhere in mind?'

'Wherever the wind blows me!' I laughed.

Chapter 30

It didn't take long to pack my few sticks of furniture and boxes ready for the return journey, but how to get them to my parents' house was proving something of an issue. Having parted company with Jay after discovering his malicious motives meant that I was a van driver down and Dad was still out of the country.

'I could help you out,' Henry offered, 'if you're really desperate, but I won't be free for a few weekends I'm afraid.'

'Thanks, Henry, I appreciate the offer. I'm sorry we haven't managed to get together.'

'So am I,' he replied, 'I really wanted you to meet Cass. I think she could be the one,' he added in a clandestine whisper, 'I really do.'

'I'm so pleased for you, Henry,' I said. 'Out of everyone I know who is still single, you are the one person who shouldn't be!'

'What about you?' Henry replied. 'We've got to get you spliced soon!'

'Oh don't worry about me,' I told him, 'when I get back from this holiday I'm buying a couple of cats and my fate will be sealed! Look, I've got to go, someone's at the door.'

'OK, but promise you'll keep me posted about this move?'

'I promise.'

'And any kittens?'

'Of course!' I laughed.

I threw my mobile on the sofa thinking I was going to have to hire a removal firm to help me out and crossed the room to answer the door. It was Rob.

'Hey, Rob,' I smiled, 'what's up? Is everything OK downstairs?'

'There's a guy in the Café asking for you,' he said shyly.

'Is there?' I asked. 'What's his name?'

I knew it couldn't be Henry because we'd just been chatting on the phone. The only other 'guy' who knew where to find me was Jay. My heart sank. What did the rat want this time?

'Sorry, I didn't ask his name,' Rob apologised, 'but he's really cute. Shall I send him up or do you want to come down?'

'Oh send him up,' I sighed, 'if it's who I think it is I can't imagine the conversation will be polite enough for the ladies in the Café.'

'Sure?'

'Yeah go on, quick before I change my mind.'

While waiting for Rob to send Jay up I wondered how he'd travelled to London and whether I could bring myself to ask him if he'd give me and my stuff a lift home.

'Make it quick,' I snapped on hearing him running up the stairs, 'I have to be somewhere.'

'Hello, Lizzie.'

Oh god. That voice. It could only be –

'How did you find me?' I gasped, spinning around. 'Who told you I was here?'

'Does it matter?'

'Of course it matters!' I gulped, my voice cracking from the shock, 'I bet Jemma told you, didn't she? Well, she had no right to. She and Tom have done enough damage already. I don't want to see you, Ben. I don't want you here. Please leave.'

'Not until you hear what I have to say.'

He looked exhausted, his brow deeply furrowed, but I didn't care for any of what he had to say. I didn't care that my stomach had done that annoying flip thing again or that my heart was hammering so hard against my ribcage that I expected to look down and see it bursting through my shirt.

'All I ever do is listen to what you have to say!' I shouted. 'And I never feel any better for it! I told you the last time you should have sent a text and saved yourself the journey.'

'I have been bloody texting!' he shouted, crossing the room and snatching my phone up off the sofa. 'Here! Look! Dozens of the bloody things stacked up unread. You left me no choice but to come and find you, Lizzie.'

'You could have phoned the Café,' I said, struggling to keep my voice level and my emotions in check.

'Look, just shut up and sit down, will you?' Ben demanded.

'No,' I said flinging open the flat door, 'just say whatever it is you think is so important and bugger off.'

'OK,' he sighed, running his hands through his hair, 'fine. Have it your way.'

I stared back at him, my chin held stubbornly high ready for the next instalment of the Ben and Natasha sob saga. Perhaps my visit had got Natasha thinking about him and now they were getting back together. Perhaps they wanted Giles and me to give it another go and make up a cosy four-some at the flat.

'It's Jemma.'

'What about Jemma?' I snapped, feeling confused.

'She's not been well,' Ben began, then stopped.

'Do you mean she's had a cold or she's been *really* ill?' I demanded, my heart hammering for a different reason.

'She's been really ill,' he said, biting his lip, 'she's pregnant, you see.'

'She's what?'

'She's pregnant, just a couple of months, but she's been trying to keep the Café going and look after Ella and everything else.'

'Oh, for god's sake, Ben!' I shouted. 'Just spit it out, will you?'

'She's in hospital,' he said finally. 'She might lose the baby.'

'Why didn't you say this as soon as you walked in?' I demanded. 'Why didn't you come sooner?'

'I wanted to but I didn't know whether I should. I didn't want to interfere. Tom and Angela had been nagging her to take it easy for weeks but she wouldn't and now, well, now she's in real trouble.'

'But she hasn't lost the baby?'

'No, but she still might. Everything's a right mess, Lizzie. Tom says they'll have to close the Cherry Tree. Angela can't manage all alone and there's no one else Jemma trusts to keep it going.'

'I don't believe this,' I sobbed, dropping down on to the sofa. 'I don't bloody believe this. None of this would have happened if I hadn't left.'

'You can't say that!' Ben frowned. 'It was us that made you leave. It was my fault that Jemma and Tom had to keep my stupid secret from you. If anyone's to blame for all this mess it's me, you know it is. Come back with me, Lizzie,' he begged. 'Come back and we'll put it all right.'

*

Apart from a freak encounter with a kitchen knife whilst parting frozen pork chops I had managed to stay relatively injury-free throughout my adult life and consequently out of hospital. Since my return to Wynbridge, however, two of the people I loved most in the world had been in-patients and forced me through the doors into that most daunting of environments.

'I know we're a bit late for visiting,' I whispered to the statuesque nurse who was standing guard outside Jemma's door, 'but we've travelled up from London and the traffic was horrific. I promise we won't be many minutes,' I pleaded, 'I just want to see her.'

'Go on then,' she said, 'but it will only be for a few minutes.'

'Thank you,' I whispered, 'I really appreciate it. Are you coming in?' I asked Ben.

He had driven me back at break-neck speed, my few belongings crammed into his battered old estate car and balanced precariously on the roof rack. We hadn't talked much, both lost in our private world of complications and regrets.

'No, I'll wait out here,' he said, plonking himself tiredly on a chair outside the door, 'and then I'll drive you to the house. Give her my love though, won't you?'

I took a deep breath and pushed open the heavy door. The lamp next to the bed cast a dim light across the sheets and Jemma's pale, sad face.

'Lizzie!' she gasped. 'Oh my god!'

'Now then,' I said sternly, 'don't start any of that or I'll be thrown out.'

I sat in the chair by her side and stroked her hand and kissed it.

'Ben's told me everything that's happened;' I said quietly, 'so don't go through it all again now. How are you feeling?'

'Better than I was,' she said, smiling weakly, 'so far so good,' she said, squeezing my hand, her few words speaking volumes.

'Why didn't you tell me?'

'I was going to after the first scan,' she said, 'like I did with Ella, remember?'

I smiled at the memory. She had taken me out for lunch and given me a card to open. It wasn't my birthday or Christmas but when the scan photo fell out of the envelope I had felt even more excited than if it was.

'I remember,' I said. 'I didn't even know you'd been trying this time round.'

'We weren't,' she laughed. 'I think we can blame this one on a night in the pub and one of Tom's bloody Mumford tributes!'

'I thought that turned you off rather than on!'

'Depends on how much I've had to drink.'

'Oh,' I laughed, 'I see.'

'I don't know how we're going to cope, though,' she said,

her fleeting smile suddenly replaced with a frown, 'there's no way I can run the Cherry Tree *and* Ella *and* a baby. It's just not possible.'

'Of course it is,' I told her firmly, 'that's what I'm here for.'

'Are you coming back?' she asked, wide-eyed. 'Are you really thinking about coming back?'

I nodded.

'But what about all the other stuff?' she asked. 'All the arguments and stupid bloody secrets?'

'Jemma,' I said, looking right at her, 'does any of that *really* matter now?'

'I don't know,' she said worriedly, 'Tom and I should have never agreed to keep Ben's secret just because he got to us first. We should have made him tell you sooner but it was just so difficult. I know you think I have the perfect life, Lizzie, and in many ways I do and I wanted you to have that too. I wanted to make sure that nothing could hurt you again but I got it all wrong. I'm so sorry.'

'No,' I said, shaking my head, 'we were all in a difficult position, each and every one of us. We were all to blame in one way or another but none of us were wholly responsible for the mess, but now you're having a baby, Jemma, another Ella, and nothing matters beyond making sure you're fit and well. Do you understand that?'

I watched as a single tear rolled down Jemma's cheek and tried to swallow away the lump in my throat.

'Now get some sleep,' I commanded, 'I'll come back tomorrow night.'

'Not in the morning?' she sniffed.

'No, of course not in the morning, you silly bugger. I'll be helping Angela at the Cherry Tree!'

I didn't think it could be possible for anyone to look more washed out than Jemma, but Tom did and the fact that Ella was already in bed and asleep, having made no fuss about going up even though she knew there was a chance I might turn up, pretty much broke my heart.

'I'm so pleased you're here, Lizzie,' Tom cried, grabbing hold of me and squeezing me tight. 'I'm so glad you agreed to come back. I don't think I've ever been so scared in my life.'

'Not even that time when Jemma's dad caught the pair of you in the garden shed?' I reminded him, trying to lighten the atmosphere.

'Not even then,' he smiled, releasing me and wiping his eyes on his shirt sleeve. 'Please tell me you're staying?' he begged.

'Of course I'm staying,' I told him.

I didn't think it was necessary to add that I didn't know how long for. There was no point making the situation any more stressful and besides I wouldn't be going anywhere until my best mate was one hundred per cent better.

'Can I stay here, though,' I asked, 'at yours, just until Mum and Dad get back?'

'Not at the flat?' Ben frowned, as he passed me a big mug of tea and a plateful of thickly sliced buttered toast.

'I thought it would be easier if I was on hand for Ella,' I lied, reaching for the marmalade, 'so Tom can focus on Jemma without having to worry.'

'Thanks, Lizzie,' Tom said gratefully, 'that would be a huge weight off my mind. Yes of course, stay as long as you want.'

I didn't dare look at Ben.

With Ella hugged, washed, dressed, fed, hugged again and dropped off at Tom's mum's house the following morning, there was nothing stopping me from rushing off to help Angela open up the Cherry Tree. Fear, excitement and a hint of trepidation bubbled through my veins as I made my way along the road, wondering if the place had changed in the few weeks I'd been away. I turned the last corner in the road and there it was; The Cherry Tree Café in all its glory and it had changed, but only a little.

Now the weather was warmer and less changeable, Tom had arranged the sets of metal tables and chairs under the canopy of the cherry tree. They were a timely reminder that the year was moving on fast.

Tom had given me his set of keys, which included one for the flat, but I had no intention of venturing up there for the time being. Working in the Café was going to be enough of a jolt. As I swung open the little picket gate and secured it on the hook behind to indicate that we were open, the Café door was flung back on its hinges and Angela ran up the path, her arms outstretched.

'I don't think I've ever been more pleased to see anyone in my whole life!' she said, pulling me into a suffocating hug, 'and that's really saying something coming from a woman whose family live on the other side of the world!'

'Hello, Angela,' I smiled, 'it's good to see you too!'

'Come on, let's get inside and get cracking. Come and see what I've got!' she said impishly.

Everything inside the Café was perfect and to be honest it didn't look like Angela had been struggling at all. I didn't dare ask just exactly how late she had been staying to make sure everything was ship-shape for the next day. The bags under her pretty eyes were proof enough that it was late.

'Here you go,' she beamed, 'all washed and pressed! I knew I'd see you in it again one day!'

I felt my throat tighten as Angela spun me around, tying my apron in place. It was every bit as pretty as I remembered and everything in the Café was as simple and straightforward as I remembered and I loved it, but I knew in my heart that it would be too much of a struggle for me to move back permanently. I'd overheard Ben telling Tom that he was definitely settling back in Wynbridge and I just didn't know how

I would cope with the risk of running into him on a daily basis.

'Thank you, Angela,' I smiled as I fondly patted the heart-shaped pocket and reached for my order book and pen from the counter. 'What would you like me to do?'

'First item on the agenda today,' Angela instructed, 'is a nice cup of tea for the workers, don't you think? It's market day today, remember? Give it an hour or so and we'll be rushed off our feet.'

We sat together at one of the tables and I ran my hands lightly over the painted chair next to me. It felt like a lifetime since I'd sanded and primed until my hands were raw. So much had happened; too much.

'Penny for them,' Angela asked as she refilled my cup.

'I couldn't possibly tell you,' I said quietly, my bottom lip trembling, 'I can't even make sense of them myself.'

Late that afternoon when I finally closed the gate and locked the door we'd sold out of practically everything and an evening of baking stretched ahead. Part of me wished I hadn't been so stubborn about the flat. Nothing would have been nicer than to pop upstairs for an invigorating shower and half an hour to recuperate before starting work again. Tom's keys weighed heavy in my pocket. The flat was drawing me in; the key to the door was my very own One Ring.

'I'm just going to nip up to the flat,' I called after Angela's retreating back.

'OK,' she shouted as she raced off home, 'I'll be back as soon as I've fed the cat and then you can pop off and see Jemma when we've got the cakes in!'

Tentatively I turned the key and pushed open the flat door. I'd been expecting the place to smell fusty and the air to be stale, but the place felt as fresh as it did the last time I was there. The majority of things were still in situ and whether it was because I was tired or whether it was something else, more than ever the little place felt like home.

A light breeze from the open window in the kitchen stirred the curtains and something on the table caught my attention. A huge vase of pale pink roses filled the tabletop, their heady perfume filling the air.

'I knew you wouldn't be able to resist.'

I spun round. Ben was standing in the hallway leaning against the wall with his hands in his pockets, his ankles crossed and a shadow of his former beard clearly visible on his chin. My stupid stomach did a loop the loop and my heart joined in the betrayal, bouncing about like a jack-in-the-box straining to be released.

'Did you want something?' I asked. 'Is everything all right? It isn't Jemma, is it?'

'Everything's fine,' he smiled, pushing himself off the wall and walking towards me. 'Tom called, the hospital has said

Jemma can come home the day after tomorrow as long as she doesn't come back to work and takes it easy at home.'

The relief was overwhelming but I would not allow myself to cry; I'd done enough of that lately.

'Well, that's great,' I said shakily, 'such a relief.'

Ben was standing just inches from me now, his gaze bearing down on me.

'Was there something else?' I swallowed.

'Just one more thing.'

'What?'

'I love you,' he smiled.

Epilogue

Waking late on a Monday, usually the first day of the working week, was a rare treat. I rolled over and blinked at the clock on the bedside table. I knew it was far later than I would usually wake; the light was a dead giveaway. Seven thirty, not all that late but to me, who was usually on the go before six these days, it felt like half the day had passed me by. I lay back and let the warm, soft breeze from the open window caress my face as gently as a lover's tender kiss. There was no noise from the Café kitchen and the murmur of distant traffic was unusually quiet.

August bank holiday weekend was upon us and I could hardly believe how much time had passed since I'd returned once again to Wynbridge and the comfort and healing warmth of family and friends. Since Jemma's pregnancy scare, Angela and I had been practically running the Café, but somehow I had still managed to oversee the crochet and knitting circles and run a dozen more crafting and sewing sessions along with some holiday classes specifically for family groups.

The sewing classes had proved so popular that I now had a growing waiting-list and we were planning to employ more help for the Café so I could focus entirely on my own side of the business. Bunting, aprons, tote bags and simple patchwork cushions adorned the shelves of the crafting area, along with a variety of crocheted mice and cleverly customised T-shirts.

I flushed with pleasure at the thought of the space so totally transformed. It was barely recognisable; the once barren bare walls sang with colour and pattern and my heart leapt at the thought that that was my office. That was where I worked now.

Even Mum had been tempted to join the weekly knit and natter session. The fact that she was a shocking knitter hadn't put her off. She was determined to get the hang of it and took my help and advice far more calmly than she would have done in the past.

'Good morning, my darling. I thought you might like breakfast in bed. You must be exhausted.'

I re-arranged my pillows and eagerly sat up ready to receive the loaded breakfast tray.

'I'm OK, actually. I think I was so tired last night I just went out like a light.'

'Tell me about it! Your snoring kept me awake half the night.'

Cheekily I stuck out my tongue and took a life-enhancing sip of hot sweet tea. Ben had moved into the flat when Jemma came home from hospital but it had taken him until last week to move into my bed. My former plan to put romance in second place was now firmly consigned to the past, just as Angela had predicted.

I was now, as my mother so prettily put it, 'blossoming' in the relationship where my individuality was cherished, my opinions mattered and my rampant curls and freckles were allowed to take centre-stage.

'How's the weather looking?' I asked hopefully, crossing my fingers and squeezing my eyes shut.

'Perfect,' Ben grinned. 'We couldn't have picked a better day for a garden party if we tried!'

The celebration had actually been all Ella's idea.

'I wish we could have a party,' she had moaned, looking out of the flat window one soggy Saturday at the end of June. 'Perhaps if we had a party the sun might shine!' she added hopefully.

So far the summer had been far from bright. Long spells of rain had arrived along with temperatures that refused to rise to bare-leg level and had pummelled everyone's spirits.

'I don't really think anyone's got time to be thinking about having a party at the moment,' I told her hurriedly, as I zipped about getting ready for the late afternoon tea and cake rush. 'I think everyone's a bit too busy, don't you?'

'Exactly,' she sighed, 'no one has time to do anything together any more.'

'What do you mean?' I frowned. 'We're together all the time.'

'I know,' she said, with a shake of her head as she tried to explain. 'What I mean is that even though we're together all the time it's only because of the Café. No one ever has time to just sit around and chat any more.'

'I thought you used to hate it when Mummy and I used to sit around and chat!' I teased, trying to make her smile but she wouldn't be distracted.

'I can't remember the last time you read me a bedtime story or played the shopping list game,' she scolded glumly.

She was right, of course; we were all together every single day but never in a social capacity. Our lives had become all work and no play and in Ella's cleverly perceptive world that had indeed made us all a little dull.

'All right,' I promised, 'if it's a party you want it's a party we'll have, but it's a secret and I'll expect you to help!'

As I stood in the Café garden admiring our combined efforts, I couldn't help but feel very pleased with Ella's suggestion. Of course the party hadn't stayed a secret but that was just as well, given the amount of work that had gone into organising it!

'How many are we expecting again?' Ben asked, as he carried out the tables and chairs and I began to dress them with fresh flowers.

Every table had ribbon-edged glass jars and my ever-popular pastel painted tin cans crammed with fresh flowers; roses and carnations in pastel shades and alchemilla which added a lime green lift and completed the look. They were a simple touch and easy to transport so every guest could take one away with them at the end of the evening.

'Well,' I said, reaching for the box of tea lights and jam-jar lanterns for later, 'let's see – Henry and Cass are definitely coming now . . .'

'I daresay you girls will all be desperate for a sight of the ring then?' Ben teased.

'Ha, ha,' I replied.

Henry and Cass had recently become engaged and I couldn't wait to see the pair of them and catch up on their news.

'And Heather and Deborah are travelling down from Norfolk.'

'With the dog?'

'Of course, you know they don't go anywhere without Angus and his knotted kerchief!'

Ben rolled his eyes.

'And then there's Angela and her family who are still here visiting from Australia.'

'And your mum, my mum and dad, Ruby, Jim and Evelyn, you, me, Jemma, Tom, Ella and bump.'

'And a partridge in a pear tree!' Ben sang.

'It does feel a bit like that, doesn't it? I grimaced. 'I hope we've made enough of everything!'

We had, of course, and the simple little gathering was a complete joy. Jemma, bump proudly on show, was the centre of attention and Ella, suddenly so grown up, was put in charge of looking after Angus and making sure he didn't pinch any of the sweet treats off the tables.

'I'm sorry about the dog,' I whispered to Tom. 'I guess this will give Ella's campaign even more ammunition now.'

Tom shook his head and laughed.

'Oh no, don't worry about that,' he smiled, 'now she has a new baby brother on the horizon the whole dog debacle has gone out of the window!'

'It's a boy?' I squealed, jumping up and down.

'Tom!'

Jemma was glowering at her husband across the garden. I clapped a hand over my mouth, realising what I had just done.

'It was supposed to be a secret,' she scolded, half laughing.

The happy news spread like wildfire amongst the guests. Tom passed round glasses of champagne and everyone gathered around the Cherry Tree where Jemma sat. Ben took my hand in his and kissed it affectionately.

'Here's to a bright and happy future at The Cherry Tree Café!' he shouted, raising his glass.

Everyone followed suit and toasted our success.

'To the future,' I smiled, taking a sip.

I looked up at Ben and slipped my arm around his waist. Finally I had found myself, and someone who loved me for just being me. Now I had found my happy ever after; now I was truly home.

Acknowledgements

If it wasn't for the love, support and encouragement of so many people *The Cherry Tree Café* still wouldn't be open for business so this is my humble, but heartfelt, thank-you to everyone who has helped hang the bunting, bake the cakes and open the door.

Firstly, thank you Paul for the precious gift of time, the first-class train travel and the never-ending supply of patience, love and understanding.

Thank you Oliver for not moaning when the TV room is out of bounds and thank you Amelia for listening when I talk at you about word counts, deadlines and plot twists.

Love and kisses to Laura, Claire and Aunty Barbara for loving Lizzie Dixon as much as I do and giving me the faith and courage to share her story with the world.

Thanks also to the RNA, the New Writers' Scheme and the many, many authors who have offered endless support and advice, along with the wonderful Book Bloggers who have championed my work and helped spread the word. I would dearly love to include names here, however there are limits and the list really would be endless.

Hugs all round for the entire Books and the City team at Simon & Schuster who, in the last twelve months, have made my literary dreams come true. An extra big squeeze for my wonderful editor Clare Hey, who has held my hand on this incredible journey and shown me how to make my story shine, and of course an extra big kiss for Sara-Jade Virtue for simply being her thoroughly fabulous self.

And finally, thank you dear readers. May your bookshelves, be they virtual or real, always be filled with fabulous fiction.

H x

Turn the page to read an extract from

Chapter 1

For what must have been the hundredth time that morning, I went back to the bedroom mirror, scrutinised my dark ponytail and wrinkled my nose at my reflection. I smoothed down the cherry-patterned skirt of my fifties-inspired dress and glanced nervously at the clock. All I needed were two tiny minutes in which to change into something a little less controversial, but it was too late. If I didn't leave right now I wouldn't make it at all. Wincing slightly, I thrust my feet into my narrow red patent heels, grabbed my bag and headed for the stairs.

'I thought you said you were going to a funeral,' frowned my housemate Helen as we collided on the landing. 'I know my brain's a bit scrambled when I'm on nights at the hospital,' she added, shaking her head, 'but I'm sure you said it was a funeral.'

'I am,' I said, 'it is. If you'd known Gwen, you'd understand,' I called over my shoulder as I rushed down the stairs.

'So I take it you haven't got time to drink this, then?' she shouted after me, holding aloft a steaming mug.

'No,' I said, flinging open the front door. 'Sorry. I'll catch up with you tomorrow, though. Sleep tight!'

Ordinarily I would have been excited by the thought of such a long trip on the bus. My heart would have been fluttering away in my chest like a trapped butterfly, thrilled by the prospect of one hundred and twenty uninterrupted minutes of luxurious people-watching, but all it could manage that morning, even as I jogged to the station, was a dull thud. Its lack of effort was a fitting reminder that this trip was all about the destination, not the journey.

My pretty but uncompromising shoes were pinching by the time I arrived at the designated bay at the bus stop and I could feel sweat prickling the back of my neck. It was going to be another unseasonal scorcher of a day, unnervingly hot for the beginning of April, and far too hot for a full skirt and net petticoats.

'Return to Wynbridge, please,' I panted as I jumped aboard the bus with just seconds to spare and clattered the money I had already carefully counted out into the tray.

'You going somewhere nice?' smiled the driver as he leant over in his seat and looked me up and down. 'Bit early in the day for a party, isn't it?' he added, as the machine spat out my ticket.

'Funeral,' I mumbled, not quite managing to return his smile.

'Oh,' he said doubtfully, 'right.'

I carefully folded and stowed away my guarantee to get home and headed for a window seat at the back. I wasn't surprised by his or Helen's reaction to my outfit, but it did go some way to chivvying my heart rate along a bit.

What if the rest of the mourners had forgotten that Gran's best friend Gwen had long held the desire that her funeral should be marked by a riot of colour and laughter rather than dull reminiscing? What if they had all decided to opt for sober, sombre black? Well, if they had, they certainly wouldn't forget my vibrant retro ensemble in a hurry. If it did turn out to be just me rocking the colour, I would no doubt be the talk of the town by the end of the day.

Gwen and my Grandmother Flora had been friends since childhood, a friendship that had spanned almost eight decades. To my utter dismay they had died within six months of each other, but even though they were no longer with me I could still sense their presence, along with their collective aura of discontent.

They had never stopped nagging me to make the most of my twenties, and when thirty was suddenly closer than my teens, they had really cranked things up a notch. Apparently the small life I had built for myself was nowhere near ambitious or exciting enough for the pensioners who in their youth had travelled the world, partied hard and left the globe littered with a string of keen suitors. As far as they were concerned, I needed to set my sights higher and take a few more risks.

Between the two of them Gwen had been the long-term party girl and had never 'settled down' in the conventional sense, but Gran had. She had married, moved away from Wynbridge and had a daughter, my mother. My arrival shortly after mum's seventeenth birthday caused quite a scandal apparently, but it was nothing compared to the gossip that started when she decided to leave me in Gran and Grandad's care and take off to Los Angeles in pursuit of a life more thrilling than the one on offer in Lincolnshire.

Her departure from our lives had been both painful and shocking and subsequently my life had been marred by an inability to truly trust anyone who entered it. However, my grandparents, although devastated to have lost contact with their only child, somehow still managed to see the good in folk and did their utmost to ensure that I enjoyed a happy and stimulating childhood, and our annual visits to stay with Gwen at Cuckoo Cottage in the Fens were the absolute highlight of my summer holidays.

The trips stopped for a while after Grandad died and then completely some years later when Gran had a stroke. However, Gwen took it upon herself to travel to see us then, bringing with her a huge, dust-encrusted carpet bag and her temperamental terrier Tiny, who was eventually replaced with the equally unpredictable Minnie. It was inconceivable to even think that these two women, whom I loved so much and who had been so instrumental in my upbringing, were now both lost to me forever.

Despite the heat, I shuddered as I thought how I had failed to achieve any of the things I had promised Gran I would get to work on. I had solemnly sworn, just days before she died, that I would start developing a proper career and pushing my ambitions further and yet here I was, six months on, and nothing had changed. Truth be told, I was too afraid to even try.

Having lived with the consequences of my mother's pursuit of her own hedonistic dreams, I hadn't dared to even think up, let alone live out, my own. But now of course, I realised with a jolt, I was completely on my own and could please myself. If only I were that brave and if only I knew what it was that I actually wanted to do with my life . . .

'This is your stop, love!' shouted the driver over the noise of the idling engine. 'Are you not getting off?'

'Yes,' I said, jumping to my feet and scrabbling to pick up my bag. 'Sorry, I didn't realise.'

'I hope it goes all right,' he said kindly as I drew level with him. 'At least you've got a nice day for it.'

'That's true,' I said as the door opened and a wave of warm air rushed in to meet me. 'She would have appreciated that.'

I stepped down on to the pavement and blinked in the bright sunshine, trying to get my bearings. Time was pressing on and if I didn't locate a taxi to take me to the church soon I'd be late.

'Lottie!'

I spun round and spotted a man rushing towards me from the other side of the market square. It took a second for my brain to believe it, but it was definitely Chris Dempster. More at home in jeans and a checked shirt and working on the fruit and vegetable stall that had been in his family for generations, he was now sporting a bright blue suit and struggling to carry the biggest bunch of balloons I'd ever seen. The spectacle was wholly unexpected, but thoroughly appreciated. At least one person had remembered, but then, given that he was such a close friend of Gwen's, I shouldn't have anticipated any different.

'You made it!' he cried. 'My goodness, look at you. It must be what,' he faltered, 'well, I can't quite recall, but it's been a while. You haven't got any taller though, have you, love?' he teased, regaining his composure. 'Are you all right?'

I swallowed hard and nodded, knowing there was no need to remind him that the last time I had seen him was at the funeral of his eldest son Shaun, who had died in a tragic motorbike accident. I willed myself not to cry and felt relieved that he had spotted me before I went in search of a taxi.

'Come on,' he puffed, taking my arm with his free hand. 'I meant to say when I last spoke to you on the phone that we'd give you a lift. I hope you can squeeze in with this lot and that frock.'

The journey to the church, wedged in the back of Chris's car with the balloons while his wife Marie sat with him in the front, was both bizarre and stiflingly hot, but as least I was going to be on time.

'Don't open the windows!' Chris bawled at Marie when she complained of the soaring temperature and faulty air conditioning. 'We'll lose the bloody lot!'

We all began to laugh and I couldn't help feeling grateful for Gwen's quirky sense of humour.

'Was this all Gwen's idea?' I asked, nodding at the bulging bunch around me.

'Of course,' confirmed Marie.

'She's certainly gone out of her way to keep everyone smiling, hasn't she?' I said, biting my lip and blinking hard.

'Oh yes,' said Chris, winking at me in the rear-view mirror. 'I've been running around like a headless chicken these last few days making sure everything's just as she wanted it. Mind you, it was a shock to discover she'd left such detailed instructions.'

'Are you sure you don't want to say anything?' asked Marie, twisting round to look at me. 'During the service, I mean. It's going to be very ad hoc so no one would mind if you got up and said a few words. After all, you're the closest to real family she had.'

'Oh no,' I said, shaking my head. 'Thank you, but no. I just couldn't face it.'

Chris had already broached the subject when we talked on the telephone. I'd said no straight away and I wasn't about to change my mind.

'I still can't believe she's gone,' tutted Marie.

'Me neither,' I whispered, wishing I'd forced myself to pay her a visit after I lost Gran, rather than putting it off on the assumption that I could come in the summer.

'But at least she hadn't been ill,' rallied Chris. 'The coroner confirmed there had been nothing untoward. You know how she would have hated to be a burden.'

'Yes,' I agreed, thinking of Gwen's stubborn streak. 'She would have loathed that.'

It had been late on a Sunday evening when Chris found my number next to Gwen's telephone in the hall and called to tell me what had happened. He explained how he had popped in during the afternoon, just as he always did on a Sunday, and found her in the deckchair under the cherry tree in her little garden. He said she just looked asleep and the Jackie Collins novel resting on her lap suggested there had been no pain or trauma; she had simply taken advantage of sitting out in the early spring sunshine and serenely slipped away.

'Right,' said Chris, pulling hard on the handbrake as we

arrived at the church and dragging me back to the present. 'Let's get this show on the road, shall we?'

'Show' turned out to be a pretty accurate description. I was deposited in the church doorway and instructed to give a balloon to as many people as I could convince to take one.

'But mind you don't get blown away,' Chris teased as he handed me the muddled strings. 'One gust of wind and a little thing like you, you'll be up, up and away!'

I appreciated his unfailing sense of humour and was moved to discover that no one actually needed convincing. The line of mourners that stretched from the church to the road were more than happy to walk down the aisle with helium-filled balloons bobbing about above their heads and it was a tribute to just how greatly Gwen was loved that not one person was wearing black.

The service was an upbeat and surprising mix of poetry and anecdotes, interspersed with a variety of music ranging from Sinatra to Queen and everything in between, and for the most part it was a jolly affair. Afterwards, in the churchyard which was awash with primroses, we stood in silence as the tiny coffin was lowered into the ground. There were tears in abundance, but then the atmosphere shifted as everyone released their balloons and watched them float away.

'Right!' shouted Chris at the top of his voice, making us all jump. 'Time to get to the pub!'

*

The Mermaid, Gwen's much-beloved watering hole, was packed to the rafters and, even though it had been a while since I had last visited, no one had forgotten who I was. That, of course, was how it worked in Wynbridge, and having been adopted long ago as Gwen's surrogate granddaughter, I was considered a token local despite the fact that I hadn't frequented the town or the pub for some time.

'What can I get you, love?' asked the burly barman. 'Lottie, isn't it?'

'Yes,' I smiled, scrambling inelegantly up on to a bar stool and inwardly cursing that they were always far too high for someone of five foot two, even if she was wearing heels. 'That's right, and you're . . .' I faltered, wracking my brains, 'John.'

'Almost,' he beamed, 'Jim, and the wife's . . .'

'Evelyn,' I cut in, 'of course.'

She wasn't the sort of woman anyone would forget in a hurry.

'It's lovely to see you again,' he said, 'even under the circumstances.'

'Likewise,' I agreed. 'I'll just have some lemonade please, with lots of ice and lemon.'

'One glass of lemonade coming up.'

It was cooler inside the pub and everyone was grateful for the gentle breeze which drifted through the open front door and out into the little garden at the back.

'You all sorted?' asked Chris, when he spotted me sitting waiting for my drink.

'Yes, thanks,' I nodded. 'Jim's just getting me some lemonade.'

'Lemonade,' he laughed as he loosened his tie and unbuttoned his shirt collar. 'I had you down as a cocktail kind of girl.'

'Don't be fooled by the outfit,' I laughed back. 'I need something that's going to quench my thirst, not knock me off my feet. I can't believe how hot it is again today.'

'Me neither,' he smiled, looking at the pint glass in his hand. 'I probably shouldn't be drinking this really. I had planned to set up the stall this afternoon.'

'You'll have to delegate,' I suggested. 'Can't you get Steve to take the reins for today?'

'Chance would be a fine thing,' he chuckled at the mention of his lad. 'He's still globetrotting with his girlfriend Ruby.'

'Of course he is,' I said, gratefully accepting the glass Jim proffered and taking a long refreshing sip. 'Gwen had mentioned that they were abroad a few months ago, but I'd forgotten.'

'They're in New Zealand at the moment,' Chris said proudly.

'How exciting,' I said, thinking that my plans for my own future, when I finally got round to making them, wouldn't be anywhere near as ambitious. 'Although if today is anything to go by I'm not sure I could cope with the heat!'

'Me neither,' he agreed. 'Give me a sharp frost and my market stall any day.'

'And what's happened to Gwen's stall?' I asked, the thought only just occurring. 'I hope it's still running?'

Gwen had run a stall on the market for years, selling all sorts of bits and pieces to raise funds for various local charities. Every day, come rain or shine, she turned out to peddle her wares and I hated the thought that now she was gone the stall would disappear too.

'Oh, don't worry about that,' said Marie, who had wandered up to join us. 'It's still going strong. Some of the WI ladies have taken it on and from what I've heard it won't be closing down. There's already a rota in the pipeline and a string of volunteers who are determined to keep it going.'

'Well, that's good,' I said, draining my glass. 'I'm relieved to hear it.'

Gwen had always worked hard, long hours and was a committed trader. It would have been a shame if her efforts fizzled out and were forgotten.

'Fancy another?' asked Chris, nodding at my glass.

I glanced at my watch, just to check I had enough time before I had to head back to the bus. The thought of returning to my meanly proportioned single room suddenly weighed heavy on my heart. I'd far rather stay where I was amongst these friendly folk, talking about Gwen and sitting out in the colourful daffodil-packed garden that I could see through the door over Chris's shoulder.

'Go on, then,' I smiled, 'you've twisted my arm, but I can't be long.'

I had just taken charge of my second glass when Evelyn took her place behind the bar and pulled sharply on the big brass bell.

'Can I have your attention please?' she called out and everyone filed in from the garden to raise their glasses to Gwen and share a moment's quiet contemplation.

It was both cheering and moving to see so many people, so gaily attired, and I couldn't help wondering how many other people in the room, or the town come to that, could have elicited such a turnout.

'While everyone is gathered!' shouted a man in his sixties, wearing a garish suit not dissimilar to Chris's, as the level of chatter began to pick up again. 'Could I just ask if there is a Miss Charlotte Foster amongst us?'

My throat went dry and I could feel my cheeks blazing.

'Miss Foster?' he called again.

'She's here,' said Chris, grabbing my arm and thrusting my hand above my head, 'this is Lottie Foster!'

books and the city
the home of female fiction
BOOKS | NEWS & EVENTS | FEATURES | AUTHOR PODCASTS | COMPETITIONS
Follow us online to be the first to hear from your favourite authors
bc
booksandthecity.co.uk
books and the city
@TeamBATC
Join our mailing list for the latest news, events and exclusive competitions
Sign up at booksandthecity.co.uk
Buy your next book directly from
Sparkle Direct
to receive 25% off & free P+P!
Call 01326 569 444
or visit sparkledirect.com
Prices and availability are subject to change without notice